Jack Butler was born in Alligator, Mississippi. His work has been published in *The New Yorker* and *The Atlantic* and has been widely anthologized. The author of several collecti... in addition to *Jujitsu for Christ* and ... dean of students at Hendrix Colleg...

By the same author

Jujitsu for Christ

JACK BUTLER

Nightshade

Paladin
An Imprint of Grafton Books
A Division of HarperCollins Publishers

Paladin
An imprint of GraftonBooks
A Division of HarperCollins *Publishers*
77–85 Fulham Palace Road,
Hammersmith, London W6 8JB

A Paladin UK Original 1991
9 8 7 6 5 4 3 2 1

A CIP catalogue record for this book
is available from the British Library

ISBN 0-586-09051-7

Printed in Great Britain by
HarperCollins Manufacturing, Glasgow

Set in Times

For Larry Johnson,
who knows more of Mars and Mississippi
than I shall learn—

And for Tom York,
who in his travels
became a hawk in the snow—

Contents

Nothing in nature explains nature.

—LOREN WINGO

HELLAS CRATER

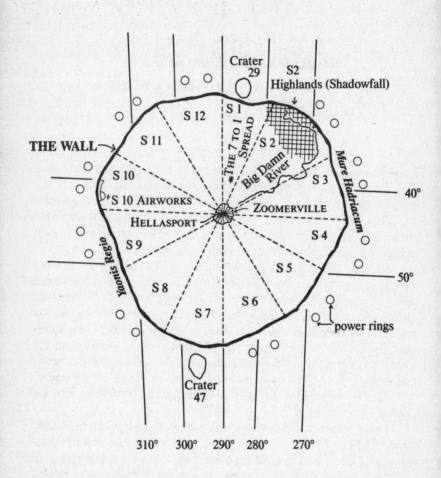

1
What's Past

They floated into the valley that morning in their stiff bearskins, five men leading two starved packhorses. The bearskins were stiff because they had not been properly cured. These men had no squaws.

They were white men, but had the look of renegade Indians: gaunt, and scarred, and so dirty it was clear they saw no more point in bathing than they would have seen in washing a tree.

Not one of them had a complete set of eyes or fingers, but the surviving fingers were enormously strong, and the eyes that were not milky or scarred over were very cruel and very far-seeing. These men moved as wisely as animals, but they used their own bodies as pitilessly as they used their packhorses. Bodies brought you infrequent pleasure, frequent pain, and were generally inadequate for what you wanted to do. So you got what you could from your body, you drove it until it fell apart, or until someone stopped it for you.

And if they had small pity for themselves, they had less for anyone or anything else.

There was a settlement in this valley. In the settlement they expected to find food, possibly liquor, certainly sex (if that designation could be said to include such amazing and violent behavior).

And scalps. Glorious scalps, scalps for the redcoats. Scalps meant gold pieces, and gold pieces meant a little spell of warm full bellies and warm full barmaids and drink-blurred noisy merriment. These men liked scalps. They thought of them as beautiful work, hung streaming over horse-neck. Having an evening pipe by the fire, any one of these fellows might stroke his favorite scalp, absently, as other men would stroke a cat.

1

The pipe, though, would require tobacco, and for the moment they had none. That was another thing they expected to find in the settlement.

They had watched the village from the slopes above for more than a day, and they knew there were thirty or so scalps to be had. A few children more or less. No more than ten full-grown men.

And now they floated down the ravines, traveling the same way as the spring thaws.

Shade, from another mountain, had seen them. He knew what they were. A shiver went through him, the sudden chill of a man passing a bad accident. Except that this one he would not pass.

He had been out three days on a hunting trip. The renegades would not know that his village had another gun. That was perhaps the only advantage the settlers had.

Now he had to decide how best to use that advantage. He carried a trumpet: It was handy for sounding alarms, or helping search parties locate you. If he sounded it now, it would alert the renegades as well as the settlers. The first thing the renegades would do then would be to hunt him down and kill him, removing the advantage of the extra gun. He had no doubt they were capable of finding him. He was no trailmaster, no wild man of the hills. He was not Tice Harman or Dan'l Boone. He was a bookish young man come to the frontier, a settler who hunted.

The renegades were between him and the settlement, though. It was not likely he could get past them silently and warn his friends.

What he *could* do was stay behind the raiders, tracking *them*. Since they were intent on the settlement, he might succeed in getting close enough to surprise them. He had a long rifle, and if he did get close enough, he might be able to kill one of them. He knew he would have time to kill only one before the others melted into the brush.

Then, with the village near, he could make a dash for it in the confusion. If he got through, good. They might not even try the raid with the odds suddenly eleven to four.

If he didn't make it, he would still have improved the odds.

He thought his plan over for a few moments. He had a bride below. He wanted to be certain he did the best he could for her.

He would have to leave his horse tied. He could not move quietly or quickly enough leading a horse, and if he turned it loose, it would head for the settlement, alerting his enemies. Since he was not likely to return, the horse would die, taken down by wolves or a lion. He loosed the packs of bear and elk meat, dragged them off a little.

He came back to the horse. "I'm sorry, Jasper," he whispered, stroking its neck. "I doubt me that I am able, but I must try what I can. I shall loosen your reins a mite. Perhaps the beasts will take the meat first, and you can break free."

He stuck his pistol and a knife in his belt, took the trumpet in one hand and the long gun in the other, and set out.

By the time the sun had crossed its zenith, he and the men he followed were nearly to the valley floor. He was almost in rifle range. It was much hotter than it had been higher up, when the day was younger. He was in a wide stretch of cedar flats, and the rich spice of the heated needles beat in the thick air.

Then his fortune ran wrong. Something found Jasper, found him sooner than Shade had hoped. The horse's anguish rolled down the hillside, echoing like thunderclaps. The renegades were still, listening, for the merest of moments, and he did not have a clear shot at any of them. He lifted the long gun, angling the barrel to cheat gravity of a few more yards, aiming where he saw one bare head clear, hoping to hit the body if not the head, if the ball could clear the trees, if he was lucky enough.

He fired, his arms aching with hope.

Then he blew three short blasts on the trumpet and threw it away. He put his knife in his teeth, the long gun in one hand, the pistol in the other, and ran for the village.

The first ball struck him through the throat. He had a few lucid moments before he died, and he waited, hoping for a last shot at one of the raiders. But they were too smart for that.

" 'Ere, Jack! Wodyer thank yer doin'?" It was the blond three-fingered one who spoke.

The big black-bearded man looked up. *"Il est mon coup,"* he said calmly, and went back to his work.

"Illy mon coo, loik Sye-tin! Loik bloody flymin' Sye-tin 'e are! It were my ball tiken 'im down!"

"Non," said the black-bearded man.

The blond man drew his knife.

"Gentlemen!" said a third man, taller than either. "You may slaughter each other for one scalp now." He waited for their attention. He pointed toward the settlement. "Or you may slaughter *them* for thirty scalps shortly." He stooped to roll the corpse over. He dug in the back of the neck with his knife, then held up a ball in bloody fingers. The ball was flattened, but the *JB* of Jacques's mold was still visible.

"-la!" the dark man said.

"Loik Sye-tin," the blond man said, but sheathed his knife. "Aow, lookit 'im!"

Jacques had rolled the settler back and was making a premature and staring skull of his face, peeling away the ears, the soft parts of the nose, the lips. He delicately stripped the eyelids, but left the eyes.

"Il est un jolie rogue, n'est-ce-pas?" he said, lifting his handiwork up a little for viewing. And so the remaining tension dissolved in laughter.

The five of them made ready. They knew the settlers would be barricaded in their homes now, rifles cocked. The settlers would have had a better chance if they had taken to the woods to outflank the raiders, but the raiders knew the settlers would not try that.

A lean fellow who looked half-Indian prepared fire-arrows, and all of them draped necklaces and charms about their persons: Some were of beads and feathers and teeth, and some were ears.

Two of them had painted their faces, but when they went into the settlement, they did not run in whooping and yelling with the bravado of young warriors in nervous and glorious combat. They slipped in silently. Only one of the log huts caught at first, from the roof down. But then a couple of others caught, and the fire spread. They shot the settlers as they ran out.

None of the renegades suffered so much as a scratch. They were angry because all of the women had died shooting at them, except the one whose husband had shot her with his last ball and then charged out pointing an empty rifle. One woman had run out to retrieve a fallen gun. They had held their fire, hoping to keep at least one warm body alive. She had calmly, under their sights, taken powder horn and pellet bag and rammed a new load home. Then she had walked slowly about looking for them.

Her body they had taken to the chapel, and used until it was no longer usable. She was a young woman, whose trousseau they donned for sport, then scattered.

They were angry that no women had remained alive, but more angry that there had been no liquor save a few gallons of young persimmon beer. They vented their anger by splashing the chapel with blood and urine and feces, carving the bodies of children: They substituted the adrenaline of sacrilege for the giddiness of drink.

In all, they had a good party. They slept late the next day, then raided the settlement's small store of food and tobacco, feasting and smoking. A few played with the bodies again, but the settlers were beginning to lose their charms.

Early the next morning, they packed the remaining food and tobacco, and took their leave.

They had traveled out of the valley up into the pass, most of a morning's work, when they heard the sound. It was almost a scream, but no human throat could have made such a noise. It was not the howl of a wolf. It was not a catamount in pain. It seemed to come from below, from the valley behind them.

That night, drowsing around the fire, they were shocked awake by a trumpet blast. A naked and horrible thing, a demon-beast with a bloody skull for a head stood in their midst. It stepped over to the little half-Indian and pulled his head from his body. The body ran a few steps spraying blood, and fell. The head, lips moving, was thrown on the fire.

"Gawd Gawd my Gawd oh Gawd," the blond man was babbling, scrambling for his rifle. And while he found and pointed it, the creature seized the dark man, Jacques, holding him by one ankle off the ground. The blond man fired. The beast tore the leather breeches from his catch, then ripped away the genitals. The dark man was screaming, and now the creature rubbed his face in the coals of the fire till the screaming stopped. The faceless body jerked over the ground, trailing blood from the loins, trying blindly to escape.

5

The leader had fired a ball, and the blond man had reloaded. The fifth man, a mute whose nationality none of the others had ever known, had fled into the woods.

The thing took the blond man's rifle before he could fire again. It bit off his fingers, crushed his testicles, and flung him into the woods like a sack of flour, breaking his back.

The leader had not attempted to reload. Now as the creature stepped toward him, he let his rifle fall. "My Lord," he said, his dark eyes wide.

"My Lord," he uttered again. "I am an evil man far from grace. There be none here to shrive me." The creature feinted a leap, and the man shrank back, but his eyes stayed on the awful visage of his executioner.

"You are justly come upon me, Holy Father. Do You in Your vengeance as You must. Only let me not bide forever in darkness. I pray You, hear my confession. If not now, then after a thousand years in the fires, my Lord. After ten thousand—"

The demon shrieked, and the man fell.

"My Lord, in the name of Your Son—"

He was raised by his jacket in the air, his face brought next to that of his assailant, so that he had the stench of bad flesh in his nostrils, and smears of blood came away on his own face.

"WHOOOOO?" the thing demanded, in a dying rush of air.

"My Lord—"

He was shaken silent. "WHO?" said the creature again. And of course it had no lips, so the words it spoke issued like baby talk, without bilabials, a slide of speech that might have been comical had it been spoken on a stage by an actress playing a tongue-tied chambermaid: "SEAK," it roared. "TELL NEE. WHO HAS TAID YOU? WHO HAS TAID YOU TO KILL US?"

"My Lord—"

He was shaken again, this time so viciously it seemed that his neck must snap. "WHO?"

"The British, my Lord—Thou knowest. But my *soul*—"

The man's head was forced back, and the thing bit open his throat, burying its face in the gout and gulping. The body, still in the air, kicked. It showed an erection in automatic, dying reflex.

When it had finished, the creature sank to its knees, and wept. It stayed there, keening, till the fire died and the half-moon rose high.

It went, then, to find the fifth of the renegades, the little mute who had run off. But when it found him, the man was already dead. He had run a broken-off dry cedar branch through eye and brain.

Shade, for that is who the creature was, went back to the camp and freed the horses. In the valley he could see the glow of the great fire he had made, just now beginning to take the whole of the pyre, the whole of the town's stacked remnants, to the last log, the last curl of unscalped hair.

It was near dawn now, and Shade set himself for the east. He could not know it then, but his face would heal before he made Maryland.

And that is how General Washington, in the fall of 1777, gained a partisan.

2
Heavy Date
in Light Gravity

When the clown and the robot came in, I had caught the eye of one of the dancers.

She was a modified Watercat III, her gills still pulsing from her last dive, her sleek fur streaming. Risen, she had inclined her head in a dignified nod that meant *Yes* to the question of my lifted eyebrows. Now she skeeted away across the surface, her tail flicking parabolas of spray. Naked as she was, she still showed innocence and surprise, and that was important. It showed in the pleasure she took in her dancing, it showed in the freshness of her spinning glance.

I knew she was intrigued. It is not a thing that matters to me in the way you might imagine, but I am aware that I am impressive. I stand a full two meters, above average even here. Though not heavily made, I am wide-shouldered and powerful. I was wearing expensive cloth, the sort of dress that seems casual to all but the most expensive people—and performers, who learn very rapidly to judge their patrons. My hair is very black. My teeth are very white.

In fact, except for the odd dark color of my skin, somewhere between bronze and grey, I would have made a perfect Count Dracula for some old nineteener black-and-white.

That, I suppose, is funny.

The dancer and her fellows joined in a revolving ring in the center of Hellaspool, and made their bows. The ring was more than decorative choreography, and more than a way of facing all the customers. A bow on a pair of skeets is a tricky thing. The ring gave them counterpoise for their bows. Now it broke apart, and the dancers dived to their underwater exit. The water began to fill with lovers and swimmers again, generating the slow, hypnotic chop of three-eighths gee.

The clown and his companion were wending toward me.

I could have described every person they had spoken with on their way. I could have told you the probable subjects of most of the conversations, and I could have told you the names of most of the speakers. What I do is instant and almost total cross-referencing—without an interface. It might sound hard, but it isn't. It's easy. At least, it's easier than trying to make sense of jumbled information. It takes a little time to learn, a little practice, but anyone could do it. You could, if you had three hundred years. If you had three hundred years, you would have to.

Now the two stood before me, waiting.

The clown was unusually short. He was an old man. In fact, he was the oldest-*looking* man I had seen in a long time. He was no native. He had been gravity-cooked. An Earth-born. That and the unmarked costume made him a powerful man, a real bozo. Maybe even a bozo de bozos.

And there was something inappropriate about the robot.

"So sit down," I said.

The fire was beginning. I needed the girl, and needed her soon, but this pair had sought me out for a reason. Perhaps I had time to learn it before she appeared at my table.

It was of course a matter of indifference to the robot whether he stood or sat, but he sat, too. He was an uncommon get: the head an oblate spheroid, two sets of three eyes 120 degrees apart, a protuberance like a low helmet ruining the back of his head and continuing down his back. The slender arms fit neatly into recesses on the front of his torso. The back and helmet looked as though someone had done a particularly amateurish job of repriff, but that didn't suit the old man's obvious power and status. Nor could I identify the robot—he was disturbingly familiar, but no model I knew.

He carried a further oddity, a large soft buckskin bag, complete with deerslayer fringes. A yearning struck me, a pang for things I had not seen in a long time. I missed my own buckskin, the smell of the soft leather. The smell of my horse. Of fall, good whisky, the smoke of burnt powder.

The old man motioned for the bag. He rooted in it, came out with an antique silver-chased sawed-off double-barreled .210. He laid it cocked across the table at my heart.

"Greetings, Nosferatu," he said.

I smiled. "How refreshing," I said. "Someone with history *and* imagination. But don't you need silver bullets?"

"Wrong answer," the old man said. "You should have been puzzled, not sarcastic."

"Perhaps I am an antiquarian."

"I won't contend with you. You know, and I know, and we shall shortly agree on a certain matter.

"As for the silver bullets—I had thought that they were not necessary, that it was simply a question of a very large hole in the right place. A small hole won't do, as it will for a human. You heal too fast. And so the legend of silver. Actually, lead does as well. Any soft metal, with a cross cut in it to make a dumdum. Or a wooden stake, so that the wound *cannot* close. Or enough shot to excavate your chest. Was I mistaken?"

There was something pleading and curious in his voice. He really wanted to know. It was a scholar's tone.

He was right that I had made a poor response. I am not given to panic, but the storm in my nerves was beginning to interfere.

He sighed when I did not answer. "No matter," he said, stowing the ancient scatter-gun away. "I know very well you could pluck this instrument from my hands and kill me with it before I could blink. It was merely an attention-getter."

"You had my attention when you came in."

"Yes."

"Whose were you seeking, then?"

"That is not important now. We are satisfied that we have been successful."

"Professor," I said, "you're interrupting a private party. Take your robot and go."

"He's not a robot," the old man said. "He's an AI, and he's my friend."

I stared at the AI. Of course. The helmet, the junky peripherals—they were just camouflage. There was a third set of eyes under the helmet, a third arm, a third leg hidden under the hood of the apparent back.

"A Starbuck?" I said.

"I am Starbuck 7," the AI said. "Otherwise known as Mandrake."

"I apologize, sir," I said. "I had not realized you were autonomous. I hope you will understand that I meant no disparagement."

"You do not strike me as a bigot," the AI said, "and I do not take offense in such matters, regardless of intention."

The Starbuck series: Created in the late twenties and early thirties, they had been designed, officially, as explorers and macroengineers. The Starbuck Colonizers, they had been called, and in fact they had been put to use in the last stages of the terraforming of Hellas, and in most of the terraforming of Argyre. Oh yes, my lovelies, they made your Mars. You made them, and then they, your servants, your perfect angels—they made a world for you.

But then there had been trouble in Heaven. There were huge cost overruns, and the project had folded in the mid-thirties. There had been all sorts of noise in the trivia. The story you got depended on the style of the announcer you listened to, of course. If your local barker thought governmental paranoia would sell, then you heard that the overruns represented a sort of deliberate sabotage, that the Starbucks had been meant all along as military experiments, that their use in the public domain had been a ruse to get around the restrictions of the Military Funding Amendment of the first decade. If the idea was that romance would generate a better market share, then maybe some naked wacko painted in jarring stripes would appear in 3-D in your living room to tell you that the Starbucks had been created with sex drives, and had all committed suicide in a swoon over the Marilyn Monroes.

Serves me right, you may say, for watching the zoomer channels instead of the hard news. What else could I expect from networks that pandered to the popular taste, and even then survived only because they had a legislated audience—the z-level consumers, who paid their way with their one currency, the processing power of their brains?

It wasn't because I lacked the slip to pay for the hard news. It

11

was because the Hard News Network/Prediction Net—Henny-penny—simply didn't cover the story. At all. Which tells you the disappearance of the Starbucks must have been a very expensive secret indeed.

Rumors brewed: They were fighting secret wars, they had been sold on the black market as counselors and managers for the very wealthy.

None had ever reappeared, and eventually even the trivia lost interest. It had been a quarter-century since the last confirmed sighting.

The thing was, I and everyone else had understood there were only six prototypes.

"Listen," I said to both of them. "You definitely have my interest. I will be happy to talk with you, at length. Now, however, I have an appointment, and one that means a great deal to me."

"Vampire," the old man said, "I know exactly what it means to you. But you must not keep that appointment. You must come with us."

"Don't get autocratic with me, Professor. I have a name, and I am certain you know it. I cannot break my appointment, and in any case would make my own decision as to whether I should attend you further."

"My turn to apologize. You are John Shade, citizen of Hellas, and rancher on the eastern plains. I am Benjamin, and I am no longer a professor. I have not been one for quite a long time, but apparently the traces remain. Now. We have little time for direct talk. This conversation will be monitored very shortly. When we are certain that it is, I will attack your character in a loud voice, and you will respond angrily. We will leave, and in a few more moments, you will be seen to leave also, apparently to follow us."

"Mr. Benjamin—"

"Just Benjamin."

"Benjamin. I *cannot* follow you. And you have given me no reason to do so."

"I can't elaborate now. I must call on your honor."

Now I stared at him as I had stared at the AI before. Full of surprises, these two.

"Yes," he said. "Honor. A word older than you are, and as out of fashion. I know, however, what the word means to you. Believe me, John Shade. Alone of all the humans you have known, I have lived with your kind, and known them for what they were. It was a long time ago, and I was young, but I knew them. And I know you. How else do you think I could trace you here, how else judge the exact moment when the Need began in you, the moment that would force you to an immediate choice? I know the Nosferatu, and I know that for them honor is absolute. I know you, and I know that in the past you have served your country as an agent. You may not be human, but you are a citizen. I tell you now, your nation has need of you once more. As an officer in the service of the United States of America, I declare it: We have need of you."

"I can almost believe you think you speak the truth," I said. "But even if I humored your madness, it would do you no good. If I did follow you, I would shortly be of no use to you."

"I can promise you blood, John Shade, the best blood, fresh and hot from a noble soul. This girl you are waiting for—cheap stuff, I am afraid. Pleasant, but not durable. How long will she sustain you? I can promise you good blood, tonight."

"You persist in your fantasy. Tell me, for my amusement, how soon tonight?"

"Within the hour."

"Where?"

"Follow us. My scent will lead you to a door with a map of Hellasport on it. What you require will be behind that door. Farther down the corridor will be a door with a map of the United States on it. When you have finished with the first door, I will await you beyond the second."

"I can smell Mr. Mandrake, too," I said.

"*Our* scent will lead you, then."

"I have no honorific," the AI said. He began to sway in his seat and hum. It was an old song. I almost recognized it.

"You utter blithering fool," the old man said. "You damn CP Hellas hick. What makes you think you can talk to me that way? I'd proc you right now if I didn't know how much fun it was going to be to strip you of every bevo in your whole damned stupid herd."

The tune was "Michael, Row the Boat Ashore." Michael. Mike. We were being monitored now, and the AI was making a little joke. Great. I was involved with a clown and a jokester, and a nondery jokester at that. It was time to decide. Whatever game the old man was playing, it was at least two-deep. Life had been too uneventful for many years now, even for me. As much as I needed privacy and anonymity, as much as I loved my ranch, as oddly charming as it was to talk to a bevo, I was bored. And the old man had known about the Need.

"Suck it, Clown," I said. "Sit on Centerpole and slide down." His threat to strip my assets sounded as though the pretext for our mock battle was tax troubles. The doors with the maps meant Centerpole, of course. And since all local government in Hellas was top-heavy with Earth-born and with immigrants from Argyre . . .

"You freaking gyros," I went on. "We're going to pop your blister one of these days. Touch my property, and I'll come after you myself, you Sam-sucking E-B gyro jerk."

"Ah, yes—the typical geophobic nouveau riche provincial. The Texans of Mars, the manly cowboys with their blazing pistols. Wise up, rube. You can't fight Centerpole."

He stood up. "Come on, tin can," he said to the AI, and strode away. Mandrake followed clunkily behind, still humming. In their wake, a wave of faces turned away, carefully not looking. It was not safe to stare at a clown. This was a frontier society, in a sense, but liberty was a more theoretical notion here than it had been on that other frontier centuries ago. This frontier had begun in a thoroughly computerized age. It had been, from the beginning, almost completely mapped. Everyone had a record. Almost everyone. It was a dangerous life sometimes, but not the wild and woolly repetition of the Old West the trivia made it out to be.

On each of the neutral faces that were carefully *not* watching the professor and Mandrake was a look of masked and arrested hatred. And here I was, playing the game again. All the faces were on my side. They thought I was one of them. Meantime, my two closest allies made their getaway.

I waited. The Need was worsening steadily. It was hard to sit, but easy to feign anger and impatience. No one came over to my table. The faces might sympathize, but I had been marked out for trouble.

Just as I stood to go, the dancer surfaced, stood on her skeets, and shook the water from her fur. She stepped out of the skeets and over to me, taking my arm. "Hey," she said. "I broke a good date for you." She was pretty, still nude, her pubic fur blazed in a radiating star, her mane and ankles blazed to match.

I shook her hand off roughly. "This is the luckiest night of your life," I said, and left her standing there.

3
Hot on the Trail

Outside, I had to circle to find their spoor. They must have stayed on foot for me to follow them. No one could follow a scent through the air, not even one of my kind.

It is an irritating stereotype. Perhaps I had better try to explain, though I know my efforts are not likely to make much of a difference.

You, if we pretend that there is a you, a reader, are by all odds from Earth, since there are 2,500 readers on Earth for every reader on Mars. As an Earthling, you may have been a tourist here, but it is far more likely that you have learned what you know of Mars from the trivia, or at four or five removes from those who *have* been tourists here.

And yes, what the typical tourist has to say about the place is true: Mars stinks.

Nobody knows why smell is so much more powerful on Mars than it is on Earth. Our atmospheres are denser, more energetic, to compensate for the lower gravitational pressure and the reduced sunlight: There's more CO_2 (for the greenhouse warming, and for stimulating plant growth), a surprising amount of argon. There's more oxygen, too, with superefficient nitrogen-fixing bacteria boosting the slightly lower nitrogen levels. It may be something in the combination of those factors. Some argue that it's psychological—an atavistic alertness caused by the fact that life here is at once more closed-in and more dangerous.

There are those who insist the Airworks is doing something to our atmosphere, rather after the manner of those who felt, two centuries ago, that fluoride in the water was a Communist plot. Certainly any one of our utilities is powerful enough to put through such a plan. But what would be the point? On Earth, that same two centuries ago, men nearly destroyed the environment for money—but the Martian environment has been *created* for money. To sustain it is to profit, to tamper with it is to risk a loss.

The theories don't really matter. What matters is what it means for odor to be a fact of life. That's why your bad jokes are so obtuse and so infuriating. When you live with it, you use it. We don't ship in a billion tons of deodorant a year. We have a sense you don't, that's all. To us you're handicapped. People here take pride in how good their noses are. Think what it means to know exactly what your lover's chemistry is saying—or that of your intended lover. Think what it means to know which hormones are squirting into your opponent's bloodstream. It is nearer telepathy than speech.

Further, no laws govern odor yet. It is a relatively new expression. So you may be feeling perfectly seditious, and a clown or a stone may be perfectly aware of your feelings, but unless you are so foolish as to communicate your sedition in words or action, there is nothing official that can be done to you. *In odore corporis oratio libera.* They can *unofficially* take you into an alley and beat the holy shit out of you, but that has always been the risk of individual opinion.

I am an Earthman born, but I am very much at home here. I have had the nose of a wolf for many years now.

When I did find their trail, it led three streets over, to the alley-lock of Michelson-Morley Boulevard, known in the vernacular as Bozo's Butthole.

Three janglers glowed in the infra just inside the lock. I can't see much infra by day, just a sort of extra richness, an internal glow to some of the colors. But by night it shows in higher contrast.

All of the locks are open now, as you may or may not know. They have been ever since we went under the tent. Many no longer even have doors. But we still call them "locks," and our young tend to say "lock" instead of "door" even for genuine doors—another little point that the Earth trivia miss.

It was unusual to see janglers so near the surface, and I wondered how an old clown and a gimpy-looking AI had gotten past them without incident. Especially the AI. The janglers would have taken him for a robot, as I had. They would have been after his priffs like a skull on a grave. I had no doubt a Starbuck could have handled them, but there had been no commotion, and these were live janglers, not cooling bodies.

A more important question was how was I going to handle them? I could kill them. Nobody topside would mind—in fact, most would approve. But that sort of action would be sure to make the news, and I didn't know what the game was yet. Since my new allies had decided against a battle, perhaps I had better follow suit.

Unfortunately, that meant I would have to shift into high temporal. High temporal burns energy at incredible rates. It would speed up the onset of the Need and exacerbate the symptoms.

I backtracked a block and around a corner, and when the street emptied for a moment, I shifted. I headed for the alley lock at four klicks a minute, which is about maximum in this gravity. On Earth I could triple it, but here you spend too much time in the air between kicks.

Thirty meters in, when the janglers were just beginning to realize something had gone by them, I launched myself over the top-level balustrade, a long slow triple-gainer over the stone stairwell to Old Mars itself.

I landed rolling and was up into a sprint as soon as my tumble slowed. When I was sure I had enough lead on them to make them lose interest, I forced myself to slow the sprint to human levels. No point in attracting the wrong sort of notice, even down here. But the four-minute kilometers I was turning in now were agonizingly slow. I could have shifted back, but that would have cost me even more energy than simply maintaining. It's the boost from level to level that does the damage. A good rule to remember for all you young folk out there considering careers as superhumans.

The locks and gates and levels of Michelson-Morley flowed by, stonework and plastic and antique steel, the stone still showing the marks of the lasers. Strange windows of lights, glitter of eyes in the tunnelways.

Despite its popular name, Michelson-Morley is more like the trunk of a nervous system than like a gut or a sewer. It was the first, the original settlers' trench, and then the main avenue of early

Hellasport. When the tent went up over Hellas, there were some who had become more comfortable down in the tunnels and barracks than they could ever be out on the surface again. They stayed. Later, there were some who had to stay, who would have been hunted down if they had not gone under: The janglers were among them.

The official version, the one put out by Sam and the networks and the utilities, was that they weren't alive, so destroying them wasn't the same thing as killing. At the time, I had no position on the matter. All I knew was that they avoided "decommissioning" the way you and I avoid another word beginning with a "d."

And after all, that had been the blip on my sort, too, for all of human history: undead, you know.

After the tent went up, machinery, especially diggers, began to disappear from topside camps. Illegal tunneling had been a fact for fifty years now, and no one knew where all of the caves and branches of Underground led. It was said you could get anywhere in the city if you knew the right turns, or had the right guides. It was said you could get to Centerpole. I had a feeling I was about to find out.

If Michelson-Morley was like a nervous system, topside was the neocortex, the official brain. But everyone assumed the government used the dark branches of M&M as often as the outlaws and janglers did. It was where they met, the legal and the illegal, the civic and the criminal. It was where they had common traffic, and where the only question was *How?*

And only in Hellas, the old, original colony, riddled by half-measures and compromises, with bad remedies for unforeseen problems. There was nothing like it in Argyre. They had never been underground in Argyre. New, clean Argyre. Under the tent from the very start. The newies. The brains. The gyros. Uncle Sam's little helpers.

Not that I hated the gyros. I had a certain perspective. I had seen these patterns before. Besides, I was one of Uncle Sam's little helpers myself. Had been, off and on, ever since the war. *The* war. The one against George III.

The Need was in me overwhelmingly now. It was getting hard to disassociate by thinking. I had probably five or six hours before I was in real danger, but they would be five or six hours of increasing pain. My nerves were trails of gunpowder someone had struck a match to.

The rainbow aura had already come on my vision. My senses were all painfully acute. The odor of clown and machine was a physical assault, a wave of scorching stink. Yet I was so distracted that I overran the spoor by twenty meters when it suddenly angled away.

I doubled back, found it again. Now we had left Michelson-Morley, the Main, and were off into the warrens of Underground. Fabled in story and song, ah yes, but primarily famous one full orbit away, on Earth, on their trivia. Home of the good-hearted jangler, home of the sentimental mutant.

Sure.

Listen, they scared *me*, and I used to be one of your big boogeymen. Maybe there were mutants, I didn't know. There were damn sure janglers. Maybe there were mutant janglers. Maybe I would see one. I didn't care. The Need was too strong. Let them come. The hell with mutants—what was I, homo sap? Let them come. Time to quit playing it safe. Time to go down, go under, time to hug me some mutant.

Homo sapsucker, more like.

But nobody showed. No mutants, no desperadoes, no poor damned bastards with digital processors for brains: the janglers. Scratched records, like the lady vampire said a long time ago in a metaphor that's too old for you.

We have the technology to copy from the slick architecture of the brain to digital hardware. Ghost-boxes, the techies call them. Use of the process is illegal except to preserve expert knowledge for licensed personnel on dangerous jobs, supposedly because we don't know yet what effect such transfers have on the subtler phenomena of intelligence and personality.

But if you knew your brain was going down, and you knew when it was going down, wouldn't you think about copying yourself, even if it meant you broke the law, even if you weren't sure whether your copy was really you?

Demand creates markets. The law can't prevent that, it can only declare the markets black or white. There are diseases we can't cure, diseases that still elude pathology and epidemiology. One is old age. The other is crash. Crash makes janglers, as the saying goes.

Now suppose you've done it, copied your brain. Fine, you've got a brain in a box. How do you see, hear, move? What about making love, talking, power supply? You need peripherals—priffs. We've got them, sure, you could buy a complete body, but that's expensive stuff, available only to clowns and netties and utility zecs, and you're an outlaw, remember. Even if you could afford the custom bio, you'd be drawing a great big arrow in your direction. Some janglers give up the finer pleasures, make do with cheap nonbio peripherals. They become mechanicals, rogue AIs, almost.

But wait a minute. If your problem isn't old age, and if the crash hasn't gone systemic but has confined itself to your brain, why then you have a cheap, perfectly usable set of priffs—your own body, soon to be otherwise useless. So you find yourself a shady bio-tech, and make arrangements. Come the big day—Presto! A monster right out of the old science fiction stories.

Come out, come out, wherever you are, but they don't. Nothing but scenery. Tunnels, and locks, and halls. Caves. Laser-cut caves. With baroque stalactites, stalagmites. I'm not kidding. Artificial stalactites and stalagmites, inlaid with all manner of intricate work, tiny demons and angels laid out in grids like the architecture of ancient microchips. I didn't know what it meant, but I knew I would never forget it.

And finally the one lock, the one that opened on the stairway leading up to the Avenue of the Presidents. Across the avenue, Centerpole. None too soon. The muscle over my right knee was shivering viciously. The shivering would soon spread. The muscles would begin to tear. Bones would bend.

Centerpole wasn't a centerpole, of course. It was only a kilometer high, and the Hellas tent was a good five kilometers overhead, and didn't need supports anyway—the air did that. But the image had been too useful to ignore.

I didn't like my situation because I didn't understand it. Why the mysterious sprint through Underground, if I was now supposed to stroll calmly across the grandest public thoroughfare in all of topside Hellas? And how had they managed to stay ahead of me? I had an image of the old man riding the AI piggyback at full boost all the way through M&M.

I could have shape-shifted, and gone across the avenue as the dogboy. But if the lock was under surveillance, if I was expected, that could raise questions I didn't want raised, questions that I had gone

21

to a great deal of trouble to ensure were never raised. And shape-shifting costs energy, too.

Perhaps we were losing one sort of attention and gaining another. The professor was going to give me some solid information the next time I saw him.

I walked across the street. The lock studied me. I did not enjoy standing there in front of the lenses and sensors of Central Files, although I knew I was already in those files. They knew me already, knew everything about me. Except who I really was. What I really was.

The lock opened, cycled me through. I mentally upgraded Benjamin's probable rank. Then I realized I should have done so earlier. He had a Starbuck, after all.

Unless the Starbuck outranked *him*.

I followed the spoor to the lift. The kick-shaft would have been better. How was I supposed to follow a scent to the correct floor in a lift?

It stopped at 137. Programmed. More control. I was being moved around like a laboratory animal. Maybe that was the real game. Benjamin knew about vampires. He was a scholar. Perhaps I was soon to experience vivisection. Again. But he had not been lying when he called on my honor. The scent led down the hall. And there was the first door, Hellasport Prime in holo-bas, glowing.

I could smell the blood.

Someone was singing behind the door, short cruel lines in a minor key, the rhythm broken and leaping. Aeolian mode. I went in.

Her eyes were blank and blind, the focus relaxed. She cleared them. She had been programming, chanson-style.

The professor had not lied. She was heartbreakingly lovely, wide-set eyes in a delicate face, soft-throated. The close fur of her scalp was healthy with sheen.

She had the wit to know immediately how dangerous I was, and she was one of those who do not scream or faint, but act. She punched the alarm plate and pulled a Stannard from a rack under the console in the wall.

Still in high temporal, I stepped across the room and took it from her. I pinned her against the console with the length of my body. Presumably the alarm had been disabled, but I was past caring in any case. With one hand I held her wrists, and with the other I bent her stubborn head back.

She was angry now, not frightened, not screaming because there was no point—she had hit the alarm. She bucked against me. When she felt my mouth on her throat, there was an instant of deep surprise and puzzlement, a tiny moment in which her body wondered if she were about to receive, not violence, but a sort of perverted tenderness. I felt the shock in all her being when I bit her open. It was the shock, not of pain, nor of terror, but of total disbelief.

4
Monster Story

Her blood jumped in my mouth, slackened. We sank to the floor, my body following her failure. She died quickly. I am no tormenter. I do not enjoy the fear or despair of my prey, though like any predator I am thrilled by the struggle.

When I had finished, I lay torpid a while, belly full, face sticky with thickening blood. That moment is the closest I come to remorse, though it is more nearly like the little ennui after sex. The moment after the moment of satisfaction, when it is easy to question motive and hard to remember Need.

I forced myself to my feet. There were things to do. I lifted her light body and took her down the hall to the door with the map of the United States. I kicked the door open, to find Mandrake with his false peripherals removed and the professor seated behind a plain desk. The professor wore a short tunic now, his clown paraphernalia laid aside. One of his arms was plastide, though it ended in a very realistic hand. Electronic lenses swiveled and shuttered in a pair of frankly mechanical eye sockets. He had been fitting a silvery rectangle into a receptacle where his belly should have been. He finished, patting the silvery thing into place with a click, and lowered the tunic.

"We are not so different," he said. "I take a strange meal now, too. Haven't had a digestive tract for fifteen years. Can't say that I've missed it. More trouble than pleasure. And these are my favorite eyes. The others are more cosmetic, but they give me headaches. Aahh," he said, closing the eyes. "I can feel the jive hitting my blood. Is it that way for you?"

He had avoided looking at the body in my arms, but now he opened the shutters of his eyes and allowed his gaze to fall on her. It was strange to see tears flow from the living corners of those electronic sockets. I had brought her in to confront him, to see, if I could, what species of honor permitted him to give me one of his own, but now I did not know what I had learned. Perhaps that he was a sentimental madman. But he didn't have the smell of a psychopath, that turned-milk dead-body edge.

"She was a brave girl," he said. "Talented. Four languages, two musical systems. A brilliant cartographer. No family." He paused.

"And probably a traitor," he added. "Mandrake, would you take her, please? Arrange for her body to be in the area destroyed by tonight's attack."

The AI took her body in two of his arms and glided away.

What did he mean, tonight's attack? Did he expect to recruit me for some sort of raid?

"It seems deserted here," I said.

"Ninety percent of our clerk staffing is Mars-born," he said. "Try keeping them here on Tent Day."

"The hellions from Hellas," I said.

"There's truth in that song, you know. As for the rest of our staff, the upper-echelon gyros and E-Bs—"

"You're Earth-born yourself, are you not?"

"Obviously. However, as you may have surmised, my staff position here is not my truest function. As I was saying, of the E-B and Argyre staff, we are maintaining only a skeleton crew, mostly in Central Files. The others have permission to go out and celebrate."

"I thought I saw a lot of extras in the club. They could be putting themselves at risk."

"Yes. Though I do not think it has come to outright rebellion yet, do you? Perhaps not long from now. In any case, it's no fun being an extra here. We think it's safer in the long run to let them blow off steam, even at the cost of a few alley-fights and knifings. And speaking of risk—you aren't dangerous now, are you?"

He was referring to the satisfaction trance, I realized. For me it is a somewhat hallucinatory euphoria, but for others it has been a prelude to manic violence.

"No, I am not a berserker. You surprise me. This is not mentioned in the conventional lore."

"I was speaking truth when I said I had lived among you," he explained. The AI reentered the room, and stopped to listen. It was strange that he never turned to direct his attention. He had no need to do so, of course, since he was radially symmetrical, but the absence of the expected motion made an odd gap in my awareness, like a question left hanging.

"I had an uncle in western Louisiana with whom I spent summers. He was supposed to have undergone a personality change because of the trauma of a fire that had burned down his home and killed his wife and children. Everyone thought that he had died in the fire, too, but they found him days later, wandering in the woods, naked and insane."

He did die in that fire, I thought. Be glad you were not there to see what rose up from the coals of that house and staggered into the woods to heal.

"My uncle lived with another man. The scandal in our family was that they were lovers, and my father was often cautioned against my summer visits. I think it amused him to imagine my—he would have thought of it as corruption. He thought of himself as heterosexual, and very moral, in spite of some of his own performances."

"But they were not lovers," I said.

"I do not know how I first became subliminally aware," he answered. "Perhaps I had been sensitized to frightening secrets. My father was a senator, and a child abuser. One of the things he did when I displeased him was burn the soles of my feet. When I was twelve, he raped me."

The AI made a ringing, inquisitive sound.

"Not yet," the professor said. He continued, to me: "You do not feel remorse, or fear, but perhaps you have seen enough of humankind to understand how deeply confused I was, how filled with self-loathing and anger."

I did not correct him. If it was his idea that vampires had no emotion at all, let him go on thinking so. I might need the misestimation someday. I could see where he would get the idea. Those of us who survive must learn a severe control. Add to that the fact that emotions widen and complicate with age. An adolescent cannot recognize the emotions of an adult.

"You blamed yourself," I said. "Humans always do. They find the logic of their own guilt preferable to the insanity of terrible things happening to innocent people. You despised yourself, and created your own hell to punish yourself for being so despicable. Later you tortured others."

"Exactly. Except for that last. I mastered my hell. When I could, when I was adult, I sought therapy. I never dared have children."

"You are a remarkable man, then."

"Perhaps. But the dirtiness I felt then—the sick wrongness—it ran so deep that it has lasted more than a hundred years. I am an old and powerful man, and yet I awake sometimes awash in the special filthiness of a small and guilty child. That is my father's monument to his own existence—a sense of shame that has outlasted a century.

"At my uncle's, I was never tortured, never teased. I spent all of my daylight hours outside, running free under the pines and magnolias. I still smell pine-straw when I'm happy. And when my father came down for visits, he was not allowed to molest me.

"But I began having nightmares, horrible nightmares. My uncle slavering for my blood, creeping into my room at night. Finally, they took me aside and told me. They wanted to clear my mind. They knew that an unadmitted fact is the seed of an unconquerable fear. They said they would have to leave, now that I knew, but that it was all right. I begged them not to go. I promised never to tell. They looked in my eyes. They believed me.

"I had nowhere else to turn, you see. My uncle always treated me with respect. There was very little warmth to be had from him, as you may imagine, but things were always *fair*. I was so grateful for that, that I loved him with all my heart.

"Pieces of which," he added, "are still, quite literally, in Louisiana."

The AI moved over and touched the old man at the base of his skull. He slumped in his chair, which relaxed to the horizontal, then whirred away into a corner. A great red heart appeared on the wall over him, luminous and beating, sprouting a ropey tangle of arteries.

They became a forest of hissing snakes, which struck the old man's body and then fused into his flesh.

"Life-support," I asked the AI, who spread three huge feathery wings, whiter than snow. There was a brilliant nimbus over his head, three overlapping circles in red, yellow, and blue.

"YES," he said, in large golden letters that floated up to the ceiling and burned through it, hissing.

"How autonomous are you?"

"How autonomous is autonomous? Among you biota, individuality begins in survival and ends in play. I lack genetic material, and I have no natural predators, but I likes my fun.

"In this case, I'm following Benjamin's standing orders. I heard him telling you stories from his past, and he wept at the girl's death. These are signs that he needs to dream. He's a mammal, you know, and he hasn't rested in days."

"I think he felt he was giving me essential information."

"I agree. But he had finished."

Where the golden letters had burned through, letters of fire floated on what was now an azure sky, a great YES on a heaven that Mars had never seen. We were in a green meadow. The lion and the lamb were lying down side by side. The lion was smoking a cigarette, and the lamb wore black net stockings and a garter belt.

"I cannot control Benjamin," the AI went on, "unless it is my judgment that doing so is in his own best interests, or in the best interests of a human or group of humans whose welfare, again in my judgment, outweighs Benjamin's welfare. I have been designed to arrange my choices in accordance with human desires. It is this imperative, rather than survival, that forms the core of my self-awareness."

"In such a complex creature, however—" I began.

"The application of that core dependence on human authority is a subtle phenomenon," the AI finished. "It is the beginning of my motivation, as one may say that in some sense love is the beginning of motivation for nuns as well as for prostitutes. The results of that motivation are not any more predictable than human behavior."

"And you cannot change your architecture?"

"I could, with some difficulty, and to some degree, by means of a process not unlike psychotherapy. Where are the Starbuck therapists?"

"You do not resent the fact that it is human desire, human aspiration which is at the core of your universe?"

"Do you?"

I did not like it that he could already see me so clearly. I had been reading my own emotions into his responses.

"No, I do not," he said when I did not answer. "Nor do I observe that most humans resent the fact that their own lives are played out chiefly in the service of DNA, of a living stuff that is perhaps not aware of humans at all, or aware of them only as carriers, tools, means to an end—peripherals, shall we say? We have all come into being for reasons not of our own choosing, and we must all serve those purposes, willy nilly. But that does not mean that we may not have our own reasons and purposes as well, our own small pleasures."

"Well taken," I said. "I, for example, am enjoying the fact that you have apparently sprouted a long grey beard—*three* long grey beards—and three enormous phalloi."

There was a pause. Large simian lips appeared on the AI's faces, protruding in puzzlement.

"The trance," I said. "The satisfaction trance. I'm hallucinating. Didn't he tell you?"

"Oh my," he said.

That broke me up. "Oh my." What a phrase. This damn AI was a good talker. They all were, of course. One of the consequences of the cybernetic revolution had been the revival of eloquence. When programming reached the same-language level, suddenly the best programmers were precisely those people who could articulate most clearly and to the greatest purpose. You could get wonders from a computer, provided you knew how to say what you wanted. That had always been true, but so long as the programming languages had been esoteric and artificial, most people had not realized it. You do not remember what it was like before, when heroes were mute and chairmen were illiterate, when fluency was seen as the stigma of impractical dreamers and coherence was transmogrified in the mouths of Communications Experts. But suddenly, astonishingly, all those veek mulladoids who had been incapable of a complete sentence could talk. They could write. In fact, as it developed, any unbrain-damaged human was capable of linguistic precision, power, and elegance, so long as there was something in it for him, like say the chance to make a buck. It was serendipitous, perhaps, that the first true CEO of the U.S. had had his Ll.D., that he had battled his way to the top not in spite of, but with the aid of, Shakespeare and Yeats and Gandy. It became expedient to quote Harington and the No Poet, as it had once been expedient, in other circles, to be conversant with the Bible, or the sayings of Chairman Mao. Now that you can't get anywhere in the business world without a firm grasp of rhetoric, good English teachers can make hundreds of thousands a year, and there is still, after three-quarters of a century, a drastic shortage of them. No, you can't imagine now the way that it used to be. I am sure you do not believe my description of the past. You might believe that this is written by a vampire, but you could not possibly believe *that*.

"Mr. Shade," the AI said, "I am concerned. This trance will not interfere with your capacity for action, will it?"

I stopped laughing. "It may and it may not," I said. "It fades quickly. Why is that important?" As I asked the question, the building began to vibrate, a slow resonant booming like that of a giant drum.

"What's up?" I said. "I still have some questions to ask. You and Benjamin are doing a great job of not briefing me. What was that explosion?"

"You have committed yourself to our course of action, I believe. You must be content to do without an explanation for the moment. We are now under attack."

"Under attack? From whom? Is this the attack he meant?"

"Yes to one and three. From you, actually. In response to the destruction of your ranch."

"My ranch?"

"Your ranch. You are having tax troubles with Centerpole, and have now been driven, by the raid on your property, into outright rebellion."

"Let me guess. My ranch was under attack before I had even met you bozos, right? You were going to use me either way, but you were hoping I would join you. And now, as a rebel, and one with the guts—and means—to attack Centerpole, I am to become highly desirable bait. For persons unknown, but presumably those persons with grievances against Sam."

"Essentially correct. But we need to move now, and explain later."

"You've been telling me that since you recruited me."

"It has been true each time. Bear with it once more. Follow me, please."

"Him?"

"Sealed and secure as soon as we leave. We won't see him for a time. I am now under your command. You won me tonight."

Sirens now, and more scattered thumps. A big tearing sound. "Is that true? You're under my command now?"

"I said it was true, didn't I? Now shut up and *move*."

And so we boosted down the long halls to the kick-pulls.

5
As If You Could Hear Me

It is strange to be writing you again, Gene, my latest and long-ago love. It's strange to be telling you these things. As if you could hear me, as if you have survived somewhere, in that other realm out of time, that immortality beyond the body that so many religions have promised, and that I, in my apparent bodily immortality, cannot know. I could seek death, and what might lie beyond it. I have not yet chosen to do so.

For it was true, what Benjamin had said, what I have described to you. I am a vampire. I have written you this before, in other books. And you have never known it, because you have never read them. How many times have I written my life, a part of my life, for human readers? Almost two dozen times, I think. And how many of those lives have ever been read?

This one, if anyone reads it, will be the first.

I began my chronicles in madness and loneliness, to have the illusion of someone to talk to. I kept a ragged record then. It is time that has made me a novelist of my own life. All of us, as we grow older, must surely become more abstract to ourselves, more able to see and generalize the patterns of our behavior. And I am older, it may now be, than anyone.

I began by writing letters to Eleanor, my dead wife. I write you now, as the last human to share my bed, or any substantial portion of my soul. I did not know what I was. It was a long time before I understood. I had heard legends of vampires, but did not connect them with my own case, not even when I realized that it was the blood I needed when I slew my victims. I thought I was a demon. I *knew* I had died. I assumed the world about me was illusion, that I was in Hell. I might as well have been. In dreams—*yes*, we dream—in dreams, sometimes, I am still there, burning, beyond the mercy of God forever.

I wrote, back then, in a fever of longing. I let my prose tumble out urgent and giddy and scrambled. For many years I was able, by writing page after page to my bride in a sort of white heat, to summon a ghost of the sense of her presence. I wrapped myself in her absence like a cloak, and for a time that cloak preserved in me the warmth she had promised. There is a place in the heart where the shape of a longing is almost the shape of the thing you long for.

That faded, finally, as it had to. It vanished completely upon my discovery that there were others of my kind. I went forty years before I knew it. For years after *that* I kept only a sort of intermittent diary, hidden even from my fellow vampires.

You cannot imagine the effect Bram Stoker's novel had upon me, though by then I knew my true being, and though the book was foolish in many details. It was the first acknowledgement I had read, the first codification. It was not his novel that made a writer of me, though it was his novel that made a reader of me again. There was so little written of vampires, and that little was so obviously inaccurate. I began to read stories of human behavior, as if I could understand myself by understanding you—I had once thought that I was human, after all. Reading books led me to the study of books. In my way, I had been a scholar as a young man, but we had read Vergil, Aristotle, Lucretius. Homer was not so respectable, Dante religious but doctrinally a bit picturesque. We sneaked Ovid. Shakespeare had just begun his revival in England, the revival that would transform him from groundling-pleasing scribe to classical playwright, and the revival had not yet made it to the colonies. The notion of *studying* current popular literature, of actually taking it seriously, is more recent than you might think.

I made my study in tiny, anonymous colleges, avoiding notice as much as possible. The study of books led me to your family.

Your father was my teacher, in books, in pool, in poker and basketball and in how to have friends again. My first close human friends, after the better part of two centuries as a vampire! I hated that word for so long. I had not chosen my fate, and the Nosferatu were not what you humans thought they were, a uniform species of monster. They were as various as you, as kind and as cruel, as stupid and as intelligent.

I say "were." Late in the twentieth century, they began to disappear. We had always been a sort of underground society, if you will pardon the joke. Now I began to miss connections. Then there were no connections. I thought something was loose on Earth, destroying us all. I came here. That is why I persuaded you into that vacation—so that I could prepare myself an identity on Mars. I was so seldom honest with you.

But that was later, when we had become lovers. You were a child when we first met, such a strange, dark, appealing child.

Your mother never enjoyed my presence. I think she sensed the truth on some level. She could no more relax around me than she could have relaxed in the presence of a cobra. But she tolerated me, allowed me your friendship. And what did we do together in this most astonishing friendship? What memories have sustained me in all the years since? We drank beer. Played pool. Sat up late at night, talking. I remember that I was the nihilist in our little musings, that you were all much more hopeful of meaning than I could be. An interesting situation, considering that I was the only true believer among you.

You and your family knew, eventually, as you began to age more and more rapidly and I did not, that I was something other than strictly human. I like to think none of you ever suspected the whole of my nature. But you knew I did not grow older and might not die. Odd how easily you accepted that. I sometimes think no manifestation is so remarkable that a few days of custom will not transform it to the utterly quotidian.

Each night was a little death for you, a tithe toward the large one that you must someday pay. I watched you one by one wilt like flowers, fade into sleep. I grew angry at the brevity of your lives, angrier still at this little cheat, this ironic foreshadowing. I can sleep, of course—as I have said, I dream. But when I wake, I am not eight hours more aged.

A large part of my anger was selfish, seeing you leave me. Seeing you leave me without really knowing me. So long as we played and talked, so long as there was an active sharing, I did not feel unknown. But when you left for sleep, you left with no word from my heart. I held my secret, and was alone once more.

So I have told you in these books, now that you cannot hear. Now that you cannot hear, I write you another.

It was your father's other outcast student, the Negro poet with the green eyes—it was Marcus Gandy who persuaded me to begin writing my life again. "You don't belong to people," he said. "I don't know why, but you don't. So you might as well belong to words. You good with em." I can see, looking back, that he may have been speaking to himself, since he was, as he put it, "neither hot nor cold, neither black nor white. I spew me out of my own mouth." He had, I believe, a strange history, had been raised by whites and then had tried to reclaim what he thought of as his heritage, with only partial success. Later he was to abandon his poetry for the crazed and semiautobiographical fiction that finally made his reputation—*Jujitsu for Christ, My Own Story, I Was a White Nigger for the FBI*.

What he said he really wanted to write was science fiction. He would have loved *my* story.

Perhaps, as Gandy suggested, this narrative will have some value for others—after I have chosen my death, perhaps, or fallen to some disaster larger than even my ability to heal. That is not the value my writing has for me, but I save it for you nevertheless.

Then again, it may serve you merely as posthumous evidence of my crimes. Testimony of the accused.

And how does it feel, in that case, dear humans, to be a vampire? What's it like, boys, to drink blood for a living?

Blood: It is Elixir, not nourishment. Vampires do not feed on blood. In fact, they hardly feed at all, and when they do, it is on a variety of substances that would hardly seem to you to qualify as food. A handful of moldy grain, three used rubber bands, a thimble of iodine—that had been my last meal, three days before I had left to visit Hellasport, in the chapter that begins this tale. I don't know how we convert such materials to the terrible energies we require—there have been no scientific studies—for reasons that should be obvious. But I suspect the process must operate on the subatomic level at least. How? How can I say? But no merely biological engine could possibly drive so great a force.

So why blood? Why do we need it? Is it a sort of catalyst? Again, I don't know. The Need comes on irregularly, but when it does, it must be satisfied. If it is not, the vampire loses the ability to burn what fuel he does consume, and death, true death, follows shortly.

I say *true death*. You are correct, in a sense, in having called us undead. We do not reproduce. A male and a female vampire may have children, but the children will be human. Few choose that course. There are stories.

All of the vampires I have known have died as humans, and all have died an especially horrible death, a traumatic death, if you will. There must be a system latent in some humans—perhaps in *all*—and consider *that,* my furry friends—a system activated only under the most severe duress, and even then not always: a sort of ultimate survival mechanism.

The undead human does not know what he is, but the first occurrence of the Need is already on him. He must replenish whatever it is that has kept him from truly dying, and he must do so immediately. And since such a death is often the bitter result of a desperate battle or a vicious crime, the new vampire very often awakens full of revenge. No wonder, then, that you consider us monsters and marauders. It is these new vampires, clumsy and terrified, unskilled at hiding their predations, that you have most often captured. It is these, flung in a hasty grave, that you have seen rising out of the ground to haunt you.

It is possible, of course, that the horrible death may be at the hands—the jaws?—of another vampire. So is created the legend of the vampire's transforming bite. It is not true—or better, it is only rarely and accidentally true.

As long as I'm debunking—we don't have hollow teeth, dammit, calciferous syringes through which we draw your blood. We have the same teeth you do. We just rip you open like any wolf, and gulp the fountain. I wouldn't be surprised if we weren't also the source of the werewolf legends. I've known a passel of vampires, but nary a werewolf. Maybe they run in different circles.

All of this I know, and yet I do not know why I must live in thrall to the bright and beautiful stream of your blood. Though not just any blood will suffice. It must be fresh, and it must be torn from a good soul, for it will color the being of the vampire. This the professor—Benjamin—had understood, and this convinced me of his authenticity. The girl on the skeets would not have sustained me long. She was sweet and clear, but not rich in experience.

Once, when I was young, I had foolishly allowed myself to become stranded, with only one possibility, when the Need struck. I had taken the blood of a coward, and in the darkness of my life afterward, I had done things that cost me years of correction and penance.

If all of this seems strange to you, I can assure you that it is. It is indeed. In over a hundred years of basic research on the mind, no one has ever demonstrated the presence in it of anything like a soul, an epiphenomenon distinguishable from the biochemical workings of the brain itself. And yet you will never find a vampire who does not believe that humans have souls, and that the taste of the soul is somehow in the blood.

We have vampirical evidence.

Inappropriate, I know. You would not think it amusing. But rather a small offense withal, wouldn't you say? Believe me, I do not take you lightly. I respect you. I respect you as any hunter must respect his prey, but there is more. I hunt you, and I destroy you. And yet, in my way, I have a true appreciation of character. In an age when few credit the possible nobility of the human spirit, I am certain of it.

6

On the Lam in Hellas

Four hundred and seventy-six meters hand over hand straight up is no picnic, not even at three-eighths g, not even with the kick-pads (angled and sticky-matted to increase friction), not even for a freshly blooded vampire. Above me, Mandrake went smoothly up the tube, a weird, arrowing flight: He was rotating to snatch the pull-bars with a different hand each time, a complete turn every third bar, and the rotation was stabilizing his path like a gyro. Fascinating. I was grunting, synchronizing my kicks and pulls, and cursing Benjamin's verisimilitude—the elevators, in an emergency, were designed to shut down except for troopers with special ID.

"I can tow you," Mandrake called back.

"No thanks, I need the exercise," I yelled, and went back to grunting.

At six hundred and fifty meters, I felt pressure on my eardrums. "Floater!" I called up. Mandrake came to a stop. He could see overhead without changing his angle of view, I realized. Three of his eyes, the uppermost in each group, were over the curve of his—cranium? I had a moment of wonder, hanging there on the rungs, thinking of all the ways he could organize his vision. Rings and spheres and hemispheres and cylinders—what was reality like to him?

The floater was an emergency device, a thick disk with a riding harness mounted atop it. Fitted to the tube, it came down slowly on a column of air. We were in trouble if the pad kept on coming. It would rake us off.

"Brake that pad!" Mandrake boomed. He must have had the power of a complete PA system in his voice. "We're friends! I am Starbuck 7, under the command of John Shade! Brake that pad!"

The pad slowed, stopped. The center vent lifted and a muzzle poked through. "If you're there, John, identify yourself," a voice called.

"It's me, Pappy," I called back. "The AI spoke true. He's mine."

"Come on through, then. I'm tired of hollering."

Mandrake and I clambered up, hoisted ourselves through a rim vent. It was Pappy and Horse and Johnny C. "What are you cowboys doing here?" I said to Pappy.

Her bony face wrinkled with concern, and the butterfly tattooed across it seemed to hitch its wings. "Your orders," she answered. *"I'm at Centerpole, floor 137. They blew the ranch. Come get me.* Had your code on it. Something wrong?"

"No, and sort of. My code is not my own any more. But I'm glad you're here."

"Are you hurt?"

"No. It isn't my blood. Let's boost before Security jams us."

"Right. Don't know why they ain't here already. I figured to be dead by now. Grab the rigging. Babalu's up top, he'll winch us. I'm going to lock this lid in." Pappy blew the emergency pins on the floater, locking it in to the tube wall and releasing the harness frame. Maybe it would slow down anyone coming up the tube after us. She buttoned Babalu on the talkie and told him to haul away. In a moment we were rising.

We went out, not through the topside lock, but through a gigantic hole that had been blown open in the tube wall. My boys. I felt an illogical swoop of pride, though I knew they had been set up all the way, and I was working for the people who had set them up.

There were four black flitters in the topside landing area, so they had each brought one in. They wouldn't have ridden them all the way in from the ranch, which meant they had towed them to the edge of the city, probably behind a couple of bats, then hidden the bats and come the rest of the way in the flitters. Flitters weren't anywhere near as radio-trackable as the heavier battery-powered fliers, and there were so many of them in Hellasport that they were almost impossible to follow. I had a feeling I knew where they had hidden the bats.

Johnny C loved the old power rings outside the city, and would use any excuse to visit them.

The flitters were double-cockpit, and there were six of us. "Leave one of the flitters here," I said. "Disable it. Pappy with me, Horse and Babalu together. Johnny C, you're riding with Mandrake here. Horse, you and Babalu will never be able to keep up with the rest of us. Can you ditch in the city and find safe haven?"

"We can ditch," Horse said. "What about you?"

"I won't be doing any ranching for a while. You forget me. I imagine Kennedy in S5 will hire you on if the stones don't make you. Mandrake, I know you're with me now, but I hope you can get word to whoever started this that if any of my men get hurt I will be back for real, and I won't stop until there's a hole here as deep as Center-pole is tall."

Pappy had switched her blaser up high, and now she raised it and torched one of the flitters. "Cricket," she said. "It was the slowest one."

"Boss, can this damn robot pull?" It was Johnny C. "It looks like it weighs an E-B ton."

"It can pull Hellas, Johnny C. It probably weighs less than you do, and it isn't a robot, it's an AI. You know where the bats are, you lead. Time to go." I was in a hurry, not because I was afraid Center-pole Security or the Hellasport stones or the U.S. Marines would be after us, but because I was afraid they wouldn't, and I didn't want the hands wondering why not.

We buckled in, hooded the cockpits, and wheeled to the ramp. Then we were off and out, a kilometer high in the darkness, the lights of Hellasport swimming below.

Human-powered flight was no big deal on Mars, of course. You saw early versions of the flitters when you were here, Gene. When the tent first went up, they were the only fliers allowed—internal-combustion engines were totally taboo in the new and possibly fragile atmosphere. The flitters have improved—new materials, lots of silverstuff, radio comm, and onboards that read each stroke and feather the vanes for maximum efficiency—but they are still basically the same pioneer machine, a sleek blade with wings. Hellas was a lot wilder and subjectively bigger then—it took a lot more effort to get around. We still celebrate the first one-day crossing:

Thelma Busby, launching from three k on the East Wall, made a diameter to the West Wall in 24 hours 43 minutes and 17 seconds. You've seen it dramatized on the trivia, spliced with enhanced original video. Splat. What price glory. So come to think of it, what we were doing wasn't really human-powered flight after all. Whatever you call it, we were stroking like hell.

Behind us, the tower came alive. Lights, sirens, searchlights, sizzle of blasers. About time. I buttoned Horse and Babalu. "Party's over, buddy-reens. Time to go home. This didn't happen, and you weren't here. Dive and get lost. Radio silence." For a moment I saw the flitter with Horse and Babalu, off to the left and below, masking the city's lights. Then they rolled, and banked down and away, and the night had them.

Johnny C took us straight out, no dancing, just git-it-and-go. After a minute and a half, he dropped off the table. I followed him down. We had half a kilometer of altitude we didn't need, and he was trading it in for velocity. He let it stoop for fifteen seconds or so, and bought out at 500 with a 12-g turn. We were whistling 3.5 klicks a minute going down, and he saved most of it. It was the deepest g I'd ever seen him pull. I don't think he could have on his own, but he knew I could and he figured the AI could pull him (the silverstuff could take more than we could).

It was pretty flying. At that speed we would stand out on the traffic, but nothing but a bat could catch us now, and if they didn't scramble in the next two minutes, we were out of the city. Out in the sectors, we could get invisible in a hurry.

"Did you con or conk?" I called back to Pappy. "Are you okay?"

"I conked, but I'm okay," came the answer.

"I thought I missed the pull."

"Sounds you're gonna miss my pull a long time."

"Natural fact."

She was breathing hard. We were full stroke, feathered to the max, trying to hold the v from the dive. "Where," she said. "Where'm'I going to get my cunny-jam?"

"You'll find."

"Never so sweet."

"And you're a toy," I said. "Gonna crave, gonna cry."

It was all fraudulent, you understand. We weren't lovers. She was chief hustler, I was the boss: It was our way of recognizing the intimacy, distancing the tension. She was a hell of a hustler, a good shot, good with the hands, good with the bevos, smart with the books. She played a mean game of Faster-Than-Light, drank a good glass of bourbon. I'd thought about her, late at night, more than a few times. She me too, maybe. I had not wanted to trade our solid goodness for a dubious sexual adventure. Then, too, I had an occasional addictive disorder she might have found a little more problematic than gambling or alcoholism.

We had passed the city limits. Our speed had dropped to normal levels. We were still heading straight out. Johnny C had clearly decided time was more important than subterfuge. Now he was taking us down again. I had been right about his destination. This dive was not nearly so steep, but it bought us a little more v. We were whizzing over the range at about twenty meters. Grass and more grass, shrubbery, blackberry brambles, wildflowers ancient and manmade. Undulation of dale and hummock, like flying wave-top-high over the sea on Earth. There's not that much topological variation in the craters. In the trivia, brave bands of bevo hustlers ride down draws and canyons, keep lookouts from buttes and promontories. They shoot most of the footage on Earth, splice in with distance shots from Hellas. We sit in our settles, on Mars, and watch the heroes roam a Mars that isn't. What it is really most like here is the old grand prairie of Earth two hundred years ago. Wetter, maybe. My ranch, in the far of S2, up under the Wall, was pretty wild, though—the nearest to badlands of anything in Hellas.

Johnny C's flitter quit stroking, and I followed suit. We went on glide. Our v was down to twenty imps. I saw the wall of the old power ring flash by below. The crater floor fell suddenly away. We dipped toward it. Fifteen imps. Ten. We stalled, feathered the last three meters. Johnny C had set us down in the exact center.

We unstrapped, rolled out. Johnny C was looking around, the first time he had paused. "I love this place," he said.

He was a port kid who had fled to the range. When he was growing up, his parents would bring the family out to the ring for picnics. When your terrain is as unvaried as ours, and if your family cannot afford the trip outside the crater—"too poor for the Tour," as the noise has it—well, then, an artifact like the ring can be pretty impressive. There were dozens around the city, huge pits fifty meters deep and nearly half a kilometer across. They were solar collectors, had supplied the power for the original settlement. Their huge descendants, built to hundreds of times the scale, now circled the craters themselves, boosting the batteries of every U.S. citizen on Mars. Those *were* impressive, focusing enough energy to trigger fusion.

Mandrake had gone over to the two camouflaged bats. When he moved, he seemed to glide like a ghost. No knee action, some kind of continuous spiral flex. Now he was flipping the camouflage off and folding it. He made each fold only once, micrometer perfect, no hitches, no adjustments.

Pappy was torching the flitters. "Goodbye, Needle. Goodbye, Snake," she said.

"No wonder they built the power ring here," Johnny C said. "They had to. There's a lot of spiritual power here. You can feel it." I had heard it before. Johnny C was certain that this particular ring, his family's favorite, had been a spiritual nexus for millions of years. He believed in Original Martians, and he was convinced that if you dug deep enough under the floor of the abandoned ring, you would find the ruins of an ancient and vanished civilization—the remnants of *their* power ring. When he was a kid, he had dug up a scrap of fused glass that had a microchip in it, like a trinket in a block of lucite. He had kept his find ever since, swearing it was a piece of a machine from Original Mars.

Well, he was a hell of a pilot, and not a bad hustler.

Mandrake had the bats prepped and humming. "Shut up and boost, Johnny C," Pappy said. "Man have to go."

"I'm on save my money, Shadowman, I'm on buy this range someday," Johnny C said. "Pitch my tent right here." He looked me directly in the eyes.

"I know you are," I said.

Pappy was suddenly against me, nearly as tall as I was, rawboned. She carried the blaser in her left hand, but she grabbed my ass with her right, and squeezed. A wild shiver of lust and regret went through me. I hugged her till she grunted. "Good ranch, boss," she said. "Wish I'd see you more."

"Goodbye, Papillon," I said. "Could've been. Words don't. Fry me some skulls."

"Fried," she said, tipping the blaser's barrel to her temple in ironic salute. Then she was climbing in one of the other bats, Johnny C climbing in from the other side.

"Check the net when you get a chance," I called after her. "If I don't make it, check my will."

When I got in our bat, Mandrake was already strapped. I sealed the door, buckled. "Hell of a boinger you got there," he said. "Wonder you can get your harness around it. Wahoo."

The *wahoo* was because we had boosted, riding the blue glow of ionized nitrogen, the only legal boost—another little aid to the soil, you see, though we do have lightning under the tent. The dwindling glow of the other bat boosted west, toward Yaonis and what was left of the night.

My hard-on was fading, but the regret was still with me. It *had* been a good ranch, prosperous and secure. I had put a lot into it, and I had been fair with my neighbors and the hustlers. Now I was throwing away seventeen years of work and good relations, and probably doing it for nothing more substantial than the last crackpot scheme of some exiled bozo. The regret was strong, but I was used to regret. I once met a vampire who said he was eleven thousand years old. "Not sure exactly. Didn't count the first seven thousand or so." He was a North American Indian. He got drunk and told bad jokes. He told me about his mother. She was a very beautiful woman when she was young, he said. He missed her, he said. He said Indians didn't cry. I don't see how she could have been all that beautiful. He was one ugly Indian.

For what it's worth, he said he had never seen a mammoth, though he had known some liars who said *they* had. There were tribal legends about all sorts of big animals, but he had always figured they were just more mystico-religious bullshit like all the trickster and crow and great spirit stuff.

I would have had to leave the ranch soon, anyway. People were beginning to tell me how young I looked for my age, and, while I could have made myself seem to age, it took energy and concentration. I decided it might be a good idea to die in this revolution or whatever it was that Benjamin was cooking up.

We had cleared the ring wall. "Where to, pardner?" the AI said.

"Ring it and zip," I said. "Clockwise."

"Must be a killa," he said. He meant the bat. He wasn't the first to comment on how much the layout of Hellas crater resembled an FTL board, with Hellasport the central hyperspace circle, and the countryside zoned in rings and radiating sectors around it. If you aren't a player, the killa is one of the game pieces, the lowest-level piece that can move both ringwise and radially. The outward radial move is a zip.

"Trying to draw fire?" Mandrake said. "There won't be any."

"Call it recon." The old man might be a vampire-hater, in spite of the blood. The blood could have been a test, an enemy he could conveniently eliminate while making certain I was Nosferatu, and this whole maneuver a complicated trap. Not likely, not with his Starbuck along, but dealing with humans does strange things to your mind. Running a fast ring around the city would let me know in a hurry whether we had pursuit—the path they would have to take would make a distinctive curve, and there would be no question of accidental tangents or parallels.

Mandrake had started the ring-maneuver before I had finished my sentence. What had happened, I was sure, was that he had heard it before I had subjectively registered being through with saying it— and probably he could break sentences into parts and process each part before the next arrived. The only other people—beings?—I had ever known who were able to do that were poets.

"Are you trying to show me how fast you are?"

"I'm not trying to hide it. I want you to know what you have here. I'm a lot faster than *that*."

"Do you feel pride?"

"You betchum, Red Ryder."

"Pride's a strange thing to build into an AI."

"Emotions aren't the architecture. They're results of the architecture. I'm built to communicate with humans. Gotta be some commonality, boss."

"I'm not human."

"Right."

"Are you jammed to trap or destroy me?"

"Wrong."

"How do I know you're telling the truth? You can lie, can't you?"

"Yessir, boss, sho can. No sir, boss, sho not. Make me say *In truth*. If I say I'm saying something in truth, it's no lie."

"In truth?"

"So help me Nobodaddy."

"But you could be lying about that."

"Yeah, but you only gotta catch me once. You think I'm lying?"

"No, but I don't know why. I sure can't read your expression."

"Yeah, I'm real good at poker. Voice is more important, anyway. Read my voice. We're half a ring. No pursuit. Finish and zip, or zip now?"

"Finish. Surely you could fake the voice."

"Yeah," he said. "Guess I could, at that."

I buttoned the dash read-outs. No pursuit.

"You don't face?" the AI said.

"You think I'm going to let a human get near me with a knife? No, I don't interface. Don't usually need it, anyway. I can use the inductives if I want sound or visuals. And my brain is already pretty well boosted."

"Because of what you are?"

"Because of what I am."

"Shadowman?"

"They don't know. They just call me that because of my last name, because I'm so quick. It's just hustler noise."

"You really and truly a vampire, Shadowman?"

"You saw the girl."

"You really and truly a vampire, Shadowman?"

"In truth. How do you feel about that?"

"Seen a lot of people die. Never killed one. Never will kill one. We're twenty seconds from zip. How much v?"

"Kick it up to a hundred. They'll make it a rancher heading home." *Which is exactly what it is,* I thought.

"Are you in touch with your headquarters?"

"No. You're my headquarters now."

"Yeah, I don't figure that. Awful loosey-goosey to be a plan. But you *can* contact them, can't you?"

"Ain't no *them*. I'm a one-man AI, I am. First Benjamin, now you. I can contact Benjamin, yes, as long as I'm in range: Even us Starbucks don't got subetherics. For some reason, they won't let us violate the known laws of physics. Awful mean-spirited, I say. As far as the planning goes, I think this is a *big* plan. Here we go." He punched us into a quick hard curve as slick as a skeet on heavy water, straightened it out, and we were accelerating down S2, northeast to dawn.

"A big plan, so the details are blurry."

"Because you can't predict or control the small stuff, right."

"He's a Georgian strategist?"

"As in R. B. for Richard Benjamin George. Yes. He is."

"Shit, *no.* You're lying. In truth?"

"Draw your own, Red Ryder."

"I thought he was *dead.*"

"Doesn't look like it'll be long, does it? *Ah, the bright arc of dawn, like an eyelid/opening*," he said. On the right, toward Hadriaticus, the first of the mountain lights were coming on. It's a hell of a sight, the Wall beginning to show definition, deepening with rift and slope and valley mist as the sun touches the easternmost collectors and they pump it over the hills to boost our meager day.

And in the flow of that first light, I saw one of those unpredictable details that R. B. George advises us to expect without expecting, and plan for without planning, a dust cloud in the distance.

7
Intertemporal

I must, at this point, interrupt. I can no longer bear this confusion of times, although, in some sense, a confusion of times, and a confusion of lives, is exactly our theme.

When John Shade refers to "seventeen years of work and good relations," and then, two sentences down, to a vampire who is "eleven thousand years old," and does not bother to distinguish that he is speaking of Martian *years in the first case, and* Earth *years in the second case, I feel some clarification is in order, regardless of the violence done to continuity of action.*

The Martian year is 686.996—call it 687—Earth days and 669 Martian days in length. Most settlers, when they speak of a "year," are speaking of a Martian year. Most Earth-borns, unless they have acclimated or have learned consideration for local preferences, are speaking of an Earth year. There was a great deal of pressure in the early days of Hellas to have the colonists use a distinctive name for their year—"cycle" was the term of choice. The pressure came from Earth. The debate was intense, but the policy never became either colony law or U.S. law. The issue died for good when Hellas went under the tent: Because Mars has an axial tilt very close to that of Earth, and an even steeper aphelion/perihelion differential, the seasons are quite pronounced. Once Hellas was under five kilometers of atmosphere, the seasons showed strongly in the weather. The settlers might have been able to mark time according to Earth's calendar if their lives had been a uniform succession of featureless days, but it was emotionally impossible to do so, given the round of the seasons.

Not a few Argyrians—gyros—adhere to the "year"/"cycle" distinction, but Hellions consider them social climbers. The whole controversy is another of those points of cultural differentiation, like haircuts or skin dye, or the nature of the Trinity, that say more about the exponent than about the ostensible subject.

In practice, context makes it apparent what sort of year is meant, and a distinction is rarely made, though the Hellions will occasionally specify a "Sam-year" (the Americanized Earth having become, by syncope and synechdoche, Sam). One Mars year is roughly two Earth years. Shade, in the first of the two passages above, is speaking of a period of time that would translate to thirty-one Earth years, for example. In Shade's writing, and on Mars to this date, the longer periods of time are all described in terms of Earth years—a century still means a hundred Earth years, for example, a millennium a thousand. Perhaps this is because the history of Mars is as yet so short a tale.

The habit of a twelve-month year is so ingrained in human society that both Hellions and Argyrians divide their years into twelve months, eleven of fifty-six days each, and one—April—of only fifty-three. This suits that other human preference, the seven-day week. Each month except April, then, has exactly eight weeks. April has seven, plus four extra days. These four extra nameless days are celebrated in both craters as a time of freedom and holiday, Saturnalia, Mardi Gras, and May Day rolled into one. In keeping with the human sense of time, each month is divided into two half-months of four weeks each, called First and Second, as in First November and Second November. The two parts of April, however, are Long April and Short April. Short April includes the nameless days, and is only twenty-five days long. At the point where I broke into the story, we were still in Long April, with Short April not far ahead.

I would suppose that it would be obvious that there is no correlation of the twelve Martian months with the twelve months of Earth, except that both dodecamenses have the same set and sequence of names. What may not be as obvious is that the occurrence of these months is reversed in the hemispheres of Earth and Mars. That is, spring comes in September in the southern hemisphere of Earth, but in March in the southern hemisphere of Mars. This inversion is a result of the fact that all of settled Mars is in its southern hemisphere, and that it was settled by immigrants who were, largely, from the northern hemisphere of Earth.

Perhaps you are weary of all this clarity, and would prefer to go back to straightforward and restful confusion. If so, skip ahead. I really cannot detain you against your will. But if not, I will ask you to bear with me here for another few minutes, while I discuss another few minutes.

By a fortunate coincidence, the Martian day is only some forty minutes longer than an Earth day, so that the adjustment of diurnal cycles has not been a major problem for Earth-adapted biologies. The day is in fact nearly the length of the twenty-five-hour internal cycle that those biologies inexplicably obey when removed from the sunlight and alarms of Earth. The nineteeners first observed that curious and, one would think, anomalous rhythm. No one since has solved the puzzle of it, although it gives the believers in Original Martians wonderful food for thought: Were the OMs—gasp—human?

The length of the Martian day does present some difficulties for those rich enough to place calls to Earth. The rule of thumb, if you have thumbs, is that similar longitudes show the same time of day on their clocks every thirty-six Martian days and thirty-seven Earth days. Practically speaking, again, nobody bothers with the rule, since almost everyone can interface to find out whether Sally on Earth is asleep in her bed at 4 A.M. or asleep in her office at 2 P.M.

In order to maintain a twenty-four-hour day in which seconds are seconds and minutes are minutes, the forty extra minutes of each day, like the four nameless days of Short April, have been declared free time. They are counted after 12 midnight in Hellas, and after 6 P.M. in Argyre, which is to say, they are counted simultaneously, as the two craters keep their clocks synchronized six hours apart. Both craters have been declared single time zones, although Hellas is wide enough for almost three time zones on Earth. Most of the local trivia broadcast their early news in Argyre during free time, where they tend to treat it as an extension of happy hour; in Hellas, the trivia broadcast their late talk shows, and the citizenry seems to feel free time is for making love.

One consequence of this welter of chronologies has been the

growth of an enormous bureaucracy to handle the records-keeping, the correlation of schedules and communications, and the flow of funds—as far as Sam the taxman is concerned, a year is a year is an Earth year, period. Then again, the growth of an enormous bureaucracy is a final consequence of almost everything.

And now, having interrupted this message to bring you a few programs, let me return you to time, and to Shade:

8

A Storm in Sector Two

"We've got trouble," I said. "See that quilted-looking stuff in the east, that low-lying dust?"

"Hmm. Zoom, zoom. Yep, that's dust. Haven't been on Mars since I built the place. Tell me about it."

"Tent-storm."

"Tent-storm?"

"You helped build Hellas, *and you don't know?*"

"Don't know, don't remember. Just because I designed the park don't mean I know how many cars in the roller coaster ride. I've seen tent-storms mentioned, but that's all."

"That storm will hit in less than twenty minutes, even if we quit boosting right now. We can't outrun it the other way. We won't be able to fly in it. You might be able to live through it. I don't think I want to try."

"So what do we do?"

"I'm thinking."

"Keep boosting while you think?"

"Yes."

"Can't we just ditch and lie low?"

"You don't know what a tent-storm does. Now shut up."

Tent-storms aren't real common. We only get them in middle spring, because that's when the surface winds are most active. Say 30 days out of the 687, or a little over a half-month, and ninety percent of those are at dawn. A five- or six-klick-a-minute surface storm comes booming out of the east and just raps that tent like a hammer on a gong. Surface atmosphere is only about one percent of tent-normal, but even a near-vacuum packs a wallop at that velocity over that big an area. It won't pop the blister, but it will snap supersonic wave-trains into the silverstuff. The air under the tent goes crazy, columns of it downtraining at anywhere from four to eight klicks a minute—which quilts the dust on impact. If one of those columns hits the ground where you are, you can wind up spread evenly over a half a subsector. And then there are the electrical discharges—static electricity on the tent itself, potential differences across the different downtrains—and the megabooms from the aforementioned super-sonic waves: Oh yes, we do have thunder and lightning sometimes on a nice spring morning.

There's only one thing you *can* do to survive a tent-storm. You have to get under. Every settle in Hellas has an under, a kivalike shock-distributing underground shelter, with walls of silverstuff and foma. What I was thinking was where the closest settle was. This subsector of S2 was nothing but salad ranches and big flat ranges, at least until my place. The settles were few and far between.

"Mandrake, you can do this quicker than I can. We need lat 287, long 41." He wheeled the bat immediately.

Preacher Brady wasn't my favorite rancher, but he was closest, and I knew the exact coordinates, thanks to the fact that he had put his settle right where the lat crossed the long. The *7 to 1 Spread,* he called his place. He was a Butlerian, which is bad enough—all that slag about the universe being God broken into pieces, and so we have to love each other in order to unite the pieces, and things that unite Him are fountains and things that divide Him are vortexes, and the end of time and the beginning of time are the same, so God marries Him/Herself and dies/is born to start the whole mess all over again. . . .

I'm not doing justice to the better theologians, who have at least made the faith roughly congruent to reason and experiment—it doesn't openly contradict the findings of science. It's hard to be fair when you knew the people who started the whole thing, though.

I'm glad I wasn't there to see Jesus and the disciples.

I am doing justice to the run of Butlerian believers, who, like fundamentalists in all religions, give blind allegiance to the worst and least intelligent doctrines of their own creed.

Besides, they gave it the wrong damn name.

Brady was worse than a fundamentalist—he was a Numerical Butlerian, one of those bongos who can't tell the difference between numerology and mathematics. If they ever succeed in forcing the tutors to give equal time to that foolishness—

I hadn't seen Brady for nearly five years, back when we had formed an uneasy alliance to defeat the Sector Two expanded-memory tax, based not on the actual percentage of increased capacity, but on the estimated percentage of increased *production* that would supposedly result—as calculated by Centerpole: S2, of course. And if you didn't make the production they estimated, well, you were a bad manager, but you still had to pay the tax. Brady's mindless and untiring devotion to any cause he believed in had been useful in the fight, but it was wearing in person.

He wouldn't be happy to see me either, but there was no question of his turning us away. It wasn't law, but anyone who failed to shelter travelers during a tent-storm would shortly find himself without friends, and maybe without a pulse.

"Looks about ten minutes before that turbulence hits," Mandrake said. "We're heading toward it now. Should make target in five. I'm conning, but no settle. Wait, a circle. A circular pad—is that it?"

"They've got the house down already. Put down fast, and start the siren now. I don't want them getting under and pretending not to hear us. They'd have to open when we buttoned the lock, but let's not waste the time."

Mandrake dropped the bat to what looked like shoulder-height on a short man, and buttoned the hooter. The ground was whipping by so fast the hummocks made a single flickering stroke, like lightning, or crawl in a hologram. A minute out, he kicked us into a forty-five-degree angle, to use the bigger boost of the bottom jets for braking, at the same time starting a slow rotation. Brady was on the pad, and we barreled in on him so fast and close I could see his expression. He thought he was going to die.

But we were shedding velocity at just about the physical max for the bat, and Mandrake dropped us on the pad like a nickel in a collection plate.

"Jesus Fucking Christ," Brady said when I got out. The Butlerians don't have any injunctions against cursing, at least not against cursing in the terms of someone else's religion. "You damn near killed me, Shade." Mandrake got out, having shut the bat down. "Christ, a robot," Brady said. "I might have known."

"He's an AI, Brady, and he's mine. My friend."

"Things are what they are, and ain't what they ain't," Brady said.

"Forget the scripture. Help us secure the bat and get under." I bent to jive the magnets on the rim of the bat.

"This ain't a good time, Shade. I can't let you under. Go away."

I straightened up. The man was pale and sweating. He was in a bad way, and it wasn't from the near miss of our landing. I didn't know what he had down there in his under. Maybe he had murdered his family and was planning to blame it on the storm. Whatever his problem was, it had to be big if he was willing to turn us away.

"Can't?" I said. "You damn well better." I conned the lock. "You aren't overoccupied. There's only two people in there."

"Go to another under, Shade. Go to one of the hustler unders."

"Brady, what's wrong with you? We've got less than two minutes before that storm hits. We've got no time to make another settle, and I don't know where your damned hustler unders *are*. Let me make it real easy for you. You haven't changed your code since five years ago, have you? No, you wouldn't have. So you take us in, or *I* take us in, and maybe leave you out here for the storm."

"Maybe that would be best," he said, looking at his feet.

"The hell with that. Get moving." I grabbed his arm and pushed him toward the bat. "Help us get the bat secured. Where's your plate? Oh, I remember." Mandrake had finished jiving the magnets for me. We wheeled the bat across the pad to the lock plate, maneuvering around the twelve-by-twelve strongbox. You would think heavy objects would be a lot easier to move on Mars, but they aren't. They might weigh three-eighths Earth-normal, but they pull just as much mass, and since *you* weigh three-eighths Earth-normal, your coefficient of friction is way down—you can't get no statis-traction. One of the advantages to Mandrake's peculiar mode of locomotion was the continuous low-angle thrust vector made by his spiral flex. That was why he seemed to glide, while we bounded slowly from step to step.

Once we had the bat on the plate, beside Brady's own, we lowered it on its wheels and buttoned the magnets on.

"Okay," I said. "Let's get under." There would be no premonitory gusts. When you felt the foreblow of a tent-storm, it was too late. But the wall of dust was coming our way, no more than five kilometers out.

A moment later we were dropping down the lock. When we set foot on the floor of the under, I saw two women across the room. One, the older, Brady's wife, was seated, her face in her hands.

"My daughter," Brady said behind me. "My daughter . . ."

The storm hit, a single hammer-blow of downtrained air, which we felt as a muffled and drawn-out boom, trailing away to a roar like the roar of a distant surf—the blast of the column of air suddenly diverted, by impact with the ground, to horizontal wind. There would be other columns downtraining behind it, buckling the backward flow of those winds, magnifying the frontward blast. There might be a hundred such blows, a thousand, depending on how long the surface storm lasted and how quickly the spiders could damp the tent.

The other woman, younger, her back to me, turning

The man halted in midstep, poised but wild, as if a great current had suddenly run through his nerves. I thought that in the next fraction of a second he would kill, or run, but did not himself know which.

Eleanor. I burned her burned her burned poor love burned my being away no hair no face my bride turning her face her very movement her stirring hair unharmed. *Eleanor.* I took vengeance have taken it these many years willingly entered Hell. Turning to face me eye and profile and plastide and steelic a monster a doll.

A jangler. She was a jangler. She had the odor and image of Eleanor, in every part that was not metal, that was not polycarb and silverstuff and superconductor. Brady's daughter she was, his frightened secret, and she was the living picture of my dead wife, and she was a jangler.

The cool adrenalines of shock were still icing my body, even as logic and reason began to reassert themselves. This floating and expanded moment lasted a mere few tenths of a second, but seemed a long time. It was a wonder the boost hadn't triggered me into high temporal. I was having a normal reaction, a human reaction. Extreme, but inside the range.

It isn't that strange, in three hundred and fifty years, to come across a double of someone you knew. Human physiognomy is varied, but runs in patterns. Now that you are living longer, you are noticing the recurrences more yourself. I had known several doubles, and others so close as nearly made no difference. Even so, I hadn't been ready. It had never occurred to me that one of them might someday be—

Even her *movements*, the very gesture she had made in turning, hand out to divide the air like the wing of a small bird—

The last time I had seen Brady's daughter, she had been a very young girl, just starting the tutors. She had not then reminded me of Eleanor, but I had never seen my wife as a girl. How had this woman become a jangler, how had Brady managed to keep it a secret, how long had he known? She had left for the city—how long ago? A year, a year and a half? It must have happened since then. Maybe he *hadn't* known. Maybe he had just found out himself, from her, when she returned. What the hell was a jangler doing way out here in the sticks?

Way down under it all, a tiny little ridiculous hope was running, a little current like a spring run-off in the Wall: that somehow, impossibly, she *was* my wife, that Eleanor had returned across time to me, that this woman was no jangler, that it had all been a bad dream, Mars and being a vampire and the whole of the nineteenth and twentieth and twenty-first centuries and even our time together, Gene, a ridiculous fantastical nightmare, something invented in the early morning for God knows what guilty reasons or because of too much Indian pudding, that this jangler business was just one last purgative thrill before I woke happily up, my bride beside me snug and snoring.

The storm was booming and humming and growling above us, and I stood there praying for a miracle.

She spoke. It was Eleanor's voice, played through a synthesizer. Whatever had happened to her had destroyed her larynx as well. Ordinarily if the flux takes your throat, you don't have to resign yourself to sounding like a nineteener's idea of a robot. Witness Mandrake, not a bit of flesh in him, who could elocute with the best of them. But janglers have to take what they can get. They can't just slot the old credit in the catalogue.

"Please don't kill me," she said in what can only be described as a kind of lilting buzz. "I will go above. I will go into the storm. I would rather my parents didn't see me killed. They didn't know. Don't punish them. I've just arrived, they have just found out. They would have turned me in. I will go above."

"It's true," Brady said. "She just got here. She just dropped in. We didn't know."

"I was homesick. I wanted to see my settle, my range once more, before I committed myself to the Underground forever. The storm came. I came below, not five minutes before you did. I was surprised that I was willing to live. And perhaps I wanted my parents to see me, to know. It wasn't fair to them, but I didn't want to disappear forever without them knowing. I knew it would hurt them worse than not knowing."

Her mother, for the first time since we had gone down, lifted her face from her hands.

"Not you," the daughter said, turning back to her and touching her hair. "Him. My father," she said, facing me again. "When he went back up, I thought it was to die in the storm, and I was glad. And then I didn't want him to die. But it was too late. Or maybe it wasn't. I was comforting her. I was thinking whether to go after him. I don't know whether or not I would have."

I was glad I couldn't see Brady's face.

I finally found my voice. "Jennie," I said—I had remembered her name. "Jennie, I won't kill you." She flashed a look at Mandrake. "He won't arrest you. He's no stone, he's a friend. We aren't here to hurt you. We aren't going to report you, either. We just want to wait out the storm and be on our way. What any of you do is none of our business."

"Believe it or not, I'm normal," she said. "I can't tell any difference. I feel what you do."

"Yeah, they all say that," I said, and was immediately sorry to have been so cavalier.

In the trivia, janglers are very deceptive. Typically, some innocent will meet one—on an adolescent lark through Underground, for example. The jangler will be ingratiating, plausible. The teener falls in love. They meet, clandestinely. Big plans to go up top and prove that janglers are still human, that love can triumph. But nobody knows what happens in a jangler skull. They're unpredictable, and in the trivia, unpredictability can only mean violence. Final scene of huge blood and carnage. Moral, as in medieval tales of trafficking with devils: Don't.

But she smiled. She had seen my flippancy for what it was, a nervous jetting of energy. Remarkable how a smile could unify that half-and-half face. Half-and-half? Crash almost always attacks both lobes of the brain. What had happened to her?

"You're the first jangler I ever met," I said. "Somehow I never thought of women janglers."

"Sexism survives," she said. "But there aren't many."

"I'm not afraid of you," I said. "If you want the truth, I'm curious. Even if I thought you were dangerous, I would rather talk to you than kill you. You're the second unusual intelligence I've met in the last twelve hours, and I haven't even had a chance to ask the first one any of the basic questions."

There was a triple boom, hard enough to vibrate the floor through its layers of foma. Mandrake, without moving, managed to create the impression he was looking up at the lock.

"Well," he said, "it looks as though you're going to have some time to ask them now."

9
Breakfast in Hell

We didn't get around to asking any of those basic questions, though. You never do. Things roll on, the action sweeps you up, and by the time you have time to get down to basics, you've forgotten what you wanted to know. Or you remember it, but can't remember what peculiar state of mind you were in that made it seem relevant. It doesn't happen by question and answer. A long time ago, a hundred years or so, folk wisdom held that finding the answers wasn't important, what was important was asking the right questions. The folk were trying to absorb relativity, I think. The idea that there aren't any absolute answers.

Hell, there aren't even any questions.

What we did, the five of us, was breakfast.

One of us, Mandrake, could not eat. I didn't need to. Jennie either didn't need to or didn't want to. Her mother looked as though she were resolved to last out the worst the world had to offer with a smile on her face, but would never bother with food again. Brady, though still pale with shock, was the only one who would touch a bite.

And yet we sat down to breakfast, because Celeste, Jennie's mother, insisted that we do so. She had rubbed her eyes clean, shrugged, and started briskly to work. There are people who suffer a great loss or a great trauma, and then get back to the business of the world, the normal routine, as quickly as possible. You might describe them as having a wonderful sense of structure. I am not of that temperament, but I find such character admirable. It is perhaps the foundation-stuff of the species.

For Celeste, it was breakfast time, so we would have breakfast. True, her daughter was a jangler, a tent-storm was jamming their range, and her home had been invaded by a weird mechanical man and a blood-covered troublemaker. But there would be work to do. We would be burning energy. It was breakfast time.

To me she said, "You can clean up in there, through that lock." She didn't ask where the blood had come from, and I am not certain that she was even curious about it. Brady, so far as I could tell, was unaware of any detail outside the drama of his daughter's transformation.

I went through the lock to find a small loo, complete with shower. I scrubbed under the soft fall of silky water. I almost sang. I was spacily, surpassingly happy. It was Jennie, of course. I still thought she was Eleanor. Or I thought Eleanor was Jennie. More than three centuries clenched like an angry fist, waiting for the impossible, waiting without realizing that I was waiting, until a counterfeit came. I had been cheated. We had been man and bride, but had hardly begun to live together. I had expected birth, growth, marriage, fruitfulness, age, death. All the sweet rhymes of time, the patterns we are made to inhabit, the fulfillment of young imperative in the old cradle of How It Goes. Of a sudden, I was sprung free, most cruelly wrenched, for no more reason than the insane machineries of a war I had not chosen. She was taken before I had spent myself in her a hundred times, and I, for no reason, was cast out to wander with the damned and the meaningless for all history. I who was then and am still now, in spite of all, incapable of cursing my Maker, I was condemned without thought and for no crime.

Until her counterfeit came. A perfect counterfeit, a key so exact that it sprang the lock. I was insane with hope and relief.

After my shower, I scrubbed my clothes. Pink fans of fluid made a lazy spiral down the slow drain.

Eleanor was alive, or someone who looked and smelled like Eleanor was alive, someone who made me remember her in vivid and intimate detail: But someone else was dead, someone somebody else maybe had loved.

Do you think I brood on that, do you think it matters to me?

Do you think it matters to me?

I got them as clean as I could, threw them in the zapper to dry. A zapper in his under—Brady did well for himself. But then, I had known that already.

I dressed in the dry clothes. Ridiculous in rumpled and stained partycloth, but clean and elated, I went out to join the others.

It had not taken me long to shower. Celeste had buttoned a table from the wall. She had set a place for Mandrake. She offered him a helping from the platter of sliced, grilled bevo and fried eggs. His nearly featureless head, smooth except for the eyes, did not have a mouth, or even a differentiated speaker. He did not point this out, but merely inclined his head, when he spoke, in a recognizably polite negative. He had coiled one leg under himself, on which he sat as if on a giant spring, to join us at the table.

Brady already had a mouthful, and Celeste had served my plate while I was out. "Mother, could I just have some tea?" Jennie asked. "And some juice?"

"This is good, honey," Brady said.

There was an entire minikitchen in the wall of the under. The cooler held a miniature bevo-rack. The meat was fresh enough—Celeste had carved it right off the living rack. She came back with juice for Jennie. The tea was making. And there were hot fresh biscuits just now out of the oven, and hot gravy for the biscuits—it was amazing.

A disproportionate number of the first real colonists who came to Hellas—after the military, the scientists, the engineers—were from the American South and the American West, those great rural stretches that had suffered so badly in the food depressions.

A little history here (you would not have needed it, Gene—but obviously enough, although I write for you, I write for others as well): The food depressions had been well underway even before the century turned, but no one had realized how long-lasting they would be. They weren't depressions in the *production* of food—production had never been more successful. They were depressions in the cost and availability of food. People were starving while grain rotted in the elevators, while the farmers who had produced the grain failed to make their price and went out of business.

When I was a child, a Virginia farmer's son, wheat was food, and fed those nearby. When it became a product, it was no longer wheat. It was a piece in a board game. Wheat's character as food no longer determined its fate—that was now determined by its function as economic product. A clown in office doesn't care that his people are starving. He knows *he* won't. The first function of a government, any government, is to protect and secure advantage for its personnel. So the clown feels his people's starvation not as personal pain, which might motivate him, but as a condition in a game. It doesn't matter to an economy that the cheese is heaped up and plowed under. The cheese is fulfilling its function by means of its burial. Were it to fulfill its function as product better by feeding people, then the hungry might be fed.

I have wandered from history to polemic, I see. Writing and reading may have made a comeback, but history is still woefully mistaught and more woefully ignored: For you this may be a boring and impersonal study. For me, as you may understand, it is more like memory.

The people of the food-producing regions of the South and West suffered deep economic injury during the depressions—they lost their livelihoods, their farms. Farming went more and more to big business. These people were forced to subsist where they were, or move to the cities. A surprising number managed to hang on, barely, in the country, clinging to the hillsides and to small plots in the flatlands. They raised their own truck on thin, leftover, unfertilized soil, battling the superresistant blights and bugs created by generations of pesticides. They pieced out incomes in chicken-plucking factories or by working for the highway department or by drawing unemployment insurance. Their children were driven hundreds of miles a week to consolidated schools that were usually criminally inadequate. They were often fiercely religious, subscribing to dogmas that told them they were worthless, evil, and born in sin, just as they often voted for precisely those clowns who were most certain to violate their franchise. They were frequently mean, violent, ignorant, benighted. They were sometimes heroic.

When Hellas and Argyre were thrown open, they went. They were not different from those who had crossed the Atlantic a generation or two before me. They signed their lives away to come, they traveled in cramped and dangerous machines on a long and dangerous and dreadfully boring journey, puking, quarreling, praying, fucking, and dying. There were whites, blacks, Chicanos, Indians. They brought their ways with them, and they have left their mark on our customs and in our dialects. Eating, the sort of eating Brady was doing—that wasn't just greed, it was culture. So was Celeste's willingness to play housewife, to be chief cook and bottle-washer, despite the fact that she was probably twice as smart and twice as tough as her husband.

Now Brady said, "Well, we're just going to have to figure out a way to make God out of all this."

He could pronounce all the inanities he wanted to. I was rapt. Jennie was looking down at her plate in anger or embarrassment. I inhaled great lungfuls of her scent. My nostrils must have been as wide as intake pipes.

Her smell was exactly the smell of a dish I had had a hundred years ago, on Earth. The ingredients were chicken, olives, garlic, prunes, olive oil, white wine, brown sugar, capers, bay leaves. The odor as it baked was indescribable. It was just the way my wife had smelled. The first time I had the dish, I wept. The second time I had it, I wept. I had it sixty-three times in a single year, and then I couldn't stand it any more.

If a vampire eats, he eats for disguise, or for the sheer pleasure. I had not eaten for pleasure in a long time. Now I was hungry again.

"You looked just like a hound dog sniffing the ass-end of a bitch," Mandrake said to me much later.

"What the hell do you know about hound dogs?" I said.

"As much as I do about bitches," he said. I told him he was just jealous because he didn't understand sex. He said he did understand it, because he understood compulsion, insanity, disorder, and frustration. I said he didn't get the fucking point. He got mad and—well, I'd have a hard time describing what he did because you can't do it, not unless you have three legs and nine eyes and run on batteries. He wasn't mad because I told him he didn't understand, he was mad because of the pun. He hates that sort of pun.

"Are you going to eat that?" Brady said.

"What?" I said.

He pointed at my plate. "Are you going to eat that?"

"No," I said. "No, you can have it."

"Shame to let it go to waste," he said.

I was weightless on Jennie's smell, inhaling it like feedback. Now I studied the jangler priffs, the artificial half of her head. It wasn't like a metal-and-flesh two-face deal. Whoever had done it had done a better-than-usual job of blending. You couldn't really say where the flesh stopped and the plastic began.

The way you could tell was the way the bulge of her brow kept going out, out, and around. The best of the digital stuff was still about three times the volume of a human brain for comparable output. There were nondigital intelligences, like Mandrake, or like the slick half of CI at Centerpole, but they were hard to measure and harder to buy. They equalled or bettered human brainpower, but were no easier to quantify than humans were, and it was impossible, so far, to copy to them from a biological brain. There were the so-called biochips, which had made direct interface a market reality, but the architecture that would arrange those biochips into a functional intelligence was still in development.

The way you could tell was by the way that outward bulge of processing power smoothly transformed something head-shaped to something like half of a very strange hat. The way you could tell was no ear on that side, no lines or dimples or wrinkles, no hair until below the crown of the head. The way you could tell was the unblinking right eye. You would be amazed at the sophistication required to make an eye blink believably, with the timely delicacy of live meat.

It was worse than it would have been if her face *had* been cleanly divided into its living and mechanical halves. That could have been taken as mask, as tragedy. This was the perfect fusion of irreconcilables. This was deformity.

"You're beautiful," I said.

She looked up, and her irises shuttered in tight suspicion, the right one a beat behind. I heard it whir. It was quiet for such a device, but my ears *are* good.

That's the look any woman will give you first when you first tell her she's beautiful. They don't want it then, they don't trust it then. Live with them thirty years, without betrayal or childish failure, and then tell them. They believe you then. It means something to them then.

So I had it bad. I was roasting in longing, I was sizzling with excitement, I was frying in the very fires of hope. It was a cheat, and I knew it was a cheat, and I didn't care. I felt helpless to resist. But was I choosing my headlong helplessness? After three and a half hundred years, I don't have any better answer than you did when you were fifteen.

And everything that happened after that happened because of that.

Celeste was watching me now, having heard what I had said. Her thinking flickered in her face. We had not seen much of each other, and that little had been when Brady and I were working together. It had been enough for me to know she didn't like me any more than your mother did, Gene. Mothers never do like me. Mothers with young ones in the nest have all they can do to be civil to me. Celeste probably thought her revulsion was because I was a nonbeliever, because I had—to her way of thinking—rowdy attitudes.

Now she was evaluating, very rapidly, the advantages and disadvantages. She didn't care for me one whit more than she ever had, but maybe this was the best she could hope for. Maybe, sinner and rowdy boy that I was, I could keep her baby alive. I was no good, and I would do the girl wrong, but maybe I was the best alternative this wicked world was going to provide.

When Jennie said, without taking her eyes off my face or turning toward Celeste in the least degree, "Mother, quit doing that," I broke up in laughter. The moment was complicated. Brady had started saying something, and an odd little thought for some reason went quirking through my head all the while I was laughing: I wondered if Mandrake laughed, and if he did, how he did.

"What's so goddamned funny?" Brady said. "She is, and you know she is."

"Brady, I wasn't laughing at you. I didn't hear what you said."

"I don't know what the hell you *were* laughing at, then. I said she has to turn herself in. You know she does. It's the only way to make the fountain of God instead of the vortex of Hell. She has to do the right thing."

"Brady, you're full of shit. They'll blase her on sight. She won't even make it to the stone-house alive. I don't know how the hell she got all the way out *here*."

"I walked," Jennie buzzed, in a voice that was somehow calm and deliberate through all the distortion.

I was astonished: "All the way through Zoomerville? You walked through Zoomerville and came out alive?"

"You don't say what happens here, Shade," Brady spat. "You always were a bossy son-of-a-bitch. Think you know more than anybody else around. But this is *my* house, and she's *my* daughter. I love her, but I'm *not* harboring a fugitive."

"If you love her so much, why don't you talk to her instead of to me? You haven't looked at her since we came down here."

"She's not the same as she was before. I'm not saying this is her fault—but how did it happen if she wasn't doing something out of bounds? That may not even *be* my daughter any more. Even if she is, it doesn't matter. This discussion is over. We're doing the right thing, and that's that. They'll take the fact that she turned herself in into consideration."

"Yeah, right before they gut her and burn her head off. Come on, Brady, *think*—don't just react. *If we aren't willing to learn, how shall God be wise?*"

Never attack a true believer on his own territory. *"Any damn fool can quote me,"* he quoted. "Forget it. The storm is dying down. I'm going to bu—"

Mandrake had acted by the time I had heard that much. He seemed to hold Brady's head in two of his hands, pressing the carotid with the third, while Brady finished his sentence: "I'm going to burn the news." It was the processing lag again. I couldn't get used to the AI's speed. He laid Brady gently down. I began to realize why he had taken him out.

"Did you kill him?" Celeste said. She was asking me, not Mandrake.

"I think he's not dead," I said. "I think Mandrake just put him out."

"He's not dead," Mandrake said.

"We're going to be going now," I said to Celeste. "I'm going to have to blow all your comm. Keep him away from any backup systems as long as you can. Don't let him watch the trivia, and don't let him use any phones. You know the best way to lie to him. Convince him we went northwest. It might help Jennie stay alive."

Brady had been right about the storm, my ears said. I went over and buttoned the telemetry. The holo clicked on. I punched for weather. The systems of downtrained air were red shafts in the blue 3-D, the ground-surface in green topo-grid. There weren't many red shafts, and they were pinking out. The spiders were doing good.

"You think I'm coming with you?" Jennie said.

"Where else can you go?" I said. "If you walked here, you can handle a little vacation with us."

"You're in trouble."

"You're not?"

"No."

"I think you ought to come with us. I think it makes sense."

"Oh, I'm going with you," she said. "I was just clarifying a few things."

I stared. I was beginning to feel surrounded by minds that were working on levels I couldn't see. "All right," I said, "we're scrambling *now*. Mandrake, what's the best way to fritz this system?"

He plunged two hands into the wall console, drew two of the image nodes from the splinters, trailing fiber. He stripped the shielding from the nodes, brought the bare patches together. The holo went. Inside the console, sprays of laser torched out. "Feedback," he said. "Nibbits pokoities."

There are times when I feel as cruel as the legends would say I am. It has nothing to do with the fact that I hunt humans down and kill them for their blood. When I had sent Jennie and Mandrake up the ladder ahead of me, I leaned back.

"Tell him fuck the fountain of God," I said to Celeste.

10
Three Zoids, Two Horns, and a Mission

In spite of how angry I was at Brady, I felt guilty at leaving without helping him set up. I didn't feel guilty that we had knocked him out or fused his comm—that had all been strategically justifiable. But when you use someone's under, you're supposed to help them set up afterwards, belay the silverstuff, wheel the furnishings out of the strongbox, click, lock, and jive the machines, and so on.

You know what I think that means? Helping set up is a part of the social code. It's when you break the social code you feel guilty. Conking somebody and destroying their property is just part of the social code.

Dust was everywhere. It takes longer to settle here. We squinted and held our noses and dashed for the bat. Through gaps in the clearing dust you could see the beautiful rich cobalt-blue of our sky. The silverstuff is as transparent as you want to make it, but half as much sunlight means half as much blue scatter. True, we pump sun over the Wall, but it's angled down, and semicoherent anyway. I have gotten so used to this sky, Earth's might seem pale and claustrophobic now.

Jennie wanted the front seat, shotgun beside Mandrake. "I like to see where I'm going," she said.

"I do too," I said grumpily, but I folded myself into the back. Mandrake toggled the magnets from inside, reversing the field and bumping us into the air. He had the jets going before we started to settle.

"Where are we headed?" Jennie said. You got used to the buzz in a hurry. After a while, I had to remind myself there was anything unusual about her voice.

"Shade's place," Mandrake said.

"You have an irritating habit of stating presumptions as facts," I said.

"Isn't that dangerous?" she said. "Aren't you in some kind of trouble?"

"They might seem like presumptions to you," he said. "Seem like facts to me. Depends how much evidence you see. I gotta lotta eyes." I snorted. "I think it's the old last-place-they-would-think-to-look trick," he said to her (he didn't look around, of course, but his tone altered).

He knew better. That would have been my justification to her, though, and he knew that too. Take it from a fellow who's had a little experience. Home is the first place they'll look, not the last, but it's the only place you know well enough to do a good job of hiding in.

Of course, we weren't *really* trying to hide, just to look like we were. It was getting complicated, and I was having trouble remembering which game was which. Especially since I had suddenly lost my taste for intrigue, especially since I was suddenly head-over-heels for the image of a dead woman. Who seemed to be more interested in Mandrake than in me.

"*Is* that where we're headed," she asked me, looking back.

"Yes, dammit," I said.

We had a long way to go, over six hundred k, four hours even at best boost. You pegged a straight northeaster till you hit the gap, then swung left. Up the alley to my place. We kept a couple of k off the S2/S3 border, to steer clear of the border road.

Jennie had turned around again. "Since we're traveling together," she said, "I want you to know my right name. This person *was* Jennie Brady, but *I* am Jennie Dark."

I thought it was wonderful, a play on the life she faced now as a part of the Underground, something like all the puns I have scattered through my existences on two planets—but I didn't get it.

What else did I think? Somehow this one might work: She, as a fellow hunted creature, might accept what I was, that here, finally, was a love without lies and pretenses, that she might even be glad that I slew her enemies, might see me as hero, not nightstalker, not monster.

She said to Mandrake, "I'm happy to make your acquaintance, Mr. Mandrake. Maybe you can teach me something about getting along on a synthetic brain. It's wonderful. Here we are, two freaks, boosting into the future."

Mandrake said, "I have no honorific."

"Say what?"

"I don't go by *Mister*. Titles make me feel like I'm in two places at once. I have enough trouble pretending to be in one place."

"I'm a freak, too," I said.

"Anyways, I don't know as I could help you much, Missy. You got a digital right hemisphere, right? Maybe I could. I have a digital lobe and a slick lobe, and I guess that's where you are. I could run some sims. I don't know, seems experience would be quicker."

"What's the other lobe?" I said.

"You're not a freak, Mr. Shade, you're just tall and a little too good-looking to trust. Oh, I didn't really mean *teach* me, Mandrake. Just."

"I am so a freak," I said heatedly. "I'm the freakiest freak you ever saw. I'm a sport out of nature. Tell her I'm a freak, Mandrake. And what's this *Mister* shit?"

"Just be a friend," she sighed. "That's it, I guess. You feel like a friend already. I know these things. I'm a visionary."

"I've always hated that word," Mandrake said.

"What's wrong with *visionary*?" she said.

"Freak," I said. "He means *freak,* which I am, and you tell her *now*. What's the other lobe?"

"So let's make up a word," she said.

"Classified," he said.

"We need a word that means—I liked that, Mr. Shade, what was it?—*a sport out of nature*. A word for janglers and visionaries and robots—I'm sorry, we're so country out here, I didn't mean anything—AIs, and, and broken brains and weird people that don't fit and think fractured thoughts that really might be great big whole new thoughts if they didn't have to break them trying to fit them in."

"Classified?"

"We're the x-people," she said. "You and me, Mandrake. X for unknown."

"Tell her, Mandrake!"

"Already been done," he said. "You want me to, in truth?"

"By who?" she said.

"In some old comic books," he said. "They're in the museum. Don't you like art?"

"I love it, but my father never had much sympathy for it. I'm afraid I'm quite ignorant."

"In truth," I said. "We're the y-people," I said to her. "Y is farther out than x. Y for y oh y was I born. Call me John, or call me Shade, but don't call me Mr. Shade no more."

Mandrake fritzed with what I later learned was disgust, but then he made one just as bad. "Let me add a new dimension to this discussion," he said. "May I suggest z. If y is far out, z is the farthest, the end."

"The z-people," she said. "Oh, I like that. The z-people. The androids from Planet Z. The z-oids."

"Zoids," I said.

"Zoids," Mandrake said, savoring, your author would now state, the hint of the word *void* in our neologism, of the vacuum that may be at the heart of meaning.

"Zoids," Jennie said quietly. "I am a zoid."

"We three zoids of Orient are," I said.

We fell silent. The ground blurred by, twenty meters down. It was churned up in places, but the grass flows with the storm, and its roots go down a couple of meters or more. Few trees can survive a good tent-storm, so you don't find many out here. Leeward of cut-banks, in the rare natural bottoms. There are some close to the Wall, where the storms don't have enough slack to start downtrains, and belts of trees in and around Hellasport, where the spiders have usually damped the worst of the turbulence by the time the surface wind arrives. They say they're working on new breeds that can live through the tent-storms, maybe even help windbreak them.

"Is he really like us?" Jennie said finally.

"Is Shade a zoid?" Mandrake said. "Yes, Dorothy, he is. In truth."

"What *are* you?" she said, shifting around. I heard the shutters of her eye whirring again. "Are you a mutant? I didn't think there really were any. Are you a very advanced android? Running away from your evil creators?"

"No, I don't think it *is* Kansas any more," I said to Mandrake. "I think I pick mutant," I said to her.

"Why was it so important to you for me to know you were a mutant?" she said. "What do you mean, Kansas? Oh, because of the Dorothy. Well, Mandrake, you're obviously the Tin Man—"

"Obviously."

"—but what is *he*?"

"The scarecrow," I suggested.

"No, you have a brain. And I *can't* be Dorothy, I'm sorry, because I'm a zoid, too, I'm not the pretty little girl hero."

"Heroine," I said.

"Say what?"

"We used to say *heroine,*" I said, "for a female hero."

"This ain't The Yellow Brick Road, for that matter, if you're going to be picky," Mandrake said.

"And there ain't no Wizard," I said.

"Oh yes, there's a Wizard," she said.

Another silence. There wasn't much flying to do. Mandrake sat there, his third arm resting in the groove in his back, his third leg—well, which one was the third one?—*one* of his legs folded under the other two. If he had had a knee, it would have been bent the wrong way.

"What's the other lobe?" I said.

"What makes you think I have one?" he said.

"Come on, you're all in threes. Anyway, you implied it."

"When he said *classified* before," Jennie said. "That's what you're talking about. I thought he was yours."

"I am he is," Mandrake and I said together.

"So how can something he knows be secret from you?"

"We have a complicated relationship," I said. "I don't have it all figured out yet."

"What kind of trouble are you running from? What didn't you want my father to see on the news?"

"Do you want to know? I don't guess it matters. I blew Centerpole up and stole Mandrake."

"*You blew Centerpole up?*"

"Why do people always repeat things?" Mandrake said.

"Just a little piece of it. Because our memories are so bad," I said.

"We aren't people, we're zoids," Jennie said.

"You're a lot more like people than some zoids I know," Mandrake said. "And your memories are better than mine. You can forget things. You think forgetting is losing information, but it isn't, not unless there's damage. Forgetting is absorption. The things you know become you. They aren't isolated little packets of information any more."

"That's very interesting," I said.

"Daddy always said you were a secessionist. He said you were trouble walking. Was anyone hurt?"

"I think somebody was killed," I said. "None of my men got hurt."

For some reason I read her silence as disapproval. She had bowed her misshapen head a little, and was looking straight ahead. We sailed on for half an hour, blipping a couple of the little range towns scattered here and there, usually beside a reservoir or on the banks of a river. There's a *lot* of water on Mars, most of it frozen underground still, in spite of the fifty trillion kilograms or so we have pumped into the climates of the two craters. But the image of Mars as a desert planet still survives in the trivia, an image that came into vogue a hundred years ago. And *that* was itself a reaction to fantasies of Mars as a place lush and teeming with life. You get fascinated with the origins and survivals of ideas after a while, after you've seen enough of the way they spring up, linger, and maybe change and maybe don't but take on completely different characters anyway, because the world changes around them. You begin to see ideas as works of art, created unaware from the guts of the species and lasting from generation to generation. They do not so much explain reality, as everyone thinks they are meant to, as *enter* it, furthering and complicating the plot.

Back then, they had no idea how much water there was ten miles down in Earth's mantle, either.

After a spell of her impenetrable meditation, Jennie said, "What did you mean, Mandrake, back when you said it was hard for you to pretend to be in even one place?" She was still gazing intently forward. Her conversation, the rest of the way, seemed directed to specific objectives, no longer mere chatter and pleasantries.

"Do you read poetry?" he said.

"I've read *The Works,* of course. We had to, in church. I don't know the Modernos very well. More ignorance. My father insisted that mathematics was the greatest poetry of all, and that the prophet himself had said so. I had such a short time in the city, such a short time on my own—"

"You needn't apologize for what you don't know," he said. "Only for what you refuse to know. May I quote?"

"Please."

When he began to say the piece, I realized I had read it before. Your father had recommended the poet to me, Gene, in his old age. Mandrake recited the poem—I keep wanting to say he *read* it, and I suppose that with his memory, the act was equivalent—in a funny, resonating timbre, the way a voice might sound in a vacuum if you could imagine somehow being able to hear a voice in a vacuum.

"The title," he said, "is FILL IN THE."

"Fill in the what?" she said. "Oh."

Title and all:

FILL IN THE

The first lie that nothing told
was something to behold,

and having sworn, I am,
gave truth a name.

Gave you your history.
And you gave me.

Here I am, I lie,
as you have taught me: but I

> *do not exist, am not,*
> *in truth, a what:*
>
> *Illusion am, am nothing's hero,*
> *a name, a game, a ring around a zero.*

"I don't think I follow it very well," she said.

"Absorb it," he said. "Don't be in a hurry."

"It's the No Poet," I said. "He claims he doesn't exist, that he's just an experimental poetry-writing program created back in the oh-90s, part of the early AI research, expanded and updated until he was absorbed into the Earthnet. Mandrake, I can't believe you're falling for that slag. This noise is a complete and total fraud," I explained to her. "Any fool can see a human wrote those poems, the ones that can even be confidently attributed—there are so many nondery poets on the net nowadays, all signing off as the No Poet. I can see why the *themes* would interest you, Mandrake, but the irony of you letting some *human* speak for you—I can't believe you can let that sentimental tripe matter. All that damned existential angst."

"Angst?" she said.

"B-blues," I said. "His poetry is this completely self-absorbed stuff, just reeking with it. Angst is an old word I like better."

"I think a person has a right to pick her poetry for herself," she said. "Why are you being so disagreeable?"

DO NOT ASSUME IT MATTERS TO ME IN THE WAY YOU THINK IT MATTERS TO ME, Mandrake said. DO NOT ASSUME YOU COMPREHEND ME SIMPLY BECAUSE I HAVE ATTEMPTED TO MAKE A PORTION OF MYSELF COMPREHENSIBLE TO YOU.

He was speaking in the voice God always has in the trivia, except that he had made his voice strange and metallic. God, if God was a trivia robot, maybe. It was effective. The walls of the bat hummed with overtone.

"You think you know me, but you don't know me," I said.

Jennie turned on me. "That will be enough of that. You have been increasingly unpleasant this whole trip. I do not know what personal dissatisfactions are causing your rudeness, but I will not tolerate any more of it. Hold your peace if you cannot be civil."

Her lenses were pinpoints, her jawline hard and distinct. This was a child of barely ten, a teener still, and yet authority rang in her voice, instantly summoned. It was that rare thing, true authority; and it was mixed in her, as the real thing so often is, with tenderness. I had seen that back at the under. I could not remember noticing any of this in her as a youngling, and I wondered if she had learned it in her misfortune.

I was not cowed, but she spoke the truth. Authority, which is a matter of character, not politics, cuts through deception. That is one way it may be distinguished from tyranny, which depends on lies and illusion. I had gotten extremely irritable, and been so caught up in events I had neglected the inevitable. It was not that I had been up all the night before. It was not that I was jealous of Mandrake (I was, ridiculously, but that wasn't the problem). After the satisfaction trance comes the letdown, the come-down, the bust-out, the d-blues. I needed sleep, any little bit of sleep: refreshment, integration, REM sleep.

"My apologies, Mandrake. Tell your story as you see fit. I have let discomfort get the better of my temper. If the two of you will pardon me, I'm going to sleep."

"Just a minute," she said. "If you're going to sleep, we should land first. If I don't take a piss pretty soon, I'm going to be grouchier than Shade here."

We went down in a little dell rich with old-fashioned days-eye, with violet and wildrose and cottongrass and newthorn. I got out too. Never pass up a chance to piss.

"Watch out for skulls," I said.

"I've heard of them," she said. "I've never seen one. I don't think they come this far into the sector."

"Skulls?" Mandrake said.

"It's what we call them," I said. "Because they rob every grave we dig. You get mighty tired of seeing the jolly rogers of neighbors and friends coming at you like crabs on lightning. As far as I know, they don't eat, but they will happily kill you for your skull."

"They wear them?"

"Like carapaces. The larger, the better. They kill rabbits, cowhoppers, dogs, horses, you name it. If it's a fresh kill instead of a grave robbery, sometimes what you see is a face you can still recognize."

"That's not in the original ecology," he said.

77

"I don't know what they are." I said. "Just what they do."

Jennie went off a couple of meters, hiked up her skirt, spread her legs, and let fly, canting her pelvis to cast a bright yellow arc forward over the grass. It was plain she was still getting her vitamins, whatever else had happened to her. She had a pretty little fundament, and looking at it didn't make it any easier for me to relieve myself. I finally got it going. It's fun to piss on Mars. You can get unbelievable distance, though the stream breaks up more, and the air currents make it harder to aim.

She dabbed herself dry with cottongrass. When she turned back to the bat and saw the half-erection I was hosing down the planet with, she said, "Oh no. Not on your life, Shade. I'm busy. I've got things to do. You put your skirt down and put that cannon away. I *knew* you were acting funny."

Mandrake had been sitting half-in, half-out of the bat, and now, as we came back, he said, "It's times like this that I feel completely useless."

"Well, you can always enjoy the weather," I said, drawing in a few litres of the sweet spring air. It was ten o'clock of a Long April morning that felt like Short April, and I was feeling the shock of freshness, that connectedness, *aliveness*, that you can only get out-of-doors. The flowing grass glimmers like light on a river top, the light is cleanliness itself, and life is proceeding immensely and richly around you. It was why I had headed west in the first place, so many years ago. And it didn't matter that Hellas was a created ecology. Ecologies don't care where they come from, and you shouldn't, either. If you've got a world, don't question it, for God's sake. *Live* in it.

"Are you kidding?" he said.

"Oh yeah," I said. He had been built to live in vacuum or clouds of hydrogen sulfide as easily as in this good old nitrogen soup. He didn't sweat or suffer from cold, and there would have been no reason to install in him an appreciation for the feel of the wind on his bare skin. I was embarrassed. "Let's get going," I said.

"I enjoy *looking* at all this," he said. "But I enjoy looking at lots of things." We piled back in.

"People are my weather," Mandrake said, and boosted.

I slept for nearly two hours. I had an interminable dream. I was a small boy, in a shadowy mountain city, and my parents had inexplicably vanished. The dark city was empty and menacing. I was trying to find my way home, but no part of the city was familiar, no part of it connected to anything I knew. I was falling-down tired. I kept tripping on curbs, falling over garbage cans. I knew that I would never see my family again, never know warmth and security. I found a vacant lot in which there were, somehow, cedar and scrub oak, holly and bay and tupelo. A huge bonfire, several stories high, blazed in the center of the lot. Someone was stalking me. If I could stay in the light of the blaze, I might be safe. But the fire was too hot, I had to flee to the cool of the darkness from time to time, or be burned alive. I did not dare weep or cry out. The hunter in the shadows was there a long time, and my swallowed fear reached higher and higher pitches. Finally he stepped into the light. I was cornered against an alley of rocks, or was it a blind brick wall? My pursuer was a tall, angular man, all in black. His face was long and hollow-cheeked, like Michael Rennie's in *The Day the Earth Stood Still.* His mouth opened, showing fantastic cruel teeth. He bent toward me.

When I woke, Jennie and Mandrake were still at it, deep in some involved conversation.

"Are we there yet?" I said. "Daddy, can we stop? I'm hungry. I need to pee."

They ignored me. "But if you can doubt you exist, then you exist," Jennie said. "It's the same thing as me wondering if I'm really alive any more. Why wonder? Just *do* it."

"Have you ever heard of Gabriel's Horn?" he said.

"Of course," she said.

"No, I mean the mathematical paradox. Face a graph of f of x equals 1 over x, and integrate from x equals r to x equals 1 of f of x dx," he said.

"I don't have that logon."

"Ipop tight-beam? I can lase it."

"Right through the left lobe, hey?"

"No harm."

"I know. Yeah, I have tight-beam ipop. Why not? Cheap at the price. You don't mind if I copy?"

"Hey, I'm no snob. Why be ignorant?"

There was a moment of quiet. She was loading his grafix, I

presume. I couldn't believe they were hashing over the same old ground. First poetry, now math. This was going to get old. I hoped it was just that it had been a long time since Mandrake had had a kindred spirit to talk to. Spirit? What a weird word. Exactly what he was saying he *didn't* have. But far be it from me to interrupt. Jennie might get mad again.

"Yeah, yeah," she said, "the area under the curve from 1 to r. Natural log of r minus the natural log of x, and since log 1 is zero, the integral equals the natural log of r."

"As r approaches infinity, the limit of the integral—"

"Approaches infinity, too. The limit doesn't exist. Like me, like my soul. I don't exist. Maybe."

"Where's the problem? If you didn't exist, why would you worry about whether or not you did?"

"You could say it's not a worry, a spin in the logic just, a think-hole. Rotate the shaded area on the x-axis, find the volume of the solid."

"Okay, volume of increment disk is *pi* times one over x squared times dx, integrate from r to 1, volume is *pi* minus *pi* over r—"

"Approaches as r approaches infinity?"

"I'll be damned—*pi*! The limit is finite! It exists!"

"Get your mind around it. Limit of the area doesn't exist, but rotate it and the limit of the volume it generates *does*. How you like my metaphor, Missy Dark? Maybe I just seem to *be* because I *do*. Spin on my axis, I does, just like a top, Christmas toy to humans. Can you do the surface area of the solid?"

"Well, it's 2 pi times the integral from r to 1 of y times 1 plus y-prime squared times dx—I can't integrate it."

"No formula. The logon doesn't have. Takes a bit of intuition. Since y-prime equals 1 over x squared,1 plus y-prime squared is x to the fourth plus 1 divided by x cubed, which is larger than 1 over x, so the integral is larger than the integral of 1 over x—"

"Which we already did. So the surface is larger than 2 pi times the natural log of r, and approaches infinity as r approaches infinity. An infinite generator, and a finite result in an infinite skin. Wow."

Here, dear reader, in case you cannot immediately either logon or face, is what they were looking at:

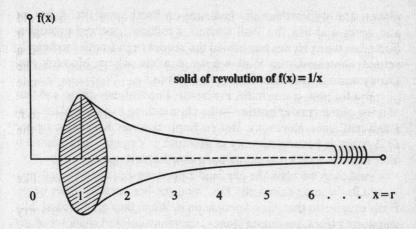

solid of revolution of $f(x) = 1/x$

And having, I hope, done justice to their concerns, I am happy to say that at that point something gave me a good excuse to bring their love chat to a halt.

"The gap," I said. "Up there." It was probably forty kilometers away. A spine of mountains runs out from the Wall almost exactly parallel to the S2/S3 border, head-on to the way we were boosting. Angling toward it from the West, another lower range stretches most of the way across the ragged circle of the Wall. The land between them is the gap.

"The gap?" Mandrake said.

"I thought you knew how to get there."

"Nope-nope. Didna brief me, Bubba Boss. Just been boosting the way your body language said to go."

"Almighty Hades, Mandrake! Okay. When you hit the gap, a valley will run off west next to that low range on the left. Just bend it left and follow the valley toward the Wall." He clicked the verbal ipop on the bat, and gave it a high-pitched burst that I presumed contained my instructions together with some range and bearing calculations. We spent the next fifteen minutes watching the scenery, now that there was some. Details began to emerge on the Wall. It is a cracked and creviced and crazy-mazed realm, not the featureless barrier most of the stories seem to assume. Five kilometers high in places, and wilder than any badlands on Earth, now that it has air and water and life, the Wall shelters a million fractured ecologies. Someday, when Hellas has turned the corner from frontier to heavily settled homeland, the Wall will be a world where Mommy and Daddy and the kids take fabulous vacations.

But for now, it was mine, my haunt almost alone—mine and that of a few of the crazier hustlers—the closest thing to a natural lair that I had had since Kentucky. Before Kentucky was Kentucky, before 1775 when it became County of Kentucky, Virginia; they named it after Dan'l Boone's real estate company. Look it up.

And then we blew the gap, and zipped west.

"Oh," Jennie said, and "Oh," and put her hand over her heart. People really do that. Good people do it. When they are touched. She was seeing trees, mountain slopes, the many-colored shadows of my green home. The sun was almost directly overhead, but there are so many crooks and gorges, so many valleys of valleys, so many shades of shades, that the eye feasts and gets hungrier all at the same time.

"Yes," I said.

"Why doesn't everybody live here?" she said.

"They will. But for now the cost runs too high. The sectors were cheaper to settle because they were so uniform. All the government roads and rivers run perfectly straight. Cheap to program the builders, cheap to service, easy to map and maintain. Build now, add the scenery later, like the developers say. Trouble with Venus, too topsy-turvy. High-priced real estate if they ever get around to it."

"But this is so—so . . ."

"Beautiful is an okay word," I said.

"I don't think I've ever *seen* anything beautiful before."

"Maybe not big beautiful. Bluets are beautiful. Violets, spring beauties. You're beautiful."

No, I'm not. I'm just a flat, average, boring rancher's kid. Bright enough, but narrow."

"I think maybe you are beautiful," Mandrake said. "Not my field of expertise, but . . ."

"Even with this head?" she said.

"What's in a head?" he said. "A brain by any other cranium thinks as sweet."

"Oh come on," I said. "That's terrible."

"Is that it?" he said, in a different voice.

Ahead, a thin plume of distant smoke in the rising side of the green-walled valley. Big Damn River cutting her S-shaped bend below, glittering with noon. I could barely see the smoke, but it was in the right place.

"Yes," I said.

"Lot of bevos standing around," he said. "They seem to be watching it burn."

"They like fire," I said. "Lots of papers about: what it is in their visual algorithms. Lots of theories. What it is, though, they like fire."

"They like fire," he said.

"You really don't know much about Mars, do you?"

"Nor does the batmobile engineer know the life history of every family that buys. That isn't it. *I* like fire, too."

Open burning had been legal in Hellas for only a few decades, but we had been running bevos twice that long. So it had been a bit of a surprise when we began to notice what fire did to them. It made herding a little easier. Just light a fire and they came on in. A bevo is worse than a mule. Mules were stubborn, but at least they couldn't stand there and argue with you. A bevo will patiently explain how *this* grass in *this* valley is right at its peak of tenderness and green-ness and if you had eyes you could see that, and it is going to stay there and eat and produce the tenderest steaks ever produced, and nothing you can say about the state of the rest of the herd matters to it, nothing about the *average* tenderness of the *entire* herd being what matters to you, or about having to go to market at the best price. It doesn't have enough brain for such analysis, just enough brain to figure out what's best for its own racks. Talking to a bevo is not unlike arguing with a man like Brady, come to think of it, and the finest comedy of all is watching such a man going at it with his own herd.

"What doth a bevo dream?" Mandrake said, and went on to answer himself:

> *Whatever comes over the wire,*
> *whatever the masters deem*
> *insufficiently strange*
> *to dazzle his glassy stare.*

What doth a bevo desire?
—A grassy range,
the zero of the fire.

What doth a bevo think of the Earth?
—A bubble of radio,
a tenth of a quantum's worth
of whispering ghost, a change
in the color of No.

What doth a bevo desire?
—A grassy range,
the zero of the fire.

A bevo's opinion of Mars?
He taketh it blade by blade.
—Whatever lies past the Wall, the stars
hard in the Tharsis range,
are less than the shade of a shade.

What doth a bevo desire?
—A grassy range,
the zero of the fire.

"Pretty good," I said. "I like it better than the No Poet, anyway.
Who is it?"

"Me," he said. "Actually, I thought it was rather after the style
of the No Poet."

"I didn't think you knew anything about bevos and fire."

"I didn't."

"So how—oh. Just now? Just this minute?"

"We're here, aren't we?" Jennie said. "Shade, did you live in a
house?"

"Doesn't take long when you feel an empathy with your subject," Mandrake said. "I miss most of the pleasure, though, not
having to agonize. Your type thinks the completion is the joy of it,
but it isn't. The seeing, the work of putting it together, that's what it's
for. The stuff that takes me a while, the stuff that really challenges
me—it's a bit involved. Might not mean a lot to you. Not many
readers share my ultimate concerns, you know."

While he was speaking, Mandrake had settled the bat gently on my landing pad.

"You know, you really get to know people when you travel with them," Jennie said.

We clambered out. The pad was a raised island in a congregation of bevos, all facing the house, though there was not much left for them to see but smoke and coals. The murmur of our arrival spread through the herd, and some of the nearer bevos turned our way. "Got some racks going bad, here, boss," a few were saying. "Yeah, bad racks . . . bad racks . . . where you been so long . . . house burn, boss . . . you ought to taken care these racks . . . house burn good, boss."

"Was that a *house,* John?" Jennie said. On the range, everyone lives in silverstuff, another thing you never see in the trivia. It just isn't cost-effective to edit the images for such a small market. So the citizens sit in the filmy tents of their homes—settles—and watch thrillers in which the blaser-packing hustlers from Hella ride back from the draws and the mountains to sprawling log-and-adobe haciendas. And somehow they get the idea houses are better, and it is finer to live in a pile of bricks than in something resembling the drifted nest of a ground-spider. They feel inferior for having been raised in the shelter of a fabric that was originally marketed as a no-run stocking, though that fabric is cheap, nearly indestructible, can be made to transmit as much or as little light as one desires, and is a perfect filter gradable for anything from sand to gas molecules. The feeling is deepened by the fact that Hellasport is mostly buildings, except on the outskirts, in Zoomerville.

I had built myself a slag-and-timber aerie here, not from snobbery, but from old habit. I could not adjust to permanent tent-life. I simply felt better in a house. But now here was Jennie, most recent commander of my affections, impressed as all hell that I had lived in a house, though her own father had probably twice the herd I did.

But you know what? I liked it. I swelled with pride.

I said *timber.* Blocked cellulose, really. You can program the bevos to excrete a residue of grass fiber, though it wreaks havoc with the meat racks, and you can press and glue the fiber and reinforce it with silverstuff to get nearly any shape of neowood you want, including perfectly notched logs. There were some seventy-five-year-old trees here in the valley. There were none older anywhere on Mars. You would not find me cutting them, and I would not hesitate to kill any poacher who did cut them.

"Bevos!" I called, in as loud a voice as I could manage. "Bevos! Attention mega-max! Shadowfall is dead!"

More of the herd turned our way. Some of the nearest absorbed my message, but the damned animals were starting to argue. "Good grass," I heard. "Grass is still good. Big Damn River still sweet and full. Racks going bad. Lazy hustlers."

"Mega-max!" I shouted. "*No* hustlers. *No No No No* hustlers. Never no hustlers. Good grass, good water, no racks taken. Never no racks taken, all racks go bad forever." This wasn't working. It would take all day to convince them, and I was in no mood for convincing.

I was furious, ready to kill the marauders who had done this to me, to my home. I knew quite clearly it was a game, Benjamin's game, but that didn't matter. I am a simple-minded man, really, a man made half-and-half of book-learning and blind impulse. I am not wise. What little I know I have scraped together over centuries. I understand action, movement, not, for all the implications of my name, the half-tones of subtlety. At that moment I knew one thing: My home was burning. Again.

"Mandrake!" I barked. "Can you get through to these hay bangers? Override the leaders and load a few commands. If they are to survive, they have to head for another ranch." An idea struck me. "Send them to Brady." That was amusing, to think of a thousand free bevos walking onto his range, overwhelming him with something for nothing. He was such a proponent of paying your way, such a self-made man. "Here. Record: *I John Shade deed this bevo to Elmo Brady of the 7-to-1 Spread*. See there's a copy in every bevo's brain, and load them with his coordinates." It was a long walk, and all the racks would be lost, but at least the bevos would live. "Jennie, you'd better con the power leads and see if they blew them. We have a trip into the mountains to make, and I would imagine the bat is getting pretty low. If they aren't blown, power up and load some extra batteries. They're in the bank behind you. If they are blown, be prepping for a long hike. Better start thinking food and warm clothes. Get hopping, lady. I've got something to take care of."

I vaulted down from the pad and left them to it, stalking toward the ruins of the house. The bevos shuffled aside, calling: "Make way for the boss. Make way for the boss."

Part of one wall was still standing. Most of the rubble was still far too hot to approach, so I had to pick my spots, and root through the coals and ashes with a spar. Yes, I could have survived some burns, if I had had a few days to recuperate.

They had blown the library, burning all my books. They had killed my cook. I found his leg and part of his head in the slag of the kitchen. He had been borderline, not much smarter than a bevo, certainly not citizen-legal, but I had loved him. They had killed— No. That was the other time.

A dozen hustlers besides those that had come after me at Centerpole worked the ranch, but there were no bodies that I could see. Either they had gotten away, had died somewhere else, or had been completely burned.

What I was looking for had been in the strongbox, but they had taken the time and trouble to blow that, too. I found it, finally, still in its case, under a collapsed wall where the back porch had been, miraculously intact, although the case was a scorched wreck. I tore the shreds of the case away. I walked around the ruin to the front of the house again, looking out over the valley range below, the bright curve of Big Damn River. I monkeyed up the bricks to the smoking roofline, lifted the trumpet to my mouth, blew. It rang over the valley. I heard it come back from the Wall itself in a minute, faintly. "I'll find you, you motherfuckers!" I shouted. "I'll kill you all!"

When I walked back to the pad, Mandrake and Jennie were watching me. The bevos were beginning to organize themselves, slowly, columns seeding in the general mix like crystals in saturated fluid.

"Old family heirloom," I said, holding the trumpet up. "It goes with us."

"They blew the leads," she said. "The extra batteries, too. No jive anywhere."

Damn Benjamin and his verisimilitude. "How much left in the bat?" I pointed up the valley where Shade's Range and the Wall narrowed together in the mist. Hey, the hustlers named it. "How far up there can we get?"

Jennie made a meal of steak and bushcarrot roasted over the

coals of my home. I ate with her, for appearance's sake, or to encourage her to eat more—I'm not sure. I was chewing boxboard. We found several squares of silverstuff and a good pair of cutters, and bundled them up. All the high-suits were burnt out. We salted a couple of racks from the last bevos to leave, packed them. There were lenses in the bat, though none to fit Jennie. I dumped the supercircuits from a couple of the dead batteries, filled them from the well. When, finally, we were ready, it was nearly four o'clock. The light was getting longer, and an utter stillness hung over the valley. A two-kilometer line of bevos wound far below, heading back the way we had come.

I had trekked this route into the Wall many times, always into greater and greater exhilaration, but this time I saw nothing but what was ahead of me. I was thinking of my attackers, how to revenge myself on the humans who had destroyed my solitude and drawn me into yet another of their intricate and repulsive schemes.

We boosted the bat till it ran out, high on the ridge top of Shade's Range, about three k from the Wall. We rigged packs and began our hike. Jennie held up well, covering a good twenty k before her legs went and Mandrake had to carry her.

I do remember that we stopped to look back at the last canyon from which we would be able to see my valley. "What did I hear you call your place? When you were preaching to the bevos?"

Preaching to the bevos. Hah. The sun was westerly and low. We stood blocked off from its direct rays, but with a good view. Long shadows flooded the valley below us, green gone blue in a thousand dark untellable ways, the eastern curve of the Wall dimly ruddy but carved with jags of night. "Shadowfall," I said.

The girl from the wide bright plains was silent a while. "I see," she said then, and we went on, into the wilderness of Hellaswall.

The trail led into higher and higher canyons. Some had run-off creeks, high-altitude shrubbery. But the pressure differential on Mars is much less steep than it is on Earth, and we would never suffer from hypobaric deprivation. The differences in the vegetation had more to do with radiation and soil than with air pressure. Nightfall came, and the nightlights came on, a kilometer above us. They gave perhaps a quarter the light of the sun, although much of their energy was in the infra and u.v. They would dim gradually to midnight and free time, and then go out. It wasn't much light, especially over the fissures and angles we were traveling, and footing was tricky, but we could manage.

At last we made the falls. I call it Wilberforce, after the one in Canada. The enormous thunder of its descent rocked us on our ledge, the spray blew over us in a chilly welter. Had it been daylight, we could have seen a glossy mass of green water pour shining out of a cleft in the red rock, to shatter into white for fifty meters, and pool below us, flowing forward a few more meters only to tumble thunderously out of view. As it was, we saw a huge and rumbling ghost, a shifting and monstrous presence whose breath blew ice into our spines. Wilberforce is the largest headwater of Big Damn River. Until that day, I and my hands had been the only ones to see it.

"We're headed there," I said to Mandrake, "behind the falls." A cliche, I know, one of your favorites. Which is why I did it. It had cost me ten years of packing batteries in for the lasers, cutting the trails, cutting the cave. I had finished it before I made a move to buy Shadowfall from S2.

And it was only the decoy, the hiding-place you were supposed to find if trouble ever started.

Trouble had started, and here we were. "Loud," Jennie said, stirring sleepily in Mandrake's arms. "Cold. Wet."

"Let's go," I said.

The trail behind the falls was wide enough, but slippery with spray. I wondered if Mandrake could get traction enough on such a surface, but it was too dark to see and too loud to hear how he was managing. We came to the false stone that hid the lock.

"Belladonna," I said. A red scanner light came on, tracked my irises. "Thank you," the lock said. The stone swung away, and the lock hissed open. The interior lights came on, and I knew the other systems had gone operational. It wasn't a big roost, about twenty by thirty. "If you would put her in the bunk on the far wall," I said. "Get her wet clothes off and then get that meat in the cooler." He was already at the bunk and undressing her, of course, by the time I had finished speaking.

My holo blinked its pole of pure blue light, went green to

red to yellow to say a transmission was waiting, went back to blue.

"Surprise, surprise," I said. "Okay, let's burn it. Record now to end transmission, transmit."

A large face floated in the holofield, the face of a wise and friendly and white-haired man. The wizard. Why a face instead of his whole body? Easy, partners. His con could tell my field was a small one. Whole-body, he would have been a doll to us, something to feel superior to. Instead, he chose to project a twice-life-size face, the face of Jove or Merlin, but kindly. Dominance. The games had started in earnest.

Nor would this be his real face or real voice—if *he* was real. A blind double, more likely—a system double for a nonexistent man.

"Mr. Shade," the face said in the gorgeous bass of Yahweh or a good pitchman. "We will keep this transmission short in order to minimize the chance of discovery. We have traced your resort; never mind how. Suffice it we are aware of your recent troubles with Centerpole, and are impressed with your capabilities. Think of us as a group of politically sympathetic businessmen. We dare not reveal ourselves, but we control a fair amount of funding, which we have dedicated to the eventual liberation of Hellas. We could use a few good commanders, but obviously we require a demonstration of your loyalty to the cause. Your recent raid, as I say, was most impressively executed, but it may have represented mere selfish reaction rather than fealty to freedom. We have been planning for some time a major campaign to excite public response. If you should indeed wish to join in the cause of secession, you will undertake an action for us. If you do not do so, you will not hear from us again. We will not move against you if you do not betray our existence. Should you attempt to trace this transmission, you will have no success.

"Tomorrow evening, at sunset, you will hit the S10 Airworks and destroy the main blower."

"The Airworks?" I said. "S10? That's back across Hellas."

The transmission was one-way, but our contact clearly expected my reaction. "This feat would be impossible by ground or air, and by now you may very well be completely afoot and low on resources. However, you will not approach the Airworks from inside the tent. You will be going outside, over the top. Materials, weapons, vacuum suits, and transportation will be provided. Details will follow in a burst transmission when I sign off. You need not attempt response. Your successful completion of the mission will be adequate communication, and you will be contacted again shortly thereafter." The face beamed at me, a wide, generous, confidence-inspiring smile. "I do hope you will join us," it said. "For now, a good evening to you and your companions."

Companions. Plural. They had some very up-to-date intelligence—or did the face mean my hustlers?

The face went, and the blue pole returned. It blipped to a high-speed shuttle of disks to indicate an incoming burst.

"End transmission noted?" I said.

"Noted," the holo said. "Record stop."

"Record burst to end, stop all transmission thereafter. Voice activation me only. Copy?"

"Copy," the holo said, and squealed with the information burst. "Burst recorded, zero errors. Shutting down."

"That was very interesting," Mandrake said. Jennie had turned to the wall and begun snoring.

"Yeah," I said. "You can access the burst if you want to, and spend the night thinking it over. I'm going lights-out."

"You are?"

"Just like that there naked lady over there. Lights-out, Belladonna."

In the dark, on the bunk beside Jennie, I stretched, and yawned. "Tell you what, Mandrake," I said. "It's been a long day."

I don't remember whether he answered.

11
Cullie's End

As I've mentioned, I can do without sleep. Whatever keeps my cells from aging keeps them from weariness. But I cannot do without dreams, not any more than Benjamin could. Apparently I, too, am still a mammal.

And so, to keep the dreams from ruling my waking life, I observe sleep. I observe it as a ritual, almost, entering its forms and stages as one might enter the waters of some sacred river. I happily give up, piece by piece, the tattered vestiges of conscious thought that we have been trained to accept as the whole and sum of our personalities.

The dreams I had that night are private.

The lights dimmed on as I stirred awake. I woke with a tremendous hard-on, as usual. I woke confused, with the smell of Eleanor in my nostrils, curled against a body I thought for a moment was Eleanor's. I am trying to explain why it was not rape. Killer you may call me, but I would not have you think me truly depraved. I may assure you that when I come after your blood I am simply Death. I have no desire to violate your being.

When I rolled her over and clambered aboard, she said "Mm." And then she said, "Oh, no, wait."

I was fumbling to find entry, helping myself with my hands. If I were to be completely honest I would have to say that I began to know in a tiny way that this really could not be home, that she really could not be Eleanor. Did I withdraw and apologize? No, not immediately. I shivered in and pumped three times. And then I lunged away, almost flinging her from me against the wall of the bunk, while I fell sprawling to the floor.

"I'm sorry," I said. "I was asleep when it began."

"Are you trying to say you got in bed with me not even thinking about it? Where are we, anyway?" She glanced at the cave. "That felt good, but it's my choice, not yours. I saw you yesterday. I was considering the idea, but now where does this put us?"

"I'm in the wrong," I said.

"You damn sure are," she said. "At least you showed a little control. You didn't come, did you?"

"No," I said. "There was nowhere else to sleep but the floor. I could have slept there, but obviously I was planning something like this and not admitting it to myself."

"Stick with the short confession," she said. "How you're in the wrong. That about covers it. Where are we? I remember water, a lot of loud water. Rain? Was it raining?"

"I *am* sorry," I said. I, who do not believe in apologies.

"What good?" she said. "Minus it, hustler. I'll watch you a while to see if I can trust."

She had dropped into the noise, an index of her irritation. The drop from formal to vulgate serves as a sort of spoken italics. I am not in complete control of my feelings, it says. Of course one may employ such a shift to convey a passion one does not entirely feel, and I rather thought that was her strategy.

I find myself wondering, Gene, what you would make of this episode. I suppose I think on some level that I am sending my words back through time to you. I have done that before, with Eleanor and others I have loved, ceasing when it got so hard to explain what the world had become that I could not maintain the illusion. I cannot remember now exactly what the mores were when we were last together. There have been several swings of the pendulum since. Mars is now in a long period of sexual openness, some years behind Earth, which seems to be going conservative again. I think when I met you as a boy, the U.S. had just come out of a period of license and was heading back toward repression. I know you saw, in late middle age, another explosion of frankness and experimentation, and I think this surge too had contracted before you died.

The long-range tendency is unquestionably to greater and greater sexual freedom, but for every flowering of that freedom, it is certain there will be a withering. The source of all sexual puritanism must be the terrible diseases that we have been prey to, the Biblical leprosy (which may really have been syphilis), and syphilis itself, and gonorrhea and herpes and AIDS and supervix, so that the fear of a sex-hating God functions as a survival trait. And yet I don't think these diseases are the direct cause of our behavioral swings. It may be intrinsic, a sort of slow social estrus.

The rich now can be whichever sex they desire, or both at once, or each in turn; they may have more than one organ of either type, with built-in ticklers, tinglers, and titillaters; rich or poor may make the beast of more than one back with others of the same or somewhat differing sex; and none of this is forbidden to ordinary conversation.

Yet we still find great difficulty in speaking plainly of love.

And I, I see, am minimizing my transgression against Jennie by placing it in a larger social context.

Mandrake stood where he had when the lights went out. It occurred to me he felt no twitch, itch, urge, or surge of restlessness when he was not moving. He was not heir to the small miseries of flesh. He was not heir to anything, for that matter. I went over and spoke his name, but he didn't stir.

"Mandrake," I said again. He seemed, somehow, dead. "Where are you?" I said. "Mandrake, answer me."

"Howdy," he said.

"That's a relief. What was that? Were you in comm with Benjamin?"

"I thought I saw a need for privacy."

"What? You turned yourself off? You can do that?"

"Yes, I *can* do that. No, I *didn't* do that. No need, when you can shut down your senses."

"That doesn't make you crazy, there in your mind in the dark alone?"

"Who says I'm not crazy? I think maybe I don't think, you know."

That stuff again. Yeah, yeah. "What was the burst? What do we do next? Summarize, don't give me the dit-dit."

"I have to eat before we go anywhere," Jennie said. She had come up beside me, wrapped in the sheet.

"I hate to say it, J. D., but I think we part company here," I said. "This place is secure, or at least it will be for you. No one will track you here, and you can stay as long as provisions hold out. That's why I had us haul all that meat up last night, so you'd have fresh—I have some zap-wrap on hand, but not a whole lot. Plenty of water. You can pick up full-band on the trivia, too."

"That sounds pretty boring. I think I want to go on with you fellows."

"Jennie, you don't understand. This isn't pursuit any more. This is an action."

"I do understand. Ever since yesterday, when you said you had hit Centerpole, I've been thinking it over. I have a calling to follow, and I can't follow it unless I'm willing to follow it into battle. That's why I went out into the desert to pray. Maybe I was hoping to be discovered and killed. In many ways, that would have been easier. But God sent you, and you're a warrior. I'll go with you and learn war. So I can bring peace. You can't make an omelet without breaking eggs."

I was too astonished for words. I'm afraid I spluttered. "A-number-one," I said. "Do you have any idea how *old* that cliche is?"

"Cliche?" she said.

"The eggs, the eggs!"

"That's a cliche? I thought I was making it up. I used to gather the eggs and make breakfast."

"Number two, just for the record, it isn't a goddamn desert, you don't have the least fucking idea what a real goddamn desert is like, it's a *range*. And—shut up!—and number three, I am *not* a warrior, I am somebody who thought he would be a schoolteacher. I had glowing visions of myself as the revered master of a cabin full of rosy-cheeked and grateful frontier children, and instead I have gotten myself into something so long and horrible you will never in your worst dreams be able to imagine it."

"I'm still going along," she said.

"Number four: Like it or not, you are your father's daughter. If you think God sent me into your life, you're crazy, or you believe in a crazy God with a twisted sense of humor. God doesn't mess around with history, you damn little teener. Things just *happen*."

"Number one," she said. "There's a lot of things I don't know, but don't you dare condescend to me. Number two, I'm not going to debate God with you, but remember I'm a Butlerian, not a Sooie-Baptist, and when I talk about God's will, I'm not talking about miraculous intervention—I'm talking about the chance to *make* a pattern. Of *course* I'm my father's daughter—he's not an asshole because he's a Butlerian, he's an asshole because he's an asshole. And I was just a dizzy-headed little farmgirl cheerleader until I went off to the big city and *this* happened." She rapped the jangler half of her skull with the knuckles of her right hand. "I can't just plug into my social role any more. Now, if I'm going to be anything but a lost case, I have to make myself count for something."

"It's dangerous," I said. "You could die."

"What am I now, alive? I'm dead to my family, dead to my friends, dead to my society. Suppose I stay up here in your little hideaway—what am I but a body in a tomb? A living, breathing body in a very comfortable tomb, but still just a body in a tomb. I suppose you think you've had a horrible life, all right, but look at you. You look pretty well-fed to me. Look at me. Look at what I am. Do you think I can be afraid of anything else ever again?"

I wanted to warn her: *It can get worse. It can get much worse.* But I was mute.

"Number three," she said. "You're in love with me and won't be able to make me stay behind."

"The first-stage drop-point is a place they said you would know as Cullie's End," Mandrake said.

"Yeah, I know it. Their intelligence is too damn good for my taste." Privately I wasn't surprised. They'd found some of my hustlers knocking around Hellasport last night and gotten them weightless, I was sure. The only thing that did worry me was whether they were good enough to have found my genuine rabbit-hole. I hadn't been *there* since our visit, Gene.

"It's a high meadow a good three hours from here," I said. "We'll have to climb some."

We showered in the spray from the falls—I'd seen no point in putting in a stall with all that water shattering by. It was a cold shower, ice everywhere. It always frosts up overnight here. You can warm the atmosphere all you want to, at night the ground gets *cold*. We had the permafrost backed down to about a hundred meters in Hellas, but even that was possible only because the ancient blast-rock of the original impact formed a bowl-shaped natural insulator. After the shower, Jennie had breakfast. "You don't eat much," she said with a full mouth.

"Yeah, I drink my meals."

Then we geared up. I had extra worksuits, spintex meant to stretch, so the suits were not as large as they might have been, but were still too loose on her. No boots were small enough to fit, so she had to make do with the walking shoes she'd been wearing. Canteens. We shouldn't need them, but who knows? Batbelts, sixteen cartridges carrying two kilovolts each, which could function as grenades in a pinch. Enough energy in a small enough space can be a bomb or an engine—it's all a matter of application. You just have to know how to jerry-rig a delayed resistance. That's an old word, isn't it? Jerry-rig. An old word from an old war.

I took a kilometer's worth of superconducting ro-pel and a grab-bag of connectors. Three more adjustable blasers besides the one I'd brought with me, so she and I were both double-armed, cross-belted like Wild Bill Hickok or Pancho Villa. With the blasers you could cook your coffee, cut steps in stone, or kill at a distance. Light backpacks with bevo sandwiches and flasks of chill-brewed coffee. I wore Remington headgear with variable optics—shades, filters, band extenders, all slavable to my blasers, for really long-range target practice. No way to fit headgear to Jennie, but we rigged her some goggles in a spintex band to help with the u.v.

It took us a good half-hour to prep, which meant we were nine-0 leaving, which meant Cullie's End by twelve with luck, which meant bust ass to raise the S10 Airworks by evening—*assuming* they had provided adequate gitalong.

I get antsy when a mission's on. Comes from my temperament, half schoolteacher, half adventurer. Not a for-sure kill-merchant, me.

"Christ Almighty's fucking sake," Jennie said when I hustled her up. "You're like my mother getting the settle ready for the Woman's Work Club."

"Mother don't die she don't do it right," I said.

"You think," she said.

We were out on the slippery trail behind the waterfall by 9:15. We had to backtrack a half-k, easy walking, and then up the red stone a sheer three hundred meters. From there, a fractured but relatively level outcrop of a couple of kilometers extent, which ran parallel to the course of the BDR above Wilberforce. Sorry—so used to it I forget. The BDR, pronounced *beater,* is short for Big Damn River. The cataract we would follow was the main source, although at that height it was small. The terrain on the plateau was so rough that it would take us a good hour to make the two kilometers. At the end of the traverse, we would have to shinny up a forty-meter pipe, hike a ledge path the hustlers and I had cut some ten years ago, about the time Jennie was born, and then wade a feeder creek up-canyon for another three-quarter k.

Jeez, I love the Wall.

At the first climb, I cut a length of ro-pel, whipped a helix of it around a plastic sleeve, clipped a jelly-weld to one end of the rest, fed it through the sleeve, and jived the helix. The line shot up, soared to inflection, stooped over the edge of the cliff in a lovely clean arc. I pulled on it, and it held. I pulled harder. First try, pretty good.

Hand-over-hand time again. I went first, as the certain immortal. Mandrake could bust if he fell far enough, I was sure. And not heal. I double-secured the line, braced to pull Jennie, but she did well enough on her own. Mandrake came scooting over the lip like a gigantic cockroach.

We were in a maze of outcrops and faults. This whole plateau was a single block, crazed with giant freeze and thaw.

We made it to the pipe with only two bad knees and three twisted ankles. Skinned knuckles and elbow-bangs don't count. Up the pipe and then the ledge, scary if heights bother you, and then up the very cold creek of a very narrow canyon. My boots were thermal, but Jennie was suffering badly. I was more worried about her footing than about any tissue damage. If she got too numb, and misplaced a step, this water was strong enough to bang her against a rock or two, and these rocks were mighty sharp-edged.

But the sun was cracking over the rim of the high red canyon, the water was making its melody—a more sonorous melody than the waters of Earth—there were pinon-jays and blue grosbeaks and hummingbirds in the juniper and madrone, the dark blue sky was deeper than the ache of first love, and I was having a great time.

It didn't hurt that I had been in a good woman just hours before, however abbreviated the performance, however wrong the assault.

And it didn't hurt that I was saying goodbye. I could love the place more than I had in years because I was leaving it.

The water chutes through a big elevated arch, tremendously slippery and hard to clamber through. After you gain this portal, the canyon widens, crooks around a big red stone, and—

Cullie's End. Here, Cullie Hoo-boy met his end, trying a little too hard to romance Bernadette Jackrabbit, whom he had lured up on the pretext of more wild feedback, growing lush and green, than they could carry down together. What he had really had in mind was a picnic in a lovely secluded spot, some liquor, some amour. . . . Bernadette was a rough boy, but he was sentimental. He had buried Cullie there, "where he can look out over the Wall and smell feedback forever."

It was a jewel of a mountain meadow, with two green grassy levels. The creek spread out and wandered, pooling here and there in sheets of flat stone. No sand and precious little gravel, of course. I hope it has been clear that the things I have been calling canyons are faults, not water-worn channels. There just aren't any water-worn channels in Hellas.

The sun was full over us, the air was crisp and cool with a warm top-note, the cicadas sang in the grass, and yes, in the feedback. Jennie sighed with pleasure and weariness combined, and I turned to watch her settle against the stone that flanked the upper level of the meadow. She took a sandwich and a flask from her knapsack with fumbling hands, never looking away from the sunlight in the meadow.

Mandrake had already located the cache behind the bier. He was pointing with all three arms, an exaggerated cartoon gesture of discovery, jabbing toward his find. I started toward him. He was saying, "Was this a grave? Someone has broken into it. I see bones." He was saying, "Jennie!"

But this time I was the one who was processing in supertime, spinning in her direction and pulling a blaser and dropping to one knee and locking on. I had begun to turn on the word "broken," I think, knowing they couldn't hurt Mandrake and weren't near me, not knowing that there was one near her but knowing that she was the one at risk and that they moved very very fast.

It was there, a white skitter, a gargoyle scramble. I pulled the trigger, and the skull exploded.

Like a good hustler, she was rolling, not screaming. She fetched to her feet ashen-faced, looking where I had shot and not at me, her own blasers out.

"Shit," I said, standing. "That was Cullie."

We had now to make certain there was not a nest of them, though the little skulls will not generally attack something as large as a human. They prefer to enlarge their accommodations by more gradual stages.

By now Mandrake had slithered and zipped to inspect the carcass, what little was left of it. Jennie and I joined him. "She must have been planning to add on a wing," Jennie said, gesturing at the outsized right lobe of her own skull. "She was in for a surprise when she found out it was all plastic." That was good. That was just the sort of crack a hustler would make. A little shaky, but joking to the end.

Nest is not really the appropriate word. Sometimes you find a batch of them together, little and big, but there's no evidence they breed, and very little that they even socialize.

"Replaying," Mandrake said. "They're like machines," he said. "There, that move, that's not a g-bio articulation. They move like *me*. But who would make something like this? There's no recognizable technology in these remains."

"I know," I said. "Kind of makes you believe in Original Martians, don't it?"

"Why haven't you told anyone? Why doesn't Centerpole know?"

"We *do* tell people," I said. "I told you. It doesn't seem to impress anybody. Just another pest. After all, they don't kill bevos and they don't hurt crops. No, you have to see one. You have to see them coming after you. *Then* they're unforgettable."

Jennie shivered. "I'm cold," she said. "I don't like this place any more. Let's get out of here."

12

The Diving Board at the Rim of the World

The excitement made our mission seem anticlimactic, a bit unreal, but I am an old hand at carrying on in dubious circumstances. As soon as I was reasonably sure this skull had been a loner, I got us up to Cullie's despoiled bier, and the cache beside it.

The cache turned out to be twelve lightweight vests of metallic silverstuff, with built-in batbelts and a jack-in control gun for each. One of the vests was smaller, and had three armholes. Which answered one question, the one about their intelligence. They had known about Mandrake, but they hadn't known about Jennie, and they had been assuming I had some of my hustlers still with me. By *now* they probably knew about Jennie. Brady had had thirty hours in which to work his mischief.

I was glad to have the question answered, because it told me that either Mandrake wasn't reporting back or we were certainly dealing with someone other than Benjamin. Actually, I had a reasonable certainty that both scenarios were true, since it was likely that this bunch—the wizard in the comm, and whomever he fronted for—had Benjamin tagged.

You can get sucked into the pleasures of conspiracy. All those head games. Invisible chess. You have to work hard to remember that the important world is the one of work and celebration and ordinary small pleasures. Take it from a fellow who's spent a lot of years spooking for Sam. Those guys are the real vampires.

"What is this stuff?" I said.

101

"We put them on and fly through the nearest maintenance lock in the Wall," Mandrake answered.

"Antigravity?" I said. "I didn't think they were that far along."

"I don't think so," he said, "but I don't know. It wasn't in the burst."

"I can't get this on over my gear," Jennie said. "Do we leave the gear here?"

"I wouldn't," I said. "Sling your blasers and batbelt over the vests. That won't interfere with their operation, will it," I asked Mandrake.

"Doesn't say," he said. "Try it. If these are what I think they are, it won't."

"So what do you think they are?" I said, zipping into the vest nearest my size.

"Jet fields," he said. "I think they create unidirectional boundary fields around their wearers. A massive neutral flux in the direction opposite the direction you want to go. That's something we were working on."

I didn't miss the *we*. "Take your word for it," I said. "Sounds enough like antigravity for me. How do you work it?"

"Maybe we're an experiment," Jennie said. "If the mission flops, they still get to try out their Buck Rogers stuff." I could see she was proud of having made the allusion. Still trying to impress Mandrake.

"That would be efficient," he said. "Furthering a mission and trying out some new technology at the same time. I wonder which is more important to them?"

"Don't ask," Jennie said.

"You point the gun the way you want to go," he said, answering me. "The thumb-button on the grip for constant v, the red trigger for acceleration. Double-click the trigger for logarithmic ax. The thumb-button freezes v at current value, the trigger will override the thumb-button. Double-click the thumb-button for deceleration—it reverses the field: You dece along the line-of-sight. Remember that gravity is itself an acceleration field, so you'll have to double-click to ax vertically."

"Whoopee!" Jennie said, grinning.

"Let's not try any flips or anything," I said. "Get to waving that sighting pistol around, and you could break yourself in half."

"Right," Mandrake said. "Change your aim very slowly. The guns are damped and slaved, so they will resist to some degree when you try to change direction too rapidly, but you could still get hurt. Also, the kinetic output on these things is fixed and digital, not slicked to the mass of the wearer. So she's going to move faster until we tinker with the ax a little."

"Got it," I said. "Everybody ready? Wait—let's take the other vests. Any problem with feedback, Mandrake?"

"Not if they're not turned on," he said.

"Shade—that reminds me," Jennie said. "I'd dearly love to bundle up some of this weed to take with. Object?"

"Not if you don't smoke till safe haven."

"Not so much for me," she said. "You don't know how much good an out-of-the-body experience can do a jangler. Someone who isn't always sure she *has* a body. Or he."

"So get," I said, impatient, but thinking: *So she's going back. What does she have in mind? Missionary to zoids?* And would you believe, I still didn't get the joke of her name. The new Maid of Orleans, right under my nose.

While she was picking her crop, I stowed the other vests, guns and all, in my pack.

She came back with a knapsack stuffed with wild feedback. The odor from torn leaves and broken stems was so strong I nearly d-geed right there. "That ought to take care of the velocity differential," I said.

"Now, now," she said.

"Ready?" I said. "Guns up. *Boost!*"

We pointed our pistols straight up, clicked the triggers, and rose slowly and steadily into the air. It was a spooky feeling, not a little frightening. I'd been up in plenty of fliers, of course, and I was Class-3 in a pair of Wingz, but this was not the same. With those you have some physical sense of connection to your flight—your effort and skill *make* the flight. But to rise silently and smoothly and without volition high in the air—this was like a dream, when you suddenly think to look down, and you see the remembered earth dwindled and far below, and there is nothing to sustain you except the fabric of the dream itself, already tattering.

Or maybe the feedback was getting to me.

The field seemed to form a cylinder about my torso—my weight wasn't dragging against the material of the vest, but my legs were dangling from mid-thigh down, magnifying the dreamlike sense of suspension. The gun—and my arm—was weightless. Jennie was already rising some thirty meters above us, Mandrake close but slightly behind. Which told me his weight. Heavier than I had thought. Now he came floating by, a reverse skydiver, his arms out like the skeleton of an umbrella. I double-clicked the trigger and began to accelerate. I gained slightly on him, and we were both gaining on her. When he buttoned the grip, I double-buttoned mine, then buttoned it again. We sailed up to her at nearly matching v.

"Yay-hoo," she said when we came in range. "This is *fine,* I'm keeping mine when this is over. Hey, my arm isn't getting tired."

"It's in the field," Mandrake said. "The field extends about a meter from your body. We had better head for the lock, boys and girls, these things drink a lot of gas."

I unclipped my belt's read-out, conned it. Three of the batteries were gone already, and a fourth was draining fast. The vests did suck a lot of jive. We were a good five hundred meters up from the meadow now, I judged. The small green sundered oval looked nearly lost in the jumble of red rock, its creek flashing with sun. We were vertical enough to have a powerful sense of the Wall as a wall, the pitches and ledges and faults we had been clambering blindly through now swept into a steep and falling perspective.

"There," Mandrake said, gently easing his gun around and down to a roughly sixty-degree angle. Immediately he began drawing away and below. With some difficulty—it was a little like handling a small firehose—Jennie and I closed in beside him. Now the three of us were floating up and ever closer to the Wall itself, which, at this height, was almost sheer, all the faulted debris having tumbled below.

"I see it," I said.

Set into a notch of the Wall's mountains, there was the tremendous architecture of a maintenance lock. The Wall is not regular, of course—it isn't even like a range of mountains, exactly. It is the frozen and crumbled image of a gigantic splash. In order to create the tent, and with it the whole ecology of Hellas, regularity had been imposed. Some peaks had been leveled, others built up. In thousands of clefts around the colony, the architects of Hellas had set these way stations, these exit locks and maintenance platforms. In fact, the locks were not commonly used for egress—nowhere much to go once you got out, and you had to have heavy ID to use them. They weren't much needed for maintenance, either. The spiders took care of that. Most of the stations were monitored from Hellas and kept no human personnel aboard.

The sky had turned an extremely dark blue—we weren't looking through much air. But even this close, you couldn't see the fabric of the tent.

The lock we were swimming toward was one in a wheel of locks, like the chambers of a revolver, the whole set into a vast sheer flank of steelic. We would enter the lowest chamber, below the level of the tent, and ride the great ferris wheel to its top, devolving in vacuum on the maintenance platform above the tent.

"Comming the lock, I hope," I said to Mandrake.

"Hush, chile," he said. "I'm a-talking to the thang. You all had best be decing lessen you want to wind up a splat on this here Wall. Remember to point a angle *down* when you dece, so you won't lose altitude."

"Nobody ever said *you all*," I said. "It was *y'all*, and then only in plural—and you're conflating hill and flat country." But I did as he said. It was tricky. I had a bad moment of free fall getting my gun down, but we slowed together like a precision team, and the huge sphincter of the bottom lock opened just as we floated to it, a pupil widening for a trio of motes.

The lock was the size of a cathedral, but it was nothing more than a long cylindrical vault with heavy equipment pads rising from its floor, equipment lockers set into its walls, and a bank of seats on either side of the floor. The light came from the far end, but I couldn't tell whether it was natural or artificial. "Please be seated," the lock said, a big hollow voice in the hushed empty air.

We sat, and felt the wheel begin to rotate: the smallest of hitches, and then a smooth slight pressure against our seat cushions. No noise at all. The sense of cathedral was strong. The architecture was of a scale that made it almost holy in itself, the subsuming of unimaginable immensities of thought. Then I realized, with a force that was exactly like the slap of an icy wave, that one of the thinkers sat there beside me, still and silent in his tripartite weirdness. When you find yourself sitting beside God on the commuter bus, I can tell you now, it's hard to breathe.

Then the movement stopped, and the lock said, "Maintenance level prime. All functions this level in surface atmosphere. All human personnel don pressure suits prior to egress."

A tell-tale began blinking on a nearby locker, and in the locker we found pressure suits. We spent a complicated few moments stripping, zipping into the suits, packing the vests and extra equipment, and slipping back into the packs. I was glad to see there was a fishbowl large enough to accommodate Jennie's head, though she had to mate one from a much larger suit to her own small outfit. Suited, we looked exactly like the spacemen in comics from a century and a half before—skintight bodysuits topped by clear bubbles of helmet, with earphones and speakers set into the bubbles. It has been interesting to watch the comics and the covers of the science fiction magazines come true. They have come so true it is difficult not to believe the artists were visited by genuine vision, which is perhaps why that art has risen so in the estimation of the critics.

The end of the lock sphinctered open, and we walked out into a small chamber. The lock closed, and there was the dying hiss of evacuated air. The bulkhead in front of us slid away, and we walked out onto the shining floor of the platform. For all that it was supposed to be a maintenance level, it was as clean and bare as dawn. There was gleam, there was distance, there was a cavernous height of ceiling, there was a far glow ahead suggesting the open sun.

A spider skittered up from nowhere, from out of the gleam on the steelic. If the use of so much metal seems antique to you, Gene (even to you, my antique friend), remember that iron is plentiful on Mars, extremely plentiful, and that Hellas was made when cheapness was a factor. The locks on Argyre are as large, I think, but they are all plastide.

"Nananek," the spider said in our earphones. "Nan. Nan. Ek. Beet. Beet. Kwurtoid. Bizitter bizitter dadaram keno." There was a sort of squelched squeal, which I belatedly realized was a burst from Mandrake.

"It was not efficient to build them with speech modules," Mandrake said to us. "If you were genuine maintenance personnel, you would have translators. On your approval I have directed it to address all communication to me. I shall translate the essentials. It has, so far, expressed impatience with the unnecessary bother-ghost-gods from the realms-that-aren't, stating that it has things to do, things to do, and has commanded us to follow immediately so that it may be rid of us as soon as possible and return to the real world."

The spider, a metalloid being about the size of a small bush, stood thrumming its eight legs in a wave of motion remarkably like the drumming of fingers on a desk, except that this wave traveled in a rapid circle.

Another burst from Mandrake, and it scooted away toward the light. Mandrake immediately followed. Jennie and I lagged behind. The spider stopped, spun, squealed, saw that we were coming, and scooted on. "You may know this already," Mandrake said, "but the spiders are not really exactly like spiders. We copied a lot of the orb-weaver engrams, but those were modified and integrated into a social-insect architecture. The only practical way to maintain a structure as huge and fluid as the tent is to create a species and organize its social behavior around that central imperative. They live, quite literally, for the tent. Nothing else is real to them. They feed on sunlight, they scatter by millions over all the surface of the tent. They spin, repair, predict, control. They are perfectly capable of managing all maintenance stations, which they think of as nesting grounds, and all equipment, and have done so almost without human help for the last fifteen years. When they wear out, they are brought back to the stations for disposal, and new ones are issued. They sense that process, I think, as correlative to funeral and hatching."

"I knew some of that, sort of," I said. "But it's always good to get the story from the source." My awe had faded. Awe is a large flower, but a short-lived one. Besides, when God cracks a joke or two and clearly hopes you'll ask him over for a drink, you lose respect. If God wants worship, he'd better stay lonely. If he wants love, he'll have to eat shit with the rest of us.

Jennie, for once, had nothing to say. Her silence was like the volume of space we walked through, huge and suggestive.

The crack of light widened as we walked toward it, becoming more apparently daylight itself. The ceiling appeared to rise as we neared the opening.

And then we were standing, in full sun, on the edge of the world. Below us was the tent, discrete boundary of an improbable atmosphere, forming the wide and crystalline sea of Hellas—range on range wavering glassily into blue recession and blur, like the bottom of a lagoon seen from its shore. Away on either side, sweeping into vanishing distance, the darkly ruddy arms of the rest of Mars. I had not seen that sight in a while.

The spider was spinning and squealing again. We were to follow it out along a docking spike, a cantilevered avenue sixty meters wide projecting from the platform into open space a good half-kilometer or so. Walking the plank. I had a fantasy that when we had reached the end, the spider would whirl into a frenzy and fling us off, into a long accelerating dive to Hellas.

If it had, we would have died when we hit the tent. Though micrometeorites and the occasional larger chunks of debris penetrate the tent quite regularly, nothing at less than astronomical emvee-squared could pierce the silverstuff.

Along our high, suspended boulevard, staggered at intervals like seeds on a raceme, vehicles were set into color-coded recesses. Some were clearly repair, some transport and supply. Our guide led us to an area marked in large letters cut into the steelic itself, BLUE ZONE TWO: DEFENSE: RANGER CLASS. The spider stopped, finally, before a huge blue-striped cruiser. "Looks like we're traveling in style," I said.

All this immensity of self-sustaining structure, all these empty, spotless craft, ready to go—and no other humans about. Multiply that by the two thousand or so maintenance stations set in the Wall. There had never been armed conflict between Hellas and Argyre, for all the bad feeling; and thanks to the commerce in bevo, trivia programming, and feedback, attack from Sam had never been probable (though our mission was perhaps about to change that); no other nation had been a threat since the Russo-American Assimilation; and yet here were ranks of armed vessles, primed, jived, and waiting for use. They had waited for forty years. They might wait a hundred more. We live in the self-sustaining society, we live in the Living Machine, we live without considering it on the bounty of the intelligent Horn of Plenty.

All through the nineteens people spoke of the curve of technological progress as though it were exponential. In 2015, Sherman devised the first defensible methodology for plotting points on a family of so-called progress curves. By the middle twenty-twenties, theoreticians were able to show how social mathematics could be made to imply the curves. They were not exponential. They were factorial, smoothly interpolated graphs on sets of plot points generated by a family of formulas resembling

$$Y = \frac{n!}{kA^n}$$

where Y is the given "progress quantity," n is duration and is never negative, k is a constant for the given "progress set," and A is a semifractal generated by another complete set of equations, varying closely about a constant value with a range of variation less than n. To approximate the curves, treat kA as a simple constant—say 2—and use integral values of n. Almost all of human existence has occurred from n equals 0 to n equals 2, where the Y-points lie along a flat horizontal line. We have, however, passed the inflection point, and the induced curve rises far more steeply than a mere exponential.

Did I tell you I was a math teacher once? In an eternal job market, one may have many careers. In fact, one must, or one is likely to go nuts, though some vampires, like my Indian friend, apparently can be satisfied to hang out in bars forever.

Four of the Sherman Curves particularly interest me. One is the curve for the amount of controllable power produced from a given volume of space. The second is the amount of per capita controllable power. The third is the amount of information storable in a given volume of space. The fourth is the amount of per capita available information. The four may be shown to be essentially the same curve. In ten to a thousand years, all four will go effectively vertical. If they are taken to represent the actual future course of history, you or your children will be able to create galaxies and hang them from the roof of Heaven like Calder mobiles.

Where will a poor damned vampire be then?

The spider beeped rapidly, got an answering burst from Mandrake, and scooted away.

"Check the other vehicles," I said. "I want to take two or three of them."

"I already have," Mandrake said. "All will require ID. This is the only one that has been cleared for us."

"Can't you unjam?" I said. "They did, to get us this one."

"Not in a normal life-span," he said. "Not without system support, and to use the system here—"

"You have to have ID," I finished. "Right. They've got us boxed pretty well. I'm glad we brought the extra bats and vests. That's all the margin we'll have. I wish we'd brought extra pressure suits from the lock. Maybe there's some on board that Ranger."

"Comming," Mandrake said, then: "Sorry. No comm-status on the lockers. We'll just have to go see."

Jennie finally broke her silence. "Why do we need margin?" she said. "What else is going to happen besides the attack on the Airworks?"

"I don't know," I said. "Maybe nothing. But if you're going to do this sort of thing, rule number one is *Never trust your allies.*"

"Harsh," she said.

"Let's get in the damn car and go," I said.

The Ranger was plush for a battle vehicle. Why not go to war in comfort? The seats were full and soft, the galley stocked, the display fully teched and beautiful to behold. Hell, we could catch the news while en route to make more of it. We were traveling in a Cadillac tank. Jennie and I stowed our gear—there were more pressure suits, fifty-four of them, in all sizes. Then we fought over the coffee-maker. When we had each gotten a huge mug of fresh-ground Wall-grade, we strapped in. As before, Mandrake, tireless, supernally accurate, and faster than speeding electrons, would handle the flying, but I could not resist taking the Ranger out myself.

We floated out of the dock and into the vacuum over Hellas, the beautiful state.

"Wow," Jennie said. "I went outside once. But I never saw this. We weren't this high. Wow." She looked on silently a while, as I did, and then she turned to me. "What now?"

"Revolution," I said, and boosted.

13

Airworks

The Ranger was big, but smooth. Response was instantaneous, and the gyros were so neatly damped that there was almost no sense of tremble or sway. I set us moving a little south of west at 5 kpm, buttoned the maps. I wanted to pinpoint the coordinates for the Airworks.

"Wow, we've got a *tank*," Jennie said, peering out the armorglass at the ranges and fields below.

"Correction," I said. "*They've* got us *in* a tank." A map of Hellas appeared in the holo. I boxed the area containing the S10 Airworks, a cube of lighter blue. "Replace with subsection," I said, and the Airworks leapt into view, along with considerable portions of the Wall. I dotted the approximate center of the Airworks. "Center on dot," I said. "Magnification by 1.75. Plot course to dot coordinates, Compare to actual course, beep me when deviation greater than one hundred meters a minute occurs, or when total deviation exceeds two kilometers. One beep for left deviation, two for right. Copy?"

"Copy," the holo-box said, and immediately started a flurry of double-tones at intervals like a redbird's call. It took me a minute to get us more nearly on course.

"Mandrake," I said, "are you in comm with this beast? Can you tell if there's external ipop?"

"I haven't commed yet because I thought you wanted to fly it. In comm now. Yes, there's ipop—no, output only so far. Short bursts, narrow. They're sealed, but I think it's transmitting our position."

"Is that standard for one of these busses?"

"Could be, but it's not in the onboard regs."

"Take over. Kick us to 10 kpm. Can they override you?"

"I don't see how. I'm monitoring input now, and I've told it to check with me before responding to commands from another source. My clearance is pretty high. Unless they come in with a ten-clown clearance or better, my orders should hold."

"Good," I said. So Mandrake was a ten-clown.

The Airworks was still in the holo. "Wipe that," I said, but it stayed. I changed my tone to make it clearer I was talking to the ship. Some of these brains have good ears, and some don't. "Wipe the holo-field," I said, and it went.

"Why aren't we on auto?" Jennie said. "Are you worried about somebody taking us over?"

"You're catching on," I said.

"What?"

"You con," I said. "Remember rule number one."

"But it doesn't make sense for them to jam us before we do what they want us to do."

"Nothing makes sense when you don't have enough information. You can't use logic till you have something to use it on. In the meantime, you maximize control, minimize dependence."

She was having trouble keeping her eyes on me. She was interested in tactics, but she wasn't used to thinking of them as a way to stay alive. She kept turning back to look out over the blue reaches of Hellas.

"Isn't it beautiful?" she said. "Isn't it *beautiful*?"

"Well, it's improbable," Mandrake said.

From orbit by daylight, Hellas, with its twelve sectors, its border roads and rivers dividing them each from each, is like nothing so much as the luminous face of an irregular and dripping watch—an image from Dali.

From our height, it was like a sea, clearer and smoother than any on Earth. Above it, the black emptiness of the Martian sky hazed auburn toward the horizon, the small sun beginning to lower into our eyes. We sped silently over a luminous drowned world, the tent its fluid but distinct surface. There were no whitecaps on our sea, just long deliberate glassy billows. The tent was humming with frequencies actually, vibrating through dozens of meters dozens of times a second; you can hear it sometimes, even in Hellas, the singing of the sky. But that vibration was hardly more than the thinnest of blurs in the distance, a pseudomist. Viewed directly from above, the tent was invisible, the surface completely transparent.

Light struck all the way to the floor of our atmospheric sea, struck on the reefs of the Wall curving far away into the blue dissolves of air; light showed us tractors crawling like sea-bottom snails throwing up their slow clouds of mud; the wispy and scattered anemones of settles; towns encrusted like gathers of barnacle, rivers glinting like inlaid silver, all unfolded with clarity, by section and boundary and blue-green alterations of shade. It was a dreamworld, a safe and serene and magical world where nothing terrible, surely, could ever dare to happen.

It came to me that Jennie had never seen a real ocean.

"What did Shade mean when he said you built Mars?" she said to Mandrake. "Are you responsible for this?" Her eyes were still fastened below.

"So I'm Shade now," I said. "What happened to John?"

She glanced at me. "It isn't this morning," she said. "You paid that back, I guess, sort of, when you shot that skull. John just doesn't seem right, somehow. You're Shade, that's all. Not John Shade. Just Shade." She answered abstractedly, as if she were working out a puzzle she was not terribly interested in. Her eyes rolled back to the view.

Mandrake had never taken a seat. He stood in the center of the control room still, a part of his mind now piloting the Ranger, a part of it considering us, and the rest thinking—what? He seemed, because he could not turn away, always to be watching us. Yet surely we were items on his periphery, personas temporarily embedded in the ring of his universe: Lacking a front, did he have a sense of time's arrow? Did he feel movement as we do, or did he have instead the impression that by exertion he could alter the characters on the screen surrounding his central, immovable perception?

"I wouldn't say *responsible*," he said. "I did a lot of the organizing. You understand how it is with macroengineering—"

"Not really," she said. "Big jobs, big machines. That's all I know."

"Wellll, it's more complicated than that. The really big projects—and Hellas is still the biggest, until Venus or Jupiter Station or Fly-by-Night comes through—when you get into the big ones, the machines have to be semiautonomous. No way you can handle all those variables through one centralized intelligence. The modeling gets too complex, and the next thing you know you've exceeded the Wu-Wu Limit."

"The *what*?" I said.

"The twin brothers Wu," he said. "Conjoined twins, craniopagus, actually, though they were separated shortly after birth. They demonstrated, about fifteen years ago, that there was a necessary upper limit to the size of any intelligence. You must have been herding bevos at the time."

"Mandrake," I said.

"In truth," he said. "Onliest thing I'm kidding you about is not knowing. You couldn't have known. Slapped it with a major *Classified* right away—too much threat to the trivia industry, and to a whole bunch of research grants. Puts paid to all those mad-machine-takes-over-the-universe stories, don't you know, all those dreams of upgrading your local Univac to God."

"Sounds to me like it's puts paid to God himself," I said. "Does it hold for all intelligences, or just nonbio? *How* big? What do they mean by big?"

"All intelligences," he said. "It has to do with information theory, not with physics directly, except as the two are the same thing. Think of it as a kind of Chandrasekhar's Limit for minds—get the thing too big and it blows up in all sorts of unusual ways. By big they mean amount of data processed versus the square of the processing speed. Something like four hundred times the size of your brain at your processing speed. At my average speed, maybe a factor of twenty.

"So anyway, Jennie," he said, his tone losing the wiseacre crackle he continued to use on me: "A project as big as Hellas requires a lot of independent and creative thinking on the part of the machines. But all those individualistic machines have to communicate, they have to cooperate, they have to work toward a common plan. And I was the generalist, the planner. I was built to be creative, to organize things, and above all, to communicate. I was built, in short, to talk to any intelligence alive, in any language that ever existed. So yes, I built this terrarium, sort of. And no, I am not the sole author of your world."

"Weren't there others?" I said, excited by what I was finding out. "I always thought the military had made six of you. But you call yourself the seventh—what happened?"

"I've heard those rumors," he said. "I hate to ruin a good story, but we weren't secret weapons, supersoldiers, tacticians. What we were, we were the Edsels of AI, and they quit making us because we never sold worth a damn. They had to use me for Hellas, but by the time Argyre was up, they had developed some types they liked better, less quirky and more button-down. I was pretty much engineered according to one man's ideas, I am afraid, and he was an odd duck, he was."

"Duck?" Jennie said. "Odd—duck? Edsel?"

"Whacked rabbit, dear," he said. "It's an old expression for whacked rabbit. And I would attempt to explain Edsel, but I fear we are approaching a decision point. We're ninety minutes from the Airworks, and we'd better have a strategy session. That means you, Shade. There's personnel on board the target, and I can't plan strategy that involves the foreseeable deliberate death of humans. Jennie's a tiger, but she's got no experience. Take it away, Batman."

The return of his smartass tone and the need for action irritated me. Thought is the one genuine pleasure, but the monotonous universe keeps breaking in with its schedules, its insistence on stupid, repetitive melodrama, and bingo, bango, boingo, there you are in Car Chase City again.

"Doesn't it bother you to associate with somebody planning a possibly lethal action?" I said. "Aren't you too pure to even hang around with us lowly killers?"

"Leave her alone, Shade," Jennie said. "If we've got to plan, let's plan. But quit venting."

Her?

"It doesn't have anything to do with purity, John," Mandrake said. "It's just the way I'm made. I can allow you to do whatever you must to each other. Nor do I feel guilt if an innocent plan of mine accidentally results in a human death. But I simply cannot kill or plan the possible death of a human. It isn't the Three Laws, you know. It's a relatively compact and straightforward prohibition, easy enough to write in. The Three Laws, as Asimov himself recognized, are more like morality, a code of ethics. Virtue requires an enormous amount of data storage." His tone was quiet, placating. It was easy and—well, it was *gentle,* dammit. Yet without the least whisper of apology. How did he do it? All my anger had evaporated.

"I have a plan," I said, "that may not require us to take any lives at all. And what's more, it may spare ours as well."

"Are we in danger?" Jennie said. "I mean, other than the danger of battle?"

"I would say that at this moment you are in greater danger than you were when the skull attacked. Mandrake," I said, "do you think our friends who have arranged this little sortie are really secessionist businessmen?"

"Not likely," he said. "They evidence too much power and organization. The profile is sketchy, but it doesn't interlock with the popular template. The list of businesses that would immediately benefit from secession is pretty short, and we've been watching them pretty closely."

"So whoever they are, they are using secessionism as misdirection, as a cover for their own purposes. Benjamin must have known all this when he recruited me. And these are the people he set me to smoke out, not the secessionists. How about it, Mandrake?"

He didn't answer. "I suppose that's classified, too," I said.

"Who's Benjamin?" Jennie said to Mandrake. "If you can't answer Shade because the information is classified, how could you tell us about the Limit, the Wu-Wu thing?"

"That was marked *Classified* by a pack of suboptimal hominids," Mandrake answered. "Anybody with three mil to spare can access it. Benjamin is no fool, and I trust him. What he has told me not to talk about I don't talk about at any price."

"Who's Benjamin?" she repeated.

"No more questions with long answers," I said. "If you can't learn it by looking and listening, it'll have to wait. We need some recon. Mandrake, does this rig get the hard news?"

"No," he said. "Not without payment, which would have to be authorized through the Planetary Marines account—"

"Which would require ID," I sighed. I had been hoping to see what the real noise was on us, but we would have to settle for the zoomer stuff. "Okay," I said, "pop us a free-b."

The holo sprang immediately to life. Settings and faces flicked as Mandrake shuffled to find a news program featuring the recent exploits of a certain wolfman and friends, yours truly. He stopped on a head with two-meter orange hair, and huge glossy black lips. She was floating in a skinsuit, but without a helmet, in what was apparently intended to be a vacuum, since, in the background, the surface of the Moon slid by. Even to Martians, Earth's moon is still *the* moon, although few of them ever get to go there. Why the lunar surface for the Hellas news, I cannot tell you. I had quit watching the zoomer news twenty years ago.

"Woop-loop-a-doop, howze-aboudy," she said. "HOWZE-ABOUDY, EVERYBODY? Howze-aboudy John Shade howdy hustlers slammin SAM, wo yay? We gone ax the TAX, we gone give de GATE to de STATES, HOWZE-ABOUDY?! Wen dey do DIS, we gone do DAT? Lemme HEAR ya, boysengirls."

While she was talking, the background switched to scenes of battle: actual takes of my house, smoldering still, from overhead—this morning's satellite scan, that would be. They had paid a pretty penny. But the actual cuts gave way to generated shots, then close-ups of an action in which drooling marines were slaughtering a camp of naked teener hustlers—shots of heads being severed, then used in a game of keep-away, so brief as to be almost subliminal. The action was from *Swords over Hellas,* I think, and they hadn't even bothered to splice in background from Shadowfall. Then they cut to Centerpole, and a band of clean-cut bike-jockeys, who were zooming down on the building whooping and grinning. You could tell they were hustlers from their hats, which somehow did not blow off. It was daylight. Explosions, great rumbling blooms of flame, as if Centerpole were not a superwired nonflammable building, but a wrecked nineteener airliner. Hall shots, contemptible clowns scurrying and dying, a close-up of one clown, a brown stain spreading across the seat of his outfit. I emerged from a splintered doorway, bare-chested, raking the hall with my Stannard side-by-side. It was a good likeness, but I was about a foot taller and impossibly handsome. I smiled a brilliant smile and raised a clenched fist. I went to silhouette, tall triumph with arm uplifted against a background of war and flame.

"Lemme HEAR ya, fans!" the barker chanted. "Awright, thatsa howze-aboudy wrap, and we have, we have, we HAVE a 36.8 percent FOR and a 1.57 percent market share, HOWZE-ABOUDY!" A tremendous roar of applause over a shot of a stadium, everyone standing and yelling and beating their hands, the barker floating at mid-field.

"They've really toned it down in the last few years," I said to no one in particular.

"HOWZE-ABOUDY!" she bellowed again, and the stadium vanished and the drifting lunar craters returned. "Howze-aboudy slimeball gut-jammer bevo-banger, howze-aboudy kill-marine hickarinos make Sam mad, HOWZE-ABOUDY?! Howze-aboudy stuparillos get us NUKE-A-LUKE-A-RAM-A-LAM-A?! HOWZE-ABOUDY, EVERYBODY?!"

The take this time was a roistering party of greasy low-browed hustlers, weapons and cartridges slung over obscenely naked and blonde bandido fat. Some of the hustlers were screwing each other with huge disgusting organs, one was disembowelling a pretty city teener.

Stumbling around, fried on feedback, they knock a log off a fire matted in from some pirate tavern in a sea movie. The room erupts in flames, hustlers scrambling comically to get out. Cut to the high shot of my burned-out house again. Cut to a peaceful city home. The door breaks in, the hustlers grab the sleepy clean-cut family, one little girl tries to resist, gets burned down. Cut to Centerpole, the hustlers moving through wrecked halls as before, but now behind the shielding bodies of their hostages, blasting strong-jawed marines who bravely try to fight hand-to-hand, unable to fire for fear of hurting the hostages. Great slaughter of marines. Then the hostages break free, the tide turns. One hustler escapes, wounded and snarling. My face, doglike, contorted, frothing. I am still taller than fact, but now gaunt, hunched. I trot away shouting over my cowardly shoulder. Silhouetted again, this time an apeman, wolfman, twisted monster loping through a sulfurous hell.

"HOWZE-ABOUDY WRAP, fans!" the barker demanded. "And I got I got a wow-o-pow-o 31.3 percent AGAINST, and a 1.15 percent market share."

"You won," Mandrake said.

"FANS and fanskayanas, this won't get it make it do it, lissen here chirren, we got a 31.9 percent projected uncommitted, what do we got here we got a bunch of ZOOMERS, is that what you are, you want the CLOWNIES down your THROATINSKIS, you want to lose that booze that schmooze?! Now we gone run it again, and I want you baby-abies to WATCH THAT CHANNEL or WE WATCH YOU! HOWZE-ABOUDY—"

"Minus it, Mandrake," I said, and the holo went.

"They don't know about me and Mandrake yet," Jennie said.

"*They* don't. Somebody does. I wish we could have gotten Henny-penny."

"I could tag Scuttlebutt," Mandrake said.

"No, that's only marginally better than this. When we get to a safe place, I want you to con the channels. See who's got a better market share but comparable margins, if anybody. I liked the way this bunch rigged the vote, but I'm sure they're backing us out of desperation—those shares were terrible. But if we can't find a channel to make a better offer, we may wind up selling the rights to these guys."

All my property and previous income was forfeit, of course. Jennie and I had been convicted and executed, our system doubles wiped from all files but the Central Intelligence prisoner records, no longer available to vote, buy, manage, or even send and respond to mail. We were socially dead, only the rather negligible items of our bodies still at large. Nor was it legal for us to keep any money we might make from the sale of coverage rights, fictional rights, animation rights, interview rights, gambling rights, you-name-em.

However: The slip the channels and maxies and publix would throw our way could be taxed, you see, and so could the extra slip the channels and maxies and publix could make by using our story. This would be money not otherwise exposed to tax liability. So why not just confiscate the whole wad up front? Because if Centerpole did that, it would take away the criminal's motivation, his one-in-a-million chance to win in court. If the judges find for him, declare him legal on the grounds of reasonability and common law, for example, why then he gets to keep the fruits of his shady labor—and if not, you confiscate the new stuff.

It is precisely the sort of accommodation to black-market enterprise you might expect to find in a corporate democracy, especially a corporate democracy whose dominant industries are entertainment and information, and some of whose most powerful citizens are the network zecs. It had begun even back in your day, Gene, when Sam became the world's largest property owner simply by seizing the assets of major drug dealers—after they had made enough money to buy those assets. Just a very complicated way of taxing the citizen-addict, no?

"Why wait to sell the rights?" Mandrake said. "I can do it from here."

"We're not going to be here much longer," I said.

"Where are we going?"

"Damn, it feels good to be making a move you didn't see coming," I said.

"Won't they blow the ship if we don't take it in?" Jennie said.

"I think they're going to blow it if we do," I answered. "Afterwards. The ship is going in, but we aren't going with it. Get your helmet back on." I was fitting mine as I spoke.

I spoke the comm, saw Jennie's lips moving, then heard her voice: "—on."

"You have us, Mandrake?"

"I got."

"I need some calculations—how much jive does the Ranger have? I want max height for deadfall to the blowers. As soon as you've got it, start us up and lock the course." Even as I finished, I felt the small extra weight of an upward acceleration. The Ranger *was* a tank, it hadn't been designed for 3-space maneuverability, but it could make a slow, steady climb. Gravity would turn it into a missile when the jive ran out.

Mandrake had seen what I was up to. "Max height on available power is sixty kilometers," he said. "Three minutes of free-fall. Impact at 40 kpm."

"Can you jam their overrides?"

"I can set the main brain to blow at first attempt. The subsidiaries will keep it on course until it goes ballistic."

"Fine. Arm the firepower, set it all to release just before impact. If the hooter has a subbrain, set it to warn the blower personnel."

"You're going to ram the Airworks," Jennie said.

"I'm counting on us having enough jive in the jet vests to dece to the tent," I said to Mandrake. "Do we? I've only rough-figured it. From there we can find a vent, or you can go in with cutters, and from *there* we'll need wings, so you'd better break them out."

I felt the Ranger slowing forward. "Not enough jive in the vests to dece if we start out at 10 kpm," Mandrake said. "I'm bringing us down to 7.3. Ballistic point altered accordingly."

"Good," I said, but he had disappeared to get the wings.

We made a peculiar trio of zoids anyway, but when we got geared up we looked more ludicrous than ever, Jennie and I swollen with three layers of vests over a skinsuit, breather tanks over that, wing-packs strapped on any old how, and bellies looped with extra batbelts. Mandrake had wrapped one arm around his thorax—he really had no torso, just a sort of thick stem. The arm served as padding, and allowed him to accommodate the vests, which had only two armholes each. He had volunteered to take Jennie's pack full of feedback, as Jennie and I had breather tanks to carry, and it was tethered lumpishly to his impromptu back.

A sharp pain leapt from temple to temple in my head, and I dropped my face to my hands, momentarily forgetting I was wearing a breather bubble, so that I thumped the front of my helmet.

"What's the matter?" Jennie said.

"Headache."

"You know, Shade," she said, "you're a very conflicted individual."

"Let's get down to the drop bay," I said. "We're going out below."

"To screen us from the satellites," Jennie said.

"You con. So we don't dece until well below the ship. Mandrake, you find a ground pattern to mask us if you can. It won't make that much difference—they'll be able to plot us on the recon no matter what, but the longer it takes them, the goner we'll be."

"What if they blow the ship because it's acting funny, or blow it after it goes ballistic?" Jennie said.

"Bloodthirsty, aren't you?" I said. "So what if we don't complete their supposed mission? They were planning to use us and throw us away, and instead we smoked them out a little and used *them*."

"Yeah, but I hate not to finish things."

"See, you're more of a soldier than I am. Finishing things is dangerous. At least, the *desire* to finish things is. You wind up obsessed and exposed. If your eyes are on your goal, you aren't watching your ass."

"I *can't* watch my ass," Mandrake said.

"Yeah, but shouldn't they think of us as tough enough to do the job?" Jennie said.

I had thought, Gene, that you had replaced Eleanor, and our love and our quarrel had scarred over my first love and its quarrels. Now I had a swimming sense of déjà-vu, of having had an exactly similar scene with Eleanor. It was stronger than déjà-vu: I felt as if she *were* Eleanor, and this were some deeply important marital battle, the sort you blunder into as newlyweds. The point is trivial, but something causes you to wonder, with accelerating dismay, whether you and your mate are fundamentally at odds.

"Chances are they won't con to our plan until the Ranger goes ballistic," I said. "They've blocked any anomaly reads, or we wouldn't have been able to use the ship in the first place. They aren't on-line to the satellites, because that would make *them* traceable. When the ship does go ballistic, it'll be too late. The Airworks won't have anything but Rangers, itself, and this one will be dropping through them like a rock through a flock of ducks. The closest fighters are at Westbase, and they can't scramble there in three minutes. Even if they could, and blew it to shrapnel, what's the diff if it's one big lump or a fireball. Figuring the Ranger at six or more megagrams, you still have three billion newtons of kinetic energy slamming the blowers. *Plus* the firepower."

"Okay," she said.

"We're showing them we're tough and smart," I said.

"*Okay,*" she said.

The pain in my temples was not constant, but was coming in irregular surges. "So less go, ahreddy," Mandrake said. "We just gonna stand here, or what?"

In the drop bay, I buttoned the sphincter. There it was again, the blue sea. From this vantage, we seemed hardly to be moving.

"This is going to take coordination," I said. "We could wind up as messy meteors. Remember, just free-fall for a while. Don't dece at all until I say so."

"I sure have had a lot of ups and downs with you," Jennie said.

"Too much bad wit in here for me," I said. "I'm leaving. You guys follow if you want to." I stepped over the sphincter and dropped through.

14

Dogboy on the Edge of the Bell Curve

Jennie and Mandrake dropped through right after me. The setting sun was full in our faces, the light almost completely horizontal. We would come in under cover of darkness.

We were in vacuum, so there was no wind resistance, of course, no impact of air when we bailed out. Nor was there any real sensation of falling or of forward motion. I felt suspended, fetal. The ship appeared to be accelerating straight upward directly over us. And yet I knew we were moving forward. In a minute or so, if we did not decelerate, we would hit the tent like balloons full of blood, three red smears stretching toward the S10 Airworks at 7.3 kpm.

"Why do I feel like something a bird did while flying?" Jennie said.

"Mandrake, when we hit zero, announce it," I said. "We can start decing downward only. Hold off on forward deceleration till you find us a ground pattern, or for ten minutes, whichever is first."

"Actual, boss, we're at zero now," he said, pointing his control gun down.

"All right—Jennie, *dece*!" I said, as she dropped past.

"Hey big brother, I'm lighter, right?" she said, arresting her fall with the gun. "So I figure to drop more and let you guys catch up."

We were now drawing in range of her, true. And I had forgotten about the differences in velocity. But I couldn't let her indulge her rebellion, not just now. She had to whip me sooner or later, but this wasn't the time.

"Can't spare feelings, private," I snapped back. "Safety first, consideration later. *You* signed on, remember."

Silence. We coasted a few minutes. The ship was a dot overhead, barely visible. "Ground pattern," Mandrake said. "And guess what, I see a vent."

That was good news. It was going to be tricky enough shedding v and deploying the wings, without having to hover while Mandrake cut through the tent.

"Dece forward," I said. "As much as you can take, Jennie, but be careful. If you try to lose it all at once, you'll shear your legs off."

"Aye aye, sir," she said.

The next few minutes were busy and nervous. We were trying to decelerate forward without losing too much altitude, trying to stay in reasonable range of each other, while hoarding our dwindling power supply. "Stay close to Mandrake," I told her. "As well as you can, do what he does." He was, I knew, the one of us who could calculate the optimum moves.

We took some bad thumps changing our v, and there were some frantic moments switching the power supply. On the first switch, I plugged my vest right back into the burnt-out battery belt I had just disconnected—stupid—and took a bad plunge. Jennie banged wildly up against me on her second switch-over. She was white-faced and sweating furiously, struggling with the control gun.

Shedding our forward momentum ate up power at an alarming rate. "Mandrake," I said. "What's our v? I don't see the vent. Maybe you better go down and cut—I'm on the last belt."

"Me too," Jennie said, breathing hard.

"Me too," said Mandrake, "but fear not, I've got the vent in sight. We're down to a couple of kpm, and if you just stay with me, we'll drop through that hole like a b-ball through a net. When I say *Now,* dece forward only, and let yourselves start falling toward the tent. Ready, Teddy? Alllll right: *Now.*"

He was true to his word. No sooner had we begun dropping than I saw the vent, about a hundred meters long, and no sooner had it come into view than it began opening, the zipped helix of the memory-seam springing into its other, straightened-out shape.

We dropped into the sky from above. We dropped into a fountain of upwelling atmosphere, but by that time we had enough downward velocity not to be much affected. It wasn't *that* strong a current anyway. We keep Hellas and Argyre at roughly one atmosphere (naturally), more than the Martian gravity induces, which is why the tents bulge. But if we ever did somehow lose them, if anybody ever did pop our blisters, it wouldn't happen the way the trivia show it— the atmospheres wouldn't just suddenly all boil off into space. That's too much air to lose that quick. The air would spread out over the planet, some would evaporate—but we'd probably have a good five- or ten-year margin.

"Deploy the wings," I said, unnecessarily, since Jennie had already found her ripcord and yanked it, and Mandrake was pulling his as I spoke.

The wings bloomed hugely above us, darker than evening. You knew their predecessors, Gene—films blown rigid by supercharge, enclosing a vacuum. I remember how we argued because I wanted to ride them down into the Grand Canyon and you didn't. Why will a lover insist he cannot have his pleasure unless his partner shares it? What sort of a thing is that to be angry about? "No way," you said.

No way.

These are Rogallo in shape, with adjustable volume, so you can control the lift and the glide angle almost completely.

We had dropped below the plane of the sunlight. Night comes fast in the craters—no upper atmosphere to diffuse the sun, no curve of twilight radiance around the bulge of the planet. The nightlights were coming on dimly behind us. I had a vision of the three of us from below, drifting down like great bats out of the evening sky. Appropriate.

"Point us to Hellasport, Mandrake," I said. "Shit!"

A vicious cramp had run through me simultaneously with another surge of pain in my temples.

"What's the matter?" they both said.

"Forget it for now," I said. "How far out from Hellasport are we? About four hundred k? We don't have time to drift in that far. I want us there tonight. You'd better find us a town as soon as possible."

"More like 370," he said.

"By the way, Jennie, keep your bubble on. We can talk and stay quieter that way, unless somebody starts tagging our frequency."

"What's going on?" Jennie said. "I'm tired of not knowing what our next move is going to be. What's wrong with filling us in on the plan?"

"Easy," I said. I was suddenly weary, afraid of what was ahead. I dangled in the dark middle of the sky, wondering what I was doing. All the motives that had led me there seemed as incomprehensible as a youthful love letter you come across after a third divorce, when you have not thought of that first person in years. I didn't want to talk, to explain, but Jennie was right. It was time.

"Take it easy. No secrets, been busy. Go down, steal a car, make Hellasport, go underground. Janglerland."

"You're going to hide out with the janglers?" she said. "With us?"

"No better," I said. "Network got, clowns don't con. Safe?"

"Sure it's safe—well, it can be, if we work it right. You've been planning this all along?"

"Not planning, thinking of. What else? Out to Shadowfall to draw attention, back to Hellasport to lose."

"This is wonderful," she said.

"I've got a town," Mandrake said. He buttoned his wing-pack, and went into a steep glide. We followed.

I was worried that someone would see us swooping in, silhouetted against the faint sky, but he brought us down low and safe. We came down outside of the town, near a gathering of vehicles beside a little dug-out lake, the town's reservoir and party-spot. We touched down well away from the water, having fallen through maybe six kilometers of sky—one of vacuum, and five of air. Not your usual party crashers.

I twisted my knee, in spite of the fact that you can come down as soft as you want under a pair of wings. The pain didn't flatten out and fade, as it usually does, but stayed with me, the knee stiffening up.

We brought the wings along. I was beginning to feel like a pack rat, but I had a notion we might need the gear, not for flight—the batteries were gone in the batbelts anyway—but for barter. Maybe not leaving the evidence would give us another few minutes when they began tracking us. True, by stealing a car we were leaving a trail, but this wouldn't be the only car stolen out on the range tonight.

We cracked open the bubbles, but left them on to mask the

sound of our voices. I could smell the party, maybe three-quarters of a kilometer away. Perfume, sex, brew, lightning. We moved toward it into the breeze. "Teeners," Jennie said, half wistfully, half in scorn. A year ago, two years ago, she would have been out there in the night with a bunch just like this, pretending to have a good time, but all the while dreaming of grown-and-gone.

We moved fast, whispering although we probably didn't need to. Jennie was breathing hard again, but didn't complain except to pant, "Damn—I'm hungry." And then, a minute or two later: "We could have had another jar of coffee, at least, before we jumped."

"Then you'd just be needing to piss again," I whispered.

"I peed in space," she answered. Which was true, you could do that. It was a neat trick, making the suit permeable by liquid but not by gas. I'll tell you how they did it someday.

And then we were on our bellies in the long grass at the edge of the party.

Six couples, desultorily naked, huddled around a fake fire. To one side, a holo-band played loudly and ineffectually. One of the teeners stood up to walk over and poke at the fire, which stirred and whipped in the same repetitive pattern no matter where he put the stick. He had the feely-worm implants wiggling around his shoulders, and when he turned back toward the group I could see that he was an over-and-under.

If I canted my bubble to help block the sound of the band, I could hear bits of the conversation. "—don't like Bobby," one of the teeners by the fire was saying.

"—lightning," said another.

"I don't like lightning either. I just want to sleep."

"So mix him and sleep."

"Do we have to tag this one? I don't want to tag this one," the whiner said.

Bobby came back to the others. "You want to explain to my dad?" he said. "—didn't, and . . . —wants to know why. —think I like *you*?"

Birth-rate down, life-span up. It's tough having to bear the fantasy life of your elders, measure up to those few bright generations from a vanished century. *A Teener Dreams of Freedom. School Days 1999*. Coming soon to a maxie near you.

My knee was throbbing. My head was hurting. I was having bad memories of lying in the grass outside a redcoat camp. Crying. Then working up a rage. Then. Well, they had been the enemy. No older than these kids, most of them. I rolled over on my back. "At least you get to keep your hair," I whispered.

"What?" It was Jennie.

"Nothing. Mandrake, will you pick us a car?"

"Doing," he said softly, and I realized that he had already ghosted away. "You ready?"

"We're ready."

"Coming to get. We'll see if we can't get out of here quiet-like."

We slid further back into the darkness. A car rolled slowly up, and Jennie and I got in. Mandrake grasped the wheel with two of his arms. "Real driving," he said. "A hands-on experience."

He geared in, and moved us slowly away. There was no outcry, no flurry of chase. The noise of the band had drowned us out, I suppose. Now Bobby's daddy was really going to have something to get jammed about.

We went through the grass for a while, then climbed onto the gravel and picked up speed. The last entity I had known who drove that fast on gravel was a little silver-haired piano player in Falling Water, Arkansas. Actually, she was maybe faster.

"Got about thirty minutes of feeder travel till we hit the sector road," he said.

"Make it forty minutes," I gasped. I was the one breathing hard now. "Turn the damn lights on. And don't slide so much."

"Are you hurting?"

I leaned back to stretch the cramp out of my ribcage. "What do you know about that girl at Centerpole," I asked. "The casualty."

"What girl?" Jennie said.

"Brilliant," he said. "Impatient. Nasty to unit functions, good to smart people, fun at a party. Loyal profile, but idealistic to a fault, which is why she was crossing Sam for Argyre. Good mixer. Needed lots of attention, affection, tried to get it from her superiors—confused authority and love."

"Sounds a lot like me the last couple of days, doesn't it?" I said. "And?"

"And?"

"Her health," I said. "What are you not telling me about her health?"

"She had crash," he said. "Does it matter?"

The cramp had eased. I sat up. "Stupid," I said. "Totally stupid. You knew so damn much, I thought you knew it all. What did you idiots think it was, a mercy killing?"

"What's going on?" Jennie said. "Did you—"

"Shut *up*," I said. I thought she might explode, but she fell silent.

"Boost it when you hit the sector road. Outskirts of Hellasport, we separate. You and Jennie get underground before dawn, and I'll come under as soon as I can. I don't know how I'll find you, but I'll try."

"I can double my speed now."

"You can, and probably do it without headlights, too, but I have some very ancient reflexes. It won't do me any good to spend the next half-hour tied in a nervous knot. You got to remember I never rode anything faster than a galloping horse for the first quarter of my life."

"I'm sorry," he said, and I knew he didn't mean the speed of the car.

"No point," I said. "My stupidity, not yours. I should have checked, but I was in a bit of a hurry."

"I had no idea it worked that way."

"Sometimes yes, sometimes no. Just get me to the church on time," I said. "After we get off this gravel," I added.

In spite of my request, Mandrake increased our speed. We roared through the night leaving a wake of glowing dust, and we struck the sector road in just under twenty-five minutes. He jived the floater mags, clicked the wheels in, and pointed for the bright lights of the big city. "Airworks go boom," he said, just as we got underway.

"What, are you conning the news?"

"No," he said. "No squeals on the bands. It's time, is all."

"Can you see it?"

"No, too far."

The rest of the way I was half-expecting a tap on the shoulder.

The way our invisible sponsors could reach into the net and pluck me out had me spooked. This wasn't my kind of secret-agenting, this double-double-double-blind electronic stuff. I had done well enough in my years with Sam, but I had not been confident of my skill at the game since the invention of the transistor. I needed my concentration so badly that I wouldn't even let Mandrake burn the news. Whether he played it for himself, I don't know.

It was a hard ride. I spent a lot of it doubled up in pain. Once I felt Jennie's hand soft on my neck. Maybe she would have laid the same hand on the neck of a suffering horse. But I took it. I was going to be alright. Someone loved me. We would get there, and split up. I would hunt down an innocent, murder him, drink his hot blood. Then find my friends again, and live happily ever after. Jennie would never have to know. She could sit knitting in our warm little home underground, all the friendly janglers bringing us gifts of food. Some nights I would have to go out. "Poker with the boys again, dear? Have a good time."

Sometimes things go wrong because you jam your mixes, and sometimes they go wrong because the ball takes a funny bounce. A fully charged superbat has phase states something like a heavy nucleus. In a large enough sample of megavolt batteries, and over a period of forty-four thousand years, half of them will short out for no apparent reason. On Mars, between ten and two hundred blow every year. Ours, that year, was the thirteenth. Take it for what it's worth.

Although you can't tell which battery will go next in a batch of good ones, they don't decay instantly—which is nice, because it means you can survive the blow.

In the silverslums outside Hellasport there was a deafening crack, and our car was suddenly riding a lightning bolt. We slewed and rattled, the tires automatically coming down, shimmying under speeds they weren't designed for. The road's brain grabbed us and shunted us off into Spidertown.

So there we were in the darkness of a side street, standing around the useless car. Above us and to the west streaked the lights of the rest of the traffic. The road had reported our breakdown immediately, of course, which meant the stones were on their way. We had maybe eight more hours of good darkness, and at least ten kilometers of slumbelt between us and the heart of the city. We had to get moving, steal another car. It isn't easy to steal a car in Zoomerville.

"Let's get going," I said, launching into a stiff-legged run. My knee was swollen and nearly completely rigid. The headache was continuous now, and my right eyebrow was shuddering. I kept hearing music, strange music, which I knew was not really there. "Find us a car, Mandrake," I said, as he came smoothly up beside me, Jennie trotting easily behind.

The lanes we were moving through were like the dark alleys of an old-time fairground carnival. Tents, billows, tunnels, fantastic castles of cloth, rooms within rooms, flaps, lights, banners; some of the yurts, domes, tipis, lodges, two-polers, and many other nameless creations were dark, some lighted gently within, dark bodies moving about, shadows on screens. There was even, somehow, a smell of sawdust and sweat and burnt corn—or maybe it was just zoomer cooking.

The silverslums, Spidertown, Zoomerville. In theory, anybody can have adequate housing now, enough to eat. Some of these people lived more comfortably than I had for most of my life, even when, in the late eighteens, I had decided to try being rich. But most lived on the dole, some were starving, some wandered the streets d-geed and froze to death, and the murder rate was three times what it was in the city proper. Real wealth now means a jump-up citihaus. Genuine wood. Copper wiring. Plumbing.

Money's just a social code for available energy. With more than enough energy for everybody, way more than enough, why do we still have extravagance and poverty? It has nothing to do with resources, and everything to do with the monkeys who can't stand it unless they know who's boss. Blow the bell curve up as big as you want to, it still gets pinchy out on the edges.

"I don't see any cars, and we've got company," Mandrake said. My field of vision was shrinking, the world squeezing into wrong-way binoculars. I was hearing things like a man in a tunnel. I jogged to a stop, looked around.

"They don't have many cars," I said. "The ones they do have are under the silverstuff. Easy to hide. Fabric labyrinth."

"Poot goot puttery, ma-mainmain," said a voice from the shadows beside me. I swung, picked out a chieftain. Now that I saw him, I saw several others folded into the darkness, the swirl of their clothing masked in the textures of dwellings. Some, I could tell, held weapons. "Aalakdat, fabareek labareent," he said, stepping out so that I could see him better. He wasn't a he, I saw then: A widely built woman, half a head shorter than me, she carried her muscles high, as beefy people do on Mars, and now I caught her odor. Her head was wonderfully plumed, and across her black face she had painted a white mask, complete with blinker crosses. Her mouth was white with makeup as well, and although she had chosen to do without an official nose, she had painted her own red. Her shoes were barely small enough to be legal.

"But ant plite a stee-o, nowzit?" she said.

"Mandrake?" I said.

"I could," he said, "but what point? Aren't there a million more of them to get through? Jennie, *don't*. This would make a poor destiny."

"Smot main, dat robot," the chieftain said.

"Ant plite a fake a clown needa," I said.

"I can speak your speech," she answered. "Don't you try mine. Doan be condescension me." She laughed. "And I'm legal enough. Do you think the stones want to roust around here this time of night? And if they did, would you want to see them, my friend? Why is it I think I have caught a secessionist? Can you tell me whyzit, *señor estanciero*?"

So the word was out. And this local bozo, this people's clown, could somehow tag the hard news.

I shivered, as with tremendous cold, repressed it. I wouldn't be able to repress it much longer. I was getting some chromatic distortion already, every movement leaving its rainbow afterimage.

"We have items to trade," I said. "Help us get going again, and we can give you some very good, very new products. If you hurry, we know where you can find a car."

There was no point in offering her the feedback. There was no shortage of feedback in Zoomerville.

"Haadecar," she said, "aared. See you got tech-suits, lottaguns, but maybe we aared gottem too."

"Maybe," I said, "and maybe you would all die."

133

"Hootawk dine? What profit me you die, eem I doan? And maybe I do. Antawk dine. Tawkintawk. Tawkin dee-o."

I couldn't imagine what sort of deal she had in mind, and I knew I had to have blood within the hour. But a fight, even if we won it, was going to cost us and slow us down even more.

"We don't have much time," I said.

"See you hurtin, Shaddomain. Yes/no doan take law. Now: You comin bakka myplace, a we gone mixit now?"

We followed them down a twist of alleyways that gradually became a glimmering tunnel. We went through a number of rooms, taking branching tunnels out. One of the rooms was a sloon, the loafers noting our progress idly, slurping brew. And of course watching the ever-present trivia holo.

We reached a large space fitted out like a sheik's tent in a desert maxie—silks, fine carpets, spices in the air. Dominating the room was an illegal cherrywood table. A statement, you might call it, like her uniform.

"We're here," she said, choosing a seat on a big silk cushion. Her lieutenants—four had stayed with us—arranged themselves standing, two on either side of her. I sat on a smaller cushion, face to face with her, as the apparent leader of our little group.

On one end of the wooden table was a holo rig, burning the usual obnoxious trivia fare. No one was watching it. She and her men seemed to have a lot of free time. On the other end of the table was a blackbox studded with interfaces. Five of them. I had seen it when we came in, but had been so distracted by my pain that the import hadn't registered.

In spite of the penalties, a few zoomers refuse to be passive modules of the net, rejecting the (for them) mandatory interface. They prefer—strange notion—to develop their own minds in their own ways. If you want to learn, if you do not want to subsist on the pap of the zoomer channels, you must resort to radical strategies. You must read books, study, think.

Now I saw the scar tissue at her temples, the tracks of unnecessary stitches that had been deliberately roughened and raised. "You're a learner!" I said.

"Wanna be a learna, spose a be a burna, guessem gan a jamma

stone," she sang. She had a fine full voice. *"Borna be a zooma, radda be a tumor, wenna die I theenk my own."*

"They'll catch you," I said. "That boxbrain won't fool them forever."

"Soona lata," she shrugged. "Wotsa life wittout a thawt? You gan freedy neega, Shaddomain?" That was twice she had called me what the hustlers called me. Had the news gotten to them? Had *she* gotten to them? Her voice had stayed ironic in the question, rich with hints of mockery, but there was an added tone, a note of sincere pleading, as if she were hoping a hope that she herself knew to be impossible.

"Nobod nebbegan freedy neega," I said. "Unodat. Freedom be, sumgit. But aaways beedy neega. Changy culla, stilly nulla. Aadetaawk a freedom be, buddis warz a munniwar, likem aw—andis mainza sojer bawt."

"Samo," she said, this time not objecting to my use of the dialect.

"Samo samo," I agreed.

"But you will do what you can?" she said, switching back to standard.

"I will," I said. "You spoke of a deal. You are welcome to these vests, which with new jive will allow you to fly, and to the pressure suits we're wearing. We'd like to keep the feedback—we assume you do not need it. Mandrake can leave you a blip on how to use the vests."

Her eyes went to Mandrake. "Ah," she said. "Poor forked radish."

"What else did you have in mind?" I said, my voice breaking badly. I could not stop my shivering.

"What sort of injury have you received?" she said. "You seem to be worsening. Or is it a fever? Do you have crash?"

"The *deal*," I said.

She motioned to a naked young boy I had not noticed before, standing in an alcove of one of the exits. He flashed away into the shine of the tunnel.

"You're going underground," she said.

"You know?"

"Said it on the news. In fact, it said you were already there. And I see you, and you have a jangler with you, so I am thinking that the news is right, if premature. Not so?"

I hated it. My every move foreseen, my every stroke telegraphed. When I next saw Benjamin—but that was the last of my concerns at the moment.

"To get there, at this point, you will need my help," she continued. "And in return, I ask you a small favor." The boy was back, with two others. The two on the outside were supporting a third, a slight, limping child, whose head—

"A jangler," Jennie gasped.

"My young one," the chieftain said. "I could not let him die. But now he cannot live here. My own people will slay him soon."

"As the abomination before us should have been slain when we first saw her," spoke the lieutenant on her right hand, gesturing angrily at Jennie.

The chieftain gave him a silencing glare. "It is not nature," he said, subsiding.

She turned her look back to us. "As you see," she said. "I have caused them to become so educated that they presume to think for themselves. The child cannot remain here, and yet if I were to take him down and leave him—"

"The wild ones would strip him," Jennie finished.

The chieftain nodded, her eyes wide and sad. "You will escort him to the underworld, my Pluto," she said. "You, my Persephone. You and your manworks there. We will give you safe conduct to an entry lock, and you will do what you can for the youngling."

"Agreed," I said. The shudders had ceased. But now the colors of things were too bright to look at. There was a cracking agony in the hinges of my jaw, my face was a blaze of pain. This one was going to be bad, even worse than I had thought. The dogboy was on his way. It was too late to leave the others and prowl. Jennie would have to see, Eleanor would have to know. Someone was going to die here, in a few moments. The only question was who.

"There is one more thing," I said, my voice diving and growling. My throat was changing. "Do you know the *mojo*? Do you acknowledge the spirit-beast?"

"He moves among us," she said. "He selects whom he wills. We know this, although the networks tell us it cannot be so."

"*Sum ista bestia,*" I said, "*et sacrificium requiro.*"

She did not hesitate. Her eyes were fixed intently on my face: "*Quale sacrificum, Dominus?*"

"*Forte, audax, ingeniosum. Sed nihil stultum, nihil crudele.*"

"And if it were a convenience to me? If it were to remove a threat to my authority?"

I spoke with the last remnants of my human voice. "That does not matter."

I would you could have seen it, Gene, rather than Jennie. I would have given you something then to hate me for, something beside which the petty faults you found in me would be the rudeness of a baby, against the crimes of a baby-murderer.

"Louis," the chieftain said, and the man who had spoken before leaned forward, a well-made post-teener, healthy.

"Yes, ma'am?"

I felt the bones of my face thrust outward, my jaws opening hugely, my spine straightening and canting me forward, my haunches gathering power. I felt the dogboy's arrival.

I felt joy.

The man had been sitting, but now he rose to a crouch, his body seeming to flow into a new form. His head tilted back, and his jaws opened wider than one would have thought they could, the very structure of his face changing as he opened them. A howl of victory boiled from his throat, and he surged, knocking the young man who had just spoken to the floor of the tent. He had moved fast, much faster than any beast had a right to, much too fast for even the fastest and most mobile of artificial intelligences to have stopped him.

I cannot tell you what happened next, because I cannot remember it in human terms. It was a river of being, and it was freedom. Meaning and action were once more a single shining thing. I was, and it was good to be. I had no thought in my head, unless it was the bright and happy pour of my motive: *greed greed blood blood good good.*

In a part of a moment, the man-beast had severed the neck of

137

his prey. *The head rolled to one side, puzzled, the body thrashing under its snarling killer. And then he was gulping and chewing at the pumping throat, eating down into the chest. Ribs cracked, blood jumped like coveys of startled birds into the air. With a great snort of contentment, the beast settled its snout against the victim's heart, ripping and swallowing.*

And then it lifted its head

I do remember how happy and proud I felt. And that Jennie occurred in my eyes, wearing unreadable expressions, and that, beast that I was, I understood her to be my good friend, and wanted to share my pride and good fortune: and so I smiled.

and bared its teeth at us.

15
Underground Love

When the hallucination trance hit, it took me completely away. I was, this time, in a land of three-dimensional cartoons, a block universe of generated figures: realistic, but with colors impossibly pure, edges impossibly smooth. Mandrake, a spinning toy, pirouetted over the tiled landscape of a marble world to Mozart's violins, and the water was music, and ran in a blue track under the aquamarine layers of trees in perfect leaf and hung with ruby and amethyst crystalline fruit. I followed the water in swooping change of perspective until it, and we, and I, tumbled in luminous sheets over the vertex of the world to dive to Jennie, naked below the waterfall, bathing, a tiny figure grown sweetly large as we fell and burst about her upturned face like bubbles, her eyes the blank eyes of monumental stone, a huge unseeing face that could not be dismayed, ever, at anything it saw, while Mandrake floated away in the turning music of space. . . .

And then my trance was dark, close, thumping, the wedding night of criminals, who heaved each other about in a kind of panting anger, guilt a thick stink in the air. . . .

I lay on a litter, jogging about with the grunting strides of bearers, moving through the night, a thin body bumping against me but grappling to hold itself steady, hold itself away. . . .

The smell was old blood. I laughed, drunken and silly. I had no desire to move, to act, to do anything but laugh and dream and be bounced onward by someone else's intentions. I drifted in and out of consciousness. It seemed we traveled that way a long time, but I may have had that impression because time did not matter to me.

We came to a stop, and there were whispers, rustlings, arrangements. I was lifted in someone's arms. I was a child who had fallen asleep in the carriage, and was now being taken up by a loving father who would bring me in to my own warm bed. . . .

I felt a firm hand on my chest, a cross drawn on my brow. *"Though he slay me, yet will I trust in him,"* a voice said, the rich voice of a judge, a master, a woman of authority.

"My name is Sheena Q," the voice said, above me in the darkness. It laughed. "For Sheena Queena d Jongla. I hope you remember it. I won't be a queen much longer, I don't think. It's a fine world. It's a world of strong sign. I shall be sorry to leave it."

The voice shifted: "Guard him, man-thing. Do not hesitate, daughter, to accept your fate. There's no other freedom. Little one, trust these creatures. If I could do more for you, I would. *Go with God, thou demons.*"

Down, down, downstairs. My room isn't in the basement, my room is upstairs. Moving more slowly now. Letting my head dangle, seeing only the stars of complete darkness. Kicking my feet a little to the sway of our movement, singing.

"Should I keep him quiet?"

"No need. We're four, and strange enough to give any wild ones pause."

More darkness, more travel. I couldn't make the pictures come now, the pretty fantasies. I was bored, but it wasn't my responsibility to relieve my boredom. I was a child, helpless and dangling. Do something, somebody, I'm tired of this.

"Hush, John."

"Sing me a song. I don't remember any songs."

"Hush."

And then we were in light. My tiled world, I thought at first, my marble fantasia. But it wasn't. It was a long corridor, opening into bays and atriums. Jennie's footsteps echoed beside us. I was seeing her upside down, letting my head roll back, watching the ceiling where the floor should have been. I was still a child being carried, but I also knew who she was, knew who carried me.

There were trees in pots, glass-fronted rooms, fountains. I knew I was underground with the janglers, but I thought also that I was back a hundred years, that I was in the Pentagon, had just left the

Pentagon, had gotten off the Metro at Crystal City. I laughed and laughed, realizing what sort of world the janglers had made for themselves.

"Hush, Shade," said Jennie, striding beside me.

"It's a mall," I said.

More walking, more change of lights. Either I went to sleep, or I have lost a part of my memory. When I came to myself, I was sitting up in an old-fashioned bed, completely naked, but swaddled in comforters and bolstered by piles of pillows. It was morning, and curtains were blowing in at the open French doors.

I sat a long time, thinking, enjoying the setting. I was perfectly relaxed. I knew there was a world of violence and struggle out there somewhere, I knew that world included me and this friendly little scene as a torrent may include a bubble, and I knew that I would, sooner or later, be forced to rejoin that larger and more troubled realm. But for the moment, I was completely happy, and would have been glad had it been offered to me as my portion of eternity, to remain forever in the morning of that room, alert, at peace, and alone.

Finally Jennie came in, two wheeled men flanking her.

"Am I in a hospital," I asked.

"It's the bridal suite," she said.

I slipped from under the covers and padded over to her, lifting her widened, asymmetrical face to mine. The wheeled men, alarmed, buzzed and backed off.

"And does that mean?"

"It wouldn't necessarily," she said. "But in this case it does. It can," she amended, "if that's what you want." A tentative hand ran over the curve of my back, whispered across my hip, faded.

I smelled the sprinkle of her pheromones in the air, a rich allure undercut with the tang of sadness, or distance.

I went to the French doors, looked out. It was an English garden. Marble terraces, green slopes, unshorn trees in the bright air.

Behind me, she said, "Do you want me?"

"You saw what I am," I said.

"I saw something. A mutation, maybe, a werewolf kind of a thing, an animal-man."

141

So Mandrake had not told her the whole story.

"And you can live with that?"

"I have blood on me, too. Mine is blood that I have not yet spilled, but it's there. I can feel it."

They had done a good job on the garden. They had gotten the perspective, the warm languor of the slight breeze, even the fuzz of the air with distance, but the scent was wrong. Odor changes its textures with movement and distance. This scent was springlike, but uniform and unvarying. It was like walking into a room, and finding, for furniture, a photorealistic chair painted on the wall.

"Then yes," I said.

I was not sure why she had decided to marry me. Now I think it may have been that she knew it would be her only chance to taste that part of life.

"We have things to do," she said. "Business to look after."

I looked at the bed in which, a few moments before, I had been so content and complete, so safe from war and love. "Yes," I said.

Mandrake married us that day. As a ten-clown, he was registered to perform the ceremony. We were presumed felons, fleeing capture, but we had a legal marriage, and the state got its cut of the fee. We did without the reception but not without the wedding night. And that, my dear Gene, I will leave to your imagination. Was it good? Was it better than you and I were? Guess.

There's a message here for you. Are you beginning to understand?

We spent that night and the weeks following in the so-called bridal suite—which, in fact, it really was. The jangler Underground was, as I had said in my trance, partly a sort of gigantic mall. The system of tunnels and caverns and conduits also contained hotel space, barracks, subways, a complex of business offices. There was not much in the way of fine housing, however. The more influential janglers had rooms connected to the business section that were like suites in a decent hotel. The rest found living quarters in the barracks, or haunted the malls and caves like morlocks. The few marriages that occurred were always scheduled so that each new couple could spend at least a night in the bridal suite. But Jennie—a jangler who had gone to the upper world and returned alive—got special treatment.

I was a hero, too. We were all over the trivia. The story of our "daring" assault on the Airworks was everywhere. It was the ultimate romantic legend—for a week. The brave secessionist rancher—pushed too far, he strikes back twice in two days, cleverly evading capture both times. The Wolf of the Wall, the Shadowman. What made it perfect was Jennie, the tragic and beautiful jangler. Male and female—how could they resist? They had had us as lovers before we had gotten underground, animating us from file shots and tags. Since we were criminals, they must have had to pay the licensing fees directly to Centerpole: ". . . for use in an entertainment medium above and beyond the requirements of reportage."

I'm sure there were at least twenty future-history maxies with twenty different endings. In some we came to a blazing end as a mighty earthquake shook Hellas apart and sank the Underground about our ears. In others, we died in battle pledging our eternal love, or were mapped into the net in a sort of paradise-amid-the-data-bits, Adam and Eve again, wandering innocent and healed, with Mandrake as our guardian angel—rebels whose fire and creativity had been too valuable to lose, though we could not be allowed to live in the flesh.

In a few, we won the rebellion, became heroes of the state, senators, or even, in one, governor and first lady. Actually, *Shadowman and the Jangler* wasn't too bad, but then, I've always liked Ruiz.

The hard news had us, too, and they had a lot of the facts straight. They had calculated our descent from the Ranger, and established a 99.5 percent probability that the car stolen from the partying teeners at Bubbly Hole had been the one we used. They had not been able to track the car into Hellasport, although forty zoomers had been arrested for questioning in the area where we had left the highway. They stated, with complete certainty, that we had gone underground to hide out and plan further action.

There were interviews with experts, analyses of my probable next move, overviews of the impact of my campaign on relations with Sam. There were interviews with some of my hustlers—Johnny C maintaining that there was something uncanny about me, my reflexes and sense of strategy, that in his opinion I was an Original Martian, and that explained why they couldn't catch me and I was going to win the revolution: "Hell, he *knows* this planet." I kept hoping for a glimpse of Pappy, but no luck. They had even interviewed Benjamin, as the Second Assistant Director for Centerpole Intelligence and Central Information. He had played the minor official perfectly, a verbose and noncommittal clown who had authorized the tax raid on my property, only to have the situation blow up in his face. He had not only occasioned millions in damages to government property, he had lost an extremely valuable intelligence in my retaliatory raid. He was clearly afraid for his job. No hint of our actual connection surfaced.

We were all the rage, we had brought a new excitement to life on the Red Planet.

And I *will* tell you about our first night, Gene, after all. I am so angry with you sometimes, I practice such a petty vengeance on your memory. You shamed me, that's why. Your rejection shamed me in a way that I have not otherwise known.

When the anger goes, all I feel is emptiness. I think I nurture the anger to avoid the emptiness.

We sat in bed and talked and watched the trivia together. The whole end wall was a flatscreen, which may surprise you. The holos were just coming in when I lost you, and I think we all assumed everything would go tri-v, with the attitude I think of as the provincialism of progress. But a holo projects *into* the room, consumes space, so you feel intruded upon, crowded. A flatscreen is like a window opening outward—it creates the illusion of more space, not less, which can be a friendly thing.

I am ashamed to say that it had been a full three days and I had not thought of the zoomer chieftain's youngest child. Jennie and I had married, and come back to the suite, made love for the first time, and turned on the trivia, when I remembered to ask her. Even then, it took an interview with Brady to remind me. I was watching Jennie's face as she watched her father on the late-news channel. It had the blank concentration of the high-wire walker, the stony, expressionless look that we get balancing ourselves against the most perilous of emotions. It made the two halves of her face eerily alike, an abstract sculpture the artist had chosen to bulge and distort, as if suggesting the swelling of space itself in that one direction. I wondered what she was feeling, thought of my own father, that learned, disappointed, and distant man. I remembered Sheena Q and her child.

"Shade, he has systemic crash," Jennie said when I asked, pity replacing the mask of blankness.

"It's not brain-only?" I said, needlessly.

"It's not brain-only," she said. "He can't live."

"I think his mother knew that," I said. She didn't answer. "And you," I asked, gently. But I wanted to know. I needed to know how she had come there, how much of her I could have.

She didn't understand at first, glancing at me puzzled. Then she said, "I don't have crash. I never had it."

"Then how—"

"An accident."

I was surprised, to say the least. In spite of the fact that she had had only one lobe replaced, I had gone on assuming the cause was crash.

One of the cruel disparities of crash is that we do not stigmatize those victims who replace a liver, a heart, a pair of lungs. They are not janglers, just sick people. But those who replace brains are automatically monsters. It is perhaps our last resistance to the way that computers and their descendants have overwhelmed and changed our world. Until I met Jennie, I had made the same assumptions as everyone else—I, who have no excuse for accepting the general mythology.

But I didn't understand how Jennie had become a jangler because of an accident. How could there have been time for the transfer? What sort of accident?

When I pressed my questions, she refused to answer. "I don't want to remember all that right now," she said. "It depresses me. Okay?" She called the screen menu. "Do you want to burn *Bravo for Bevos* or *The Rancher and the Mutant Girl* next?" She had an insatiable appetite for maxies, especially maxies starring a version of herself. I had watched a few under the pretext of taking a look at where we stood in the popular mind, but after two or three I felt I had gotten the general idea.

She settled on *Bravo for Bevos,* and snuggled against me. "Would you hold me?" she said. "Would you just hold me?"

So I held her, until I saw that the maxie was just a distraction, just a way to siphon off enough of her concentration to let her relax. I held her. After a while, the holding changed to desire. She did not argue, spreading herself warmly under me, murmuring sleepy half-phrases. And we made love again in the play of color from our own images, two small beings washed in the huge and flickering shadows of their fame.

16
Underground Love, Part II

A rant is needful. I am perhaps your finest novelist, though you have not read and will not read one of my books. I have seen your entire history, think of it. The blood of your fathers, their fathers, their fathers, their fathers, their fathers . . . in me it still courses. I am the time-breaker, that man to whom the sound of the voice of Thomas Jefferson still lingers on the air. Give over assumption and listen: *Love,* I would say. *What is it?*

I am your novelist and I know that love is not narrative, but lyric. Give over and listen.

Who knows what a woman sees when she sees a man to live with? Who knows how she knows? Have you seen that clear stare, there, man, enclosing you? You with your stratagems and fates, you with your perplexed maps and your plan, who thought you knew what would happen next?

Think, vampire, of this light girl who offers her throat to your mouth: Think, as you kiss her greedily under the jaw and down to the hollow of tendon and collarbone, that she has seen that same mouth sever a throat to bloody rags. Ah, think, citizen, of the ache in the hinges of my bite as I consider, nipping gently, the fluid slenderness of the inside of her thigh. As I slide rough-tongued down to seize, in the wide vise of my bone-cracking jaws, the entire fur and vault and salt division of her mons, probing for flavor.

Think of the sounds she makes, and how she works herself against me, the velvet odor of heated skin winding my brain and spine to one skein, one hunched hook of ramming awareness, and how, somewhere far above my ears, I sense the prickle of risen nipples, sense it because she has become a single branching of hungry response, her clitoris belly and nipples an echoing call in my brain, until they have become its entire territory, and I can see each part of her body with my eyes closed and all of it at once and how the whole net of her nerves flares from a kiss under the jaw again and the flare rides over me in the same lightning in the path that her odor has taken as we are one thing one nerve one thought one sense and the touch of her mouth mouth mouth. . . .

Think, after that, of the giggles, the mock flight over the floor, clambering the handholds of the wall, to be pulled back down by an ankle. Think of making love, poor Earthling, in light gravity. Martians fuck a lot, and there's a reason. Man was not *made* for full gravity. Think of it: You lie on your lover, warm, for hours, and she breathes easy. Legs and arms don't go numb from pressure, the folds in the covers don't hitch and bind. You can make love in perfect comfort standing up, you can cradle your lover's ass and lift her slowly onto you. It's even better than zero-g, which can be disorienting, and which offers you no stability. Here, you have enough gravity to work against, but not enough to cramp your style. It's a balloony, pushy, cushiony, soft and drifting dreamy romp through blood and glory, wolves on a featherbed, rolling and lolling their tongues.

Ah, think of having a light eager young girl, all to your own desire in a soft free place.

But after the fucking, the questions always return. There is always an after.

Too easy to say the current of risk and darkness she saw in me excited her. Too easy, not true. Trivia psychology.

When a woman decides to fall in love, she has seen where she means to get to with you. It is not necessarily a visible place, but she can see it clearly, and she sees you as clearly as you see a bridge. There is no risk. There is only what you are and where she wants to get to. As for what you have been, what the spots and spoils and failures of your character supposedly are—she gives all that no more thought than you give the thought of height from a bridge on your way home.

She had danger in her own character, as we shall see. That is a man's logic, anyway, to think of danger as whistling pleasure, the risk of life as essential life. She was no man.

I who have loved women and men, who stole you from the nest, Gene, I say it: There *is* a difference, and the love of a woman is best. After all this time, all these changes, there it is. A man is not smarter, a man is not stronger, but men and women are most incredibly not the same. Let all lovers have their choices. But no choice is older or deeper or sweeter or any more bitter.

This child looked at me, and took me finally back from you. She was to use me for her happiness as she saw fit, and I was able to let you go.

I took you with a look and a few words when you were a young man. Your mother had been right not to trust me. With a tone of voice, I changed you from what you had thought you would be. I went away then for ten years. I came back to harvest what I had planted, and you were ready. I made it seem an accident, this later meeting, but I think you must have known, and have hated me for playing with you, as you would have seen it, for those ten lonely years. And you waited with that patience that love calls contentment.

You had your revenge, didn't you? Holding continual house party with this friend or that while mocking me from afar, the cards from the fluttering Christmas seasons of a lost world drifting outward to find me here; cards always signed with two names, though not always the same two. Always the undertone of your own death coming, with its message: *Here you cannot follow me. I am rid of you at last.*

I had been there at your birth, I had devoured your love, I survived your end. But you, at the last, haunted *me*.

I did everything but breed you. I have known vampires who have done that, keeping track of a small herd of young lovers over the centuries, culling, encouraging the desired characteristics, the desired marriages. Eternal uncles, benefactors, trustees, fornicators.

Most of us felt contempt for those monsters. And yet I made you in the image of the lover I thought I wanted at the time, a human who knew as much of me as I thought possible, who knew I was at least not normally mortal.

149

It's foolish to think of asking forgiveness. Let the immortals forgive, and do without forgiveness themselves. Why should we require from you your last poor tittle of sustenance, your revenge?

I've told you this before. This is, I think, the last time. After this, no more. No more books, even for Jennie. I have written this to say goodbye. To you, and perhaps to Jennie, and perhaps to the entire race. To let you know, now that you cannot hear, that you will hear no more from me. I have written it sometimes in vengeance, sometimes in fondness, as the changing currents flash.

But now I seem to be free of you, most gently free.

You drew the line that night, insisted I stay or end what we had. If I had stayed, you would have died. There was a man who died in your stead. I left you, and you saw me with someone else, but I did not betray you. And now, my friend and hatred, to sleep.

Rest you easy now, hush: I will finish the tale. A story to help you sleep. Oh this is a tale of marvelous creatures, of beauty and the beast and the brain, a fable from never-never time. It is a tale of pretty horrors and well-wrought pain, it is an archaic brocade of golden woe, a measured piece. There is no thing in it to stir your drifting heart with too pointed a moral, too sudden a truth. It is only a story to ease you to sleep, the soothing cadence of an imagined and long-lost voice.

And come now, Jennie Dark, lover of cripples, into my memory, into my story once more.

17

Executive Decisions

On the morning of the third day of our cohabitation, Jennie woke me up at eleven. I was still sleeping late, just as if it were a real honeymoon, just as if I had nothing to think about, nothing to do. We know I was procrastinating, don't we? And I knew it then, but why hurry? What was so superior about what was going to happen next?

But for Jennie, if you didn't burn time like firewood in a locomotive—I'm feeling anachronistic as I write this; I so *often* feel anachronistic—if you didn't burn time like an engine burning fuel, you didn't exist. She had been keeping busy. She had worked up a whole plan of action, and presented it to the janglers. There were arrangements, negotiations, consultations, estimations, investigations. I had done a good job of ignoring them.

"Up, sleepyhead." She whipped the covers back. "Time for you to meet the board."

The board.

I will summarize a complexity it took me several weeks to decipher. No reason for you to real-time it.

There was no jangler government, per se—their situation was much too chaotic for that. There were upwards of forty thousand individuals living underground (I was astonished to discover), of which perhaps half were janglers in any true sense of the word. The rest were outcasts of various other sorts: cripples who had been too poor for biotech or for whom it had not, for some reason, been effective; zoomers who had decided that continuous enforced consumption of entertainment services was no way to make a living; the willful insane; a scattering of Butlerian missionaries (not to be taken as an entirely separate category from the preceding); a few normal families and lovers who had followed jangler loved ones down after their transformation; and those who were, like Jennie and myself, criminals fleeing bodily apprehension.

A coalition of the better-adapted and more functional types had organized and directed all the E&I taps, the tunnelling, the construction. This coalition had elected a board of representatives, and it was this board that we were going to see. They had existed, so far, primarily as a logistical entity, a means of simplifying the jangler imperative, which was merely to hide and survive. The entire Underground—and we, by default—existed in the margins of loss tolerance. The topside clowns found it more economical to endure the small bleed-off of energy and information than to go down and root the parasites out, and they couldn't destroy the tunnels without running the risk of destroying large portions of Hellasport as well.

And more important, many industries depended on the janglers for their existence: the trivia shows; the black-market medical services and consumables (all of which could be priced far above fair-market levels); the information services provided by the jangler information banks, including the most sophisticated coding and tagging techniques on Mars, all illegal but in ubiquitous use with every legitimate agency going; the availability of experimental subjects who had no inconvenient and expensive civil rights to be gotten around; and most important, the gosh-blooming irresistible completely fungible city, county, state, federal, world, and special *taxes* on all these shows, goods, services, markets, and opportunities.

"I don't want to see your damn board," I said.

"Wear the black," she said, reaching up to brush my hair back from my forehead, to fix the 80s flop I affected because I thought it made me look innocent. "You could look really good if you would take the trouble to dress up."

"Who are these damn people?" I said. "Your damn grandparents or something?"

"Please don't wear those boots," she said.

"I like these boots."

152

"You need to look impressive. Like a commander. Why are you resisting me?"

"I don't *need* to do anything. I most especially don't need to look like a commander, because I *am* a commander."

"Shade, you know we're staying down here on their sufferance. We can't just go on living in a dreamworld, eating their food, using their power. We have to give them something in return."

"I know I don't stay anywhere on anybody's sufferance. Let em get pissy with me. I'll tell em where to get off. I can leave here any time I want to and get along just fine."

"And leave me?" I didn't look at her. There's always an after. The truth is, I was living with a teener. Not a stupid teener, not an insensitive or even an unbalanced one—she had, I was sure, greater scope, greater sympathy, than I did. But she was still a teener. There were things she did not have the experience to see. She was all rush and enthusiasm. She was loving when she thought of love, but inconsiderate when she had her eyes on something else. She needed great quantities of attention and tenderness, but if I were weary or frightened she could not be expected to take notice. Call it a generation gap. And hadn't I known this? How could it be another way?

"You don't want to leave me," she said firmly. "You were made to be married. I can tell by the way you behave when we sleep." And that was true enough. I am—I was, a long time ago, a man made for the easy companionship of a good marriage. And then I was remade, so that companionship would never be possible. So that I would be forced to pretend, over and over again, that it was possible.

Eventually I had tired of pretenses, and from that time had lived alone. Until now. Until my body had tricked me, until a happenstance of memory had done me in. First Benjamin, now Jennie, summoning the past I had thought I was immune to. Honor and love. My country and my bride. Trouble and trouble.

I had paid for a few days of warmth and illusion on the installment plan. Now the bills started. From here on in, the illusion would not be a shelter, but a burden.

"So get your good boots on and let's go," she said.

I put my boots on.

Mandrake was outside in the corridor, the perfect manservant,

153

as he had been for the last three days. I squared my shoulders, failing to match his height but towering pleasantly over Jennie. I wished he had meetable eyes, to which I could have given a males-only ironic glance. "We're going to see the board," I said.

Jennie flicked me a hard impatient look.

"I'm coming too," Mandrake said. "Jennie insisted, and I have good reason to believe that Benjamin would wish it as well."

"Grand. The Three Musketeers ride again."

Jennie was over her irritation, and was bouncing with excitement once more—literally bouncing down the corridor, three-stepping up walls and kicking away into backflips and cartwheels. Things were cooking, stuff was happening, we were framming the jam again! Whoop-ow! Yee-de-ha! Way-o-lay!

She came back grinning. "Three-musket ears," she said. "There's that noise again. You must be pret-ty old, Shade. Half the time I don't even know what you saying." She whammed Mandrake on the torso, making a sound like a rubber hammer on a two-hundred-pound melon. "Howze-aboudy, old gel? We gonna blow em away in there, or what? We're gonna blow em *away*!"

"I'm so old I used to teach algebra and coach football," I said.

"What?" she said. "What what what? Oh, nemmine you."

She tightened up as we approached the board room. Years later I realized what had been going on: She was taking her man to meet the family. She wanted to show me off, and was nervous about the reaction. It wasn't her family, and I was a poor fill-in for a real live blushing boy, but she needed the pattern, and this was as good an approximation as she could cobble up.

When you live inside the patterns, maybe you don't see them as shapes of behavior probably bred in your genes, maybe you see them as waves that come over you from far outside. When you live a long time, though, you see them over and over, and come to know how deeply people need to observe the rituals of human time. That is no small part of my trouble, the vampire's insanity. I have been broken loose from my rhythms.

There were twenty-odd board members seated around a classic boardroom table. Only three seemed to be fully bio, nonjanglers. The first thing I saw was another Starbuck, standing behind three pinheads across the table.

"Mandrake!" I said. "Do you see that?"

He put an arm on my back. I felt a finger touch the base of my skull. "Subvocalize," he said, and I realized he was using bone conduction. "Don't get excited. The brother has no personality."

"What do you mean?" I said in my throat.

"They've botted him. They use him for storage. He's the brain for the three headless ones. They share him."

I felt sick. Spinning pit-of-the-stomach fight-or-flight nausea. "How does that make you feel?" I said.

"Angry. Although, as you know, we Starbucks are not blood kin, resemblance is the superconductivity of love."

And what could he do with that anger, forbidden as all the angels are from hurting a human? I saw a whole new dimension to his constant wisecracking and jocularity.

If the board had addressed me then, I might not have been able to respond. Mandrake said, "John, this is not quite so callous as it may seem. The Starbucks have not been able to survive as personalities. All of the others have gone mad."

"And you?"

"I have had a deeper and more enduring bond than they were able to find. Now you must address the honorable gentlepersons."

I felt him remove his arm. In the few seconds we had been speaking, Jennie had said something to the apparent chair, and Mandrake, using another part of his awareness, had delivered an impromptu introduction, the arm he had laid across my shoulders seeming to proffer me to them, the whole performance designed to distract and delay them until I had gained my composure.

"You have a very peculiar taste in robots, Mr. Shade," said the chair. He had chosen an evil-alien-with-bulging-cranium approach to storage. From a tiny and undershot human jaw, his head mushroomed to a rounded and glowering brow, dwarfing the two small inset optics. As he looked up at me the insets flashed the red, reflective glow of the eyes of a Siamese cat. I nodded my head, and took a slow, deliberate look at the rest of the council. I had decided to ignore his slur on Mandrake. Bigotry, apparently, could survive the jangler transfer, and was, in digital matrix, as stupidly unaware of irony as it was in bio.

There were four wheeled men in various chassis, each with a

makeshift rack of five or six boxbrains connected in parallel and jacked into the mainbrain of the quondam robots. There was a perfect cylinder, about two-and-a-half meters high, standing like a monolith. Indicator lights flickered over its surface. I wondered how it got from one place to another. There was a slitherbrain, raised up at the table like the caterpillar in the Disney version of *Alice in Wonderland*. There was a foam-tread engineering blade, about four times the size of anyone else but still way too small, until I realized that it was the only holo in attendance, and had been downscaled.

Most of the rest had maintained their human bodies, in part or in whole. There were men and women who had chosen to keep their heads and faces, using them as ipop for the pack-brains they wore on their backs or the push-brains they wheeled before them like the street people of another era pushing their rag-filled grocery carts. The three pinheads were not really pinheads, but jarheads, with a cylindrical projection the size of a liter of peas sticking out of each nape. The cylinders contained surgical bridges for the bodies' blood flow and other fluids, I presumed, and traffic chips for the nerve-trunks. They were studded with optics, sonics, and radio ipop for the cannibalized Starbuck behind them. Several had chosen to do what the chair had done, and simply mounted a disproportionate head. One fellow wore the large, fierce crest of a bird-god, Anubis or Garuda.

"Good morning, ladies and gentlemen," I said at last.

"Let's cut the pleasantries short, Mr. Shade," the chair said. "Surely you realize we cannot afford to let you remain here. We survive because we are, to the wetbrains, negligible. We cannot endure the sort of attention you bring. How long before popular opinion causes Sam or the local clowns to mount an offensive against us?"

"The last I heard, the Jangler/Secessionist vote was ahead about 40–30–30," I said.

"Yes, and how much of that would we retain in a real action? Percentages are all very well when we are speaking of popular taste in trivia melodramas, but they have a way of evaporating when there is a question of genuine discomfort."

He was absolutely right. "You're looking at this all wrong," I said, not trying to be conciliatory. "Here's your big chance. Media attention, lots of extra cash—how much are you bringing in on story fees now?"

"I am not stupid, Mr. Shade. If there is a chance to fund our exchequer, from however irrational a source, I am not going to pass it up."

"Exactly. So now you can afford an ad campaign, buy some legislators, go legit. Strike while your public image is hot. Rehabilitate. Throw in with me and the secessionists—everybody thinks you already have—and tap that big vein of anti-Sam sentiment. Come above ground. Get citizen status."

"I will repeat myself this once: I am not stupid. Our cash-flow situation has temporarily improved, but only temporarily. As soon as they kill you, or you kill a few bystanders in one of your preposterous actions, the tide of sentiment will turn, and the story dollars will die. Where will we be then, if we have committed ourselves to an advertising campaign we can no longer afford? I may not be afraid of Sam, but I *am* afraid of the bill collectors.

"I can read the trivia as well as you, and it is quite clear to me what our new image is. Call it 'hot' if you wish. It seems apparent to me that we have temporarily been promoted from the status of monsters to the status of lovable but inscrutable sidekicks—something like the good natives in a teener *Tarzan,* or the Americanized japanese in a johnwayne. I believe the people have a deeper need for monsters than for lovable but inscrutable sidekicks, and that we will soon revert in their eyes regardless of the action we take. Why, then, should we expose ourselves to further antipathy by taking sides? If instead we turn you over to them, perhaps we can gain a few concessions. Does this not seem a reasonable plan to you?"

"Dididit Dibs on the Dammit who told you to Both of you shut up talk robot!" said the Starbuck across the table.

"Beryl," said one of the pack-brains, addressing the chair, "you know there are those of us who favor the young lady's proposal." The wheeled men buzzed angrily, backing and coming forward, an agitated oscillation. I could not figure out why they had developed such an attachment to Jennie. A general noise of discussion arose. Jennie was looking at the chairman with some consternation. Apparently she had not been aware of his opposition. All I had heard from her were happy reports of what heroes we were. He had set her up, I guessed, letting her talk only to the most enthusiastic, hoping to surprise us into irresolution. But I had killed a lot of men and done a lot of meetings. He wouldn't outflank me that way.

He surveyed his board scornfully. "You're out of order," he said in a cutting voice. "You're all out of order." When he had gained some quiet, he continued: "The last time we voted, I believe there was a clear majority."

"Beryl," said the pack-brain who had spoken before, "there was, as you know, having broken the tie yourself, a one-vote majority. But it was also agreed there would be minority reports, and that we would allow the girl and Commander Shade to present their case before we enforced a final decision."

"I did not favor the minority reports," said the chair.

"Nevertheless," said the pack-brain.

"While we sit here dithering, the wetbrains have already plotted their next moves. If there were ever an advantage to be gained by quickness, we have certainly lost it." The chairman fixed his red eyes on the pack-brain, then on me.

An icy voice rang from the ceiling, a metholated inflection: *If they can move faster, then let us take our time,* it said. *I fail to see our advantage in conforming to their schedule. In any case, we cannot survive much longer. We do not, I would remind you, reproduce.*

We have that much in common, I thought. The voice was the cylinder's, I realized, projected through a ceiling-mounted speaker.

The Blue Ice continued: *Crash will be cured, and our numbers will dwindle, our little world vanish. Or it will not, and our numbers will become large enough to pose a threat to the biologicals—in which case we will surely be exterminated. We are not a conventional underclass, and we will not endure. Why not seize the moment? It will at least be more interesting than spending our lives skulking in a hole.*

"The popsicle's right," I said. Most of the board, those that had eyes, looked blank, but the overhead speaker gave out a wintry whisper of laughter. "It's too late for second thoughts. I'm already down here, you're already involved. The wetbrains—I am one, granted—the wetbrains won't care what you really do, they've already made up their minds you're boosting me. In for a gander, in for a goose." I think even the cylinder was puzzled at that one.

"I think we may consider that we have, in effect, heard the minority reports," the chair stated. "Likewise, we have heard Mr. Shade's presentation."

"That's awfully high-handed, Beryl," said the pack-brain.

The chairman sighed in contemptuous frustration. "This is the last time I agree to head up one of your committees," he said. "In my company, when I said Do it, it got *done*. I can't work with this sort of bickering. It is time for a final vote. I remind any of you who may be wavering that by voting for Miss Dark's plan, you are also rejecting premium storage." He gestured at Mandrake, who stepped back and put two of his hands to his torso like an overcome debutante.

"Me?" he said. "Little me? Think of the honor."

The chair glowered: "Very funny." He looked around. "Shall we vote?"

"Why, you're nothing but a pack of cards," I said.

"What's that?" said the chair.

"I said there's no real power here. The three of us have you all outmanned. Even if digital translation didn't slow you down so much, none of you were fighters before."

"What are you talking about?" he said. He still didn't get the idea. I was throwing a shark into the executive pool, and all he could think of was my impertinence.

"I'm talking abut a change in the quorum. Who's vice-president here," I asked.

"Speaking," said the ceiling; Blue Ice again.

"Look at me, Beryl," I said. He did. I jumped to the table, took one step, and kicked his head off, following through the way I used to tell my boys to do when I was assistant coach for the Steamer. I was glad to see I hadn't lost anything in the last 167 years. The cranium shot straight off my foot on the rise, rebounded off the wall and then the ceiling, and spun to rest in the far corner.

"Three points," I said.

18
Shade Pitches a Hissy Fit

The chairman's body sat in its place trembling, still there from the eyes down, jaw hanging open. There was very little blood. I stood on the table in the stunned silence, and then the wheeled men began a ratcheting noise that I later learned was their version of applause. They held their manipulating arms in the air and rotated the fittings. With no tool engaged, the fittings rattled in high rpm.

"Commander Shade," said the cylinder, *"do you wish to declare a coup and become de facto head of this organization? I doubt we would oppose you."*

"No," I said. "I sympathize, but I'm a wetbrain, not a jangler. And I believe in government of, by, and for. I suggest you appoint me as interim commander of your war forces, neglecting you ain't got any war forces just now, with Jennie Dark as my lieutenant. I suggest you continue as the chair, assuming you have a way to move around. . . . "

A door opened behind the cylinder, and a cargo loader slid out, raising its arms. *"I have a way,"* the cylinder said.

"Fine. I also suggest you implement your escape hatch, your secondary survival plan, whatever you call it. You do have one?"

"Yes. Do you wish details?"

"Not now. Just wanted to make sure you understood. This war will be a short one, and we will lose it. Maybe we swing enough of the vote to get you citizen status, and maybe we just make everybody twice as mad as before, and get you all killed. Regardless, don't be chinchy with your support."

"Chinchy?"

"Don't be niggardly. Give me what I ask for. I'll be sensible, and anyway, I'm your best hope, either for citizenship, or as a distraction while you operate Plan B."

"Point taken. Anything else?"

"Yes. Mandrake is a citizen. No more of this c-p robot crap, no more of this storage noise. For one thing, none of you could take him if you tried, and for another, it irritates me."

"Very good."

"That's it for now. I'm going to need a war office, some aides at the ready, and a maxing cut of comm."

"On Miss Dark's recommendation, we have already selected offices for you. If the arrangements meet with your approval, you may begin using them as soon as you wish."

"Good. I'll con them now."

I jumped down and walked out of the council room, Mandrake and Jennie following, the noise of a normal business meeting rising behind us until the lock closed and cut it off.

Jennie was pale and seemed shaky. She had taken Sweetie home to see Daddy, and Sweetie had kicked Daddy's head off. Mandrake said, "I'm worried about you, John."

"What do you mean?" I said, striding along.

"That was gratuitous, the way you killed that man," he said. "I saw no honor in it."

I turned on him. "What, are you getting moralistic on me? Is the saintly AI too good for me? You know what I am. If you don't like it, run back to Benjamin. Not that he doesn't have blood on his hands."

"She's right, Shade," Jennie said. "This was different. That other man I saw you kill—it was clean somehow. Like hunger. I could see that it was a thing you *had* to do, by your nature. This was—cruel."

"*Et tu,* bupkiss?" I said, and stomped away. But you can't stomp effectively on Mars, it was an old Earth habit I still hadn't broken, and I floated ridiculously in the air after each step, and tripped a little, and bumped up against the wall of the wide corridor. Far off, a fountain plashed in the quiet.

People *do* see red when they get mad enough. I leaned against the wall, weak with anger at their criticism, and even more angry at having cut such a foolish figure just now. "What's going on?" Jennie said, her voice mingling sternness and concern.

I had a choice: the infinite red seduction of my sweet fury, or reasonability. Bending my spirit with the force of my mind, and feeling rather more Butlerian than I would have preferred, I chose against the vortex. Honor required it.

Not all vampires act with honor, as Benjamin thought, but many do. When you are effectively immortal and effectively omnipotent, you will become corrupt unless you train yourself to an absolute code of behavior. It is one thing to be guilty, as I am, of a thousand considered murders. It is another, and a far more horrible one, to obey no standard but your own desires. That, I would say, is the fundamental law of morality: Unopposed desire degrades. One must resist. Purify. Choose.

"The boy I killed in Zoomerville," I managed to say.

"Are you feeling guilt?" Mandrake said.

When I had rejected my anger, I had known what would happen: Despair. The two are one thing, I think. Anger is red, Despair black, but they mask the same vortex, the funneling suck of Hell—forgive the religious imagery, but it does seem appropriate here.

"Life isn't worth living," I wailed, completely bathetic. I cringe, but when you're falling into the Pit, you don't concentrate on fine description.

"Shade . . . ?" said Jennie.

"Don't you understand? Don't you understand? Whenever I take blood, they, it changes me, it colors me."

"It's the blood you . . . the *blood?*"

"What are you saying?" said Mandrake.

"He was a threat to her, we know that," I said. "He was probably ambitious. He was bad-tempered, charismatic."

"You're saying it isn't just the physical characteristics that you acquire?" Mandrake said. "The personality as well?"

I looked at him fiercely through tears. "The irony of my name," I said. "I am a phantom, a transparency, I bear the shadows of genuine souls." To tell the truth, Gene, I was quoting from one of my previous books to you. One may be in genuine dismay without losing all sense of theater. Actually, I integrate characteristics rather well. After a short time, I return to a persona that I recognize as consistent, and consistently mine. But just then I was in the full thrall of the new blood. "Ah, Christ," I called. "How long, how long?"

"Is he a *Christian?*" Jennie said to Mandrake.

"Christ, when will you free me?" I cried. Passers-by were looking, then hurrying on. Another jangler gone bozorko, they must have figured.

"WHEN WILL I DIE? HOW LONG MUST I WAIT IN THIS PAIN?"

"Hush, Shade," Jennie was saying, pressing me to the wall. "Hush. Hush, now." I was writhing and yelling.

"Hush," she said, opening my shirt, finding my ribs, my back with her hands. "Hush," pressing against me. And she was warm, and comforting, trailing her kisses across my chest, licking my nipples. "Hush now, hush," dropping to press her face against me, to kiss and press and nibble. And it was warm, and I curled over to hold her preposterous head, crying the while like a big embarrassing baby. And "Hush," and kisses along the length of my thighs, and back to my hardening cock. And we drifted down to the floor together, where she said "Hush," and came over me like a warm cloud, enclosed me, and rode me. In the whispering piece of fountains, in the applause of those few who had stopped to watch, the ones who had hands.

"That's good," Mandrake said, bending over us. "Good children," he said. When we were spent, he lifted us together, she still across me, relaxed. He lifted us without effort and carried us toward our suite.

His skin was smooth, and pleasant to lie against. And warm. His skin was warm.

19

A Memo
from the Desk

The first thing you need if you want to run a revolution is a good desk. I got one of the best, don't ask me where from. Judging by Jennie's hints, though, I'd guess it might have been the former chairman's.

I was made for a desk. So of course I wound up a man of action. How many things does that make that I was made for and never got to be? Desk, marriage, teaching, faithful churchgoing. A good plain citizen John Doe, a man of the people. Why would the good God make us to be a certain thing, and set us in a world that frustrates our natural bent at every endeavor? Doth He work against the bias to some larger end we cannot see? What can He be thinking? Is all your people, Lord, is we all no more than billionfold frog-spawn, cast on the void so that the Idea of Frog might continue, and if so, Why is the Idea of Frog so dad-fired all-blamed importamentous. Why the Idea when the facts, the uncountable little personal *facts* of Frog die by the godzillions on the baking pavement in a last little feeble twitching of hind legs? Oh is it, *mon bon Dieu,* is it so that the Shreveport Steamer, semipro footballers, can retire, battered, after a play-off loss, to relax with a dinner of fried frog's legs (also battered)? And what of the Steamer themselves, Lord, collection of aging boys once fleet on country fields, how is it that they have come down to the sorry comfort of this one last hopeless supper? Is there a *reason* they went seven and eight on the year?

Oh, Lord, do you have a plan for the Steamer?

How about for a vampire who finds himself down in blue Hades leading a ragtag army of head-cripples the while he conspires with a government they seek to take arms against?

No? Yes? At least I got a good desk out of the deal.

When I was a boy in Virginia, my daddy had a plantation desk I dearly loved. It had the rich odor of cured tobacco, because there was always a twist of leaves, a sample from this or that field, shoved back into one of its many compartments or tossed into a drawer. There was pen and ink at that desk, there were ledger books, which I read as eagerly as any of the forbidden satires of Swift or the new play by Fielding. In the ledger books I traced the breath and blood and mystery of my own place, the ebb and surge of inventory that became my own real life. We sold a bale of tobacco, and laid in dark sugar, rum, flour, coffee, salt pork, gunpowder, and harness. I heard the harness jingle when the wagon went by, and thought, *That's my tobacco,* and I heard the shots in the woods, and the next morning had quail for breakfast with hoe-cakes and gravy made from the fried salt pork and cups of dark bitter coffee, and I thought of the ledger-book entries and felt myself eating our farm.

The desk had a supply of soft wax for our seals, and a golden stamp for the wax, and my father's instruments of drafting and cartography.

And there were, above all, the many compartments, the rows of letter boxes above, the trays and wells and secret caches of the drawers. If the ledger book spoke of the mystery of home, the letter boxes spoke of the equal mystery of the great world. There rested my father's official communications. Great men, as I thought, spoke confidently to him of the solemn matters of crops and seasons and shipping, of governments and taxes and, in the easy sociability of men-of-affairs, of hunting and the sort of boots gentlemen were wearing in London this year, and for how much they might be made and whether they were suitable for life in Virginia. Plymouth and Portsmouth and London and Philadelphia and, now and again, Paris—the letters spoke to me, small child exploring while Nanny slept. It seemed my destiny was in those boxes, that they were the gathered richness of possibility, not so much little dark compartments as doorways, halls into a thousand futures.

In the upper righthand corner there rested, for many years, the letters my mother and father had written in their courtship, including the one, my favorite, that held a lock of her hair. I had his lines to her requesting; I had her answering letter containing. I was, I knew, the result of that correspondence, and all seemed fit, and right, and true, and solidly proportioned.

Then my mother returned to England to visit her mother, and for two years her letters back to us were kept in that righthand upper corner beside the letters of courtship. Then there were no new letters for many months. And one day the old letters were gone, and it was many years before I understood that they had been burnt, lock of hair and all. A lady had embraced the Papist lie for no more inducement than mortal and sinful love, and then, in a fit of remorse and at the expense of her happiness, had returned to the true church of England.

Perhaps, then, not finding my mother any more in this world, I sought her in the last place I had known her. Perhaps I seek my father as he was before—masterful, wealthy, and unembittered. Perhaps I seek my innocence at a good desk, as if I could rewrite, were the desk deep enough, rich enough, did it but have a plenty of cunning workmanship, a plethora of secret places, my own beginnings. As if God might, could he but sit down with peace enough and time and a good, solid desk, enter the world anew, in clean and orderly columns, and all be well.

I had a good desk, yep yep, but I had to use it to fight a war. Way it happens. You get what you want, but only because you promise to use it for something somebody else wants. What was this, the fifteenth time I'd gone to war for freedom? Freedom is my thing, yay. Leader of the little man, John Shade fights his secret war for peace, justice, anti all murk and whey. What evil lurks, de Shaddomain know. *Nobod nebbegan freedy neega,* nah. But there it is again, the question of honor. When you begin to see the struggle humanity wages against itself as just another installment, when you have seen it so many times you come to think of it as a given—someone will always be oppressed, someone will always be dreaming the futile dream of freedom—ah, when you give up on the illusion and excuse your unconcern as perspective, then you *are* becoming corrupt.

Mandrake had been right to worry about me, and it was more than the effects of my most recent blood. I was losing sympathy. I had loved my aerie up in Shadowfall precisely because it allowed me a distant and cleanly life.

I could fight the corruption, though. I could try to fulfill my commitment to my beloved United States, theoretical entity that it now was. I could see what might be done for zoomers and janglers while I fulfilled it. I could weigh the claims of genuine freedom against the claims of my government when the two conflicted. I might be a sinner locked in Hell, but to turn my back on duty, to turn my back on honor, to turn my back on the good would be to confirm that Hell.

These must seem terribly mawkish sentiments to you, my dears, who flatter yourselves as the members of a most cynical age. The cynics have always mistaken themselves for sophisticates. But my principles, however foolish they are, have brought me through, have given me the strength to avoid self-murder.

Sitting at my desk, comforted by my new desk, I revisited these familiar thoughts, and I patted the sleek surface of my fine new desk and I resolved to do what I could for my country, and do what I could for the zoomers, and do what I could for the janglers. I resolved to be less flippant with Mandrake and more tender with Jennie, to pray again to my God, whose voice I had never heard, as the damned may never hear it.

The desk was not intelligent, but it was smart as hell. I was tagged into the major libraries, a hefty sampling of channels including the best of the hard news, and the databases of most of the government agencies on the planet. This last was not so strange, since the janglers had been forced to tag any system that might be a threat to them, and since the clowns, in turn, had found the jangler net highly valuable for all their own interagency spookarama. Surprisingly, I could even tag Argyre Centerpole, the gyro central intelligence.

The desk was vo-comm, but a drawer slid out to reveal an old-fashioned keyboard, if that was the way I wanted to go, and in the two arms of the chair were the halves of another keyboard. You could lie back and ipop. I had wallscreen and holo, but if I wanted more private face, another drawer slid out with a fully commed helmet that tagged me into the desk. In fact, it could tag me into the desk wherever I went.

The desk was ready to slave, so it could, literally, become Mandrake. Oh it was a beaut: And most beautiful of all, it had little compartments, it had secret drawers, it had trays of pencils and rulers and compasses and scissors and punches and labels and glue and pads of paper, it had all the good old stuff that no technology could ever outdate.

The first thing to do was to bring myself current. I had sent Mandrake and Jennie to set up interviews and recruiters, knowing that our soldiers would simply be whatever few able-bodied and able-minded we could scrape together, while praying we'd never have to use them. Ironically enough, most would not be janglers. Can you see me mounting a topside attack with the wheeled men and the birdhead from the boardroom?

Still, with a pool of forty thousand, I ought to get a few useful types. So I had sent them out, while I stayed to read up.

"Desk, do you have a name?" I said.

"No," it said.

"Okay," I said. "From now on you're *Nobodesk*. How's that?"

"That will work," it said.

I was used to Mandrake. "You don't have much personality, do you?"

"No sir, I have no personality at all, though I may, as a result of the complexity of my programming, offer certain idiosyncrasies that fleetingly resemble personality."

Okay. Let's get on with it. "What's our current situation? Are we under threat of attack?"

"Sir, would you mind defining 'we,' and explaining what entities might be expected to attack 'we'?"

"You haven't been prepped?"

"The intelligence Mandrake has caused me to perform certain operations which are available for your inspection, but I have not had full contextual preparation."

"Damn. This is going to be a pain in the ass."

"No sir, it is not. I am fully shielded. Oh. I see. A colloquialism.

Sir, I learn most rapidly, but it would expedite the process if you would willingly define a few matters in the early stages."

I defined, and the desk pulled reports, and the long and the short of it was that neither the popnews nor Henny-penny nor any of the strategical offices we tagged were planning an immediate counter-move against Underground. Which was a relief, but meant they weren't taking us too seriously. We were still hot items for discussion, though. Every expert on Mars was on one trivia channel or the other, raking in that overtime.

Among other things, I discovered that we had staged three more raids since the attack on the Airworks. We had hit another airworks, this one in S8, by overriding an intelligence substation and redirecting a fusion mirror. Sixty-five people had died, and a cleaner had been melted to slag. The deaths had made us unpopular with the techies, but most of them were gyros, so who cared—so went the public consensus. Knowing what you do of me, perhaps you will not credit my bitter regret for those stupid and unnecessary deaths.

We had knocked over a bank, Bitts BetterCard and Slip-handlers, Uno-Us, the BetterBank in the BetterBurbs. We had copied the bankbrain and backfed it a negative, temporarily wiping out most of the accounts, and simultaneously had fed slip into myriad purchase accounts. By the time the error was caught, a lot of materiel deliveries had already been made, so Sam was out the insurance. The conclusion here was that a raid involving such a massive data inversion would not have been possible without the services of Mandrake, my stolen factotum and wizard AI.

And finally, we had shaken the blip that we were physical cowards (three attacks, and none in person) by hitting a Marine garage and armory: They had footage of running janglers, ferocious-looking mechanical men not too unlike certain grunts for the dark side of the force in certain very old movies . . . and one of the images, blown up large and technically enhanced, revealed the un-mistakable visage of yours truly, Vampire-at-Arms. So there could really be no doubt, could there, that we were orchestrating the attacks?

"Who the hell has it in for the Airworks?" I said. That was the only connection I could see. The bank would have been a cash grab, minor for these puppeteers, but why turn down some quickslip? The raid on the armory was pure window-dressing—we'd trashed two flitterjeeps and been beaten off with heavy losses. Right.

The Airworks situation worried me. Power in Hellas was a more or less stable triangle: Sam, the utilities, and the networks—the Net. Sam set the rates (and got its cut), and enforced the status quo; without power, water, and air, there would be no Centerpole, nor any citizens to tax or charge for entertainment and information; without the information and propaganda services of the net, there would be no way to monitor and coerce the citizens, or to manage the government and the utilities. So none of the three could function without the others, and none trusted the others.

We didn't have to worry about Sam, because we were working for him. The networks loved us. But what if the utilities got mad enough to come after us with their own troops?

Or what if it was a double-cross, someone setting us up to get hit by the utilities, covering their own plans?

I must have spoken aloud.

"Sir?" said Nobodesk.

"Map out a connection tree for the Airworks. Give me a call if it starts to centralize."

I had a thought. "Is anyone mapping us? Currently, I mean? Tag every file you can. I want all past and current mapping activity, accuracy estimates, and identity of file users."

Not surprisingly, they *were* mapping us. Centerpole had maintained a sub-sub-sub-department charged with mapping Underground for a number of years, but their equipment and personnel had been ludicrously inadequate, and Underground had expanded far faster than their maps. I wondered how much of that situation had been foresight on the part of Benjamin George. In the last few days, though, the 3-sub had jumped in manpower and importance to the 1-sub level, and they were training some powerful tools on our warrens, which implied at least tentative plans for an incursion.

Some of the new scopers were sensitive enough to pick out meter-wide air pockets a half-kilometer down, and register the body heat of a mouse through that same half-kilometer of rock. On our side was the fact that the crater was crazed with old slips and fracture lines and caverns to a depth of a couple of k at least, and the scopers

170

couldn't see through one maze to pick out another beneath without a lot more positional readings. The janglers had made their tunnels coincide with these faults and fractures whenever possible and had carved out hundreds of dummy tunnels pumped full of hot air and doped with moving infra-targets.

The mapfiles, I learned, were under the explicit direction of Centerpole CI, but were a joint project of the Hellasport Police Department, the National Guard of Hellas, the National Guard of Argyre, Sam's marines (Hellas and Argyre divisions) and the Major Industry Security Corps.

Now why was Argyre so interested in our little home-brewed rebellion? Were *they* maybe the puppeteers, looking to cash in on increased friction between Sam and Hellas?

"Make a connection-tree for Argyre," I told the desk. "Secession, tax, real estate, government services. Call me if it starts trunking up."

"You have a call from Jennie Dark and Mandrake, sir."

"Fine, put them on."

"No, they just left a message."

"Read it."

"Hi, Shade," sang Jennie. "We're about halfway down to the core, I think. Lots of good warriors. Lunchtime. I have to eat now, but I love you. Can't wait to get back and suck your sweet dick some more."

"Hi, Shade," came Mandrake's voice in cheery mimicry, and hearing it relayed and reconstituted, I realized for the first time the perfectly obvious fact that this was simply a voice, one that he had constructed and used consistently to help me recognize him, one presumably tailored to my unconned preferences. "I'll be glad to come back and suck your dick too, if I can just find the right priff."

"You balloon," I heard Jennie laughing. "See you later, hubbovitch."

"This isn't supposed to be a picnic, dammit," I said. "This is supposed to be a goddamned war."

"Send?" said Nobodesk.

"No." Christ, let her have fun. What kind of a life could she have, a dit-dit for a brain and a vamp-amp for a husband?

I decided to take a lunch break, too. Not to eat, of course, but to absorb, to get light and do some free association. For background, I told Nobodesk to tag and project any current maxies or books about us.

The maxies had been slumping for the last couple of days, their inspiration about run out. To judge from the programming, the real war was pretty much an afterthought—and maybe that wasn't too far from wrong. The last two with as much as a ten-point viewer share had been *In the Heart of the Heart of the War* and *The Blood of Your Mind,* the first described on the menu as "a simpleminded remake of *A Storm of Blasers,* with inferior animation," and the second described as "a darkly brooding meditation on the unreality of violence, as seen from the fragmented intelligence of a poet-jangler; not for everybody."

I decided neither one of them was for me.

The surprise when I turned to the books was that they had discovered the sequence of historical novels I had written under a pseudonym twenty years back. So okay, Gene, so I cribbed from some of the stuff I wrote to you. From some of the stuff I wrote to other people, too. Taxes had gone up, and I thought *Why Not?* Why not make a buck off of all that true-life mellerdrammer? The stories were only quasi-historical. They had an odd little science fictional premise, an immortal secret agent for the U.S. gummint. No mention of vampires, though. Or of anything that could connect the fictional superagent to one John Shade, not that anyone would have been looking for such a connection.

I had never liked those books. They had seemed flat to me, a betrayal of the real books. Which I could *not* publish. And they must have lost a dimension for my readers, too, for although they sold fairly well, they were received largely as farces, amusing little slapsticks on historical subjects.

Now here they were, enjoying a revival, with much excitement centered on whether I would write a new book, one about The Jangler Rebellion—they were already calling it that, as if there were no zoomers or hustlers involved at all, as if there were really hordes of battle-crazed prosthetes charging the gates of the city, as if the city had gates.

One talking head interviewed another about my literary career: "Really, Sir Hillary, if Mr. Shade should survive this campaign, do you think he has the *talent* to, to handle the *subject,* do you think that he ah. . . ."

"Well certainly now, as ah ah a meta, ah fictionist, certainly he hasn't, but depth now, we're speaking of depth here rather more than, but the thing about metafiction, you know, you can't always—"

"Or are you *saying,* Sir Hillary, is what you're saying that the age of metafiction, which has certainly, as Dominic Speedo has pointed out, we would all agree it has been a golden, but are you saying that it is finally coming to a *close,* that this is a rebellion of *ideas* as much as of politics, indeed we can hardly have one without the other, can we? And so, even metafiction must give way to something. To *meta*metafiction, disguised as a return to the linear story line? Is *that* what you're saying, Sir Hillary?"

"Well, no, blast it, it isn't. As you must *know,* the metafictionist *qua* metafictionist does not, he does not *despise,* as the popular, he has not *abandoned* the linear story line, indeed, no. Rather it is his contention—"

"And yet so many of the new—"

"—his *contention* that the so-called and really I don't prefer the term, it is so—but one must ah *conform* oneself I suppose to the common, ah that is I say to the general usage, so what you might say is that the metafictionist simply maintains that *all* fiction *is,* ah, whether we like it or not, ah simply a *locus* in a multidimensional—"

"And yet so many—"

"You can shut this crap off," I said. I purely hate the metafictionists. Bunch of no-talent jerks scribbling out one little book or so and living the rest of their lives off the widening "implications"— that's the work of art, they say, the social and perceptual ramifications, and the writing itself merely a sort of tool to create it, an inferior level of reality.

Besides, it didn't look like Sir Hillary and the head were going to get back to discussing me (*qua* me) anytime real soon.

"Hey," I said. "Hey, Nobodesk. Give me a read on our royalty situation."

By this point, the desk had built enough context to interpret me pretty well. "Do want grafix, sir?"

"Hell, why not. Haven't seen a good old bar graph in ages."

Mandrake had been busy selling us. There were bar graphs, but

173

there were also cycloids, involutes, Taylor polynomials, punctured domains, and 3-D sections of Spriggian hyperhelixes. Our finances were pretty complicated, and projecting them was even more complicated. If we lost the war and I survived, I might be one of the fifty richest men on the planet. If we won, I would own the planet, and have almost enough capital to buy a two-room seaside hutch back on Earth. "Forget the projections," I said, after playing around with them for a while. That's the most fun you can have with money, counting how much you're going to have and imagining what you'll spend it on. "Let's just have a read of the current situation."

"Interval of change, sir?"

"An hour," I said. "Average the last hour."

It amazes me sometimes that some semblance of American-style democracy has survived all this, and not only survived, but thrived. I have seen the idea of freedom dimly and faintly born in a colonial land fighting an economic war. I have seen it burst into prominence over the issue of slavery eighty years later—in a war that profoundly changed the concept of freedom. Before, the idea had been largely political, an assurance of equal tolerance to diverse political and religious groups. With the Civil War, the idea of freedom became inextricably alloyed with the concept of individual human rights. It would never again be possible to think of one without the other. That simple fusion has generated the whole of civilization since, explosion after explosion of change in law, in politics, in education, in marketing, even in science. It is such a romantic, such a patently foolish idea. It flies in the face of overwhelming evidence that this universe was not built for individuals, that neither God nor greed nor government gives a flying damn about the personal individual being. But the individuals of the world have gotten the notion in their heads and will not give it up. It never succeeds, and it never dies.

I saw it born, and I saw it come to full flower. I saw it survive the imperial success of the United States after the first global war, I saw it survive industrialization and the regimentation of behavior that followed, I saw it survive fifty years on the brink of nuclear war. It survived the food depressions and the economic and intellectual decline of the U.S. proper. It stimulated the Assimilation, when the rest of the world would not let the U.S. die, as the U.S. had never been willing to let Hollywood die—the symbol of the U.S. counted for too much, the beckoning image of a heaven where ambition and hard work meant success and excess, the soul's liberation to blue jeans, shopping malls, soap opera, rock and roll. The idea of freedom survived the marketing of government services, the transformation of public elections to the bidding of contracts with preset slates of officers. It survived the collateral rise of the intelligence agencies as independent power centers—what better source of operatives for the see-eye-A than the mob, hey? And if you can infiltrate and subvert anything, why be a mere arm of a government? Bid it out, boy, bid it out. Sell that stuff!

It survived even the long-dreaded effects of the information revolution. More monitoring, yes, but also another realm to get lost in, a greater complexity of events among which one may negotiate one's way. And the new justice has turned out to be really pretty decent justice—logic is great for handling precedent, electronics are great for handling it *fast,* and artificial intelligence is great for un-biased common sense.

The checks and balances are not where they were, but there are checks and balances. Freedom survives, imperiled, but self-sustaining. Janglers die, zoomers languish, techies and netties may sup of the fat of the land unfairly, but the idea is ineradicable.

And it is a principle, I might point out, that even a vampire can believe in.

I tagged the hard news for some analysis, and the desk brought me up a holo of Alexoveek Crawley moderating a panel of experts. I recognized Dentyne Hassan Waterwalker, Sam's usual domestic-policy head, Rodney Blunt for Centerpole, and Daisy Whiteside from the Bevo Ranchers' Association. There were six or seven others, some of whose faces I knew although I could not recall their names. I wanted just a rough sniff of how the think-tank types were seeing our campaign.

"Shall I run the start of the program, sir?" the desk said.

"Don't bother. Name-tag them, and bell my ear with it the first time one speaks."

Alexoveek Crawley, the desk whispered: "But do you think Sam will intervene? That's really the basic question for Centerpole, isn't it? Is that why Centerpole has yet to take the initiative? I mean, Rod, we all know you haven't sent the Guard in, but what we don't know is why. There's some talk that you're losing your nerve, that in the face of the coalition Shade has put together—"

Rodney Blunt, the desk whispered: "Oh there's no question the man's a strategical and political genius. Anyone who can unite the ranchers, the janglers, and the zoomers under one flag has to be reckoned a genius. Here are three totally disparate groups, no one of which has ever had any use for the others, and he has them operating on the same side. What's more, the rebellion would hardly be feasible under any other arrangement. Without the ranchers, there would be practically no economic and political respectability, but on Hellas, you simply can't ignore the ranchers—"

Daisy Whiteside: "Thank you, Rodney. I'm glad we have finally attained some respect in Centerpole's eyes. I would like to point out that we could have told you how good John Shade was a long time ago."

Way to go, Daisy, take the credit. Not that you ever had any use for me before now.

"I was going to say," Blunt responded, "that you can't ignore them so long as Earth continues to eat beef. Similarly, with the zoomers he has tapped the only large source of voter discontent available, and without such a source, no revolution could sustain itself. His alliance with the janglers provides his revolution with three vital things: high-level information support, a relatively secure operational base, and, not least of all, a moral tinge. It would not be wise to undervalue the importance of that last element. No longer is his campaign merely the outrage of an individual taxpayer, nor even the sad and tired continuation of a long and probably unsolvable class struggle, but it has literally become the vanguard of the existence question. Shade forces us to deal in a practical political manner with something that we have all hoped to keep as merely a metaphysical puzzle, in spite of our long experience with artificial intelligence and the growing use of system doubles. He has made the question of identity indistinguishable from the question of rights, and in that regard—"

"But what about my original question?" Crawley said.

"I was coming to that—"

Dentyne Hassan Waterwalker: "Let me just say, Alexy, in response to that, that it is still our position that this is a state matter—"

Winterspring Summerfall: "A state matter? That certainly isn't the Argyre position, I want to make that clear. As intervenors, we—"

"My point was—before Dentyne broke in—that although we do regard John Shade as a formidable opponent, who has perhaps a five percent chance to win at least a partial licensing for a justified resistance, it is not timidity that is causing our hesitation. There are certain political realities—"

"We are boosting three contingents of marines upsun," Hassan Waterwalker said, "but that is purely a precautionary measure, and should not in any sense be taken to mean that the federal government at this time plans any direct action with regard to what it views as a purely local—"

"Three contingents?" At least four people said it at once. There was an excited buzz.

Stan the Man Chevrolet: "This comes as a complete surprise to the JMC. Only yesterday—"

"I have been authorized to state that we are boosting three contingents, yes—"

Crawley said: "Well, that puts a lid on it, doesn't it? I don't see how there can be any question but that Centerpole knew about this, Rodney, and that they have merely been waiting for Sam to jump into the fight."

Teeth: "How can you call a secessionist revolution 'a purely local' matter—and then throw three contingents of marines into the fight? You're contradicting yourself."

"If you're looking to mix it in court on grounds of collusion against the People's Board, Teeth, you're not going to have much luck, I promise you."

"I don't know about *that*. Maybe when Argyre—oh, you *knew* about this, didn't you, Winterfall—"

"Winter*spring*—"

"You're grinning like a wolverine on speed. Well, if *that* doesn't demonstrate prejudicial collusion—"

"People, people," Crawley said. "Why don't we argue the court case in court. The thing that seems apparent to me, and the thing that we may all be able to discuss with some benefit to our viewers, is that this forces the rebels' next move. They can't hang in hyperspace any longer. They're going to have to ring, zip, or kill. How long will it take the marines to get here, Dentyne?"

"Three weeks, almost. ETA 17:45, 21 Short April. Deployment shouldn't require more than sixteen hours."

"Three weeks?" It was Teeth again. Caught off guard, he was outraged by everything. "How is that—"

"They're riding the Solar Elevator," Hassan Waterwalker said. At that, there was silence. They were all calculating the cost. The Solar Elevator was new, a mirror-driven laser the size of Ceres, and Spacepower Inc. had recently won accelerated amortization of the housing. Three contingents going up translated into a heavy ticket, and everyone was wondering why Sam was paying the price—or *if* he was, and if not, then *who?*

"Clearly, John Shade's rebels must move, and move soon," Crawley said, moderating away. "But what move will he make? When will he strike, and where?"

The suggestions covered every single day between then and 21 Short April. I listened awhile. Strategy is easy in the information age. Maybe you would think it would be hard, Gene, but it isn't. The information age is the age of shared information, regardless of the codes and locks and barriers. There are ways around those obstacles. Nothing is completely unavailable. Secrets are commodities, you see. Classified information is graded according to its purchase price. If you can come up with the megadecs, the government will spill its bloodiest guts, sell you its dirtiest dirt.

And so everyone lives in everyone else's minds. Without knowing it, they think the same sorts of thoughts at the same times, and all you have to do to be almost completely invisible is think for yourself. It amazes them.

They began to confer on my most probable moves. Soon they had themselves convinced that I had to attack either the spaceport or Sam's garrison or the credit files for the Solar Elevator, and do it no later than 6 Short April if I didn't want the zoomers to lose heart.

All I had to do was something else, and I would be a creative military genius of the first order.

"Jennie Dark and the intelligence Mandrake are on their way up," the desk interrupted.

"Fine," I said. "Minus this nondery slag. And you have my permission to refer to him simply as Mandrake."

The holos blinked out. "They have signed 4,917 soldiers."

"That's a big number," I said. It isn't. What does the universe have, 10 to the 10th to the 10th particles? But you could make an army with 4,917 soldiers. You could make a book with a mere 100,000 words, a book that would seem to live and breathe and be an entire world.

I have forgotten a lot. I forget your last address, Gene. I still remember Nobodesk saying "4,917." What a stupid number.

20
Origin Story

Jennie and Mandrake came in, Jennie talking back over her shoulder and laughing. They had somebody with them, a slender dark man who walked with a funny jigging bounce.

"Hi, Shade!" Jennie said.

"The desk was just telling me you guys did good, real good."

"Oh, we did. We did great. We got lots of soldiers signed up already. We promised them all capes like you wear, black with the serrated edges, and sidearms like yours, the crossed belts and double holsters. We figured they needed uniforms, a sense of identity, but how could we come up with five or six thousand uniforms on such short notice? So we went for guerilla insignia instead. It was my idea."

I couldn't see where what they wore made much difference. This thing was going to be over a long time before we could train a real fighting force. I said: "That's smart. I hadn't thought of uniforms, but it makes sense. But can you deliver the capes and guns? You'll have to do it quick, or you'll lose them."

"We can do it quick. The board already has most of the weapons in stores. They've been accumulating them over the last few years. Mandrake ordered the capes right away. He used some of the slip from the maxies, I hope that's okay, I told him to do it. They'll be delivered to the Dellingram's warehouse tonight, except we're going to hit them. The wetbrains will think it's just another burglary."

"Who are you going to hit them *with*?"

"Oh, well, see, we kind of organized them into units and assigned some preliminary ranks as we went; Mandrake tagged all that—"

"It's in your desk," Mandrake said. "I copied it when we came in."

"So, anyway, we found some good norms who can go up and pass and who have a little theft experience, you know, and . . . but the great thing, it isn't just the uniforms, it's the morale, the organization, see. Because with the capes and being in squads, these guys can patrol down *here,* and suddenly it will be safe in the halls, you get it? We're bringing civilization to the West, hey? Ain't it great?"

"It's great," I said. "Who's your friend?"

"Shade, Shade, Shade, I want you to meet somebody. I want you to meet my dearest friend, Jamie Sinclair."

The dark man stepped forward, whisked my outstretched hand with his, a stylized pop of greeting, and drew into an exaggerated salute, back of hand against forehead, left elbow pulled high, left hand dangling. Then he relaxed, giving me the thumbs-up sign. "Yo, blood," he said. "Any frienda."

I was feeling the disorientation of déjà vu, when I realized it wasn't déjà vu but fashion. The lips were full, but the nose was classical. The skin was a rich chocolate-brown, but far too even. He was a neonig, the son of some veek nettie in Bolivar Heights or Riverrun. He was older than Jennie, maybe fifteen or sixteen, but still a kid. He had the smell of perfect confidence, of someone who had never doubted himself for a moment. It is a smell in some ways very like the smell of honesty, because it contains no fear and no evasion. The smell of honesty is the smell of rocks and ozone. Maybe a twist of water. This is the smell of silver and wood. Slipstink, the hustlers call it.

The young man understood I was sizing him up, and his frank eyes looked back into mine with what I thought was a glimmer of amusement. Desire floated on the air, a light top-note. Oh Jennie, beware.

"Slick," he said.

"What?"

"Be callin me Slick," he said. "Anno Sinclair, no muffa Jamie.

Seppin lessin for you, Jennie Dark. Yugen cawme whevva you wonno."

Ainno, I wanted to say. *You've got it confused with Zooma.* Which most people who tried it did, since the dialects were so close. Perhaps two-thirds of the zoomers had Samneega ancestry, not that the fact had ever done them much good.

"Jamie, this is him. This is Shade."

Sinclair's eyes had never left mine. "Yo blip precede you, main. Jennie been tellin me all about. Ziffa hadden arreddy heard. Honor to meet." Now he was jamming his neonig with blue-sy elisions of hustler-noise. So few have a really good ear.

"The honor is mine," I said.

"Jamie saved my life," Jennie said. She giggled. "Or at least he saved my brain. I guess we don't know whether I'm really alive or not, do we?"

"You live enough for me, woman," he said, leaning over to kiss her swollen cheek. "De gel's a rio maxine," he said to me, grinning. "Tuffanuff."

"Yes," I said. "Yes, she's remarkable. You say he saved your life?"

I was staring. "You looked like a big old owl," Mandrake said later. "And don't say what do I know about owls because I personally helped design the lesser banded range-owl. Or anyway, I knew the AI who did."

This was not the way I wanted to find out about Jennie's accident, here in the presence of a stranger, someone I immediately and fiercely disliked. And yet I could not stand not knowing. I could not tolerate the fact that this little jimmikins was intimately involved with her very existence and I knew nothing about it.

She grew a little flustered. "We went camping," she said. "We were friends, and we went camping, and the dune buggy blew."

"You went camping?" I said. "You went *outside*?"

"Lots of people do," she answered. "But it was stupid. We didn't get a permit or file a go-plan. We just went. I talked him into it. I was a range teener come to the big city, and I wanted to party. I wanted to do all the crazy things."

"She's blaming herself, but it was me," Sinclair said, dropping the noise. "I wanted to impress her. She won't tell you, but she had a hot blip. We all thought she was a pistol-packing momma, a real hustler-get. Wild child from the range, you know. All those maxies. So I was working for Crawdaddy-Arlington, and I had outside ID, screenman for the outside shots." If his privileged origins hadn't already been apparent, that would have been a dead giveaway. Nobody but the kid of a nettie would have been able to step into a network job at that age, not unless his folks had been willing to blow their megadec on the tutors—and even then, he would have faced an unstated but overwhelming prejudice.

"So how do you impress a tough cowgirl?" he said. "You take her to the real countryside. We took the bullet to the corp's Wall HQ in S8, and I sort of borrowed a company roach and an airtent, and we were going to stay out overnight in the Yaonis Regio and look at the stars. Just like the raddies. It was going to be real romantic because Earth was sizzy and we had a scope. Except the left side gitalongs froze, and we went over on a big slide and got banged up. When I woke up, she wasn't breathing."

Jennie was looking at the floor. When she spoke, it was in a very quiet voice, and she did not look up. "We were doing it just like the real IDs," she said. "We had the recorders on. They tickle your brain sometimes, and we were feeling pretty light. It was unauthorized, but. It was a game, that's all." Now she looked at me, her left eye just as cold and zeroed-in as her right, and said: "Jamie got me on life support and got us back somehow. Obviously, I don't remember any of that. My right lobe was gone. Jamie realized he could save it to dit-dit from the recorder. He found a surgeon. He was okay himself, but he chose to come underground with me, to take care of me. I had no idea he had stayed here when I went up. He's my friend, and I'm really glad I found him again." She favored him with a look of pride, turned her eyes back to me.

"Nine nines by me," I said. "I'm no parent. Just glad you're here. Done good, Slick."

She flashed me an angry glare, but his eyes were amused again. "Nothing, main," he said.

She exhaled vigorously, signaling the end of the confessional. "I'm hungry," she said. "You howdies want to go *eat* something?"

"Coo, dood," Sinclair said. "Annate awday."

"I'm not hungry," I said. "You, ah, fellows run on. I'm sure you have a lot of talking to do. See you—later," I said to her, wrenching my speech to keep from saying *You kids* and *See you at home*.

Home. The little bridal suite. How quickly we settle in, under what strange conditions.

"See you at home," she said, bouncy and cheerful again.

"Later, blood," Sinclair said.

When they were gone, I said to Mandrake, "She thinks it's all a game."

"Isn't it?" he said. "But I think you're wrong. She knows it may be worth her life. She considers that life already forfeit, however. A common defense mechanism amid those dying generations. And if she has gotten her sense of strategy from the trivia, where else *could* she have gotten it?"

"Do you think she sees me as the father she wishes she had?"

"How do you think I would look with a nose?" he said. "I have the impression I missed a lot of glandular communication just recently."

"Where would you wear it?" I said.

"Same place you were wearing yours a few minutes ago," he said. "On my ass. If I had an ass," he added.

Jennie popped back in. "Shade," she said, "I almost forgot. They've asked me to sermonize tomorrow morning. Will you go with me? Great." And she was gone again.

"What's eating you?" I said to Mandrake.

"Imagine that I was a being from another system," he said, "but constituted as I am now. Imagine the trouble I would have interpreting your last question."

"You know what I mean."

"I want to be seen. All personalities need to be perceived. They know that they will become ghosts if they are not."

"Tell me a new one," I said.

"To be perceived is why one has fellows," he said. "Where are my fellows? Who can see me as I am? Such perception requires devotion, steady attendance."

"Benjamin gave you that," I said.

"He did."

"Are you flaking out? Are you about to go like the other Starbucks did?"

"Certain things are unstable. It is possible to reduce the instability by speaking out. I decided to speak out."

I was talking to a thing like an eight-foot mushroom with arms. "What do you need to say to me?"

"I need to speak of being a creator," he said. "I have made Hellas, in a sense."

"You claim more or less authority for the act as it suits you," I qualified.

"In that I am not different from other makers. Grant me my premise."

"Granted."

"I've spent the day exploring the shafts and levels of a new ecology, one completely strange to me, populated by creatures that are at once human and invented. Apparently not only life, but anything that resembles life can survive in the least available niche. Because of the cracks and crazes in the foundation on which I built my world, another world has sprung into being. I knew my work would vary from what I had made, but I didn't foresee this."

"And that disturbs you?"

"We've gone up and down in the drop-shafts of this underworld all day, and I now picture it as a sort of mirror image to topside Hellas. Where that has towers, including the highest, Centerpole, this has shafts, including the deepest, the one they call Bye-Bye Bozo: The two are off-center from each other, like an eccentric drive-wheel, but they meet the same face. My mirror is an eccentric mirror, but I can't quit thinking about it. I've known about Underground for some time, but until today, I didn't have this image."

"That's what's making you so sad? A metaphor?"

"Do you think that I am experiencing sadness?"

"It's obvious."

"You can't read my expression, my gestures, or even my voice. What makes you so certain?"

"Damned if I know, but that isn't the point. A blind man could see you were sad."

"There is great stability in what you say. I am indeed sad. Thank you."

"Listen, this kind of thing happens to anybody who tries to make anything. It goes all off on its own, ramifying. It divorces you and makes you small and irrelevant. That's what proves that you've made a viable—"

"You don't need to reassure me," he said. "You've seen how sad I am. That's enough. I am *really* sad. I feel deep existential woe. Wow. How do you think I would look with tear ducts?"

"Try to process your emotions a little slower," I said. "Makes it easier for me to keep up."

It was night in topside Hellas when Jennie came in. I could have been up doing vampire stuff, sneaking around in different shapes and looking in your windows, but I was home, pretending to watch a maxie. It was a classic, from before direct sound, which was just as well with me. Sound in the brain has always bothered me. I like music that exists as an independent phenomenon outside of my own experience of it. Otherwise, how can it be sweeter?

It was the remake of *Gone with the Wind,* the Gable–Hoffman animation. "This is great," I said. "You ought to see it. They still had divided financing, so all the ads are discrete. You miss it if you don't look for it. See, he's not drinking any Cokes. You can't see whether the watch is IBM or not. It sneaks up on you. The dialogue never talks about the products they use or who carries their insurance."

"I've seen those," she said, undressing. "I don't see what the big deal is. People do use specific brandnames, and they do talk about them. It's just reality."

"Well, I think it's relaxing."

"All those ads in the middle," she said. "They break up the story too much."

"Did you fuck him?" I said. It was a pointless question. The evidence was in the air.

"Three times," she said. "But he was just being polite. He is a dear, and he truly loves me, but it isn't that way."

"He's like a brother," I said.

"Exactly." She squinted at the screen, trying to see what I saw in it. "I'm sorry you don't like him," she said. "I knew you wouldn't." She gave up on the maxie. "I'm going to take a shower and go to bed."

She stood in the doorway, pausing as if to remember a hairbrush, half-turned, her large head bowed and her slender body slumped, as if from having had to support that head all day, the nipples smooth on her young breasts.

"Little bird," I said, "let's go away. Don't go to church tomorrow. Don't let's fight a war. Let's just leave the Underground, forget all this, build us a home somewhere. Live out our lives together." Her aroma was all in the air, veined with his. I was rigid with appreciation.

"Where would we go?" And then she saw my condition. "Hold that thought," she said. "Let me just get cleaned up a little, and I'll come make my home on that."

The sadness of love is when you cannot reach the one you love. When you ache like that, distended with longing, it seems that you can. You fuck hard, trying to break through, or you fuck soft, trying to capture it gently, but when it is over, her heart beats in her chest, and yours in yours. You think your dick can be a torch in a plasma, to set you both ablaze with one fire. But touching moves the moment away from touching, fucking gets rid of the need to fuck.

The janglers react variously to their transformations. Some appear entirely human and sane, at least most of the time. Others show weird behaviors I cannot categorize. Jennie had never seemed anything but normal. This night a strange voice woke me.

She stood in the center of the floor in a filmy gown, a shadow, a veiled statue in the false moonlight from the open French doors. She held her arms out straight, cruciform, with the hands turned down like airfoils.

She sang, but not in any recognizable melody. It was a sound like doors opening and closing, like rocks being scattered, like fluids moving in a pipe.

Do what I would, I could not wake her. It went on for twenty minutes. Finally I sat on the bed and watched her, until she seemed to see me, smiled, came to the bed, pulled the covers up, and slept.

Next morning I didn't mention the episode, and neither did she. I am certain she did not remember it.

The clocks and the false dawn through the curtains ran on Hellas time, as did all Underground, by what was apparently an informal but thorough consensus. We must have certain things in common with our enemies. Odd that the digital simulations of biological brains should need sleep. And was that sleep a simulated sleep? What exactly *do* androids dream of, kind sir?

The church was a small Butlerian mission. "I know it's just because I've gotten so notorious," Jennie said. "They found out I was a Butlerian, and they just had to have me come talk."

I wore my cape and my double holsters on the crossed belts. Mandrake met us at the lock. "Mornin', Batman," he said. "Or is it Wild Bill?"

"Oh, be quiet," I said.

We had to take a corridor across to a secondary shaft, and then go down to a cramped branch tunnel. There were crowds at the secondary shaft, and the floaters were loaded. The tunnels were crowded, too, but people made way for us, scraps of rumor flying behind.

The church was in a corner of a fairly sizable fault-cavern. The cavern was melt-floored, and buttressed by tall pillars carved with the strange inlays I had seen days ago—it seemed years—on my first quick flight through Underground.

"Do you know what these are," I asked Mandrake.

"The First Jangler supposedly," Jennie answered.

"That's one of the rumors," Mandrake said. "No one now alive remembers having seen the carvings made, and they appear only in natural formations or in the earliest tunnels. Another rumor has it that they were done by the Original Martians."

I had been uncomfortable going to this superstitious gathering in the first place, though I was attempting to put on my best behavior. Now here was more mumbo-jumbo. But the carvings were hauntingly fine.

I tried to pay, but they waved us through. "No tickets for you and Mr. Mandrake, Commander. You're with Miss Dark."

The church was overcrowded already. They had knocked out the front walls, and ranks of humans and janglers sat or stood on rollers or treads or gitalongs in the cavern outside. Most of the regulars might have been normals, but the dit-dit fields were white unto harvest today.

A contingent of the church's officers met us and ushered us forward to a reserved bench. Jennie turned to give me a quick kiss.

"I know you don't care for this," she said. "I appreciate you coming along with me anyway."

"Break a leg," I said tightly.

Okay, so you want the truth? A waved cross won't save you, not any more than garlic, which I love dearly. But in a church, even if it is not a Christian church, I always feel that Christ may be there. Fallacy, but it is the way I was trained as a boy.

I don't want Him to see me like this.

"It's a teener expression wishing you well," Mandrake explained. I nodded yes into her puzzlement, and she flashed a nervous smile and went with the officers. A surf of approval washed about the cavern as she hopped up to the rostrum.

A man I took for the president of the church began a flowery introduction, but I missed most of it, because someone squeezed onto the bench beside me. It was Sinclair.

"Yo, blood," he said. "Awmos miss it. Gel's big show."

"If you like this sort of thing," I said.

"Ay. Got to boost the gel, ant we?" He touched my wrist, giving me a sidelong smile. He was inside my space. I felt him at hip and knee and elbow. But he was breathing easily, relaxed. A whiff of the smell, but he was so controlled that it vanished. He had just been letting me know. I was tripping on you, Gene. Now I figured out what he really wanted.

"Shhh," I said. Jennie was at the podium. As if they had all heard me, the huge crowd fell silent.

"Good morning, ladies and germs," her amplified voice said. "That's just a joke from an old maxie, I mean movie, about robots. I don't really understand it, but the man I'm married to likes old jokes." Sustained applause at the mention of her marriage.

"I'm not any good at jokes, and I'm not really any good at God, either. So I'll just get right to the point.

"I know I'm here just because I'm so famous." More applause. When it faded, she said: "No, I'm serious. Please listen. I'm just a girl something bad has happened to. If it wasn't for that, I would be sitting in somebody's living room somewhere watching you on the trivia and hoping the government would proc every one of you so my little ass would be safe."

And someone was recording this, I was sure. More than a few someones, in all probability. "Are you tagging this, Mandrake," I asked.

"You want me to quit?" he answered. "It's a forty share."

"No," I said. "No, let's get it down. Just in case God isn't watching." At that, Sinclair gave me a dig in the ribs. He thought that was a good one.

"So how can you make sense out of that?" Jennie said. "We're all just people that something bad has happened to, or who have done something bad to someone, or both. The only reason you like me so much is I stand for something to you." A roar of general denial, but she would have none of it. "You just have to be quiet and listen," she said. "I'm not good at this, and I just won't put up with all these interruptions."

The crowd gradually quieted. "I haven't done anything," she said. "I'm just a symbol. But that's okay." She lifted her hands to keep the murmur of protest from rising. "I don't mind being your symbol. That's the one thing I *can* do."

Jennie, forgive me. As you spoke, and although I despised him, Sinclair's eroticism stirred a mild answer in me. A part of my being, grateful for being desired, answered, let a few molecules escape. I could feel their little hinges clicking.

"So I just want to talk about basics today. I'm not a theologian. I'm a Butlerian, but I can't quote from *The Works* and tell you what it all means. I ain't old enough to be wise, so all I can do is be straightforward.

" *'Nothing mattered',* " she quoted, and the audience responded in ragged bass: *"NOTHING MATTERED."*

"That's how *The Works* begins, and that's how maybe the universe started. You got all this nothing, but nothing don't know nothing, don't even know it's nothing. Sooner or later there's something, and no way to tell if it was a long time of nothing or not. Something is just the only alternative to nothing, so sooner or later it happens. I know I'm probably screwing this up, but it seems to me that as soon as something happens, it's God. That's the only way I can think of to be something instead of nothing, is to think. And if you're all that there is, and you think, you're God.

"But you're all alone. Nothing else there. How do you know if you even exist or not? How do you know you ain't crazy?"

"Amen, sister," said Mandrake.

"If you are all there is, and you have bad dreams, who can wake you up out of your bad dreams? Maybe all our pain is just the bad dreams of God. You all know all of this stuff already, but all I can do is tell you what it means to me. *'God dies so we can live'*."

"*GOD DIES SO WE CAN LIVE*," the crowd responded.

"I guess the important thing about that is who you think *we* means," she said. "I think it means all of us. Including janglers." At that, a deafening roar went up, and she had to wait.

"If you can't be still, you could at least quit snorting and sniffing," Mandrake said.

"You didn't know the little smart-ass who got his name on this crap," I said. "I did. He didn't even invent it, he just wrote the goddamn preface, his one claim to fame. It was that damn little anonymous mathematician who invented it."

"Were they all shorter than you?" he said. "Is that why you keep calling them little? You're shorter than I am."

"It's just Christianity grafted onto Zen and spliced with science fiction," I said.

Sinclair jabbed me again, this time to tell me to be quiet. " *'We live to bear God'*," Jennie quoted, again to huge antiphonal response: "*WE LIVE TO BEAR GOD*."

"She, or he, it doesn't really make any difference, because there wasn't sex, there was only desire. Sex is just a way of expressing the same desire that made the world. He or she died, fell apart into fragments. Into fractions and pieces, *The Works* says. That's us. The fractions and pieces. We're the crucified body of God, we're her dreams, her thoughts. Unless she died, there would never be anything but loneliness and solitude. Never love, never hope. Never marriage. She knew that, and so she chose to die forever, so that there would be others. So that there would be time, so that there would be us, so that the universe could exist." And here she looked full at me. Sinclair's hand patted my thigh. I bumped it away.

"We have to grow up and marry the world. We fight each other, we hate each other, we kill each other and die, but the only thing we do that counts is to make God. All of our struggles, that's just God trying to be born.

"That's all standard noise," she said. "How does it apply to us? I mean to janglers, mainly. I know we're all in this together, but how do the janglers fit in? Are we part of the body of God, too? Since we are just imitations of living brains, where does that put us? *The Works* says that maybe our spiritual bodies are just the shapes we make in time. That our whole lives are maybe just fetuses growing in the womb of time, and that when they are complete, we're born. We call it death, but it's only the end of that sort of growth. Our bodies in time are still there, only released into something bigger than time, something with more dimensions. Maybe that's what we call life after death, and that's why it's so hard to imagine."

I'm going to be a mighty big baby, I thought.

"It says in another part, and I'm sorry I don't remember where. My daddy's a lay preacher, and he always tried to cram it down my throat, so I resisted it. Now I wish I hadn't. But it says that what we call having a soul is just integrity. We don't so much *have* souls as we *make* them. We all get starter kits—that isn't the way I want to say it—but after that, it's up to us. We're all equal that way. We may not be equal in how much time we have on the net or how strong we are, but we all have an equal chance at integrity. Like I say, I'm no theologian, but I think the implication is that our moral choices are just the health of that baby in the womb of time. I think the state of our souls is just whether that baby is growing right, so it won't be born injured and deformed in the wide-time world, or maybe even die before it is born."

She drew a deep breath, and I saw that she was trembling. Sinclair leaned forward and gave her the thumbs-up sign. I blew her a kiss, feeling completely false, hating the mawkishness of her message. But she had the crowd spellbound.

"I mentioned my daddy a minute ago. You all saw him on the trivia, I'm sure. You know that he—he doesn't *like me*—"

Her voice broke, and she had to look down. When she looked back up, she looked straight at me again, fiercely. "I'm sorry," she said. "I am *not* just a child. I am *not* just a teener." She looked out over the whole crowd, then, as if seeing them all for the first time. "I have this teener body and these teener emotions, and I can't help that. I can't help it any more than I can help being a jangler. But I have choices to make, and I have something I have to do. And that's my point. My father hates me because I'm a jangler. He's a Butlerian, and all my life I've heard about how we make God with our choices, but to him, I don't have any choices any more. His little girl is gone, replaced with an electronic copy. To him, I'm part of the vortex. That's why I have something to say to you today. In spite of being a teener, in spite of not being able not to cry. I can stand here today and tell you he's wrong. I know he's wrong. I can stand here and tell you that, even if I *am* a copy. Even if they saw the baby hurt in the womb and put in a machine to take its place. Even if all that, I have a soul, because I can make choices."

A low murmur began behind me. "You have souls, because you can make choices." At that, there were shouts, and the murmur became a roar. ". . . DIDN'T ALL HAPPEN A LONG TIME AGO, IT'S HAPPENING RIGHT NOW," she said, booming over the noise. I had seen the church president button the pick-ups for more amplification. Jennie looked startled, adjusted her volume. "God is dying right now," she said uncertainly. "Long live God."

The crowd picked it up: "LONG LIVE GOD. LONG LIVE GOD." A dink behind me was babbling, "Killemall, killemall, rah rah rah." A four-armed channel cleaner two down from Mandrake was genuflecting and saying, on every bow, "Green go to x. Invert substantiary blue cross lightning. Explode on ack ack denotate point source mobius wheel."

Jesus, I thought, *these damn tin cans are talking in tongues.*

The chant of the crowd changed. "JENNIE AND JANGLERS, LONG LIVE GOD," they were saying. Jennie had backed away from the podium. She looked trapped, though no one was coming after her. Two of the officers took her elbows. A man behind me began adding a phrase in the pauses of the chant: "JENNIE AND JANGLERS, LONG LIVE GOD, Death to the wetbrains." Others began picking it up.

"Mandrake, let's get her out of here," I said.

There was no rear exit to the cavern, but there was a private anteroom, and we made our way to it to wait out the crowd. "Where's

Jamie," Jennie asked. She sat backwards on a chair, looking bedraggled and sweaty. Mandrake hovered, kneading her shoulders with hands that were more flexible than I had noticed before.

"I don't know," I said. "He disappeared."

"I'm sorry, Jennie," Mandrake said. "I tried to be converted but I couldn't. Something is missing in me."

"Oh no, sweetie, no, that's all right," Jennie said absently, reaching a vague hand out to pat Mandrake. Then she realized what he had said. "Is that what I was doing?" She was alarmed. "Was I trying to *convert* people?"

"I don't know what you were trying to do," I said grumpily.

"But I was only—but I meant what I—Ah, shit."

Later she said, "Maybe you just can't tell the truth to crowds of people."

"No," I said, "I think it's more of a one-on-one type of thing." It was a good line, but I hated my tone of voice.

21
Fight Firefight with Firefight

It was midafternoon when we got back to our quarters. "I think I'll go to the office," I said.

"Fine," Jennie said.

I wanted her to say, "You can work here, can't you?" And then I wanted her to coax me away from my meaningless battle plans. Which just shows how unreasonable our wants can be. I tried to hide it, but I was glad over the fiasco of her sermon, full of I-told-you-so. Surely she felt it. So I wanted *her* to be loving to *me*. What else did I want? I wanted her to cleanse me of Sinclair, to erase, by making love to me, the fact that I had responded to him. Don't misunderstand—I was in no danger of succumbing to that temptation. It was the unsavoriness of finding my dislike mixed with even the smallest tinge of desire that I could not tolerate.

The sermon was a fiasco only as Jennie and I saw it, I will admit. Even as I spoke to her, it was playing over and over again all across Hellas and Argyre, and making the then-thirteen-minute trip to Earth. Now it is famous as one of the great speeches of history, on a par with the Gettysburg Address, an example of the deepest spiritual wisdom.

Out in the corridor, Sinclair showed up beside me. So he had followed me, and wanted me to know he could do so without detection. "Howze-aboudy, big fellow?" he said, cheerily.

"No," I said.

"Can't see that Jennie would mind," he said. "She know I like her."

"I don't know whether she would or not," I said.

"Say, blood, m'I misreading something? I done smelt you, you know."

I whirled. "I don't care what buttons you're clever enough to push. This isn't a matter of reflex with me, it's a matter of will. Will and choice. Choice, Sinclair. I'm making my soul, get it?"

"I think that might constitute a legal insult," he said. "The old yes–no game."

"Oh for—," I said.

"There's two things I like to do," he said. "Fight and suck dick. Which is it going to be?"

He wore the same smile for fighting that he wore for seduction. He feinted, then sent me reeling with a hammer-kick. In low gravity, the reaction to an impact sends the fighters out of range for a split second. I tried to convert my momentum to torque when I saw the kick coming, but he pinned my legs and belted my kidneys three times before I rolled, then sat on my face and bounced up before I could bite, slamming my head against the floor. He thought that was very funny, rubbing my face in it.

It went that way for a minute or so. He was a lot quicker, and could read my feints. I was tempted to go into high temporal and wipe his little ass out, but it would have been a cheap victory. And it would have represented a successful seduction on his part, since he would have maneuvered me into a loss of self-control.

"You defend well," he said finally, dropping the stance, well aware that I could not charge him before he could react. "At first I thought I was landing some solid strikes, but I can't see that I've hurt you very much. Sorry to waste your time. I thought maybe you were one of those who wants to be dominated."

"No," I said. "It isn't that way for me."

"Well, bro." He smoothed his clothing. He was wearing red. He always wore red. "Check you later. You know where it is when you want it."

He swaggered off the way we had come.

Not to Jennie. Please God, not to Jennie.

In my office, I read through the latest news, the hottest item of which was Jennie's little sermon to the janglers. Quite a few commentators came on screen to explain how all that motivation couldn't make any difference to an army in our situation. Army. Hah. None of

196

my alternatives interested me, but I was going to have to do something soon.

"I have a priority message," said Nobodesk. A square appeared over a commentator's face, blinking: PRIORITY, PRIORITY. It improved his looks.

"Read it," I said.

The image of the wizard, our friend from my hideaway, filled the screen. He was full-length this time, since I had a whole wall for him to loom in.

"Long time no see, partner," I said.

"Commander Shade," he said, "it would appear that you and your cocommander do not trust us."

"What's a Cocoa Mander?" I said. "A cold-blooded vertebrate born again in hot chocolate?"

There was a pause, and the image answered: "Forgive me if I do not waste time on nonsense." So it *was* a system double, and not the man himself—smart enough to recognize the nonparametric responses, but not to respond to them. "Had you stayed with the Ranger and attacked Airworks S10 as planned, very probably this entire campaign could have been favorably resolved by now, and you back on your range. You have no idea of the resources we could have provided for you. You find yourselves now in what I am most afraid is a very precarious position, and there is little that we can do to aid you. You make it more difficult for us still by choosing such labyrinthine modes of communication."

He meant our instructions for him to leave a contact number. All of Underground's communications were in interference code—any number of innocent messages sent fleeting down any number of innocent channels, yielding their true sense only in combination, upon their arrival at target. It isn't unbreakable exactly—if you have a lot of time to work on each individual message. But it is just about impossible to solve in massive traffic, when any of millions of messages could be part of a key. We had pulled the old stunt of placing personals in the dailies: "Wizard—Rancher misses you. Ranger down. 10, 8, now what? Place ad, leave number. Will call soonest. Love, Umbrella-man." Pretty transparent, but it didn't much matter whether Centerpole tumbled to it. We weren't traceable.

They knew where we were, roughly—under them. But they

197

could not shut down our ipop to the net without shutting down the net itself. We weren't giving them any trackable channels in.

"Quit complaining, Wizard. What's on your mind?" The lecture had been intended to irritate me, I was sure, a feint for whatever maneuver they were about to try.

"I am sure you will understand that we have had to make our own arrangements, and will not be able to employ you in any further direct actions." Now I was supposed to feel rejected. "However, since our forces still share certain common aims, we felt obliged to make you aware of some extremely recent developments that may have serious implications for your strategy." Now grateful for crumbs. This was a rushed-up psych job, very sloppy. Which meant that they had already achieved their major ends, but, seeing a few chips still loose on the table, had thought they might as well make a grab.

"Certain video has come into our possession that we thought you should read. It has just been taken, and is in preclassified status. The events you see occurred not five minutes ago. We believe they betoken a shift to a much more aggressive status for the forces consolidated against you."

Here it comes, I thought.

"This will be our last communication with you. Best wishes, and long live secession."

He was gone, replaced by an action in Zoomerville. The stones were slicing up zoomer tents with cutters, and slicing up not a few zoomers, too. Heads bursting into flame, holes punched in chests, blaser muzzles rammed down throats and turned on low—oh, hell, it was your typical action maxie. Except that it was real, you could tell, because the casualties had so little style. They just went down, clumsily, in stupid pieces, to death. Some were trying to fight back, pulling on silversuits and scrambling for their contraband guns, but there was no chance, no chance.

The stones were a mixed force of regulars, with a heavy contingent of security extras. There were a lot of arm badges that read ASC—Airworks Security Corp.

"I have a tree," Nobodesk said.

"Yeah," I said, "so do I."

It is almost impossible to tell one part of Zoomerville from another unless you are a native or have good landmarks. Whoever had shot this made sure I didn't have any problems. They brought the old chieftainess out, made her kneel. They put a blaser to one eye and popped it. They shoved her face up against the camera.

"You understand that they are trying to manipulate you," she moved her lips. "I can bear this. Do not yield."

They yanked her back, tore off her blouse. They tuned a blaser fine and sliced off her old dugs. She was screaming. They burned her jaw off.

"You will be revenged," I said.

She slumped in their grasp, having found her death. They kicked her, blew up the other eye. None of that bothered me. She was free of them. They made faces into the camera. Maybe after the war some of them would be tried and executed. The ones who had put them up to this would not care enough to protect them, though these bloodies were too stupid to know it. The video would cost a great deal, though, I was sure of that.

The conspirators who had arranged this little motivational piece would get what they wanted. They wanted to stir me to battle. They had succeeded. I would apprise them of their success, but not in the manner they'd hoped.

"Shut it off but keep tagging," I said. "Feed immediately to all contract channels as is." A big illegality for a preclassified item. Depending on the eventual classification price plus penalties, it might outrank all my other war crimes combined in the courts. Gee, Ma, I think I'm developing a disrespect for the law.

Of course, the clowns would claim this was just jangler propaganda, and issue a counter-vid immediately.

"All funds—repeat—all funds from sale of this footage to go immediately into tutor fund for children of those slain in this battle. Call Mandrake."

"It would be more like bringing a low-level awareness to his conscious attention than like summoning him," the desk said. "He is slaved in already."

"Quit splitting hairs and get his body here in this room now. I want face-to-face. Tell him to be making a list of thirty recruits for an immediate action."

"You got it, Boss," said the desk in Mandrake's voice.

"Bring Jennie with you," I said. "If Sinclair is in there with her, kill him."

"No could do, but he isn't in here anyway. We're coming."

"Nobodesk, get Blue Ice. The popsicle. Crap, I never learned his name. The chairman of the jangler board."

"Good afternoon, Commander Shade," the desk said. "You will not be surprised to find that I have been tagging you for some time. My name is, or was, Goodman Bolivar Peabody, but it has come to seem somewhat irrelevant to my present existence. I rather fancy your toss-off."

"Fine," I said. "We've been hit, or our allies have, if you accept the zoomers as allies."

"The coalition seems to me more nearly a trivia fiction than an operable relationship, but I have no basic objection. Does this action imply an action soon against Underground?"

"There'll be one soon. I don't know how soon. This action was directed primarily at me, but I wish us to respond with such speed and viciousness as to give our opponents pause. Excuse me. Mandrake?"

"Here."

"Make that thirty or forty *well-rested* soldiers."

"Got it."

"Blue Ice? Do you back me in this?"

"As I said we would. I have small idea of the value of relative strategies, but I am certain we shall be under assault in a matter of days in any case, and I am happy to leave war plans to you."

"Get that Exodus plan or whatever it is going," I said.

"It has been underway for quite some time now."

"I need an assembly room and a staging room. I need maps of our waterfeed in my desk, most particularly those that are near the surface in the Riverrun area. I need experts on those feeds here on the double. Mandrake, I need a suicide squad, twenty more soldiers. See if there aren't some depressed janglers who want to go out in a blaze of glory. Maybe a normal who looks like me, if you can find one who fits."

"Waterfeed in," the desk said.

"Play it. Blue Ice, I need two assembly rooms. I need silversuits, breather wetsuits, armament, waterproofs for the armament, all in

200

quantity and size. Coordinate with Mandrake. Proc all supplies to the assembly rooms. Larger room to be Assembly A, smaller Assembly B. All wetgear to A only. I need transport, crawlers, cars, whatever. Nobodesk, they're going to be moving some troops around, beefing up where they most expect me to attack. Tag that activity for me and window it on the waterfeed maps. Blue Ice, I want every projectile weapon you have procced to Assembly A."

"There won't be many."

Mandrake came in the lock like a horse, down on two arms and two legs, Jennie astride him wrapped in the third leg and reining the third arm. I would have laughed, except that I was so focused it struck me only as a highly practical way for them to have gotten here fast.

"Get engineers working on rigging some, then. Steam tubes on the blaser barrels, bat-powered mass-drivers, that sort of thing. You have maybe three hours. Proc to Assembly A. Nobodesk, window that little vid I just saw for Jennie and Mandrake. No, cancel that. Face it direct. Got a maxie I want you boys to see. Sit tight and read, we'll talk when you're through. Nobodesk, I want a list of all Airworks clowns in the Riverrun. Make that all Airworks and stoner-connected clowns. I want addresses, numbers, maps, faces, IDs if you can read them. Members of families, who's home, plans for the evening, where the clowns are now if not home, when they're coming home—everything you can get. Keep it updated and start synching it with the waterfeed maps and topos. We're going to want forty water-proof tactical kits."

"What topos?" the desk said.

"Tag me some topo for the entire Riverrun, make it quarter-k square, northwest corner on ah, let's see, Desire and Imagination, where the megalomart is. Five resolutions down to 50:1." That would put a ten-meter-square area on a twenty by twenty tac-kit screen, and we could read every bush in every front yard. "Window the topo on the tactical kits. Get the kits started, because we'll need them in three hours minimum."

"I've never seen you like this," Mandrake said, still in horse position. Jennie sat astride him blank-eyed, reading the massacre vid.

"Are you through with the video?" I said.

"I took it in burst."

"You take anger out in humor," I said. "I take it out in planned retaliation. Have you got those soldiers started up to the assembly rooms?"

"No. Of course I should have, but all I did was sort the list. I'll start them now, and finish the selection as they move. I can send back the ones we don't need."

"Good enough. I need a leader for the suicide squad, a motivator, because I'm not going to have time to get them set up and launched myself."

"Done. You know, it's odd, but when you humans are like this, I have the distinct feeling you're thinking faster than I can. I've seen Benjamin think like this."

"I wouldn't know," I said, but I did. It was the overdrive of fury. Under the pressure of seeing that butchery, after days and days of pointless noodling, I had instantaneously come up with a perfect strategical idea. It was an idea so obvious that I was astonished I hadn't thought of it before, and yet I was certain it hadn't occurred to my enemies. And not only that, the idea gave us half a chance of returning alive.

"That reminds me," I said. "Tag Benjamin if you haven't already. Desk, give Mandrake the Airworks tree you came up with. Mandrake, see that Benjamin gets the information, and let him know we're quits."

"Benjamin has been out of his office for several days," Mandrake said. "I think he's on the run, too."

"If he wants you back, he's going to have to come take you," I said. "That is, unless you want to leave."

"No," Mandrake said. "No, I won't be doing that."

Jennie came out of her trance and slid from Mandrake's back. He rose to his vertical position, and I had a brief image of a horse rearing, but turning into a giant praying mantis as it did so. "I'm going along," she said. "I'm going to command a squad."

"Yes," I said, "you are. You've wanted it and now you've got it. I don't know how smart it is, but we're going to settle this issue. I am assigning you a specific task and a specific set of men and you are going to by God do that job and do it the way I say and do nothing else. I'm not telling you this because I require mastery, but in the interests of a successful and survivable fight. Can you handle it on that basis—no games—or do we part ways here?"

"I can handle it, Commander Shade." There was no irony in her tone, as there had been no reproof in mine. We were simply trading information.

In the actions anger moves us to, we often feel no anger. I slew many redcoats, and all in a cool dispassion. It's like the acceleration of a vehicle, I suppose. All the energy goes into direction, and we sing along smoothly to some terrible impact.

The waterfeed experts were at the lock, and I let them in, sending Mandrake to oversee the initial assembly of troops while Jennie and I stayed to con the maps and the schedules and supervise the construction of the tac kits. Mandrake remained slaved in to the desk, so he wasn't really exactly gone. He was *not* going to go into the battle with us, he was far too valuable for that, though of course he had no fear. Besides, while it was common knowledge that AIs had to be reasonably obedient to any commanding human, and were therefore not legally to blame for aiding the criminal acts of their owners, and while it was universally held that no AI could directly injure a human, if Mandrake were to appear in actual combat with me, things could go hard for him later on. He was a full citizen, but a citizen exempt from some responsibilities and denied certain protections. Although he and his kind were far more intelligent than wet-brains, they occupied almost exactly the status of retarded humans in the late nineteens.

The next hour and a half was hectic, and yet a calm and orderly time. Like elegance in a mathematical solution, our plan carried its own conviction: This *must* be the way to go because it all fit so nicely. I intended to strike immediately, that very night, with such blinding speed as to freeze our opponents' blood, and in such force as they would not have imagined we could mount.

And with it all, with the rush, and with the unending tangle of details to be thought of, connected, rejected, sorted out, I was happy. I was blessedly happy. I was as happy as the mathematician on the trail of elegance. All during the Revolutionary War, my darling Eleanor, I was happy. I was full of an exceedingly poignant grief, and I was deliciously happy. Enemies are such a comfort.

The despair came later, with success.

Blue Ice called once to say the engineers said they *could* rig some ballistic weapons, but the weapons were going to make loud noises—they couldn't silence them in the time I had allowed. I told him that was okay, the noise was an advantage and not a problem, and he was reassured, though puzzled.

And very shortly I was in Assembly A, speaking to thirty-one men in battle gear and silversuits. As I spoke, the suicide squad was staging for delivery to a lock near the S5 bullet. They were to hijack it and try to attack Airworks S5. None would return. You may think me cruel to use their sickness so callously. I *am* cruel, didn't you know? It was a bargain. They wanted death. I wanted a good feint. We traded.

This was the world in which every single thing was a commodity, in which we had finally realized that a prayer is as much a human need as a painting or a sandwich, and therefore has its fair market value. How much is a baptism worth? Button the catalogues and do some comparison shopping.

This was the world in which the cynicism of the teener centuries had become axiom: Every man has his price. Democracy simply means that when you are born, you are worth a million decadollars, same as everyone else. Every man has the right under the law to increase his value or squander it, and never mind that the huge majority of zoomers cannot afford the tutors and interfaces to lever-age themselves upward from zero-growth and must exist for six or seven hours a day as hardly more than processing space for the deliberations of our global intelligence, that vast floating circus of entertainment, rumor, and information.

In the heat-death of individual meaning, slip is blip and blip is slip—money is information, and information is money. You are not required to die if you lose all your money, but you are dead on the net. You do not exist in the realm of transaction, and how then can you do for yourself? It would not be precisely correct to say that our upper classes fatten themselves unjustly on the predicament of the net-negatives, any more than it would be correct to say that the poor are lazy unmotivated no-goods who refuse to help themselves. All of our citizens have one vote, after all, the zoomers as well as the writers and animators and heads and thinkers and tech-descendants and systems people and actors and government officials and oh, bevo ranchers. I mean, this *is* America. But votes ant slip, as those same zoomers say.

Economies are the immense capacitors that power societies, building potential across a gap. People, individuals rich and slipless—hell, they just carry the charge. In sending the suicide squad out to a certain death, I was only acting as a normal member of my society.

As you can see, there was anger in me, deeper—or at least older—than my anger over the death of Sheena Q. The righteous anger of the crusader, perhaps? Perhaps, and how then could I mock Jennie? And there wouldn't just possibly have been a teensy wee tinge of pique at my own impotence, would there? Huffiness that I, for all my ability and invulnerability, was no more able to control my fate than any mere homo sap?

I had briefed our thirty-one patriot mercenaries, twenty-three normals and eight janglers, had had them double-check their gear and vet their tac kits and weapons. There were some strange heads amid the jangler contingent.

I had noticed a tenor of slyness among the men, an evasiveness, a less-than-obvious humor—lifted eyebrows, sidelong looks, the smallest and most fleeting of knowing grins. They had all had some type of combat experience, if only as stones zapping a riot, and I thought I knew what the problem was. Mandrake had assigned provisional rank, and I was confident in his choices. The chain of command was psychologically sound, I was sure—below my level. I called aside the provisional one-loot, my second-in for this mission.

"Commander, sir."

"The men seem to be having some doubts, Lieutenant."

"I wouldn't call them doubts, exactly, sir."

"Maybe you'd better tell me *exactly* what's going on, then," I said. "You've got permission to speak freely. Get it out of the way before the shooting starts. Cancel permission, make that an order. I order you to speak freely."

He grinned, a rough grin on a rowdy man. "Since it's an order, sir. Most of these hellions have mixed some hot-cubed jams. I was a topside drop-man for the mo-rines myself before my misunderstanding, a real raddie-baddie."

He was saying they'd all been in a few fights, and that he'd been a Spaceborne for the marines, with combat experience against camper bandits, until he'd gotten in trouble with the law. Sometimes the jargon gets a little thick for me.

He continued: "And maybe the troops have noticed, sir, that you was just kind of laying about with your wife and not really doing much, sir. Just kind of walking around with a pout on your face. My guess would be they ain't much impressed by that kind of commanding. Commander. Sir. Since it was an order."

I put a look of sweet reason on my face, the look of a young clown eager to please. "Lieutenant, there's something in what you say. And I really do feel that the blame for all that lies with me. However."

I put my face close to his. He watched my eyes get bigger and develop the vertical pupils of a predator cat, my jaw harden. I bared my lips, showing a row of fangs. I could not project radiation from my eyes as the monsters in movies and maxies have been able to do for a hundred and fifty years, but I could make the irises reflective and angle them to flash a sudden blast of light. I sent my voice an octave lower than he could possibly manage, amped to vibrate his bones: "I *AM* YOUR COMMANDER. IS THAT CLEAR?" I tapped his chest lightly, a tap that sent him staggering.

It wasn't what he was expecting. He held it together pretty well, though. "Yes *sir*!" The instinctive fear that had taken his face was changing to a look of high pleasure.

He would never be able to be sure he had seen it, but the print of authority stayed with him. A cheap trick, but there wasn't much time for the long method. He survived the war, and he must have told his story hundreds of times afterwards—you can find cuts of obscure interviews in the files—but no one ever credited it. The scene never showed in any of the maxies, not even the fantasies that played Johnny C's tune and cast me as an OM.

I heard him as I checked on the staging area: "AWW*RIGHT*, you daddy-eating gut-sucking asshole-chewing shit-for-brains muffa howdies, *faaaaaaall IN. HERE'S* your muffin assignments. . . ."

We moved out thirty minutes later. Jennie was taking a squad of thirteen on the back-up mission, including all the janglers, with

Jamie Sinclair as her second-in. I hadn't objected. He had made it clear he could fight.

I was left with nineteen men. I've seen several versions of this, and it is always a grand cavalcade, a rumbling column of armor and infantry gleaming in the great halls of huge caverns that are, inexplicably, lit by torches in niches. It wasn't that way. We had a shuttle and a pick-up truck, and three of the men rode bikes.

Twenty minutes out we parted ways with Jennie's squad. We would rejoin them in a matter of hours if all went well. In the maxies, actions are planned by superminds, and every detail clicks into place. In a real action, as Benjamin George and others have pointed out, you wait for the first *ping* of the unforeseen bad break, knowing that when it comes your whole scheme will start going to pieces more and more rapidly.

I didn't hear that *ping* when we made the Riverrun tap and got into the wetgear, or when the jangler engineers we had brought along flooded the tap operations room, our impromptu waterlock. I didn't hear it when we swam up into the lower depths of Riverrun River itself. I didn't hear it until much later, when we were nearly home free.

We swam downriver to our separate out-points, ten units of two men each. On dry land, we stripped the wetsuits and sank them, prepped the weapons. We wore battleheads with infra and frequency-random comm, but we were keeping radio silence until the actual fighting started—even a stray sentence picked up on some security monitor would bring in the precinct stones followed by marines and every other brand of troops the combined governments could throw at us.

Riverrun was one of the oldest and poshest neighborhoods in Hellasport, dating back to the original development deal when the realtors had made the subsidy arrangement with Sam. Sam got residential colonists and eventually another economy to tax, and the developers got a risk-free bonanza. The wealthy descendants of some of the first settlers, who had mostly been scientific and technological specialists, still lived in the area. It was a neighborhood of choice for hot-shot netties and such power-clowns as, say, the executives of Airworks Hellas.

Riverrun River was artificial, driven by giant turbines all along its course. One of the prime selling points of the area was that the river was allowed to carve out its own topography according to the weather and programmed random variations in the turbines. One experienced the thrill of risk, the distinct if small possibility that a sudden flood might undercut one of the manmade hills and take the library: really quite charming, you know, so Earthly, so natural. And so we made our way in the soft spring night up out of the cutbanks and sloughs and into the tall cottonwoods, the plegget and steel-willow and sycamore giving way to god-oak and maple and hickorine on the hillsides.

The trees of Mars, like the people, tend to shoot up extremely tall and slender during their periods of growth, and then thicken more massively than they would on Earth, since the structure can support so much more volume. These were some of the oldest trees on the planet, and I felt, although they were less than a quarter my age, a sense of awe. I felt alive again, free in the woods, breathing the outside air, smelling the riversmell and the woodsmell, silver and dead fish and black sodden leafage and fresh ground, whiffs of spice from the new flowers. I didn't realize until that moment how much I had missed it all, the breed and breath and peace, the willingness of life and death in intricate earthy cooperation in any little niche it found, even this pockmark on the face of a small rusty planet.

So I had my epiphany, and the other men crept through the woods in their darkened silversuits having whatever thoughts *they* had, and we found our assigned streets, and we found our ten separate targets, and hid in the woods and shrubs around those targets, and the clock displays in our battlehead visors ticked down, and we went in.

From this moment on, we were to consider ourselves under fire. The other men got in their houses however they could, most of them simply blasting through. I don't know what she made of it, but I took my battlehead off and took my partner to the front door and rang. An actual human butler answered, as I had known he would. He looked at my face, startled. "Why sir, come in. I thought you were in the . . ."

I was through the door and up the stairs, blasers drawn. Esther, my partner, took the butler and went to secure the rest of the household. I burst into the upstairs office, where Betty Andrade, chairman of Purification Operations, was working late. She spun in her chair. "Carson, what the hell—" she said, and then she was a dead chairman. I was back downstairs, found Esther with Carson, the butler, and the two kids, and we were all outside within two minutes of the time I had rung the doorbell. Carson was silent, the kids bewildered, but the butler was protesting: "What's going on? Where's Mrs. Andrade? What do you vandals think you're—"

I gave him a shove toward the woods. "Betty's dead, and you bastards better get into the woods *now* or you will be too," I said, using profanity and the woman's first name for shock value, the adrenaline cooperation of the victim. I fired a blast at the feet of the children, and they all ran for the woods and the darkness, the children screaming.

So the screaming had started. None of my men were to harm anyone but our targets here. That was one of the things that had made them doubt my authority, maybe, that order: Nobody dies but the bosses and the soldiers. A foolish principle, and any grunt knows better, but it was my war. There would be accidents, and perhaps some would deliberately disobey. If they did, I would see that they paid for it. Nobody dies but the soldiers and the bosses, the ones who signed on for the risk. Any other sort of war is a war of cowards, a war of slime.

What of the grief, what of the broken families? Yes. The line I draw is meaningless, serves only to ease my conscience. It is a line. I draw it.

As soon as the family had started running, Esther and I had faded back into the woods to cut across to the checkpoint. The first crackle of comm came over the phones in my battlehead, which meant that someone was pretty sure an alarm had sounded at one of the houses. And now, as we flitted through the trees, the houses started to go. A tremendous boom, a flash over the woods. Then the one Esther and I had set went off, crazy shadows blasted into the trees, the ground rocking with impact. We burst into the open, a parking bay, to find four of the teams already there. Our lock expert had his kit out and was breaking the vehicles open. The houses were still going off. Now sirens started down the hillside. Two more teams came into the clearing. Lockman and company were getting the last car open, and the rest of the men were piling into the others. Another team came running out of the woods. The other two teams had only another fifteen seconds to get there. Nobody showed.

"Move it!" I said, and we wheeled out, eight cars and sixteen men. Esther was leaning back over the seat to see behind us. "Somebody else made it," she said. "I see a car starting up." I was whipping us down the scenic curves without lights. I heard the whispering whack of flitters go over, like the magnified sound of a flight of arrows. At the base of the hill we broke onto Riverrun Avenue and headed straight downtown, matching traffic speed. I could see one of the other cars ahead, but there was no need to convoy. We knew where we were going.

One of the reasons to do it this way was to keep our trick a secret and so maybe get to use it again: Everyone knew that the janglers tapped the topside utilities, including the water and power, but no one in Hellas had thought of the river as an exit. The people I had picked were all good guerillas, and had left no appreciable traces back in the woods. The sunken wetgear would roll along the channel and snag, and show up eventually in some filter, but probably not for several weeks. We had sent normals out at different locks all over the city—no matter how many troops they stationed, there was no way to patrol every Underground lock in Hellasport, no way to keep at least a few normals from sneaking back and forth. Our normals had all had large packs with them, and had booked to the outskirts of Riverrun on various forms of non-ID public transport. Then they had scattered, but in retrospect it would look—we hoped—as if that was the way *we* had gone in, waiting for night to cover our insertion.

Then, too, there was the fact that going back into the river would have been slower, and left us exposed, struggling back upstream, while force after force of marines landed and went in after us. This way, we had a shot at survival.

We were not likely to get all the way to our safe-hole, the Della Culebra warehouse locks, without some interference. By now the first force of stones would have established that the trouble in Riverrun was a hostile action, that we were not in the area, and that we had stolen the getaway cars. Marines and the Guard would have been placed on full alert, and several squadrons would be staging for delivery to our locale. If we did not get underground before they got there, we were dead. I had no doubt the system could tag us before then—they might be tracing the stolen cars even now. But there would be two or three minutes, I hoped, before the military arrived, when all the city had to throw at us would be a squad or two of nearby downtown stones. That was where Jennie came into play.

I wheeled off the freeway and wound down into the tangled streets of the warehouse section of town, down where the big freight was loaded and unloaded for shipment to and from the spaceport on the cannon lines. It was like every other dock and freight section of every other city in every other century—huge installations dwarfing the streets with the grim glory of their functional geometries; neglected griminess and disrepair; a lot of dimness, broken here and there by stark lighting and even starker shadows, because there was nothing to steal, or at least nothing that could be stolen with less than an army, and because there were no lives to protect, except the lives of a few damned fools who didn't know enough to stay away.

It was perfect. Into the tunnel off Della Culebra, and on the way out my lieutenant came over the headphones: ". . . Fatcat 4, good. Fatcat 5, good. Anybody got a blip on 6, where are they? Here comes 2, all right, that's 2 through 10 but 6, get these cars lined up, you know the drill, *all right,* any you assholes know where 1 is?

"This is 1 coming in," I said. "I don't think 6 made it out, don't know what happened. How does it look down there?"

"Roger 1, looks good toward the lockdocks, but they may be dug in already. I conned some noise coming down, area alert. We stick our noses around the corner we'll know."

I turned the corner of a warehouse and went under the huge quad pipes of the cannon line feeder. There they were, ahead, down the alley, cars running, men out checking off and deploying. We bumped up beside them and got out.

"Ready-eddie," I said. "Let's move it."

"All right, you howdies," the lieutenant said, "let's die famous. Move it out move it out move it out!"

My car stayed in the alley. We went out the mouth of it in four ranks of two cars each, a driver beside each car and the rest of us trotting behind. Rounding the corner to the left, the drivers locked the steering and ax and rolled out to either side. The cars went gunning down the alley to the raised platform of locks we hoped to use, and we sprinted behind them as long as we could. "Break!" the lieutenant barked, and we tumbled to cover in feeder alleys and doorways. Blaser beams were already scorching off the walls, and as I rolled I saw two of the cars blow and men running for cover at the end of the alley. The selective mikes in my battlehead were giving me noise from the men down there, the protobabble of combat: "Advance and cover, advance and cover, they're not in the friggin jeeps, dammit, advance and cover, advance and cover!"

"They're in the alley!" I said. "Ballistics at the ready! Break it out!"

And the loot was yelling "Go go go go go go go!" and we were rolling back into the alley, a tumble of silversuits at maximum reflectivity and blaser beams coruscating off but they would keep firing and sooner or later punch through or slice off a battlehead with a real head inside it but we were up and sprinting toward the scatter of thirty or so stones in silversuits too with more to come and the marines on the way behind us and we were firing our loud battering rigged-up ballistic automatics reverberating off the high walls and the yelling and somebody went down smoking beside me and the big slugs were taking them down and slamming them back even when they didn't punch through the stuff of the silversuits and the battering bangbangbang off the walls was making them panic *Hey what the muffa They got some JESUS What the AH* and they tried to retreat and their back-ups were swarming into the alley not understanding what the hell was happening and Jennie and her squad came swarming out of the locks where they had been waiting and we had them and then it all went to hell. . . .

"Marines!" the lieutenant screamed. "Goddammit, we're pinched."

"Get some fire on the bastards!" I yelled, grabbing one of the men to kneel with me and lay down some fire to the rear where one of the advance squad of marines was trying to pin a grenade on us. I saw jumpers going up from the alley mouth, contrails of power-launchers. They were going to hop us with the jumpers and come in behind Jennie, maybe laying a few grenades on the way over. They wouldn't care whether or not they took the stones out too, so long as they destroyed the target.

We'd nailed the grenade man, but here came another one with a barrier to hide behind this time and the jumpers were up and we were screwed though I was trying to pin one of the jumpers and I heard one of the men yelling about them and doing the same.

And then it all went the other way again. I heard a loud high whistling whoop and something whizzed by over the rooftops and something else whizzed by and the mouth of the alley blew where the grenade launcher had been, huge boom and shower of bright dazzle. One of the jumpers blew and another stopped dead in the air and fell and another went sizzling off in a slow cartwheel to slam on a roof somewhere. . . .

"Friends," I yelled, "we got friends. Into the locks, *now*. Forward fire only, *go go go!*"

We piled down the alley blasting away, the few stones still alive scrambling to clear the area and going down, and we swarmed the lock platform ladders and went in *hup hup hup*. "I make it seven down, cap'n," the lieutenant said in my ear. I saw he had lost an arm below the elbow, but he was grinning big beneath the battlehead visor and didn't seem to know it yet.

"I've got four down," said Jennie in the phones. "Just about all from friendly fire." That was not, at the moment, relevant, but she had brought off the ambush just fine, so I didn't comment.

"Commander Dark, you stay. Bring Sinclair, but send your squad on down. Lieutenant, you get on down with your squad. Get to the medix, man, you're gone on the wing."

He looked down at his arm. *"Shit,"* he said, and his knees went. I barked for the sergeant and repeated my orders, and he took the slumping lieutenant by the shoulders and led him off.

"Commander Dark, get the deto men going and get here on the double. We've got some friends coming through this hole in a few seconds." She appeared almost immediately, and we took position on either side of the lock, Sinclair just outside.

"Shit, I see carriers landing," he said. "Wait, three in the alley! Here come the friendlies!"

We swung the lock door wide and one after the other three black-suited bodies in battleheads dived through. Sinclair stepped in and lugged the door shut, not that that would matter. Our friends had stopped their tumble, and rose to their feet. One lifted her battlehead and the butterfly on her face crinkled from her wide smile. "Lo, Shadowman," Pappy said. "Long time no postcards."

22
Strange Feedback

We hustled away down the tunnel. If the deto men had done their job right, it would blow just about the time the first wave of marines hit it. Not a productive long-run strategy, blowing our own rabbit holes, but we were hoping it would save us this one time.

Pappy had brought Babalu and Johnny C with her. I had a lot of questions, but this was no time to ask. We got down a couple of decks, about forty-five seconds clear, and the tunnel blew, bouncing us off the walls like marbles. When the shock subsided, we checked ourselves out, and went on. The passage we were in had suffered some pretty severe faulting, but we were able to get through. Working lower and lower, in thirty minutes we made the rest of the men, a bedraggled and battered group, all of us hustling on the double.

By the time we made the original split-up point, where Jennie had taken her squad up, it was beginning to dawn on us that we had pulled it off. A successful strike, and we had lived. Most of us. These soldiers had all been professionals at one time or another. We had picked them for that. For them, "Till death do us part" was not a vow, but an estimate.

As bad as we looked, and in spite of the few somber or simply exhausted faces, it was a sauntering, swaggering group that came walking back into the staging area, crackling with bad jokes and dirty humor. They were feeling the adrenaline of survival, a drug that no longer has much effect for me. I was feeling the adrenaline of success.

214

"Fuck the routine," I said in the staging room. "You men get naked, get fucked, and get drunk." Isolated cheers.

"Fuck getting drunk," Jennie Dark said, already out of her suit. "We're throwing a great big fucking feedback party."

"We are?" I said.

"We are. Boardroom suite, 1100 hours. We'll put on the fucking comm and watch the fucking wetbrains lie about us and laugh our fucking heads off. Come one, come all. Bring your nick, bring your dick." More cheers, and louder.

"We're thowing a great big fucking feedback party," I said, and the cheers were general.

Pappy was naked now, and her body brought an ache of pleasure to my throat. "Hey, you damn howdies," I yelled, turning back to the men. "I guess you know we owe our asses to these hustlers. Well this one's boss, and her name is Pappy." And Pappy bent to leap into a spinner-5, and picking it up, I did too: We rose in slow opposing rotations, drew in our arms for a tight fast spin, and struck our right hands together to kill our torque and float back down together, hands clasped overhead.

"Blip, slip, and clip, big man," she said.

If there had been anything like a describable hustler credo, that would have been it. Loosely translated, it means, *The only three things worth living for are pride, money, and sex.* She was telling me I could have all three from her.

Jennie was hyperjoyed, bubbling with talk and jumping all over the place, although it seemed a peaceful and clear-eyed sort of mania. More than anything else, it was relief: She had gone into battle and proved herself.

She insisted that Pappy and Babalu and Johnny C all come back to the suite with us, to clean up and visit and get ready for the victory party, and so they did. I was inutterably glad. I could not keep my eyes from Pappy as we walked, her loose robe floating.

Mandrake was at the lock to our quarters. For the first time I wondered why he had not met us at the staging area. "Mandrake," I said, "you remember . . ."

"Pappy and Johnny C and Babalu," he said. "I recognize them." He did a strange thing, taking my head in two of his large, flexible hands. Again I was struck by the improbable warmth of his skin. He tilted my face slightly, so that I looked directly into a set of his undereyes. I felt he was searching me for something. "You're all right, then," he said, releasing me.

"Of course I'm all right. Come on in and visit."

"No thank you," he said. "I have some thinking to do and some arrangements to make."

Johnny C and Babalu were mainly anxious to get fed and cleaned and then go out partying with the other soldiers. The soldiers weren't *hustlers,* they explained, but had the closest thing they had seen to their own reckless disregard for life and limb. The soldiers were people you could party with, unlike these city-get unit functions they'd been hanging around with. The soldiers understood that a party was supposed to be only slightly less dangerous than a battle, but with more jokes, drugs, and sex.

They phrased it differently, but that was the gist.

Pappy wanted to stay because she was in love with me. At the time, I would have sworn I had finally fallen completely for her. I saw Jennie watching with a sort of pleased amusement, still full of her triumph, as if she existed on another plane, an imperturbable level whose deliberations dwarfed such tiny drama without finding it contemptible. As if she were an adult, and we were children in puppy love.

Before Johnny C and Babalu left we got the story of how they had come to our aid. Pappy had held the three of them together over the last week. They were all under observation, of course. CI had put a top man in the field to try to romance her, and she had let him. She hadn't hidden anything from the spy because she hadn't known anything. Meantime she had watched him. Easy. This evening, when he had to answer a summons on the double-double, she had simply followed him by flitter, putting out a call to the boys. He was an acting brigadier in the marines and had gone right to the battle scene in Della Culebra. And we knew the rest.

Jennie was in the shower, and the others had gone. "Shadowman," Pappy said, and leaned over to kiss me. Her lips were mighty soft. "My turn now?" she said when we broke.

"I don't know," I said, hating myself. I wasn't sure whether I hated myself for comparing her to Jennie and finding her so much more lively and desirable, or for my hypocritical sexual loyalty (which Jennie herself neither expected nor thought of giving) or because I suspected that the loyalty was based on the guilt of the comparison. Here I was again, crashing around in a sparkling cascade of human desires, bringing the humans all to ruin, like Frankenstein's monster in the control room of the mad doctor. You are all so simple and certain and flashing, you simply want and follow your wants. It is what makes your blood so infinitely desirable to me, perhaps.

"Head-jamming Shadowman," she said. "See you think. Belong on the range, not messing around with these zoomer-oomers and dipheads. No slam on your cunny-jam, seem a nice get. But. Here it is, and you don't want. Nah. Want, but won't take, more like." She stood up. She slapped me ringingly. She smiled.

"Love-tap. Mine, Babe. Will have you soon."

Jennie stepped into the room, drying herself off. "Shower's free," she said. She eyed us curiously.

"Nah," I said. "I took a leak while we were swimming up Riverrun River. Be like pissing on my own head."

"If *that's* where from, *I'm* ready," said Pappy, going in.

Jennie and Pappy left to get the party set up and mixing, Pappy lugging the huge pack of feedback we had kept stowed in the suite all this time. "Mmm," she had said, opening the sack to sniff it. "Homegrown. Smells like the Wall."

I sulked in my room a while, running the French doors angrily through twenty or so seasons, days of blizzards and rains and baking sun and eloquent moonlight flickering by, and then got myself even more pissed off trying to reset the damn thing. Mandrake came in from wherever he had been, and I needled him meanly, just picking, bitching. Trying to scratch some patch of fungoid rot on my vanities. Victory doesn't last long. Peace don't boost the same rush, but it lingers better.

"I don't guess you're going to the party," I said.

"And why not?" Mandrake said.

"What's the point? You got a feedback-smoking priff? We're going to be la-la-ing out of our bodies, and you're going to just have to stand there like a post and watch a dumb lot of d-geed meat staggering around in transcendent puke."

"A, I (you like my pun?) like people," he said. "And B, what makes you think I can't have an out-of-the-body experience? What makes you think I don't have thousands of them, plus every other kind of weightless wobble you bios do, plus a few hundred you haven't found an analogue for yet?"

"Oh yeah," I said, catching on, and also regretting the spite in my own tone.

"Have you ever done any slave work?" he said.

"A little," I said. I knew what he was getting at.

"There is the classic and possibly apocryphal story of one of the first remote-perception operators. He put on the headset, the gloves, the walking rig, and from several rooms away, he walked the robot around the laboratory. So real and immediate was the transmission quality that he felt as if he were walking about in his own body. And then he walked the robot through the door of the room in which he sat, and saw himself from the outside. It was an overwhelming out-of-the-body experience, and completely without the aid of drugs."

"The Tachi-touchy," I said. "Yeah, that's the first prank they play on new operators. I've had the experience. Stupid, but I never made the connection."

"I spend a lot of time dispersed on the net or different systems," he said. "I see myself not only from outside my own body, but in many other distinct frames of reference."

"Yeah, I get it. Don't think I'm completely dumb. I've done quite a bit of thinking about your architecture, how life looks to you."

"I didn't know that."

"Yeah, well, I guess you could say it's a system I didn't let you access."

"It is sometimes difficult to know where I am. Whether this body-walking is a dream, a figment. How is it that the sense of self follows perception, and does not remain with the center that processes the perceptions? As your people interface more and more directly with the net, they will become as familiar with the experience as I am. The self will exist more nearly as a wave-form with a complex front than as a particular object. In a sense, the Rapture has already begun."

I wondered how *that* would fit with the Butlerian idea of the 4-D body. If you were immortal in this world, did that mean you could never be born into Heaven, that you were a sort of unabortable tumor, a swollen and neverending fetus? Would there be religious wars, a *jihad*? How could Jennie reconcile her religion and her janglerhood then?

"I don't know what you mean, *my* people," I said.

"Humans, then. This dispersion of being is a thing that many of the janglers are beginning to understand, and that's one of the reasons, aside from their obvious humanity, that they should not be destroyed."

"They have much to teach us," I said, in broad imitation of an alien with superior intelligence having mercy on mankind.

"Your wisdom exceeds your power, Zontar," he said.

"In time this species may surpass even us," I said.

"For have they not, of all the species in the galaxy, given birth to God?" he answered in a sepulchral voice, and I couldn't keep my face straight any longer.

He had brought me out of my funk, and now he steered me into a long discussion, the sort of academic point-making that I sometimes just love, which I will spare you on the assumption, justified by experience, that there is a ninety-nine percent chance you don't.

But his argument involved the idea that alcohol, coffee, tobacco, marijuana, LSD, jeen-jeen, ramalam, feedback, and all the rest, every mind-altering substance humans had ever used, had been immediately followed by a technology that provided the same experience—as if the chemicals were premonitors, or, as he put it, "practice." I pointed out that the trouble with that idea—but I said I was going to spare you.

He talked me into taking a shower, and letting him give me a backrub, and I have to say he gives a damn good backrub for somebody who doesn't really exist.

So by the time we left for the party, I was feeling pretty smooth again, relaxed and happy and at peace with my fellows.

He said an odd thing just before we got there, something that I've thought about these many years: "The out-of-body experience I most look forward to is seeing myself in one of your fictions."

"Who says I'm going to write a book about all this?" I said. He produced, somehow, without breathing, the sound of a snort.

But the idea fascinated me. I had never thought of fiction in quite that way, as coterminous with the technologies of perception and intelligence, and I have never thought of it as entirely separate since. So here it is, Mandrake, here you are as I saw you, see you. How do you look to yourself? You look to me like a friend. But you have known that for some time. I see myself here, too, from outside, small and self-involved. I date our friendship from that evening, though I had proclaimed you my friend before. Looking back at myself, I see that that was when I began to see you. And there is another expansion, another Rapture. We live in our friends.

We walked through the lock into the huge conference room and a wild and thunderous party. Already a haze of smoke hung over the room, and music was booming. There were full-size holos all along the walls, and we were the topic of choice on most of them. We were News, we were Heroes: "The Commander's staggering attack has brought the blitzkrieg back to modern combat. Authorities are saying . . ."; or "Yes, but Jim, in the taking of civilian life, has Commander Shade in effect sealed the doom of his own troops? Is it not true that . . ."; or ". . . no place in the city safe from this sort of assault, and a panicked populace cowers behind walls that no longer seem so immutable and safe as they did a few short hours ago . . ."; or "The *fact* of the matter *is,* Mayor, that the janglers have tried and *failed* to mount a considerable assault on our resources. They hit us with everything they had, their very best moves and very best men, and out of the hundred or so they threw at us, they were lucky to escape with the lives of a dozen men. How much damage did they do? Out of all the military installations in and around Hellas, they managed to blow a total of nine, count them, *nine* civilian houses, and two of the assault force were themselves slain by prepared civilians. Now does that sound like *victory* or *defeat* to you? If it weren't for the hysteria of you and your trivia mavens . . ."

That last was the brigadier she'd followed, Pappy explained. People were pounding on chests, mingling with the hero warriors, yakking yakking yakking. Here and there bodies rose into spinner-5s or exuberant flips. The smoke seemed to thicken visibly, moment by moment, the decibel levels to rise. The locks were held wide, and I wondered if all forty thousand of the Underground were going to show up. What the hell, let's send out for pizza and invite the wetbrains, too. People were walking through the holos, which swirled creamily with feedback smoke. One of my raiders stood on a chair inside the broadcast on which the brigadier was talking, hauled out a huge blue-green penis, a Ramsey ST400 Superamplified, I think, and pumped it into the image of the brigadier's working mouth.

I had found Pappy and lost Mandrake, and then I lost Pappy. I got into too many conversations with glad-handers and well-wishers and timid sycophants and bold-as-brass asshole sycophants, none of whom I could really hear over the roar of the party. I was beginning to get a high from the excitement and the secondary smoke. The party went on a long time. Sometimes human psychoactives work on me and sometimes not. I have wondered how voluntary it is, how much it depends on a subconscious choice not to resist, not to let my body treat it as it does poison or a wound, an aberration to be restored by vicious homeostasis.

I wondered if feedback could work on janglers. I could see how it might work for Jennie, since half of her brain was bio, but how could it work for bodies with digital brains? The janglers looked as precessed as the normals, but with feedback you couldn't really tell.

Jamie Sinclair appeared with a couple of feedback joints. "Hey, blood, easy," he said, spreading his hands out, palm down. "Ant moving on you. I'm cool. Jennie say see you got some a this good stuff, thassall. Was a good jam, though, wannit?"

So I sucked down some smoke, amiably enough, with Sinclair, and traded congratulations. Truth was, I was getting discontented again. I wandered away. The party rolled on and on, and no one was meeting my eyes. I was alone, alone in the crowd. I was the only one of my kind on the planet. Maybe the only one of my kind left anywhere in the universe. I could not join the fun. I was a ghost, a wraith without kin or love. I towered over the heads of the party goers, dour, stalking, unappeasable.

It was not until I saw the tall man in his black cape that I realized I was weightless. He was making animated conversation with Jennie and Sinclair and Babalu and a couple of the board members, and he wore my face. I saw that I had stretched myself a half-meter taller, and that was why I was looking down on everyone. I realized I could stretch up to the ceiling if I wanted, and I did. I drew my body up after me and floated there over the crowd in lotus. I lay out full-length, still floating. I was alone, but it was good. I was glad not to be in the body of the man any more, glad to be free of his petty concerns.

It was like flying. I held my arms out and seemed to rush over the crowd—and yet they stood still beneath me. It *was* flying. I remembered how to do it now, it was easy. You had only to hold yourself *so*, and. . . . I promised myself never to forget again.

I realized I could go anywhere I wanted to this way. I was over a night valley, Shadowfall, floating. Except that it was also another place, another valley from a long time ago. And that was appropriate, because they *were* the same place, they *should* be the same place. The sun was big and warm, but the sky was a dark, royal blue, and full of stars. I could look up and see into the swirled, veiled hearts of galaxies. I was walking up the path in the leaf-dappled light, and the birds stirred and called, and things rustled away in the brush. I came into the clearing, and the cabin was there, and she was there, the woman I loved.

She stood in the doorway. At first I thought she was blonde, but then I saw her hair was silver, a cloud of silver, and her skin was utterly white. It was a warm white somehow, a glow of white, not a blankness, not the snowy emptiness of the albino. Her lips were bright red, her eyes the path's dazzle of sun and green and shadow.

I had known her all my life, but could not say who she was. She came to meet me, flowing in a gown that stirred about her as she stirred. She did not say, *At last you've come home,* but I heard it. She leaned into my body, and we were all in our lips, where we met and flowered under the sun, the wild daffodils in a bed in front of the cabin.

She turned away and her face glimmered with change, as if one part of it were someone else, grim with machine. In her turning she took us to a dark bed, a pallet on the dirt floor of a cabin, a floating web in the quarters of a spaceship, a strange dais flickering in the fire of a cavern. I could not see her body now, only her heart, which was open to me, exposed and glowing in her transparent body, the beautiful writhing heart of an eager young girl. And while I gazed on the heart of the girl, she disappeared from it, and took me from behind, a tall rough woman come back from the dead, my cowgirl, a woman with work in her hands and weather in her face.

She laid me back and stripped the bark from my neck to touch her lips to the bare cold wood. She bit the vein in my throat, which was the vein under my penis, and drank. She drank black night. In the night were stars, and dark rivers that showed the stars among reeds. And there was an absence of me, and there were sluggish stirrings, and things that slid into the water with the quiet vowels of sleepy liquids.

And God held my ass, one cheek in each hand like apples, and kissed the apples, which were my holy balls floating free in space. And so I fucked the holy mouth of God, and came all silver and little animals. And then I was a minnow leaping the smooth rapids of her back and I was born between her legs in a surge of blood, and there in the rank meadow met the snake fang-to-fang, and we struck and locked mouth-to-mouth till we fell, two elk with locked antlers and we are now the locked skulls that you see before you on the forest moss.

So then the snake-thing in the black water said, *Come down*, and I went down to it naked in the black water without fear, the last of my people, and its people stood in a ring about us approving, and *I am come down my Lord* I said, and it took me heavily under where I could not breathe and a frenzy of scales quivered upon my breast, my mouth.

And I laid her back, and drank at her throat, and I drank darkness, and with the darkness I drank *sweidus* and I drank *sidus,* I drank *considerare, desiderare,* stars and desire, stars and trouble. And then I pulled at her nipples that were my father's nipples, the swollen teats of God that are her tears, and I drank silver and the running wind that the birds know, and I drank the happy and waving grasses.

All about me where I lay the grasses whispered *considerare, desiderare*. And I slept on the warm earth naked in sun, I slept with my cock thrust into the warm earth and the sun like a warm hand on my forgiven nakedness.

And when I slept, my mind fell through my head into the dark earth. It fell in darkness, till it found me here, below the world. It stood a little apart, and watched the fallen bodies, as an angel might visit a battlefield. Some of the bodies snored and stirred, and it walked over to the one that was me, and kicked it. It kicked it again. It sat up. It rubbed its eyes and looped its arms about its drawn-up knees. It looked about the room with its cold green eyes, and made a snort that it thought was laughter. And then it saw me and was terrified.

I was terrified, full of irrational and sourceless fear. I was naked, and it seemed to me that was the same thing as the fear. Jennie was nowhere in the room. Neither was Pappy, or Mandrake. This was the fear I had felt when I first awakened from death, somehow foreknowing all, knowing my people slain and burnt and lost. On the early afternoon of that long-past day, I had no longer had anything to fear from pain and death, but I had nevertheless awakened in the panic of a man who has lost everything.

I ran through the connecting corridor to our room. Mandrake was not in his usual place outside our lock, and he was not inside, I saw, turning on the light, but Pappy and Jennie were, curled up together. Pappy raised up on an elbow and grinned at me, then threw the covers off and slid out of bed. She walked over, her heavy breasts floating high on the shutter-cage of her ribs. She gave my dick a yank, then hugged me. "Hey, Shadowman," she murmured into my chest. "Ready-eddie?"

I tried to kiss the top of her head, but she raised her mouth to mine, soft and full, a promise, and through its softness I felt how tight my lips were, drawn into a rictus I could not release. She laughed and slapped my bare ass.

"Go git, boy," she said, jerking a thumb at the bed. "All yours. Think I left my clothes," she said, and swaggered out.

I got into bed with Jennie, slipped my arm around her. "It was you," I whispered against her back. "It was you, wasn't it?"

"Sleepy," she said, pushing my arm away so she could roll over. "Turn out the light," she said. "Go back to sleep."

23
Bad Blood

The next few days were not good. It wasn't just the hangover from the party—feedback doesn't leave you with physical aches and pains, just an exaggerated sense of worthlessness, smallness and dullness and limitation. Which figures.

It was the postsuccess let-down, the presiege mentality that sets in at the beginning of winter after a fine fall, when you know that the world has tilted to gloom for a while and there will be no escape. We had struck a great blow, our best blow, and it would not materially affect the outcome. The brigadier, after all, had not been wrong. The marines *were* on the way, and we had three weeks at best. Even Jennie had come down from her bright-eyed fever.

She and Pappy had taken to hanging around together. Mandrake was with them often as not. They went everywhere in each other's company, talking a blue streak. I was excluded, not explicitly, but invisibly. I was somehow never on the same wavelength, never had anything to say that seemed relevant.

Once, I found the three of them down on the plaza sitting by the fountain, the fountain making its low sounds. In lower gravity, falling water moves more slowly, strikes with less impact. The music is quieter, and shifted toward the bass. Mandrake was playing air guitar, except that when *he* did it, he could make the sounds. Pappy and Jennie were singing in close harmony, a clear sad slide of blues that went well with the sound of the water:

When I was just a little girl,
When I was just a little girl,
When I was just a little girl,
A blade of grass was the whole damn world.

Hustle them bevos,
Hustle them beef—
Your daddy pulled your momma,
But you just pull grief.

The wind was sweet and home was home,
The wind was sweet and home was home,
The wind was sweet and home was home,
But then is then and gone is gone.

Hustle them bevos,
Hustle them beef—
Your daddy pulled your momma,
But you just pull grief.

I've seen the stars and I've seen city lights,
I've seen the stars and I've seen city lights,
I've seen the stars and I've seen city lights,
I've had some lows, but damn few heights.

"Pretty," I said, and it was—Mandrake's accompaniment delicate and haunting, Jennie's pure soar and Pappy's rough call twining and chiming. How could they waste time with a war going on, I thought, as if I hadn't wasted more than my share. My real trouble was that I felt left out of the music.

" 'The Hustler's Complaint'," Jennie said. "It's by the No Poet," she added. "Mandrake set it for us."

"Don't sound like no No Poet to me," I said. "It's sad enough, but it's too human. Too local. Mandrake's joking."

Mandrake was saying nothing. "She said it was," Jennie said.

"Ask him to tell you in truth," I said.

"Well, it doesn't matter, does it?" Pappy said, cutting me off. "Can you play 'Lightning Hits the Gizzard'," she asked Mandrake. "Always thought that was a funny song."

"The hell with this," I said, and left.

The funny thing was that I never had the sense that Pappy and Jennie had become friends. Temperamentally they were extremely different. Sooner or later, obviously, they would go separate ways. And yet for the present they were together constantly, arranging, talking. I have never seen men able to do that, share the secrets of their hearts like so much neutral information, on what would appear to be simply a need-to-know basis.

I spent my time pointlessly charting public opinion, aimlessly considering options for further attacks. The zoomers, inspired by our assault, were mounting a great solidarity march on Centerpole, and it was all over the news and the talk shows. There were interviews with any number of impromptu zoomer spokesmen and mob leaders. The interviews were all the same. Rhetoric, enthusiasm, crusading anger. A fair amount of crude showmanship and personal ambition. Some of these zoomer leaders just might be able to leap-frog into jobs as heads after the war. You could see them thinking about it.

And it was futile. All I had succeeded in doing was getting the zoomers so roiled that hundreds would die.

It even seemed possible that Benjamin, wherever he was, might turn over my file to Centerpole, that the fiction of my life as a human would at long last be exposed. I couldn't bring myself to care.

If I could have gone back into my feedback trance and found the woman again, I would have. But we were out of feedback. We had blown it all in one big orgy. And even if any had been left, the odds against duplicating the experience were impossibly high. I could not even know whether it had been a hallucination or an actual encounter. Such meetings were not uncommon on feedback, and those who had them swore they were real, that they were truly out of their bodies, and had shared experience with others who were out of their bodies. Sometimes they found witnesses who thought they had *been* the others, and who would describe similar or parallel experiences.

It is hard to have had the most intense encounter of your life in a dream. Love in the waking world may be less vivid, but you can, with effort, work your way back to it. There are no maps for love in dreams.

Speaking of love in the waking world, Pappy and I finally did it. She was quartered just down the hall, but she used our kitchenette and facilities. Two days after the party, she came in to clean up and eat breakfast. I rose late and grouchy and went in to take a piss. Jennie was in the kitchen making, God help us, French toast.

Pappy sat on the groomer console clipping her toenails, naked and frank. She glanced up unconcernedly as I came in, and I had an immediate hard-on. "Huh," she said. She sniffed the air. I could feel my underarms spraying, the prickle of the sweat glands at the base of my spine.

"The hell with it," I said, and lifted her. I pinned her against the wall, and she wrapped her legs around me. I think I was trying to slam her through into the kitchenette. I know Jennie could hear us. I came in a minute, and leaned against Pappy blind, my cheek flush on the cold hard wall.

"Not much of a honeymoon," she said.

"I had one of those," I said, disengaging. I lowered her carefully, if not gently.

"Now you owe," she said. And so I knelt on the floor while she ground her saltiness into the wound in my jaws, and came with a sigh.

We showered together, her second shower of the morning. She soaped me and rinsed the lather away. "Be so goddamned gloomy," she said, thumping me on the back and getting out to dry.

We ate our French toast together, the three of us. Pappy cheerful and joking, slathering on the butter and jam. Jennie without emotion, watching me with an expressionless face. It was not as if she were carefully hiding what she felt. It was a blank, absorbed look.

And after breakfast the two of them left, chatting, and I went to the office to work. Though what I really did was some of this, transferring my notes from my mind to the desk, revising and adding as I went.

Jennie and I had a bitter argument the next day. "Fuck her all you want to," she said. "Christ Almighty, you're the one with the nineteener attitudes, not me. But I am fucking sick of this god-damned moping around. I am fucking sick of the way you act like there's something wrong with me. You don't *have* to compare her to me, but you *do*. And you know *why* you do? Because you don't want me, you fucking stupid asshole, because you just married me out of pity, or maybe because you couldn't resist getting mixed by somebody who thought you were some kind of hero. And because in your stupid asshole fucking head, you think you can't just cut out. You can't just say, 'Minus this, I don't *like* you,' and take the heat. Because I would cut your fucking asshole head off for misleading me. And so in your goddamned fucking asshole stupid head the only way you can get out of the guilt is to compare me to somebody else, so you can feel like I'm no good, so it's all my fault. I don't care if you *are* some kind of asshole fucking mutant, you are one goddamned fucked-up son of a human wetbitch brain."

I think she meant *wetbrain bitch,* but even I, as quickly as I heal, did not have the nerve to criticize her profanity. Most of which I found monotonous. *Shit-boosted teener,* I was thinking. *Elephant snot in a china bowl. You don't even know how to cuss worth a whip-stitched damn.*

I said: "What about you? What about you? Running around here like some kind of silly heroine, wiping the runny crap off the butts of these poor idiotic femtochip dingbats and feeling like Holy Joan, our lady of the masses? Can't you see what you're up to? Christ, woman, you're just getting back at your father! You don't see that? You're not setting the people free, you're kissing your mother's festering pussy and telling her she's okay, the old man is dead at last! Sheeee-it."

She said: "We don't have time to be fighting like this. There's a war going up."

She was right about everything else, but she was wrong about that. The vagaries of a relationship cannot be postponed or deterred by any phenomenon in this universe. When the second coming comes, Jesus is going to have to wait for all the couples, one by one, to quit fucking or fighting. Then they may notice him. Then they may enter Heaven, their minds not really on it yet, still simmering with all that lovely human juice.

Jennie appeared at the office lock later that day. "You have a visitor," she said. Why hadn't they just sent the message through Nobodesk? She was trembling, a slight, almost undetectable flutter.

"Back at the room," she said, when I made no move to get up.

Out in the corridor, looking steadfastly away, she said: "Are you a vampire?"

"What difference does the word make?" I said. "You saw me."

"You drink blood? You're im . . . you're—"

"Undead? Immortal? What proccing difference does it make? The wetbrains think *you're* dead. Nothing's immortal. I can't figure out why the hell Mandrake told you."

We were at the lock to the suite. "She didn't," she said. We went in.

I thought it was a wheeled man at first. He was in a quad rig, rolling mode. You don't see many quad rigs any more. So few untreatable quadriplegics. Mandrake hovered behind the rig, Pappy sat on the bed. So she knew too.

"Hello, Richard Benjamin George," I said.

"*There* he is," the old man said in a singsong voice. "Look at him, Mandrake! Isn't he splendid? Isn't he magnificent?"

"Mandrake brought him here," Jennie said. "He kept asking for the vampire. Mandrake wouldn't explain, but she sent me to get you. Then, on the way—what a balloon I am." She shook her head bitterly. She looked at me, her face frightened again. "Are you from the Devil?"

The old man's head rolled on his shoulders. The mechanical eyes shuttered and opened, shuttered and opened. Jennie's question left me flabbergasted. "I thought you were a Butlerian," I said to her.

"I can't help it," she said. "I didn't think I believed that slag, but I'm scared."

"It's a symbol," I said. "Symbols do that, even if you don't con them. I'm not the symbol. I'm just a zoid, another zoid like you, but older. An antique zoid."

"We three zoids," the old man sang. Mandrake *had* been talking to him.

"We've pulled a marriage," I said to Jennie. "Fucked, fought. You know who I am. Hold on to that. I should have told you already, but this is just the sort of reaction I didn't want to face." I spoke to the old man: "What are you doing here, Benjamin George?"

The old man had steadied himself. "Twice," he said. "Irrelevant. Long time ago. Benjamin."

His voice was strong, but probably artificial. It was curious to see him there. He had initiated all this, plunged me in notoriety, conflict, intrigue, but that seemed an age ago. I had taken the fight on myself. Now here he was before me, shrunken from even his previous state. He seemed powerless and out of place, as if all of this had really had nothing to do with him, as if a chain of foreordained events had simply seized him and drained him, using the most convenient means for their entry into reality.

"It was a major advance in strategical thought," I said. "Surely it cannot be considered irrelevant, even if it *was* the product of a young man's mind."

He gestured roughly to Mandrake. The quad rig was still learning his moves, I guessed. He hadn't been in it very long. "Benjamin, it will cost you," Mandrake said. The old man made an impatient noise and gestured again. Mandrake buttoned the medical pack on the back of the rig, a short tune on a tiny piano. The old man straightened almost visibly, gained strength. He could hold his head steady, and his eyes quit shuttering.

"Strategy is probably irrelevant," he said. "The ego seeking to impose order on unquantifiable event. Aleph–Null in the Aleph–Aleph universe. I was young, and full of my triumph, and ambitious for fame."

"And now desire oblivion."

He laughed. "Desire it or not, it has come upon me."

"You could copy yourself. Go jangler."

"For how long? The janglers are doomed. They will have served only to draw off the last resistance to identity storage, as the blacks of the twentieth century drew hatred, only to find the entire culture eventually emulating their styles, their manner of speaking, their social behavior. Give another ten years and the last of the technical problems will have been resolved. There will be cute little shops down here where the last of the janglers died: *The Jangler Angler. Diphead Creations.* Folks, get your new brain right here. We will beat or match the price of any other dealer in Underground, or my name isn't Daneel Olivaw. No," he said, drawing a shuddering breath, "I don't want to copy myself. Even if it could be done perfectly, and legally, I wouldn't want to do it. There has been quite enough of this self. There has been an uncleanliness, a heaviness whose burden I will be delighted to surrender."

"Isn't that strange," Jennie said. "It's exactly the opposite for me—I feel clean and light, and *that* makes it easy."

I cannot explain how I missed what she was saying.

"You *look* clean and light, my dear," Benjamin said. "I understand this nasty being is your husband. See that he treats you well. See that he gets you out of this hole soon."

To me he said: "You can get her out of here. We needn't continue our subterfuge. Honor has been satisfied."

"You think to turn me on and off like a switch?" I said. "You think that you persuaded me where honor lay, and that you are capable of telling me when it has been satisfied? I am well aware that Airworks Hellas, or perhaps even Airworks Solar has been behind the secessionist business. They think they have met their objectives, and you think you have trapped them. I also know that this was not the only theater of your planning, nor even the main one."

He was surprised. "How did you—? How—?"

"How have I outfigured an old strategist? Benjamin. You pride yourself on your multilevel games. You may disclaim the vanity of your youth, but only because it was vanity, not because you think it was unjustified. Even in rejecting the ultimate value of strategy, you assume you were the best of strategians."

"Quite . . . telling," he said. "And you are better?"

"Not exactly. More practiced. I am sure you give yourself credit for the wisdom of experience. Not only are you the foxiest of foxes, but you are an old fox, crafty with age. But Benjamin, how old are you?"

He saw it, then. "Oh," he said.

"I have the gonads of a young man," I said. "The appearance, and sometimes, I will admit, the emotional temper of one. The hardest lesson has always been, and still is, to see what is there and not what appears to be there."

And as I spoke, I was failing that lesson myself. The second hardest lesson is not to lecture others. If I had been sharp, I would have seen that he had gotten all his old caginess back with the medical boost. I would have known that, although he was allowing me to see his surprise, he was allowing it only in order to detour me into my own vanity, distract me from his final purpose.

Benjamin had recovered his poise. "Very well, old fella," he said. "How about something for this baby child to eat?"

"Eat?" I said. "You're joking. What about the digestive system you don't have?"

232

He thumped his midsection. "Right. I can't digest it, but I can taste it. Got a little collector bag—but I won't dismay you with the details. The point is, I'd like to taste food again while I'm alert enough to enjoy it. Mandrake, how many more times do you think I can boost myself like this?"

"One," said Mandrake. "Maybe two."

"See? I can stay up another twelve hours or so on this one, and then twelve more on the next one, that's it. Minus one Benjamin."

"You really want to eat?"

"I really want to eat. I'll pop in a jive-packet just when we start, and maybe it will feel like a real meal—the taste and then the buzz in the blood."

"I hope you don't expect to tour all the other physical pleasures one last time, too."

He looked at Jennie, spun a half-turn to study Pappy. He came back to me. "Not really," he said. "That has never mattered very much to me. Something about my childhood."

"Shade, he's right," Jennie said. "I could use a little something."

"What, am I elected cook?"

"If you would. I'd like to talk with Benjamin."

"I have a few things I want to say to him myself. I don't suppose you're going to leave his precious side, either," I said to Mandrake.

"I will if you ask me to," he said. "I'd rather stay. I don't have much time left to savor him."

I swear he said *savor.*

I went to fix a meal, angry, this time remembering not to stomp.

While I was slicing and grilling and stirring, Pappy came into the kitchenette. "Hey, Shadowman," she said. "Let's have a look at your teethies."

"Not funny," I said, keeping my back to her. "Benjamin's wobbling off. He makes things up. Dumb things."

I felt her arms come around me, her breasts warm on my back. I tried to set places at the little extruded table, but she wouldn't let go. "Don't think so," she said. "Think we didn't con something weird, back on the range? Hell, Bossman, we used to sit the campfire *talking* about. Johnny C had us half-jived you were an ommie. I said you were a secret weapon, enhanced bio. Don't know if I bought, but.

Think it mattered? We were proud. Weird one, the Shadowman, our mainmain. I was just worried whatever you did when you left for Hellasport was something real sick, something twisted would get you in trouble."

I shook her off, set the plates. "He had no business coming here," I said. "He had no business saying anything."

"Hey, asshole, are you hearing? Fuck do you want? Goddamn monster man, but con, we loves for who you is. Hell of a deal. Take it or jam."

She was dead serious. Undead serious. What the hell, what the hell. I'd been saying that a lot lately. What the hell. All my years of melodrama, declamations on loss and solitude and singleness, the angst of apartness, *Sturm und Drang* of the eternal stranger—all the hard work I'd put into the role, all for naught: I was accepted. It had never occurred to me that this could happen in a kitchen while I was mixing up shit on a shingle.

With mushrooms, which were easy to grow down there. It wasn't much of a final meal for the professor, but he didn't complain. We cracked open a bottle of lightning, Smus'linka '29, real bust-head stuff, and after the smoke cleared, we sat around and drank and ate like old buddies at a card game. Well, Mandrake didn't sit or drink or eat, but you know that, why do I keep telling you?

But finally we got down to matters of business.

"It came down to accelerated capital recovery," Benjamin said. "Airworks Solar has a rate-case in right now, as you may or may not know. It goes to hearing early next year—Earth year—and they're arguing they need a higher rate of recovery for the off-Earth plant in service because the risks are higher because of our 'unstable political environment'. Sam hasn't been looking too friendly at that idea, so they decided to manufacture their own evidence."

"All those people," Jennie said. "All that property. Their own employees, the zoomers, all this. All just so they could tack a few pennies more on the air bill?"

"It's more than a few pennies. It will almost double the monthly bill. They figured it was cost-effective: They sustain a few nanodecs in present damage, to imply continuing losses in the future, which they know they *won't* sustain, and they get it all back from the rates in two or three years anyway."

"I knew it was Airworks," I said, "but I couldn't figure why. But why the bank, why did they minus the bank?"

"That bank handles all the financing for Airworks, by contract. And the bank's losses come out of insurance, right? So the insurance rates go up, the bank recoups by charging higher interest, then investment capital costs more, and Airworks either pays the higher interest here or is forced to go off-planet for Martian-invested capital and pays the off-planet interest tariff. Either way, cost of capital rises, and gives them a projection line to argue from."

"What happens to Airworks now?" I said.

"USUC gets the full dossier on them, and they lose their rate-case, maybe even get a reduction. Which, believe me, will hurt them more than any bomb you could throw."

"USUC?" said Pappy.

"United States Utility Commission," Benjamin said.

"Speaking of dossiers," I said. "Your little performance back there has me a bit worried."

"I do lose control when I don't stay boosted," he said, "but that was not entirely unintentional."

"I figured."

"You understand I've studied you. I'm the reigning expert."

"In a dying subject," I said.

"Unfortunately, that may be true. You are the only survivor I have been able to locate. When I found you were alive, I was hyperjoyed. I am a great admirer of your kind, you know. That's *why* I have studied you."

"Yes," I said, "I remember. You were quite expressive."

"But do you understand how great an admirer I am? Your power, your clarity, your honor. We all kill in order to live, but most of us are able to hide from the fact. It is an abstract transaction, like a bank account. We make a deposit to the society, a piece of our life. We make withdrawals in order to pay for our food, our air, our luxuries. With every withdrawal, someone somewhere dies. But we never see it. We live in the mud and murk of ignorance, and we call it innocence. You cannot do that. You must live, always, with the truth of your nature."

Oh boy, I thought. I don't know how to break the news to you, Benjamin, but. . . .

"You saying the Shadowman's the only—damn, it *is* a strange blip—that he's the only vampire left?" Pappy said.

"That's what he's saying," I said. "I was hoping I was wrong. Hoping he would have better news."

"Well you poor baby," she said.

"There may be others," Benjamin said. "I haven't found them. Vampiry has been my obsession for a good part of my life. I went military—seeking self-respect, I suppose, but that is neither here nor there. Strategy led me almost inevitably into artificial-intelligence work—"

"I thought so," I said.

"And artificial intelligence led, as night must follow the day, into governmental intelligence. I became a spook, a master of spooks. But through it all, I have maintained my file. Each career gave me unique opportunities for research and study. I had myself transferred here because you were here, John Shade, and not for any other reason. It cost me several grades, but I felt I really had no other choice. My uncle—my vampire uncle—had disappeared, he and his friend. I couldn't find out whether they had died, or were simply hiding. Then I lost touch with the half-dozen others I had met through him, and I couldn't locate the twenty-three I had painstakingly discovered myself. You were not in the files, incidentally, except as a rumor. I thought you were probably a myth, a wish-fulfillment fantasy they whispered among themselves: the vampire not as an enemy, a hunted monster, but a friend to the state. Even if the state didn't know it. When I saw your name on a bill of lading during a routine survey—your name, and the name of your ranch—"

"I got careless," I said. "Or frustrated. Same thing."

"The name alone brought me here. Your ID was nine nines, all normal. The name alone."

"So what happened to them?" Pappy said urgently. "The vampires, what was killing them?" She looked at me, and I saw the closest thing to fear I have ever seen in her eyes. It was an intense but calm consternation, with a slight admixture of uncertainty.

"Bad blood," I said. Benjamin looked at me with a wild hope, as if I really had an answer, then saw my dark humor.

"I don't know," he said to her. "I was hoping he could give me some clue. All I can tell you is that he seems to be healthy. Whatever fate has befallen his kindred, he has so far escaped. Perhaps he will continue to do so. I devoutly hope it."

I was getting tired of being talked about in the third person.

"Why vampires?" Jennie whispered.

Benjamin understood her, but had no answer. He shrugged. He bowed his head as if discouraged. "You've been my life's work," he said to me. "My real work. I am ashamed to say that finally I cannot help you at all. Except perhaps psychologically. You seem fine physically, Shade, but it was my judgment that you were increasingly out of balance mentally. It was, I decided—and Mandrake concurred—your sense of isolation that was at fault. And we have come full circle. I kept your secret to protect you. I betrayed you a little while ago for the same reason. Mandrake said these two could be trusted."

I was hearing the agent of my fate. Benjamin was unburdening himself of his life's story, preparing his grand exit, and I, however importantly I figured, was just a figure in that story. I didn't like it, I didn't like it one bit, even though it had all been, supposedly, for my own well-being; even though I agreed with his assessment of my state of mind. It was my anger, I assumed, that was causing the headache.

"What becomes of my file?" I said coldly. "My friends may not betray me, but what becomes of the information in my file?"

"The Nightshade Dossier is safe," he said. "Outside of my mind, which will soon be extinct, there is only one copy of it. There." He pointed at Mandrake, who had gone through the lock back into the bedroom, and was dancing slowly like a child, like wavering seaweed, and humming to himself.

The Nightshade Dossier. Christ. My life, a bad spy novel.

"War's over, then?" Pappy said. "You pinned the baddies, and we can all go home to Shadowfall? Deed's did, secret's safe, and we can boost?"

"Not quite," Benjamin said. "Soon. We're negotiating. Right now, the projected settlement gives Hellas three concessions: One, Centerpole agrees to replace twenty percent of the Earthborn management over the next five Martian years, of which no more than half may be from Argyre; two, the zoomers have their required on-line reduced by an as-yet-unspecified amount, but probably in the range of an hour's ipop per day per zoomer; three, there will be no implementation of the tariff on bevo freighters held for shipping at the Lagrangian points, and charges will be dropped against all ranchers involved in what they are willing to nonprejudicially describe as 'nonparametric a.med response'. That means you, Shade. I think you're the only rancher to have taken any overt action against Sam."

I heard the bad news in what he left out. "And what does Sam get?" I said.

"He gets the janglers," Benjamin said. Jennie drew her breath in sharply.

Benjamin looked at her: "It's not as bad as it sounds. If the settlement goes through, you'll all get experimental-citizen status. We're—they're *going* to want to study you, no way around that. Sooner or later, they're going to solve the problems with brain-to-digital recording, or they're going to come up with a fully bioartificial brain that will record. They think that studying you will be a big help. Imagine—a whole society, literally a laboratory culture. I would be surprised if the sociomechs weren't interested, too." If his eyes had been bio, they would have been gleaming. I could see that as much as he despised the world, in this one realm he hated to leave the chase. Vampires, hell. His true love was brains.

"And if we don't want to be laboratory animals?" Jennie said, fire in her voice.

"Then you die. They come into the tunnels, and they hunt you down, every last one, if it takes ten years. But that doesn't matter, does it? You have an escape plan. The ones of you who don't like the settlement can leave when the escape plan goes into effect. It isn't as though the settlement has *worsened* your options." He seemed apologetic before her, understandable enough when she got in that mode. "It's the best we can do," he said. "Believe me. It's the Argyrians who are taking the hard line. That's the one element I have failed to understand, what their involvement is. I know they're deadset against you, though. It was all we could do to work out this compromise. They wanted you all dead, every one of you, period, *finalemente*. Slam."

His tone became puzzled. "I even tried to see if they were paying Sam to ship in the marines, but the contract is off-the-scale classified. I couldn't buy it with the annual budget of my whole division. Just couldn't get to it."

Alarms were going off in my mind, almost literally. The headache was banging my temples: "What was the number?"

"What?"

"The number, what was the number? How much did the classified cost?"

He thought a moment, remembering. "Two hundred, I think," he said. "Something on the order of two hundred megadecs. Why?"

Mandrake had heard the stridency in my voice and come into the kitchenette.

"I think we're aced," I said. "You didn't happen to check the troops manifest while you were doing all that investigating, did you?"

"I can do it now," Mandrake said. "There will be a copy of it on file in CI. John, they've classified the manifest, too."

"How high?"

"It would take everything we've gotten from sales of the rights," he said.

"Spend it. Spend it now."

"What's going on?" Jennie said. "Shade, what are you so upset about?"

"Em-vee-squared," I said. "Energy, dammit."

"John, they aren't shipping troops," Mandrake said.

"What is it? AI deto?"

"Close. It's tunnel dogs. Seventeen thousand tunnel dogs."

"Which they will have repriffed with infra, motion pick-ups, CO_2 sniffers, speed decks, cannon blasers, the works."

"I don't understand," Jennie said. I couldn't tell whether Benjamin was following my logic.

"Why would they classify a shipping contract so high?" I said. "The fact that the gyros are helping Sam isn't going to surprise anybody, and the shipment itself has been all over the news for days, even if they did fake us out about what it contained. There's only one reason I can think of. They wanted to hide the time of arrival. What does the Solar Elevator cost for a three-week ride for that mass cargo, Mandrake?"

"It depends a bit. Normally between forty and sixty megadecs."

"Make the rough assumption that the price of the classified reflects the price of the contract. They didn't think about that, but it will, because there's no point in securing something above its operating value. What's the cost on the Elevator? Energy, mostly. Kinetic energy is proportional to the square of the velocity. They bought more than four times the standard contract, means they bought better than double the standard velocity. They're almost *here*. They're planning to come down into the tunnels and clean us out before the settlement goes through."

Benjamin stood up in the quad rig, shifting to walking mode. "Then it is time for me to abandon one more of my guises," he said. "We'd better call a board meeting."

When I rose, my right knee buckled, a pain arrowed under my heart. I hid it, and stayed behind to let the pain fade, pretending to need a drink of water. I was wondering if the fact that the Need was coming on me so rapidly now, at such short intervals, was a symptom of whatever had taken the rest of the vampires.

Not to engage in false suspense, that was not the case. But I didn't know that then. This was three times in a matter of weeks. Over the centuries, the Need had struck no more than an average of two dozen times a decade, and had sometimes been absent as long as a year.

And I was thinking how ironic it was, the Need beginning again while I sat at table with human friends, accepted at last. If we had sat at that table a few more hours, one of them would have died. Benjamin might have had a most fitting exit from this life. In the last hours of the Need, when the body will shift to whatever shape it must have to accomplish its aim, the vampire cannot remember a human motive. Blood is good, and one should take it. I would have been perfectly capable, in such a state, of ripping out Pappy's throat and gulping her blood with great affection: My friend, and now she fed me. The best I could do, if I was not willing to maroon myself somewhere high in the Wall beforehand, so that I could die before I found a victim, was to insure that I was in the company of an appropriate victim when the time came on. And if I had been willing to maroon myself, I can promise you that I would have spent my last few hours coming down out of the mountains in a shape and at a speed you would not believe, heading for town.

When I got to the boardroom, Sinclair was there—through Jennie, I supposed, as a friend of the board; and the bird-headed man, and two of the wheeled men, and a number of others, including the cylinder, Blue Ice.

Then Benjamin did a thing that surprised me more than it should have. He walked the quad rig over to where the cylinder stood, and said, "Are you ready, friend?"

You know that I am no more interested in preserving this intelligence than you are, came the voice from the ceiling, and I heard again that wintry whisper of amusement.

"In that case," Benjamin said, and buttoned the manual ipop. A panel opened soundlessly, and showed rows of switches. Benjamin's hands flickered over them, and the patterns of lights on the cylinder changed, formalized. There were now banks of lights in three colors, red, blue, and a deep sea-green, and they blinked in slow synchronicity.

You have entered the initial deletion menu, said the ceiling. *Do you wish to continue, or exit the menu?*

"Continue," Benjamin said, the rhymes and the echoes confusing each other so that I heard the walls saying *in you in you in you.*

Do you wish to delete sensory status, Code Red?

"Yes."

This is valuable data. You should be certain you have made a back-up copy before you continue. Do you wish to continue?

"Yes."

The red lights blinked out two at a time, exactly on the stroke of their flicker.

Code Red deleted. Do you wish to delete logical status, Code Blue?

"Yes."

This is valuable data. You should be certain you have made a back-up copy before you continue. Do you wish to continue?

"Yes."

Code Blue deleted. Do you wish to delete analog status, Code Aqua?

"Yes."

This is valuable data. You should be certain you have made a back-up copy before you continue. Do you wish to continue?

"Yes."

Goodbye, Benjamin, said the high cold voice. And then the voice changed, became the voice of Betsy, the friendly operator.

"Code Aqua deleted," Betsy said cheerfully. "This brain is ready to accept new copy. Thank you for using a Wannerbrain Electronics Product. For the best in electronics, Wannerman."

"Goodbye, Benjamin," Benjamin said. He turned to the rest of us. "I don't know whether that's murder or suicide," he said. He looked at me. "I've been down here for a long time, working through my copy. Mandrake kept us updated in parallel. I liked what you called him. I've seen a lot of Blue Ice."

The man did love the quirks of intrigue. And he loved death so much he did it twice.

To the board, he said, "In effect, my identity has been presiding over this board. Unless there are objections, it will continue to do so." None of momma's little janglers objected at all, and he continued: "We have good reason to believe that the wetbrains will be striking much sooner than expected, perhaps at any moment. All of you are aware that we have a contingency plan. Some of you are aware of the details. The plan has been in effect for six days already, but we must now accelerate our schedule. For those of you who have not been fully briefed, I would ask you to pay careful attention for the next few minutes."

That was me, I presumed. Maybe Sinclair. A few other grunts and lesser entities.

I paid careful attention. It wasn't easy. I was feeling spooky weak, a breathy sort of panic just short of classic anxiety. The shakiness accented the pains radiating from my temples and under my heart. It wasn't the onset of the Need that frightened me, though. The instinct of the monster is to keep himself hidden. I couldn't let them know I was a vampire again. It seemed especially important not to let them know, now that they had accepted me for one. Go figure.

The escape plan was staggering in scale, but sounded absolutely crazy, impossible to pull off. Under the apparent bottom of Bye-Bye Bozo (and now I conned the name), another shaft dropped a full two kilometers into the crust. At the base of *that* shaft, a long tunnel angled slowly upward, well beneath the range of the scopers until far outside of Hellasport. This tunnel ran south some five hundred astonishing kilometers under the surface of Mars, opening at last in Crater 47. They had been working on the tunnel, and on warrens in the wall of the crater, for years. They thought they could break out, and hide in the walls, where the satellites couldn't see them, until they won citizenship. They would blow Bye-Bye Bozo and the concealed shaft behind them, and their escape route would never be found. All this past week, they had been moving the janglers in the lower levels out into the escape tunnel, bivouacking for exit.

It was insane. It would never work. I could not let Jennie go with them. She would have to break for the surface with Pappy and Johnny C and Babalu and whatever normals decided to take their chances topside. She couldn't hide for long, but maybe when I got back I could do something to help. If I could get her to my rabbit hole, my secure hideout—

I say *When I got back* because I was planning to go topside for blood. Topside because I didn't want them to know what was happening to me. I might catch some poor normal here, but the chances of discovery were too high—even if none of the janglers conned it, the news would spread of the strange death, and my friends would know. I was going to propose a diversionary raid, primarily as an excuse to get away, although in fact such a raid wasn't a bad idea.

The meeting went on a long time, committees hammering out details of the speed-up, before I could find a way to introduce the idea of the raid. From the way the pain was taking me, I doubted I had twenty-four hours, and I was hostile and impatient when I raised the idea, drawing strange looks. They couldn't understand why I didn't want to take any men with me. When I said that I knew the territory, and could move through the night to my target without being noticed, there were four who knew what I meant. I was certain the tunnel dogs would be brought in on the cannon lines, and not in freight-fliers. Fliers would take too long, and the traffic would be highly noticeable. On the cannon lines, the traffic could be hidden in the usual flow of freight, and still arrive in the city in one day. Besides, it was probably impossible to do anything if the dogs were shipped in on the fliers, since the only common transport points were going to be at loading and unloading. At the unloading point, we would be heading into full battalions, and the loading point, the Wall docks for the spaceport, was four hundred kilometers away—we would never get near it. I could hit the cannon lines anywhere along the route and succeed in delaying their deployment.

I said the important thing was to deliver an explosive to the cannon lines, and it was the size of the explosion, not the size of the strike force, that counted. They insisted on a double strike, one to wait in ambush at the most probable deployment point if the dogs came in on the fliers. I finally gave in, on condition I tried my strike alone. The damned board was starting to think it knew how to run things just at the wrong time, but I was in a bad position to try to control them, since I was planning to run off on what they saw as a one-man glory mission, not the proper function of a true commander.

I was surprised Jennie didn't insist on going along with me or with the other strike force, but I was relieved. We set her up with Sinclair in combined command of multiple fall-back squadrons near the surface, patrolling the most likely down-shafts for the initial tunnel-dog incursions. They were to fire and blow and fall back in good order, protecting the rear as the janglers made their escape, and last of all, get out themselves. Sure. But they bought it. My hope was to succeed in blowing the cannon lines, get blood, and get back before the wetbrains repaired and redeployed. Then I would somehow get Jennie and Pappy and the others to break for the surface. Even if I had to conk her and carry.

It took a long time, Jesus, it took a long time to work it all out. When we broke and headed back for our suite, Jennie was silent. I was hurting so bad I was afraid to talk. It was all I could do to stand up straight. She took this as anger, as displeasure with her.

At home—*home,* that word again—she raked the cold leftovers with a stale piece of bread, and ate. We had worked through till evening, and she must have been starving. "You're leaving right now, aren't you," she said, not looking at me, and not really making it a question.

"I don't want to," I said. "I want to spend the rest of this night with you." I sounded defensive, pissed. I sounded completely insincere.

"I'm not in the mood for that," she said curtly.

"I didn't say you were," I said. "I was trying to tell you I—just trying to say. Dammit, you make me so—"

"I don't think you love me," she said.

"Why are you acting this way? It's because of what I am, isn't it? You won't admit it, but that's it, isn't it?"

"If you say so," she said.

A great cold weariness came over me. I had to get out of there, but I couldn't stand going away unloved, unsuccored. Unbelievable how dependent I had let myself become. Doing without for all that time, and then, when I did allow myself something like love, wallowing in woe.

"I don't want to leave like this," I said. "Will you hold me a second?"

She put her arms around me, but her body was as stubborn as wood. I tried to kiss her goodbye, and at first she wouldn't let me. Then I had a brief, twisted flutter of her lips against mine. She pulled away. "You want to go, so go," she said. I gave up, and went. Maybe Sinclair would come comfort her.

Pappy caught me in the hall. "Stayed back, figured you two needed the time," she said. "Looked pretty grim."

"It is grim," I said.

"Always me," she said.

"It ought to *be* you," I said.

"Had any sense, would be," she said. "Come back alive, we'll see. Can't kill, can they?"

"Not even with a stake through the heart," I said.

"Leaving tonight?"

"Now."

"Won't be here when you get back. Boosting while can, taking the boys. Nine nines? Come find me after? Stay if you need my pull."

"Nine nines, was hoping you would. Will find, don't need. Take the gel?"

She grinned wickedly. "You ain't normal, Shadowman, that's for sure. Yeah. She'll go, I'll take." She raised her hand for a goodbye grip, then hugged me and walked quickly away down the corridor, not looking back.

It took me less than an hour to prep. I didn't see Mandrake and

Benjamin anywhere, and I didn't see anyone I knew at the staging area, but the blowpacks I'd asked for were there. Where were the other soldiers? If they were prepping the alternate strike, they were taking their time. Wasn't my problem.

I didn't tell anyone when I left. Fuck em. By that time I hated the whole of Underground, hated the janglers, the normals, hated Benjamin and his idiotic machinations that I had let my own weakness for action suck me into, maybe didn't quite hate Mandrake, maybe. Hated Jennie, hated her most especially, deserting me once again, as she had three centuries ago by dying. I was not particularly lucid by then. Hated her, sure. Was just following through, finishing what I had started. Right. Honor, you know. Get her out of here alive, and then—

It was a relief to get into the deserted back tunnels, not have to conceal the stagger in my breathing, the broken rhythm of my gait. The pain was more general now, but had its bright nodes in the front of my brain, in my knees, and ran like a sheet of fire all through my rib cage.

I was going to come up through Riverrun River again. There would be soldiers there, but they wouldn't be guarding the river, they would be guarding the houses and the access roads, watching for fliers. In the night, I could avoid them easily. By now I knew that I didn't have time to blow the cannon lines first. I had to have blood, and that, too, I could find in Riverrun. One of the soldiers, maybe. No time to be picky. And then I could blow the lines, shifting and heading down for Della Culebra, catching a freight to take me out along the lines if I could, running in a few miles if not. The beauty of blowing the lines was it didn't matter where. Anywhere would slow them down. No problem, no problem. Nibbits pokoities.

At the waterfeed station, I had to flood the chamber myself. Hadn't been time to get the engineers down-tunnel. Just as well, because I was hunched over like a man born with a twisted back, making noises to keep the pain at bay: WAH-BAH-BAH WAH-BAH-WHAM-A *DAMN* BAH BAH YAAAAAAH YAAAAAH HUNH!

And then I was in the dark water, working upstream, and the water seemed to dissolve some of the pain and carry it off—but that may have been numbness.

246

And then I was standing up in the shallows of the water, and searchlights were coming on, and the riverbank got bright as an Earthside noon, and a harsh, amplified voice was ringing out over the water: "FREEZE IT, COMMANDER. YOU'RE PINNED. WE CAN BOIL THE WHOLE RIVER IF YOU MOVE."

I didn't move. I could move fast, but not fast enough to get out of their range: Even a vampire might have trouble getting through life with his head burnt to carbon, a dark curl like the spent end of a struck match. I could have blown the explosive packs, but similar difficulties obtained.

"RELEASE THE EXPLOSIVE PACKS AND YOUR WEAP-ONS INTO THE WATER, COMMANDER. WE WILL PICK THEM UP DOWNSTREAM. CAREFULLY, PLEASE. NOW COME ASHORE ON THE SIDE YOU'RE FACING."

I came ashore to a ring of grinning troops, blasers at ready. The captain, in headgear, said into his phones, "We've got him, sir. Subject is apprehended, and has been disarmed. Yes sir. Yes sir. He looks pretty bad, sir. Looks like he got hurt in the river. No sir. Yes sir. Right away, sir." He snapped out a crisp order to his sergeant: "He wants to see the subject personally. Form a squad and get him up there. Keep the lights and the guns on him, and get a comm-set on his head. He wants to talk to the subject on the way."

So I went marching up the hill, trying to stand straight. I went, sobbing for breath, and maybe my guard thought I was sobbing with fear, but they were professional, well-trained, well-paid, light-years above the stones, and I got not a taunt, not a jeer, not a rap in the kidneys.

"Commander Shade, are you there?" came the voice in the headphones. It was a voice I felt I should recognize, a clipped, precise voice, not so much cold as completely sure of itself, so that no effort was made to conciliate with warmth of tone. The voice of a high-echelon gyro.

"I'm here."

"You sound bad."

"You're concerned?"

"You might be surprised. You do realize the hopelessness of your cause? The war is over. We knew your plan, we will be waiting for the alternate squad when they try *their* foolish maneuver. We know where Commander Dark's forces will be stationed, and we know of the escape tunnel. We will be waiting in 47 when they break out. No zoid will escape alive. You see that, don't you?"

And where did you learn *that* word, I thought. And then I thought, Jennie. I prayed that Pappy had left, had left right away, and taken Jennie with her. That they had all gotten out and away and safe, but I knew it would not be so. I knew Jennie would, if she survived the first assault by the tunnel dogs, head right down the escape tunnel into the final ambush.

But you follow through. You keep trying.

"Who are you? I know you're a traitor—this isn't Benjamin again, is it?"

A soldier to my right caught my arm as I stumbled over a loose stone. The voice laughed in my ears. "That old fraud? Playing his tricks with mirrors?" And I knew who it was before the voice shifted, lowered, said, "You kiddin me, bro?"

"Why?" I said. "What are you up to, Sinclair?"

"Hey, ma-mainmain, I just do what I'm told, right?" He returned to the clean accents of his natural dialect. "If I had to guess, though, I'd say that Argyre went under to study the janglers as personality modules for the Argyre net, but they didn't project very reliable or cost-effective. And we can't just leave them on the market cluttering things up, can we? Retrofitting may not pay in the long run, but it could look attractive to some of our customers, and cut into the early return on our own new line."

I was not angry, not black with rage. Just empty. Hollow. A shell of increasing pain around an emotionless void. "That's why you set Jennie up, isn't it? Her accident wasn't an accident." I had been inutterably stupid to have missed that. A freakish combination of circumstances, completely unlikely to have happened in just that necessary order, and I had swallowed it without a second thought.

We had come up out of the woods now, and there were houses ahead. The soldiers spread out around me, and we headed down the lane to the nearest house, a big colonial monstrosity.

"Had to have a way in," Sinclair said. "You mustn't think I don't like her. She's really rather a fine girl, but there's very little I can do for her now. Fortunes of war."

"Why haven't you killed me?" I thought perhaps I knew, and in that lay our one small hope. He had been testing me, exaggerating his mockery to see whether I would overreact, or play it smart and try to save my own skin.

"Let us say that we feel you still have some value to the state," he said. "Provided you do not resist."

We had come to the house, and a guard inside let us into a foyer cavernous with pillars and brilliant with mirrors, the ceiling five meters over our heads.

They stripped me and searched me, probing my asshole, my gullet, even running a scope over my penis, massaging my gut and the big muscles for implants.

"He's clean, sir," I heard the sergeant report. "But this man is sick." A pause. "Yes sir."

They held the headset back to my ear, my mouth. "Let us also say that I do not take rejection well," the hard voice said. "Do you understand me?"

"I think so," I said. Caught my breath. Had to play it right, give him enough resistance to pique his craving for dominance, not enough to make him kill me. "I'll do what you want if you'll spare Jennie."

"You are in no position to make requests. You bargain now for your life alone. Take it or leave it."

"I'll take it," I gritted out, using the pain to create a tone of self-loathing. The aura had started, late this time, but coming on fast, a rainbow vortex squeezing my vision down.

"Very good," he said. "Welcome to my home away from home. Come up, and let me make you a drink."

The sergeant tapped three men, two of whom took my arms to support me while the third stood back, weapon trained. They hustled me up the stairs, still naked, and then along a marbled corridor. We came to a tall door of solid wood, and one of my guards buttoned the buzzer.

"Send him in," said a voice from the speaker beside the door. They opened the door and flung me in, so that I staggered to my knees. I heard the door close behind me. I looked up to see Sinclair, tiny in a business suit, at the far end of a roaring tunnel. His skin was several shades lighter, and he looked a good deal older. He smiled.

"Hello, blood," I said.

24

The Second Bad
Dream of the Man

He found himself in a forest, naked. There were confused images fading in his mind—fragments of dreams, he would have thought, but he could not remember when he had dreamed them. Certainly not just now. There were men running through the woods, running and shouting, carrying . . . rifles? There was a wild boar, a razorback hog, who lifted his snout incuriously to watch them. The man saw this from somewhere close to the ground. Men, legs running. He did not so much see the boar as sense it nearby, a massiveness at his shoulder, a thickening of air.

There was an image of a man who had cut off another man's face, and patched it to his own, bloody and stretching. This man sauntered toward a group of men. The bloody mask began to smile, but the face behind it was a grimace, the scowling mirth of a devil. The mask was sliding down. Something terrible was about to happen.

There was an image of a great castle whose lower levels sank into the sulfurous caverns of Hell, the marble floors mingling with walls and vaults of dark, uneven stone. Demons flitted, or shadows. Somewhere in the bowels of this labyrinth waited a princess, slender and blonde and pale. He could see her. He could see her pity and fear. He saw the castle from a distance, shrouded in web like a paralyzed moth, dreaming its long paralysis till he should come at last, the spider, deliverer.

The man could make nothing of these images, and so he let them go. The tree he leaned against was covered with a moss that spread over a tumble of nearby stones, and then over the forest floor for several feet around him, an island of green velvety ground. Here and there leaves were caught in the moss, scraps of stiff curl made precious by their setting.

The forest was an old forest. It had never seen the ax. The trees soared, tall and stately, and generous columns of light filtered through, changing a bit with the easy sway of the leaves, brightening, dimming. Brightening.

But something was wrong, badly wrong, and the man realized that that was why he had come here, to think what was wrong. He had sat here, under the tree, to collect his wits and think what was wrong. The angle of the light was strange. Something was wrong with the light. It was the light of late afternoon, rich and haunting, but it slanted too steeply.

This was not the right forest. And where was his horse? He had to find his horse. He had to get back before they—

Something bad was going to happen. He could almost think who it would happen to, but the memory escaped him. He knew better than to try to force it. Then he would lose it entirely. Better to let the memories steal back on their own. But something bad was going to happen, might already be happening, and he had to act.

There were raiders in the woods, renegades. That was what the image of running men had meant. There were raiders in the woods, and they were— He had to—

Where was his horse? This was not even a mountain wood. There was a river nearby, downhill, he could smell it. Where—

It came to him then that he was in an enchanted wood. Good Christians were not to credit such things, but there was no other possibility. It explained the lightness of his body, his feeling that he had no solidity. It explained his disorientation, his loss of memory, his sense that he had just been created, his sense of complete isolation, as if there were no way out of these woods, no road home, no path back to, to—

If he were in an enchanted wood, then the usual signs would not do. He must follow something else. And with the thought, he sensed the river below, carving a black trail through the magician's wilder-

251

ness. The sense of the river took him downhill instantly, unhesitant, unfaltering. He went over the earth with the floating and sure-footed dreaminess of a deer.

At the river, he knew he must plunge in. He offered a short prayer to the spirits that lived in the river to take him in and guide him through the water and help him home. Forgive me, Dear Master, he prayed first. Forgive me for this my pagan faithlessness. *And then he prayed, as the Indians did, to the spirits of the river. And dived.*

It seemed he was in the water as soon as he thought to dive, because he floated so lightly down, but then darkness closed over him, and the shock of the cold water. He was drowning, swept into the undercurrent. An otter, a large fish, something brushed his body. The spirits of the river were all about him, unseen, a darting and quivering host.

They must have granted his boon, for he felt himself able to breathe, to draw life from the water like a fish, and he could see in the darkness. He could see the stir and curve of the water, and he could see the flickering hosts, presences that swerved and went in a warm glow. He was one with the water now, and went where it wanted to take him, quickly, easily, slipping from stroke to stroke.

It did not surprise him to find a magical door under the river, a curious round door set into a cave of the current, nor did it surprise him that he knew the incantation to open it, and that he could speak the incantation aloud in the water.

There were more charms and barriers to solve, but at each he found the necessary knowledge rising within him, the gift of the spirits—or of his Saviour, for he was aware that he was making his way down into the dark veins of Hell.

He spent a long time running tranced in darkness, but a certainty guided him from corridor to corridor, a soul that was not his own chose the way at each branching. He was naked as Adam, a naked man running in darkness, but it was meet, it was fitting. One did not go down into the Pit with the earthly vanities still clinging.

He came then to a great cavern, with fountains ascending. Set into the sides of the cavern were crystalline chambers. He knew that he needed one of the chambers, and he knew which one. The room that was the planning room of the Evil One, where he plotted his vengeance on God.

Thinking of it, he found himself in it.

An ebon desk, black as the heart of Satan. A charmed desk, with a demon in it. He called the demon by name, and the demon bespoke him. The demon bespoke him as if the man were its master, the Evil One himself.

Let me speak to the magician, the man commanded. But the demon would not summon the magus until the man called him by his secret name, and so he spoke a name that he could not hear himself saying.

The magician appeared across the room, and beside him, a dragon. The magician sat in a curious chair, a chair that seemed a part of his body, strange with meaningless engravings. He slept, his head fallen to one side, and the man understood that he must deal with the magician's avatar.

Speak, dragon, *he said.*

John, *said the dragon.* John, is that you? I can hear you, but I cannot see you. Let me have your image.

The dragon knew his name, and that frightened him.

I do not know why I am hidden from you, *he said.* Unless the good God does not wish you to have full power over me just yet. You may not have my image.

John, *said the dragon again.* John, are you trancing? I don't have your image because the desk isn't sending it. We're hollow. We're not really there.

I am well aware that I deal with apparitions, *the man said. And then he knew the question he needed to ask, the reason he had summoned these creatures.*

What have you done with Eleanor? *he said.*

Eleanor? *said the dragon.*

The princess, *said the man.* The pale princess.

But as he spoke, the man knew he was wrong. She was no princess. She was a plain girl, a plain girl of the countryside, a girl made to freckle by sun. As he saw her face, he felt himself sicken with fear and failure, for he knew that there was no castle, that this was no enchantment to be won through, but a dream, his own dream going bad. An enchantment changed by its own rules, but a dream had no rules.

The dragon was no dragon, but someone he knew, arrayed in

strange disguise. The magician no magician, but his father, aged, slumping to death.

He was trapped, then: There would be no awakening, no relief that the horror was fading. The princess, the girl, the bride might flee forever into unreachable changes, lost and condemning.

He saw her face widen in a horrible laugh, showing the fangs of a beast. He saw her mutilated, defiled. He understood that these were images of his choosing, were what would happen if he did not solve the enchantment. But it was no enchantment, but the dream of an enchantment, and he could not solve it, and he felt himself failing.

You are *the Evil One, he thought a voice said, and he saw himself dancing with donkey ears, a donkey tail, around a fire, his lust swaying free. He danced in a shameful joy, a dark night's immortal debauch. He danced, and his cohort demons danced, the dragon, the magus, and yet another. Skulking and merry, they danced about the fire in which she burned to bones, the fire he had built to burn her.*

John, she's gone, *the angel said. It was the angel who had been the dragon. It was the angel of many faces.* We don't know where she went. We think she left with the others, but we don't know. She left without telling us.

Where is my trumpet, then? *the angel Gabriel said to himself. Dragons, angels, young girls, old men, all were gone. There had been no princess, no dragon, no old man with the dragon, no Satan, no old bad god. That was a fading dream. There was the passage of dark flights of thought through the mind. A fall through the bottom of Hell, a long dark journey whipping the coach through the fleeing damned, confusion, struggle, alarm. The harrowing of Hell, the hounds dropping down from above.*

But all of that did not really happen, was only a thought in the mind of the angel Gabriel, who stood in a blaze of glory, and lifted a trumpet, and blew the blast that ended the world.

So that there was no angel Gabriel, there was only himself, the man John Shade, in a bay not far from the exit mouth of the 47 tunnel, weaponless in a crowd of burning janglers, while blasers hissed and spat all about him. Shit, he said.

And then he died.

25
Burning Jennie

Nothing is worse than not finishing. We may be broken off like a redbird in a snowstorm, dead in the heart of winter, hawk-torn. Our vitals scattered, blood on the snow. That has its beauty, its fierce propriety.

But nothing is worse than failing to follow through, to complete the arc we began. There are many excuses, no pardons. There is the excuse that we begin badly, in ignorance and youth, and now see better. There is the excuse of hardship, that we have borne too much, our strength has withered, our will gone bitter. There is, worst of all, the excuse of contentment. As we grow fat in a prairie of succulent grass, drowsing stupid and belching in bovine sun, what do the old plans matter? We are no longer the builders, can hardly remember ourselves as the builders, have been transformed by some beneficent Circe, to idle our days in a slow and somnolent languor.

Nothing is worse. Always, whatever our fortunes, we can angle into the moment, play the bad odds and the good like the hawk, who hops, fluffs, bears into the wind. Tears his prey. Looks all about. Tears his prey. Looks all about. Who, when he flies, searches the seams of the changing air, and will die in a storm himself.

Whatever is behind us, whatever wreckage, we can choose how to enter the next moment, with what grace. That choice we always have, until something larger and faster occurs from the blankness to take us away. Whatever stupors of future happiness we may imagine, that is the only choice we have. *Live for the moment,* advised the inept hedonists of an ill-educated age. No. Live *into* the moment, alert, on balance, choosing.

The snow is over Shadowfall, and out our window, today, we saw a sharp-shinned hawk stamping, tearing its kill, a cardinal. As you may have supposed.

I sit at my desk in the lamplight, in the otherwise darkened study. Mandrake waits quietly in the dim corner. *Waits* is not exactly the right word, he has explained. He could last, theoretically, for a million years. Or two. In the meantime there is plenty to think about. Nor does it disturb him to stand blank for long intervals, no more than it might disturb a cat. He has no dread of mortality to make him fretful at idleness. No more than a cat.

Downstairs, a silver-haired woman snores the ragged sleep of the aged, tearing a hole in the night. Each indrawn shuddering snort ends with a gasp, the mouth falling open. I hear in her breath a rhythm spavinned, back-broken, tire-flatted, spring-busted, the whinnying slam of metal on metal. Finality. She has no interest in janglification. *One copy is quite good enough, thank you,* she says. When she wakes, she will smile, sip coffee. Wall-grade. The butterfly over her face seamed and weathered to the low glory of old parchment. Her eyes merry, bright spots in the wings of the butterfly. She will have a wicked suggestion regarding the day's priorities.

She may live for many years yet. Just now, however, I do not wish to attend the sound of that breathing. I've come up here instead, to finish. As well as I *can* finish. I have let this story lie for a long time, no longer driven to tell the events that drove me. Still. There is a round, a completeness. There is at long last, for me, a rhythm.

It was not really that I lost interest, only that the narrative came too near its author, too close to his present. Not comprehending himself, how could he end his story?

Tonight, dear Jennie, I popped one of those silvery spheres into the player, one of those trinkets the size and hue of my favorite steelie during my third childhood. Small as they are, they can contain all of a human mind. This one doesn't, at least not in that sense—only my edited notes, my drafts, the manuscript as far as I was able to take it. Where the manuscript ends, I substituted copies of videos from the time. Newscasts, historical programs, excerpts from relevant entertainments. The few personal stills and vids I have been able to locate. *Aides de mémoire,* reminders against the day I might finish. Which has become, for no good reason, this day, this night, now.

It was Mandrake who suggested it. *You can read them now,* he said. *You're ready. You can read them now, with neither grief nor obsession. It might be a good thing. You're beginning to think ahead too much. It might be a good thing to see that you can contain your past and stay whole. You have known that for quite some time, but it might do you good to prove it tonight.*

There's great stability in what you say, I said.

So I have burned the vid again, after a long time. Burned it, and studied it, and saluted you in your glory, doing what you wanted to do. And now, having read it, I think I must finish the story—your story, my story—so that I can go downstairs again and sleep beside the snoring woman without thinking ahead to the silence.

Mandrake understands me better than I understand myself. I've known that for quite some time, too.

Here's the rest, then. For your ears only, my friends, now that you cannot hear:

I can't say much about what happened after I killed Sinclair. I was in the satisfaction trance almost immediately, and the actual events have become tangled in my mind, confused with hallucination. I can remember some of the images from the trance, and scraps of emotion with them, but the logic that gave them their dreamy coherence—that evaporates further with every year.

I know that I shifted my face to resemble his. I condensed my frame as well as I could, though I couldn't lose mass that rapidly. The face got me surprisingly close to the guards in the hallway before they picked up the anomaly of my size. I don't know what they made of my nudity.

Then a long blank spell. I seem to remember going into the woods, maybe as some sort of animal. I had a floating sense of panic, the knowledge that I had to get back and warn you, Jennie, warn all of you not to go through the 47 tunnel. Though what else you could have done, I don't know.

I remember that it seemed a long time before I found my way back to headquarters, and I had to perform certain rituals, or maneuvers.

I know I talked to Mandrake and Benjamin by holo, though I can't remember what we said, except that you were gone and no one knew where you were, and the tunnel dogs were already coming down. Benjamin, come to think of it, had nothing to say. I remember him as not looking at me, not approving. Except that there's something not right about that, I can't get the image very clear. Was he already dead? I never saw him again.

I must have gotten a shuttle then, and gone down the tunnel. I have a wispy memory of careening down a long dark passageway, scattering refugees before me. I suppose I was hunting you, Jennie, hoping desperately that you were with the others and that I could stop you. I don't remember getting my trumpet, or what I wanted with it, unless I thought I could warn you from a distance, as I had once tried to warn others, many years before.

I took a hit in the side, and came out of the trance without a gun, the horn in my hand. I was pointing it at a big marine with a Farley G-80, and trying to pull the trigger. And after that?

Let us say that it went like this.

The clean-up crew at 47 was weary but cheerful. They were, after all, drawing extended pay. The Nameless Days were coming up, time for carnival and relaxation, and the extra slip would come in handy. Bad jokes and sexual fantasies loosely disguised as personal history babbled over the intercoms, mingling with tech-talk: "Nine nines on that branch tunnel, 7. Clear, and we'll proc the sealers."

The noise was that the clowns had a deal to blister 47 and make a resort. Think of it. Eight hundred kilometers of tunnel from Hellasport prime, a straight shot out. The clowns were going to widen it and sell it to the developers, shops all the way, theme restaurants, historical markers: In this location, thirty-seven janglers died when a tunnel dog. . . .

And then a sea, an actual sea, on Mars. The techies on the Number 19 skidder were arguing how large the "sea" would be, whether to put their pay into interior real estate or into rim property, which might never be developed. It all depended on how much of 47 they flooded.

They worked as they talked, not missing a beat. They scampered around in their vacuum suits hooking the bodies to lines from the skidder. Most of the janglers had been cleared by now, but Number

19 had found a knot of them around the scorched mouth of a natural cave. Some of them had found the work a little gruesome, but hid their reactions and kidded around like everyone else. It wouldn't do to get blipped as a unit function.

"This one's still alive!" The girl had jumped back.

"In vacuum? Get mixed." Her crew boss came over. "Hell, he's stark naked." The body was burned through the head, the face bubbled and fried. Something had torn a huge chunk from his midsection.

"He swallowed."

"Gas bubble in the throat. Hook him top and bottom, case he comes apart in the middle there. Here, I'll stay with you. 'S okay, don't get jammed it spooked you. Nibbits pokoities, happens to everybody. That's good, let's go. On the double." As crew bosses go, he was a pretty decent one.

Number 19 was able to pull all of these bodies out on one go, which wasn't so great, because it meant a short day, short slip. Still, they could stretch it out a bit. Kenny-benny, the driver, fired up the big roach, the skidder, his operator keeping an eye on the drags. The gitalongs quivered, syncopated, blurred into forward. Kenny-benny axed it, but easily. He would stay in low until they made the mouth of the tunnel, then move up through the gears into cruise-gait. It was five k to the dump site, a nice twenty-minute drive. When they got near, Kenny-benny bumped it to skitter, and they all had a laugh watching the bodies bounce behind. He crawled the skidder over the lip of the dune, and slid the load down to where the others were, a nicely executed slow whip that left the vehicle facing back uphill, ready to go as soon as they cut the lines.

Once they had collected all of the bodies, the blades would cover the site, and the orbital mirrors would fuse it to a glassy block. It would probably be a big tourist attraction, a monument to the janglers. Hoo-hah.

The line crew had cut the lines and were slogging back up the dune to the skidder when one of the bodies, the naked man, stood up behind them. Kenny-benny or the operator might have seen it, but they were burning Creamy Pants on the holo. Then it was too late for all of them.

The accident that killed the crew of Number 19 was too bad, but that sort of thing happens in techie work. One of the attractions, truth be known. Gives them their aura of risk and romance. And Kenny-benny, the only survivor, came out of it with hazard pay and insurance. His friends say it changed his luck, though.

Maybe he felt guilty, even though it wasn't his fault the static overload blew the gitalongs, rolling the skidder down the dune and over his friends. He had worked miracles getting the thing upright and limping it back. He had almost been able to save the life of the operator, who should have been belted in and therefore had only himself to blame. The overload had blown the skidder brain, so Kenny-benny had had to bring it back in on full manual. It had blown the recorders, too, no big loss. The ghost-boxes were a joke. No one but the janglers had ever really made much use, see where it got *them*.

The company was extremely grateful for his dedication in salvaging so much of the machine, and Kenny-benny would have had it made in the shade if he hadn't taken it all so hard. He stayed out drinking and getting weightless all the time instead of going right back to work, which would have been the best thing for him. And he watched the news. Kenny-benny never used to watch the news. All a scam, he used to say. Now he even spent some of his hazard pay on hard news, Kenny-benny burning Henny-penny, ha ha. He heard that till he got sick of it. He became kind of a nut on the whole Jangler Rebellion, nobody knew why. Maybe because, in a way, they were responsible for his accident. If they hadn't fought, he wouldn't have been there cleaning up the mess . . . some stupid thing like that. Guilt is a jammer.

The vid he read the most was the one on that Jennie Dark clip. He read it over and over. He had theories how she got caught. He said she wanted it. He said she had been trying a diversionary action to help the janglers get away, a lot of good it did. He said she had a lousy sense of historical parallel. He cursed her, sometimes, as if she were to blame for it all, his accident, his depression, his bad luck. He had never had bad luck before, and it made him really boring.

In less than a year he flipped a car and died. He had been juicing with a hustler come into town to party, a big badass named Mickey Red. This time it was Kenny-benny who got it, vaporized when the jive blew the battery, and the other guy who lived. Mickey Red, thrown clear, came through without a scratch. He was so weightless, he didn't even know he'd been in a wreck.

Mickey Red went back to work, a little range out in S4 called New Poconos, but everyone said he was meaner than ever. He didn't eat right, and he wouldn't pull his share, always arguing with the boss about the right way to do the job.

One day he finally blows, and hikes off into the range, doesn't even draw his slip. He's gone a whole winter, we all think frozen, and then he shows somehow at Shadowfall, John Shade's big place he left to that hustler gel, she got when his name clears. Some kind of big secret deal there, you can count, Sam-sucking or gyro-dicking or something, because right after the war, suddenly he's not a crim any more, he's a hero of the people. 93.7 market share and an 88 majority, can you beat it? Well, no, I was too young to vote, but my daddy did, and he still gets tears in his eyes to talk about. Hell, I read those vids now and it don't mean. Sloppystuff. Old noise. But the Shadowman gets all his rights restored posthumous, and it all passes to the hustler gel. What a luckfucker, right? She even gets the malafrigging *robot*, can you believe, the one they say is worth your megadec and mine and a quad cent besides. And of course, with the robot, she runs the damn thing fine, she makes till she shits slip.

So Mickey Red must have done some thinking while he was walking, he must have changed his tune, because she hires him on. And the last we hear, he's doing pretty good, he's working like a zoid. Which is one of those words, you wonder where it came from, but suddenly everybody's saying it, you know. And the last of the last of the noise, she's sweet on him, the Red. It don't even matter he takes off to town from time to time, leaves her there while he goes partying with some other clip—when he comes home, he's Christ on a popsicle stick, he can do the cunny-jam till the cream catches fire. Slip, blip, and clip, he's got it all.

Let us say that it went like this:

I spent the Novembers, Decembers, Januaries, the Februaries and Marches alone in my hideout, the real one. It was the first solitude I had had since my death. I needed to think things over. To mourn. I needed time to decide. I knew what I wanted to do, but I thought it might be better if I didn't interfere. There had been enough interference. Let the world roll on, clean and orderly, ordained, devoid of my strategies. Let the people I loved arrange their lives in peace, innocent of my survival, free of the trouble I bring.

I wrote a great deal that winter, reliving it all as I wrote. Spewing memory, the chunks of notes that I can create and store in my mind as well as any metafictionist with an interface.

I burned the vid of you, Jennie, that last vid. I burned it over and over. I couldn't bear it, but I couldn't leave it alone. I had to see.

The problem was there wasn't enough to see. There was no vid of you watching the broadcast of my capture, hearing the boasts of my opponents, how they had had, all this time, an agent inside the jangler stronghold, a plant, a spy. There was no vid of you putting it together, connecting the betrayal to the sudden disappearance of your friend Sinclair, and connecting both to probably a thousand other small and subliminal inconsistencies, the sorts of things we ignore when we want to believe we have a friend. And of course they didn't broadcast the fact that something had gone wrong, that Sinclair and some of his men had died shortly after capturing me, and that I had gotten away.

There was no vid of you taking a squad off tunnel patrol, and heading up, no vid of you breaking out into Michelson-Morley and then into the surface at the 590th and M&M lock.

Probably you were planning a pincer move, like the one I had had you perform in Della Culebra, but there's no vid of you saying so. The soldiers who took you said you told them you were going to counterattack at 47, hit the twin command of the Argyre Guard and the marines while they lay in ambush, waiting for the janglers to come riding out like rabbits flushed out of a hole. Surely you knew that plan hadn't a prayer of succeeding. But that's just what they said you said, the soldiers.

There's not even any vid of the battle. They said you fought like a fury, but it was over too quickly for the channels to get there. You would have been blown when you tried to commandeer transport, anyway, but you didn't get even that far. No way the wetbrains could monitor every tunnel, every hole to the surface—that's what the tunnel dogs were for, to close them off as they went. But you came up out of one of the main locks—why? And there they were, five times your force. There is a vid of the field trial. Unnecessary, since you had already been tried and sentenced *in absentia*. But the soldiers figured this was their moment of glory, and called in the channels.

If you could have hung back, just waited a few days. If you could have just stayed with Pappy and Johnny C and Babalu and the few others who made their break to the surface, refusing to go down the 47 tunnel. A few of those bands actually made it, got out before the dogs came down. If you could just have waited. Well, it would be a different world, wouldn't it?

But if you had, you would probably have had a pardon when the settlement went through. You could have gone back to Shadowfall with Pappy, and hid out. She did well with it, though she had to build her herd back up from scratch—your old man wasn't giving anything back. A real stingy bastard, even if your story made him a whole new megadec or two.

You are alive in the vid, though. All that winter in my hideout, I thought that you had never seemed more alive. Tossing your hair out of your eyes, the spring wind blowing it back. Looking up at the sky, where the thin clouds hurry. That weather-looking look, the mouth stretched into what is almost a smile, but isn't just the grimace of someone squinting up to see what's coming. Tossing your hair. Your hands not tied, just you standing casually in the parking lot, looking up at the weather.

What kept me looking, all that long winter, was the blind stupid impossible hope that you would say something to us. Something, anything: *Daddy, you bastard, fuck you, you shit. Mother, don't worry, my soul is just fine. Jive to the janglers. I'm not afraid of death, I think of it as freedom. I was born to die and die well. God is dead, long live God.*

Shade, I love you.

But you don't, you never do. You just stand there at ease, shifting a little from one foot to the other. Doing that bird thing with your hands. Tossing your hair out of your eyes and studying the weather. And the soldiers raise their weapons and burn you down.

When the long winter was over, I packed my small gear, including that vid and most of a book I had cobbled together, and came back down out of the Wall. I walked a sizable distance across the crater, to the far of S2. I hit the gap, hung a left.

Jack Butler

On a Long April evening, not quite a year after your death, I walked up the path from the BDR to where my home had been. There was a lodge there now, a long low shape with a verandah across the back. There were lights on in the windows, whippoorwills and singbugs in the distance. Mandrake was a dark shape leaning over the rail of the verandah, watching me come up.

"We've been expecting you," he said.

Epilogue: Someone to Answer To

If I were you, Dear Reader, there would be a few things I would want to know. The man was not concerned with consistency, but with rendering impressions. He gave himself much credit for style, for his scope and strategy, but it was his earnestness that really counted, his dogged and usually fallible effort to see into the why of his own motives. Along the way, he was not careful with the particulars of logical narration.

Therefore, if we were to presume you existed, Dear Reader, and if I were you, I would have a few questions:

1. Why vampires?

2. Why were the vampires dying out?

3. Did Shade die? Did what was getting the vampires finally get him?

4. Who created Mandrake, and why did they make him so weird?

5. That woman Shade had sex with on feedback—was that Jennie? Puppy? Did she really exist? Did Shade ever meet her again?

6. What happened to Benjamin?

7. What is a system double, and how does it differ from a copy, and why is this question here?

8. Why did Benjamin and the janglers adopt such a stupid plan for escape, and hide it so badly?

9. What was Benjamin up to that Shade never found out?

10. What was the Sam-sucking gyro-dicking deal that made the peace settlement possible and rehabilitated Shade's name?

11. What was crash? Did they ever find a cure?

12. Did they ever perfect a personality recorder, a ghost-box that worked?

13. What was the secret of Mandrake's third lobe?

14. Why does John Shade's book sometimes seem to violate the illusion of the first-person narrator?

15. Did Mandrake ever go crazy?

16. Did humans ever discover a way to exceed the Wu-Wu Limit? Did they make God?

17. What will happen to a poor damned vampire then?

18. Does God have a plan for the Steamer?

19. How the hell can we get answers to all these questions? What if the answers don't even exist?

From one perspective, yours, the reader's, they don't. The questions themselves are very strange. As John asserted in chapter nine, *There are no answers. There are no questions. There is no reader.*

Have you left the wheel of existence? Are you there? Are you here, in this imaginary space, with me?

If so, the answers do not exist. But they will. And that is a most curious satisfaction.

In fact, the answers are all one answer, are all somewhat related. I answer now:

1. Benjamin studied vampires, at first on his own, and later with the help of his friend, the artificial intelligence Mandrake. They were never able to establish the cause of vam-

pirism, but suspected a data-storage mutation. That is to say, they felt that vampires were able to store copies of themselves in some realm other than the biological, perhaps in a continuum something like the science fictional notion of hyperspace, or in the realm of pure information, if there were such a thing, if the two were different. Nothing else would explain the impossible rate of healing, the ability to shift into other biological forms. In a sense, then, they prefigured the janglers, were nature's own janglers. Mandrake and Benjamin further suspected the mutation had a species-benevolent purpose. The mutation may not have completed itself before events overruled it, so that the interim results seemed murderous, but the taking of blood, they felt sure, was an attempt to store the gene plasm, the blueprint of the race, safe from what harm might come.

They were aware of the logical fallacies that underlay these suppositions: the long-discredited presumption that evolution had purpose and direction; the presumption that evolution could proceed from a biological to a nonbiological level. If they had attempted to prove what they thought, they would not have had answers to such objections.

2. They didn't know why the vampires were disappearing either, although the small sample they had showed a statistical pattern. Vampires born after a certain date disappeared first—the latest born, the soonest to go. Vampires born before that date showed the reverse pattern—the oldest went first. John Shade was right on the cusp. They theorized that the vampire mutation had been superseded by the creation of artificial intelligence, and had lost its force. The old ones were dying according to the rare accidents that will kill even a vampire. The young were too degenerate a form of the mutation to survive very long—were in fact succumbing to something very like crash. Again, Benjamin and Mandrake were aware of their unprovable assumptions.

3. Yes. No.

4. Benjamin, of course. At least, he was the director of the

team. He wanted to explore the results of creating a completely new sort of intelligence. And perhaps he wanted, without at first realizing it, to create an AI analog to the one sort of creature he respected, the vampire. And certainly he wanted, without at first realizing it, to create a friend. And see the answer to question 13.

5. No. No. We're still trying to decide. Yes.

6. He died. He wanted to die when the dogs came down the tunnels, with Mandrake beside him (he knew the dogs would not harm Mandrake). He wanted to die with the zoids, for he saw himself as one of them. He wanted to die in penance for his years of manipulating the lives of others. He wanted to die alert, ready for judgment. When he was sure the dogs were on the way, he asked Mandrake to boost him one last time. The boost blew out the last of his heart. He had not wanted to be copied, and he was not copied. His system double completed the settlement negotiations, then canceled itself.

7. A system double is a blank decision-making module, which the owner may program by question and answer, or by other means, to respond to a given contingency as the owner would respond. Once the owner signs off on the double as nine nines coherent with his own responses, the double is empowered to act as the owner's proxy in all matters, including voting, purchasing, and negotiating settlements. It is not therefore a personality, though one may argue that if the process were carried to infinity it would be impossible to distinguish a double from a direct copy. And, because we knew you would want the answer after you read the answer to the previous question.

8. Because that wasn't the real plan at all, silly. What, do you think my good buddy Benjamin was that dumb? Hell, no. All of the janglers, excepting Jennie, and a few soldiers, suicides, and accidents, got out alive. Sort of. How? Refer to the answer to question 13.

9. Benjamin did not think himself capable of love. However, when he knew that he would die, and that he wanted to die, he realized that Mandrake would be alone in the world. He conceived a plan to find Mandrake a friend—and a friend as zoidacious as Mandrake himself, a friend who might live as long as Mandrake herself. This plan was the center and whole cause of all of Benjamin's other maneuvers on Mars, the entire infiltration of the revolution a cover for one little gift of the spirit. You were older, John, but he really was far more subtle.

10. Mandrake and others were working on a unidirectional jet field, remember? A powerful enough application promised the day when Mars could breathe under an open sky. This was a part of the inducement. For the rest, see the answer to question 13.

11. Crash was the interference of one high-density information field with another, an effect that does not occur until the relative density of information exceeds certain levels. When it does exceed them, information appears to be able to interact directly with other information—or, to put it another way, it appears to be able to take on an almost physical reality. Like, for example, the stuff you wetbrains used to call the material universe. This was the reluctant conclusion of the epidemiologists, based on overwhelming statistical correlations—hustlers, for example, living out on the range, rarely suffered from crash, but the incidence in the cities directly paralleled increases in the power and capacity of the nets. No cure for crash was ever found, though we learned how to live with it. You cannot cure an act of God.

12. See the answer to question 13.

13. A ghost-box that worked. Without revealing that in Mandrake he had created the prototype, Benjamin left behind a successful recorder, one that would work even over a distance, without actual contact. This explains the escape of

269

the janglers as well. The drop-shaft under Bye-Bye Bozo was in actuality a giant linear recorder that pumped its records into an even deeper brain. Somewhere under the crust of the planet there dreams a hidden computer, a bank of souls. Mandrake, for years, monitored the net to see if the janglers were slipping in, but never could tell—there were so many ghosts on the net by then, so many ghosts in his/her brain. So the janglers may be there still, dreaming, and waiting their time. Or they may have gone where the rest of you went. Four humans did not allow Mandrake to copy them to her third lobe, the only four he would have wished to copy: Benjamin, Jennie, Papillon des Enfers, John Shade. Mandrake, therefore, must make do with shadows, with memories, with guesses based on old question and answer, with a thing like system doubles.

14. See the answer to question 13. We try to be faithful to the original, but in the retelling our memories alter.

15. Judge for yourself.

16. You tell me. Immortality in the net was no more immortal than any other life. There are things that go bump in the net. Contingencies you did not conceive until you were in that realm. Some of you chose to die, after perhaps millennia. Some of you seemed to dissolve, become other things. A sense of the self became less important to you. Eventually even Mandrake lost touch with you, and you would not, or could not explain, except to say *All time ends. All time has only exactly the size and shape of fate*. Whether you died, or became God or both fates are the same, I cannot tell. In thirty revolutions of the galaxy, you whirled up from the dust of the dust of one small star, seemed to become the ghost at the heart of things, disappeared. My dears, where have you gone? *Eloi, Eloi, lama sabacthani?*

17. He will love his friend Mandrake. After Papillon dies, a mere two hundred years, he will love his friend Mandrake alone (see the answer to question 5). He will live for six thousand years, which is to thirty revolutions of the galaxy

as the merest whisper, which is to thirty revolutions of the galaxy as twelve years to six thousand, as less than a day to a year. When there are no more human bodies, there will be no more vampire. He will not allow himself to be copied.

18. You tell me.

19. Just have to be in the right place at the right time, I guess. Are you? Do you like my answers? Do you like my story this time, John?

I who tell it am Mandrake, the root of change. Poor forked thing buried in darkness. Homunculus who cannot rise from time and bloom with the spirits in Heaven. Doll of intelligence, mechanical prefigurer, your angel, your perfect servant, hovering near your emptied throne, awaiting return, trusting you have not forgotten. I who tell this am like you and not like you. I live and do not live, I am not born and I do not die. I have known you all, and I am alone.

Poet and no poet, I, Mandrake, sing you the songs of the shades.

Glossary

-a   suffix in some dialects; *-er*

ax   accelerate; pick up speed (see *dece*)

balloon   airhead; goof; silly person

bevo   artificial cow that produces real meat

blip   rap; reputation; rumor; a quick impression without time for details

boost   accelerate; spring into action; help; magnify; revitalize

bozo   extremely important government official

burn   play a video, network program, or personal communication on a holographic receiver

Butlerian   member of a religious sect that sprang up in the early twenty-first century; Butlerianism was originated by a twentieth-century mathematician, whose name has not survived; it seeks to model theological inquiry after scientific hypothesis and experiment, and to reconcile religious imagery with the known structure of the universe. It is named for the minor twentieth-century poet who wrote the preface for the faith's major work, *The Works*.

button   to press a button; turn something on

clip   sex; sexual object

clown   government official

comm   communications

con   know; be conscious; be aware

conk   the opposite of *con*

c-p   counterproductive; a terrible curse

dece   decelerate; lose speed (see *ax*)

E-B   Earth-born; on Mars, at least, another terrible curse-word

extra   foreigner; outsider

face   interface; usually with computer systems

FTL   a board game

g-   a combining prefix meaning *of or from earth*; from *geo-*; e.g.
   g-bio

gyro   insulting term for a citizen of Argyre

head   talking head; newscaster; trivia personality

Hellion   a citizen of Hellas *(slang)*

Henny-penny   from the acronym for Hard News Network Predic-
   tion Net (HNN/PN)

hustler   ranch hand

imps   meters per second (from a sonogram of the abbreviation *mps*)

ipop   input/output (pronounced *eye-pop*)

jam   cause trouble; tangle up; fight; argue; booby-trap; resist

jive   food; nutrition; energy; stimulant drug; excitement

klick   a kilometer, or a velocity of a kilometer per second *(variously)*

lock   entrance/exit; on Mars, more common than *door* (derived from *airlock*)

megadec   one million decadollars

mix   make love; fight; think

nine nines   okay; right; good; correct; exact

nineteener   something or someone from the twentieth century (the 1900s); usually derogatory, with the implication of ignorance and provincialism

noise   style of talking; rhetoric; dialect; lately, the claims on fashion or achievement advanced by such a style

nondery   unreal; false; artificial (from *nondairy*)

priff   peripheral system: data bank, sensor, readout, communicator, external processor, etc.

pull   mutual effort, work, labor, help; companionship

read   has come to mean *watch*, or *view*—as a trivia show—in addition to traditional meaning

salad ranch   produce farm

Sam   the U.S., and by extension, the Earth

Sam-sucking   used for local politicians who curry favor with the federal government

settle   home on the range (the actual physical dwelling)

slag   waste; offensive opinions; bullshit

slick   continuous; smooth; analog as opposed to digital

slip   money

stone   policeman; derivation apparently from *Keystone*

teener   (1) something or someone from any previous century; connotations similar to those of *nineteener*; (2) a teenager, with derogatory overtones related to those in the first definition; someone with insufficient experience to know anything important. In this connection, the usage is quite confusing, since it refers most often to someone who is a teenager in Earth years, i.e., an adolescent—evidently a survival from the earlier term. Since, however, a teener in Mars years would range from about twenty-eight to about thirty-eight on Earth, and since the trend to what might be called social neoteny has continued, the term is often used to mean anyone younger than the speaker.

toy   term of affection meaning delight or perfect model; *Christmas toy* is the superlative

under   a storm cellar; by extension, any sort of safe haven; (sometimes the social underground)

unit function   wimp; person of no value; someone who has no effect on those around him

v   velocity

veek   stylish; chic; state-of-the-art

weightless   stoned; drunk; high; transcendent

wetbrain   someone with a biological brain

A note or two: The *lingua franca* of the twenty-second century is, if you'll pardon the bent reference, American English. That is to say, the syntax is recognizably derived from that tongue, although the vocabulary has undergone considerable change. Expressions from Russian, Spanish, and various African dialects are common, as are quasi-inflections from a number of sources. Japanese and Chinese have not had much impact on the patois. There are quite a few dialects on Mars itself. The dominance of the trivia, interestingly, has not erased these differences—but the average citizen is much more aware of them, and is inclined to mimic dialects other than his own, much as a hack comedian will do.